"Morgan?" sa

Morgan frowned   Is that you?"

"Yes," she answered, her voice flat.

"You caught me at the airport," said Morgan. "I'm waiting for my flight."

"Where are you going?" Claire asked.

Morgan felt a moment of annoyance. She knew that Claire was overwhelmed by her new baby, by all that had happened, but Morgan had told her repeatedly how much she was looking forward to this trip. "I'm going to England. Remember?"

There was a silence at the other end. "Right," said Claire at last. "That's right. Never mind. I'm sorry."

"It's okay. I'm glad you called," said Morgan. "I have time to talk."

There was silence again at Claire's end.

"Claire? What's going on?" Morgan asked.

"It's Guy," she said. "And..." Her voice cracked. "Drew."

"What about Guy and Drew?" Morgan asked, her heart beating fast.

"They're...dead," said Claire.

"They're dead?" Morgan cried. Chills ran through her, criss-crossing her arms and legs. "Oh, my God. Claire... Oh, my God."

PATRICIA MACDONALD's
suspenseful tales have captivated readers
across America, as well as in France, where
she is a #1 bestselling author. Her previous
novels include the Edgar Award–nominated
The Unforgiven. She currently resides with her
husband and daughter in New Jersey, where she
is working on her next novel.

PATRICIA MACDONALD

FROM CRADLE TO GRAVE

W♦RLDWIDE®

TORONTO • NEW YORK • LONDON
AMSTERDAM • PARIS • SYDNEY • HAMBURG
STOCKHOLM • ATHENS • TOKYO • MILAN
MADRID • WARSAW • BUDAPEST • AUCKLAND

To Alice Early,
My friend of fifty years. This one's for you...

Recycling programs
for this product may
not exist in your area.

ISBN-13: 978-0-373-06261-4

FROM CRADLE TO GRAVE

Copyright © 2009 by Patricia Bourgeau

A Worldwide Library Suspense/December 2011

First published by Severn House Publishers.

www.Harlequin.com

Printed in U.S.A.

FROM CRADLE
TO GRAVE

Thanks to Rick Pass, Sandy Thomson
and Carmen Alvarez, who answered all my
questions, and to my daughter, Sara, who heard
me out, and told me I better start over again.

ONE

MORGAN ADAIR RANG THE BELL at the reception desk of the Captain's House. While she waited for the owner to appear, she walked across the antique-filled parlor to the French doors which led to the side porch. The day was unseasonably mild and the doors were open. She stepped outside, and inhaled the autumn air redolent of burning leaves and the tang of salt spray. Morgan lived and worked in New York City, but she often felt assaulted by city life, and it sometimes seemed to Morgan that she had been born in the wrong era—that she would have been better suited to life in the countryside in the late nineteenth century. This oceanside guest house had a little of that feeling of another time, another era.

A graduate student at Hershman College in Brooklyn, Morgan would be traveling, next week, to the beautiful English Lake District to finish the last of her research for her PhD thesis on the English essayist and feminist Harriet Martineau. Martineau had lived the last years of her life in Ambleside on the shores of Lake Windermere and Morgan planned to spend some time at the Knoll, the Victorian house which the prolific writer had called home. She could hardly wait.

The prospect of the trip was made all the more exciting by the fact that she would be spending much of her time there with Simon Edgerton, a poet who had guest-lectured at Hershman last Spring. During Simon's time at Hershman, Morgan had been assigned to work as his assistant. Their academic relationship became an ever-escalating flirtation. When she told him that she would be coming to England to do her research, he offered to accompany her to the Lake District. Struggling to conceal her delight, Morgan could not accept his offer quickly enough. She was already picturing a Jane Austen-worthy scenario—their old-fashioned courtship consummated in that romantic setting. She was counting the days.

In the meantime, it was undeniably pleasant to be in this seaside town, in this quaint house on an autumn weekend.

On the internet, she had found this guest house, one of the few still open in late October, and booked a room. West Briar was one of three towns referred to as the Briars, here on New York's Long Island shoreline. It did not have the same wealth or cachet as its near neighbors, the Hamptons, but the Briars were, nonetheless, a coveted summer haven. Now, the season was over, and West Briar had resumed its sleepy, rural character.

'Hello,' called a voice from inside the house. Morgan came back in off the porch and smiled at the tall woman with a stylishly cut bob, half glasses and a cardigan draped over her shoulders, who was now behind the antique front desk.

'Hi there,' said Morgan. 'I'm on my way out, but I brought down my card.' She held out the plastic credit card to the innkeeper, who, with her arms full of clean towels, had knocked on the door to Morgan's room earlier to apologetically ask Morgan to stop by the desk with her card for imprinting when she came through the lobby again.

The innkeeper reached for the card, looking sheepish. 'I'm so sorry to put you out, Miss Adair. I should have made an imprint when you arrived this morning.

I'm just scattered. All my help has gone back to college and I'm expecting company today—the daughter of an old friend—so I'm a little distracted. How's the room? Are you comfortable?' she asked solicitously.

'Very comfortable. It's charming,' said Morgan. 'You have a lovely place here. Are you open all year?'

'No,' said the woman, shaking her head. 'Actually, this is our last weekend open. My husband and I go down to Sarasota for the winters.'

'That sounds like a good schedule to have,' said Morgan.

'Oh, it is. Although I always miss this place. I'm always glad to get back. Is this your first visit to West Briar?' the woman asked.

'No,' said Morgan. 'But I usually stay at my friend's house. I just thought that they didn't need a houseguest this weekend.'

The innkeeper pointed to the box wrapped in pale blue with a white ribbon which Morgan carried under her arm. 'Ah, I see. Wedding?' she asked.

'Baptism, actually. I'm the godmother,' said Morgan proudly.

'Oh. Well, congratulations. And you look very pretty,' she said in an approving, motherly tone.

Morgan glanced into the silver framed mirror behind the desk. When she drove out from her Brooklyn apartment this morning and checked into the guest house, she was still wearing her running clothes. She had showered and changed in her room. Now, glancing at her reflection she had to admit that she did clean up well. She wore her shiny, chestnut-hued hair in long, loose waves, and she had forgone the tailored jackets and pants she normally wore for work, and chosen a short, swingy dress in a pale shade of olive. The color flattered her hair and complexion and the dress showed off her legs. 'Thanks. It's an important day,' Morgan said.

The innkeeper handed her back her card and smiled. 'A christening. It certainly is. Well, you have a wonderful day,' she said.

THE MAILBOX AT THE END of the Boltons' driveway was festooned with blue and white balloons tied to the mailbox post with long, curling ribbons. Baby motifs—rattles and carriages and cunning teddy bears—were printed on the balloons, which danced in the autumn breeze. Colorful leaves from the mature trees in the yard joined in the dance, twirling down on to the long front lawn. Claire's gray cat, Dusty, sat on the front step of the brown cedar-shake cottage, alertly watching the leaves fall, poised to spring if any leaf tried to land there. The burnished sunlight threw a pattern of dappled shadows across the lawn. Morgan opened the white gate and started up the stone pathway to the front door. Dusty jumped off the step as she approached and watched from his hiding place in a bed of zinnias beneath the window. As Morgan raised her fist to knock she heard the thin, plaintive sound of a baby's cry.

Although it was the most normal of sounds, the audible evidence of all that was new and hopeful, Morgan immediately felt a knot tighten in her stomach. This was her third visit since the birth, early in September, of Claire and Guy's son, Drew. The first visit she had come bearing gifts, energy to help, and a heart full of happiness. It had been a shock then to see the anxiety in her best friend's eyes. 'I don't know how to take care of him,' Claire had whispered. She looked exhausted, the dark circles under her eyes like sooty smudges on her wan face.

Although clueless about babies, Morgan had peppered

Claire with reassurances while she took over every chore she could manage including getting up at night with the baby. The second visit had come weeks later, when Guy, a chef who ran a catering business that serviced all the best parties in the Briars, called her in a panic.

'Claire doesn't bathe. She won't get out of bed,' he said. 'Morgan, maybe you can talk to her. I don't know what to do.' Morgan posted a notice on the door of her shared office at Hershman College, saying that she would not be available for her tutorials, and had rushed out to West Briar. Guy had not been exaggerating. For four days Morgan helped out with the chores, and tried to reassure Claire that everything would be fine. She had gently urged her friend to see a doctor, get some medication for her baby blues.

Now the baby was six weeks old, and the day of his christening had arrived. But the persistent sound of the baby's wails made Morgan uneasy. She could visualize Claire's panic, her agitation. It doesn't necessarily mean anything is wrong, Morgan told herself. Babies cry. She knocked on the door and in a moment it was opened by Guy Bolton. One look at the strain in Guy's face told her that the situation had not improved.

'Morgan,' he said. 'I'm glad you're here. Come on in.' Morgan followed Guy into the house. It was cozy and charming, a seaside cottage, decorated with warmth and flair and now clearly ready for a party. The dining room table was covered with wine glasses, serving dishes, piles of utensils, plates and napkins. The rich aroma of a *pot-au-feu* emanated from the kitchen, and there were flowers arranged with autumn leaves, and candles on every surface.

Parties were Guy's business. He was a chef who had trained in France and worked for six years at a highly respected restaurant in Lyon. The master chef there had gifted him with a set of exquisite Sabatier carving knives when he left his service. Once back at home, Guy had many offers to be the head chef at fine restaurants. He decided instead to open and operate a catering business in Briarwood that served the Briars and his business was a great success. Clearly, he had brought all his culinary skills to bear in preparing for his son's baptism.

'Guy, everything looks wonderful,' said Morgan sincerely. 'The food smells fantastic.'

Guy frowned and ran a hand through his dark, wavy hair.

'I think we're ready,' he said. He was a slim, handsome man with broad face, sensuous dark eyes and full lips. Today he wore a blue shirt with the sleeves rolled up, dark pants and a foulard tie, with a white chef's apron tied around his narrow waist. Eighteen months ago, when Morgan first met him, he had just fallen head over heels in love with Morgan's best friend, Claire. In those days, his joy was catchy and intoxicating.

'Is there anything left to do?' Morgan asked, putting her present on a pile of presents on the sideboard. 'It looks like you've done it all.'

'Maybe you could get through to Claire,' he said grimly.

'How's she doing?' Morgan asked.

'She doesn't want to come.'

'Oh dear,' said Morgan. She reached out and put her fingers lightly on Guy's forearm. He flinched. 'I'm sorry, Guy,' she said. 'I'd hoped…'

'Yeah, me too,' he said. His dark eyes glistened. He rubbed the heels of his hands against his eyes and took a deep breath. 'I don't know what to do.'

'Has she seen her doctor? Did she get some medication?' Morgan asked.

'She doesn't want to leave the house,' Guy said. 'She makes the appointments and then she breaks them.'

'It's hard. I know it. But these blues are not that uncommon, you know, for new mothers. It'll pass.' She said this with some authority. Alarmed by Claire's mental state, she had done some research on the internet about post-partum depression.

'Will it?' he said in a flat tone.

A stove timer dinged in the kitchen. 'Excuse me,' said Guy. 'I have to get that. I'm trying to get everything out and on the table before we leave. So people can come in and just serve themselves. I probably should have arranged to have Drew christened at home. But you know Claire. She wanted to do it at the church,' he said.

Morgan understood. All her life, Claire had retained a childlike faith which Morgan found hard to fathom. Despite their closeness, their many similarities, it was a profound difference between them. Morgan's turbulent, disrupted childhood had made her cynical, to say the least. One of the reasons she had been attracted to Harriet Martineau as the subject of her doctoral thesis was that highly educated woman's rationalistic rejection of religious teachings.

But Claire had stayed with her faith despite the difficult life she and her impoverished single mother had known. When, before Drew was even born, Claire had asked Morgan to be her baby's godmother, Morgan had felt bound by conscience to remind her friend that she was not a churchgoer, and not, perhaps, the best person to entrust with her baby's religious upbringing. Claire had brushed off Morgan's objections. 'I want my baby to have a godmother who will always care for him, or her, if anything happens to me. And that's you.'

Those late days of Claire's pregnancy had been such a happy, optimistic time for Claire and her husband. They had even talked about selling their West Briar cottage and moving to Provence, which they both adored. Now, Morgan's heart ached at the bewilderment in Guy's voice, the misery in his eyes. 'It'll work out fine,' said Morgan. 'Look, we'll get her ready and get her over there. Don't you worry,' she said briskly. 'Leave Claire to me.'

Guy looked at her. Hope and skepticism fluctuated in his gaze.

'Go on. I'll just go tell her that I'm here,' she said firmly. As Guy returned to the kitchen, Morgan went down the hall to Guy and Claire's room, and tapped gently on the door. 'Claire? It's me. Morgan. Can I come in?' Without waiting for an answer, Morgan opened the door.

The smell of unwashed linens and sour milk hung in the stale, still air. Morgan frowned, trying to adjust her eyes to the darkened room. She could hear the baby's cries of misery. She stepped tentatively inside. Her vision began to adjust. Claire, who had worked, before her pregnancy, as an edgy computer graphic artist in Manhattan, was clad in a stained gray T-shirt and underpants. She was sitting up in bed, the bedclothes wadded around her slender hips, absently rocking the wailing baby in her arms.

'Hi honey,' Morgan said gently. 'Do you mind if I let a little light in here?'

Claire shrugged. 'I don't care.'

Morgan walked over to the windows and pushed open the curtains. The pale autumn light crept into the room. Morgan walked over to the bed, and sat down on the edge. Now that the curtains were open, she could see that Claire's dark eyes were bright with tears, and there were tears rolling down her elegant cheekbones, dripping from her small, square jaw. Claire did not bother to wipe them away.

Morgan's heart sank at the sight of her friend's face. 'Oh, Claire,' Morgan said. 'Not any better?'

'It's no use,' said Claire.

'Come on, now,' said Morgan gently, giving Claire's shoulders a brief squeeze. 'It just takes some getting used to.'

Claire shook her head. 'No, you don't know,' she insisted. 'I'm a bad mother. Nothing I do is right. I feed him. I change him. He just keeps on crying.'

'Here, let me hold him,' said Morgan. She reached for the baby, and Claire released him without protest. Morgan pressed the trembling little body gently to her shoulder. The baby continued to cry and hiccup, but the force of his protests diminished.

'Hey, little guy,' she crooned.

'You see,' said Claire. 'He'd rather be with you.'

Morgan frowned. 'Don't be silly. I'm just a novelty.'

Claire closed her eyes and slid back down under the covers. Morgan had known Claire since their first day of junior high school in a small farming community in upstate New York. Morgan, whose father was a diplomat, had been raised in Malaysia. Her parents died in a hotel bombing and Morgan was sent back to live with an aunt and uncle who clearly didn't want her. On Morgan's first day of school, so bewildering and alien after her years abroad, a skinny, acne-covered girl with glasses, who stood a head taller than anyone else in the class, sat down beside her in the lunchroom and asked her if she liked *Lord of the Rings*. Claire. It was a moment of relief that

Morgan would never forget—the revelation of a kindred soul.

They had shared innumerable experiences in the years since then—from the triumphant to the devastating. But even when Claire's mother, her only family, died during her senior year in college, Morgan thought, Claire had not seemed so hopeless.

'Guy's got everything ready,' said Morgan.

'I know. He's been a saint,' said Claire. 'I don't know how he stands it. I'm sure he wishes he'd never met me.'

'How can you even say that?' Morgan asked. 'He adores you.' As she spoke, she could hear the wistful pang in her own voice. When she had told Claire about her flirtation with Simon, Claire had said gently, 'This doesn't seem right to me. I mean, I don't know of a guy who wouldn't have made a move by now.' Morgan had protested that Simon probably didn't want to violate protocol, being a guest lecturer at the college and Morgan still a grad student. She proudly pointed out that they were going to be spending time together in England. Of course her flirtation with Simon would seem tepid compared to the dramatic passions of Claire's life.

Claire and Guy had met when Guy catered Claire's engagement party to another man—Sandy Raymond, a dot-com mogul who got rich from Workability, the internet employment site he founded. Sandy had hired Claire to do the graphics for his site, and he began to woo her soon thereafter, proposing during a vacation in Spain. Their engagement party took place at his summer home in West Briar. It had been a bittersweet occasion for Morgan. She and Claire shared an apartment, and she knew that this night marked the end of an era—their era as room-mates and travelers, sharing exotic adventures and late night ice cream runs, and building castles in the air. Claire was about to begin a very different kind of life as the wife of a dot-com millionaire. The event was glamorous. All the trees were lit with fairy lights, a jazz combo played, and the champagne flowed.

At some point in the evening, Morgan stepped out on to the patio behind Sandy's beautiful house and saw Claire, in her blush pink silk party dress, standing on the stone steps, deep in earnest conversation with a gorgeous man in a food-stained chef's jacket. The very next day, Claire told her that she was afraid it would be a mistake to marry Sandy, and she was going to give him his ring back. It had only taken her one night to realize that she had met the man she truly was meant to marry. Guy's proposal, their wedding and Claire's pregnancy had followed in a happy whirlwind. Morgan made no secret of it—she envied Claire that commitment, that certainty. 'You're the love of his life,' said Morgan. 'You and that baby.'

'I know,' said Claire in a small voice.

'He wants this day to be perfect. Mainly for your sake. If it were up to Guy, I don't think he'd care that much about having Drew christened.'

'I know,' said Claire wearily. 'He avoids these family occasions. He's done it all for me.'

'I know it's tough, but you've got to pull yourself together for this.'

'Morgan, you just can't imagine how…helpless I feel.' Morgan looked down at the baby in her arms and realized that Drew had fallen asleep. Carefully, she placed him in his bassinet by Claire's bed. Then she turned back to Claire. 'Look, you and I are always honest with each other. And we've always tried to help each other through the tough times, right? Now, this one is tough. But when you put your mind to it, you can do anything. And I'm right here to back you up. You can do it,' said Morgan firmly. 'You have to do it. For Drew.'

Claire let out a sob. 'Oh, Morgan,' she wailed. 'Oh, I love him so much.'

Morgan recognized this as capitulation. 'Of course you do.'

'I don't want to fail him…' she said, wiping away her tears.

'And you won't. You'll see,' said Morgan, although Claire's helpless tears made her feel queasy with anxiety. 'Now, come on,' Morgan said, bending over the bedside table to switch on the lamp, 'Get it together. I'll run you a bath and you soak a little bit, while I'll get into that closet and find you something beautiful to wear. You're going to be the best-looking mom in all of West Briar. Trust me. It'll be all right. You'll see.'

TWO

MORGAN SAT IN THE BACK SEAT, beside the baby who was strapped into his car seat, while Claire, pale in the face and unsteady as a fawn, but clean, made-up, and wearing a short, navy silk sheath and a pair of pointy-toed, low-heeled pumps, sat beside her husband, who drove as if he had a car full of uncartoned eggs.

Morgan could see Claire's delicate profile from where she sat, and she watched for changes that would indicate an imminent meltdown. But Claire was maintaining a shaky equilibrium, commenting on the beautiful autumn day and asking Guy questions about the baptism itself.

'I talked to Father Lawrence about it. He promised me it would be short. No long service or anything,' said Guy.

'Good,' Claire murmured, and then lapsed into silence. They pulled up in front of the simple, white, wooden congregational church which stood beside a cemetery with a wrought-iron gate. Morgan recognized it. It reminded her of an old New England-style whaling church and it was the church where Claire and Guy's wedding had taken place. They all got out of the car, and made their way slowly up the church steps and down the center aisle of the meeting house-style room. There were two banks of wooden pews, and a choir loft above. Today, there was no choir in the loft. The other guests were already assembled in two rows in the front.

Morgan recognized most of the people in the church from Claire's wedding, and she remembered much that

Claire had told her about them. She handed the baby to
Guy and sat down beside Guy's sister, Lucy, a short,
pudgy woman with soft, white skin and flyaway blond
hair and glasses. Lucy suffered from the genetic disorder Prader-Willi syndrome. In its extreme form, Prader-
Willi led to obesity, mood disorders and retardation. Lucy,
however, had a mild form of the condition and was of
normal intelligence. She lived alone with two dogs and
collected shells from the beach which she crafted into
picture frames, boxes and other knick-knacks for a local
store called Shellshack. Her love life, if she had one, was
secretive, but there was speculation in the family that
she might be asexual—another frequent complication of
Prader-Willi.

Because the disorder was passed through paternal
genes, Claire was advised by her obstetrician to go, early
in her pregnancy, for genetic counseling. As she sat in the
waiting room, reading a magazine, Lucy emerged from
the counselor's office and walked right by Claire without
seeing her. Although Claire was very curious to see her
sister-in-law there, among a group of expectant mothers,
she never mentioned it to Lucy. Guy, who had little to do
with his sister, could offer no explanation.

On the other side of Lucy, holding her hand, was Guy's
stepmother, Astrid. Beside Astrid was Guy's father, Dick
Bolton. Dick, though in his mid-fifties, still liked to surf
in his free time, and had the tanned, fit look of a lifelong
beach enthusiast. He was still handsome, and looked like
a larger, more muscular version of his son. Soon after
Dick was first married, in his early twenties, he had
bought a run-down beach-front bungalow and turned it
into a surfers' lunch spot called the Lobster Shack. Over
the years, the runaway success of the tiny, beachfront bar
had spawned a retail business called Lobster Shack Sea-

foods. Dick affected a laid-back, 'no worries' persona, never wearing a tie, or foregoing a chance to stop and have a cocktail while the sun set. But, in truth, he was a demanding, impatient man whose short temper had made both his children wary of him. Astrid was Dick's second wife whom he had met when he took Guy and Lucy to a tiny island in the Dutch Antilles to recuperate after their mother, his first wife, died after a short, fierce bout with cancer. Dick had picked the hotel out of a book about Caribbean trips on a shoestring. Astrid's parents, Dutch nationals, owned and ran the small hotel and Astrid, a tanned, lissome blonde who wore her platinum hair, even then, in an old-fashioned crown of braids, worked for her parents as everything from receptionist to informal tour guide. While ten-year-old Lucy played alone on the beach and her teenaged brother, Guy, learned to dive, Dick courted the lovely Astrid with her tranquil, lilac-blue eyes. After an indecently short courtship—only the length of the vacation—Dick and Astrid were married and Astrid returned to West Briar, now a wife and the stepmother of two stunned, angry youngsters.

According to Claire, everyone in West Briar was shocked by Dick's hasty remarriage. But Astrid helped out in her husband's business and treated the children, especially Lucy, with a motherly tenderness. She tirelessly provided the care Lucy needed for her condition, making sure the girl had the proper diet, physical therapy, and medication she required. Astrid also was an advocate and regular attendee at conferences devoted to Lucy's disorder. Guy, at fifteen the older of the two children, remained diffident in the face of his stepmother's kindness, but Lucy quickly grew devoted to her.

Morgan also recognized a few of Guy and Claire's friends. Donna Riccio and her husband, a salesman who was often on the road, lived across the street from Guy and Claire. They had a one-year-old at home, and Donna had advised Claire often on what to expect in her first year of parenthood. But, after Drew was born, and Claire confessed her depression, Donna said, 'I don't know what you mean. I was happy when I had my baby.' Claire had not confided in her since.

Morgan avoided the gaze of Earl Fitzhugh, universally known as Fitz, who was Guy's longtime best friend, and soon to be Drew's godfather. Even though she did not look at him, Morgan's face flamed just to be in his company again. Fitz, a wrestling coach at the local high school, was tousle-headed, with boyish good looks. He had been best man at Claire and Guy's wedding while Morgan was the maid of honor. He had looked handsome in his tuxedo that day, and Morgan felt seductive with her hair in a casual upsweep and her figure curvy in a low-cut satin gown. Thrown together by the events surrounding the wedding they had flirted for two days, drunk too much champagne at the reception and ended up in a feverish, awkward coupling in the back of Fitz's car.

Afterwards, Morgan felt a little ashamed of herself to have acted so wantonly, especially with a friend of Guy's. But she told herself that it was nothing to be ashamed of—these sorts of things happened at weddings all the time. She decided to regard it as a moment of spontaneity, apt for the occasion. She had not seen or spoken to Fitz since. Now, she had to share the godparent title with him. She planned to act like an adult, treat that encounter like the meaningless fling that it was, and avoid any mention of it. She could feel Fitz's gaze on her but Morgan did not look back at him.

'Good morning,' said Father Lawrence, the bespectacled, gray-haired minister who had officiated at Claire and Guy's wedding. 'Good to have you all here today. Can I have the godparents come up to the font with the parents?' he asked. Morgan realized that meant her and Fitz. She stood up and edged past Lucy out of the pew. As she mounted the step to the altar, she nearly bumped into Fitz, who winked at her lasciviously. How juvenile, Morgan thought, and then she tripped on the step, blushed, and joined the others at the font. Father Lawrence began the baptismal rite. As she listened and responded to the ritual questions, Morgan kept her eyes on the baby. When at last she looked up, she noticed, out of the corner of her eye, a movement in the empty choir loft. She hadn't seen anyone there when she came in. But there was definitely someone there now, seated in the shadows of the last row. Morgan peered, and then frowned in recognition.

Claire noticed the look on Morgan's face. 'What?' she whispered.

Morgan shook her head, and looked down at Drew, who was yawning and clenching his little fists. Although she had only met him two or three times, she was certain she had correctly identified the man in the balcony. But if it *was* Sandy Raymond, Claire's ex-fiancé, here at the christening, she did not want Claire to know it, or to look up and see him. At that moment, Father Lawrence told Claire to hold the baby and he began to pour the water over the child's head. By some miracle, the baby did not cry, and Claire actually smiled, as the minister pronounced him baptized and the small group of well-wishers began to clap.

'Guy and Claire and, of course, Drew, want to invite you all to their house for a small celebration,' said the minister with a broad smile when the applause subsided. Everyone stood up, and Morgan glanced back up at the balcony, but Sandy Raymond, if indeed it had been Sandy Raymond, was nowhere to be seen.

THEY MADE THE SHORT DRIVE back to the cottage. It had been Guy's house when Claire met him. Dick Bolton had given the cottage to his son, and a similar house, half a mile away, to his daughter, Lucy, some years earlier. His gifts showed foresight. Property in the Briars was now too expensive for young people to afford. Morgan watched as the houses of West Briar flashed by, each one more charming than the last, with expensive cars in the driveways, and swimming pools tucked discreetly in verdant backyards.

As they pulled past the balloon-decorated mailbox into the driveway, the first car to arrive, Morgan noticed a black motorcycle parked behind her car in front of the house. Claire said, 'Honey, who's that?'

A pale, thin girl with a stud in her nose, her dyed black hair streaked pink and secured in a messy twist in a hairclip, sat on the front steps of the cottage. She was wearing a leather jacket, filthy jeans, and heavy black boots. Her hands were festooned with rings, including a large, black onyx ring on her forefinger. An overstuffed backpack was slumped on the steps beside her as well as a black motorcycle helmet with a red rose painted across the visor.

Guy stopped the car, and stared across the lawn at her. 'Who is that girl? What is she doing on our steps?' said Claire. She opened the car door and got out. Slowly, Guy got out of the driver's side. Morgan unhooked the baby from his car seat, lifted him up to her shoulder, and emerged awkwardly from the back seat.

The girl on the front steps stood up, wiped her hands nervously on her jeans. She ambled toward Guy, clearly trying to look nonchalant, but her gaze was shy and hopeful.

'Guy?' she asked.

Claire looked in bewilderment from the scruffy girl to her husband.

Guy's face was ashen. He shook his head, as if he could somehow ward the girl off by denying her presence.

'It's me. It's Eden,' the girl said, her voice catching slightly. She had a soft, Southern accent.

'Eden. What…What are you doing here?' said Guy. The girl affected a bright smile which looked strained. 'I heard I had a brother,' she said. 'I came to see him.' The girl was standing close to Morgan. Morgan could see that she had flawless skin the color of parchment, and small, slightly yellowed teeth. She turned to Morgan and she had the foul breath of someone who hadn't eaten in too long a time. She pointed to the bundle in Morgan's arms. 'Can I hold the baby?'

Morgan instinctively cupped her hand around the back of the baby's head. 'I'm not his mother,' she said apologetically. She glanced at Claire, who seemed to be teetering on her low heels. 'Claire is his mother.' The girl turned and looked questioningly at Claire.

Behind her, Morgan could hear car doors slamming as the other guests arrived, parked on the street and began to walk toward the house. Claire's eyes widened, and she looked helplessly from the girl to her husband.

'Who told you about the baby?' Guy demanded.

The girl looked confused. 'A…friend saw the birth announcement. She thought I'd want to know so she sent it to me.' Eden's voice sounded high and anxious. 'Why?'

'You shouldn't be here, Eden,' Guy said. 'I'm sorry, but this is a very bad time.'

Claire began to sway slightly. 'Guy?' she said. 'Who is this?'

The girl looked directly at Claire. She shook her head in disbelief, and her voice was plaintive. 'Doesn't she know about me?' Eden asked.

Guy avoided Claire's panic-filled eyes. 'Claire,' he said grimly. 'This is Eden Summers. She's...my daughter.'

Claire looked from Guy's face back to the teenager. Then she let out a little cry of anguish. She looked as if she was about to collapse. Morgan wanted to help her, but she was still holding the baby. Without another word, Claire turned and fled into the house.

For a moment, Guy seemed to be torn between speaking to this teenaged intruder or following his wife. Then, Guy made up his mind and rushed into the house after Claire as the arriving guests watched, mouths agape.

'Who is this?' Dick Bolton asked, confused. He looked casually elegant in a black turtleneck and a tweed jacket.

Astrid murmured into her husband's ear.

'Oh, for God's sake,' said Dick angrily. He turned on the girl. 'Look sweetie, if you're trying to get to know this family, this is not the way to do it—showing up here out of the blue.'

'It's not her fault,' Lucy protested indignantly. 'Guy should have said something.'

Eden's chin trembled, but her gaze had grown steely. 'It's my brother's baptism,' she insisted, her voice shaking.

Dick shook his head. 'I'm not trying to be cruel. But you should go back to Kentucky...or wherever it is you come from.'

'West Virginia,' the girl said bitterly.

'Dick, let's be nice,' Astrid pleaded in her charmingly

accented voice. Looking pained, she offered the girl her hand. 'I'm Astrid. It's nice to meet you.'

Eden shook her hand briefly.

'Astrid.' Dick yelped. 'This is ridiculous. This girl does not belong here. Can't you make her leave?' he said.

'Darling, it's not my place,' Astrid murmured.

Lucy turned on her father. Her mild, almond-shaped eyes were uncharacteristically ablaze. 'Dad. You act like she's a criminal. She's got a right to be here.'

Dick shook his head. 'I'm sorry. Not after all her grandparents put my son through. This is just wrong.'

Astrid, dressed in a sky-blue knit suit, was holding a beribboned package.

'Astrid. Take the present inside,' he said. 'And meet me at the car.' Dick turned away. Then, he made a detour over to where Morgan stood, holding the baby. He rubbed his index finger over the baby's delicate head. 'You be a good boy, Drew Richard Bolton. I'll see you soon.'

Astrid, gripping the package, walked up the pathway and into the house.

Eden's face was frozen into an expressionless mask. She did her best to avoid meeting the curious gazes of the guests.

'Lucy, what is this all about?' Morgan asked in a low voice. 'Who is this girl?'

Lucy rolled her eyes. 'You heard her. She's Guy's daughter.'

'How come I've never heard of her before? Claire didn't know anything about any daughter.'

Lucy shook her head. 'He should have told her. That's just like Guy. He doesn't care about anyone else's feelings.'

'The girl said she was from West Virginia. Does her mother live in West Virginia…?'

'No. Her grandparents. She was raised by her grand-parents. Kimba died on their honeymoon.'

'Their honeymoon!' Morgan exclaimed. 'Guy was married before?'

Lucy looked disgusted. 'For about one week. They got married after Eden was born.'

The front door of the cottage opened, and Astrid came outside, minus her present.

She walked over to where Lucy stood with Morgan, the heels of her shoes sinking into the lawn. She opened her arms to Lucy and squeezed her in a brief embrace.

'Poor Claire,' said Lucy. 'How's she doing?'

Astrid shook her head and rubbed Lucy's small fingers in her own, well-manicured hand. 'I didn't see Claire. I only spoke to your brother for a few seconds. He's very… upset. He's prepared a banquet in there. I wish your father would be reasonable…' Astrid's voice trailed away. She glanced back at the guests who were waiting by their cars, uncertain how to proceed.

'Why is he being so horrible to Eden?' Lucy asked her stepmother plaintively.

Astrid sighed. 'He doesn't mean to be horrible. He doesn't know how to act. The situation is so…awkward.'

Fitz ambled up to where they were standing, his hands shoved in the pockets of his khaki pants. 'Enter the bad fairy,' he said in a low voice with a hint of a smile.

'Not funny,' said Morgan under her breath.

'I'm sorry, Astrid, but I blame Guy for this. This is typical of him. You know he only thinks of himself. Maybe I should just go home to the dogs,' said Lucy.

'Please Lucy,' said Astrid, wrapping an arm around her step-daughter's shoulders. 'It's Drew's christening. Your brother had no way of knowing this would happen. You mustn't be too hard on him. He needs our support. You know that. We're a family. We help each other. Right?'

Lucy nodded reluctantly.

'Anyway, darling, somebody had to stand by him. I can't defy your father's wishes. Won't you go in there? For me? Please?'

Lucy sighed. 'Oh, all right. But just because I feel sorry for Eden.' Lucy turned to her newfound niece, who was standing helplessly by, her humiliation obvious from a slash of pink across each of her cheekbones. 'Eden, why don't you come on inside?' she asked gruffly.

Eden shrugged without looking up. Lucy walked over and took her gently by the arm. 'Come on. There's food in there. You look like you need to eat. I'm your aunt by the way,' she said. 'I'm Lucy.'

'That's my girl,' said Astrid to Lucy. She brushed the feathery white bangs off of Lucy's forehead and leaned down to plant a kiss there. Morgan couldn't help noticing that Lucy's coloring was so similar to Astrid's that they truly looked like mother and daughter. Then Astrid turned to Eden. 'Your Aunt Lucy here will look after you.'

'I'll look after her,' Lucy repeated grimly.

Morgan joined the other guests who, following Lucy's lead, stepped uneasily into the house. Guy was taking the lids off of chafing dishes. 'Please, eat,' he said. Fitz did not hesitate. He walked over to the pile of plates, picked one up, and began to survey the buffet. Other guests followed suit. While Lucy filled two plates, Eden sat down stiffly on a chair by the door, watching Guy, who did not meet her gaze.

Morgan slipped out of the room and took the now-squirming baby down the hallway. Drew had begun to cry in earnest. 'It's all right, baby,' she said. 'It's OK.'

She opened the door to the master bedroom. In the dim, gray light from the window she could see Claire, lying across the rumpled bed, still in her dress. Claire looked up and seemed almost frightened at the sight of her squalling baby.

'Claire, I think he needs to nurse,' said Morgan.

Claire sat up on the bed and unbuttoned the front of her dress listlessly, as if she were disrobing for a doctor's exam. Morgan handed her the baby and Claire held him to her breast. Drew latched on greedily and was quiet.

Morgan sat down beside her friend. Claire looked stunned. Morgan rubbed her back awkwardly. 'Claire, I am so sorry about all this. What a shock.'

Tears coursed down Claire's cheeks as she looked at Drew's head. 'He's a liar.'

'You mean Guy? Well, I don't blame you for feeling that way. Obviously, he should have told you,' said Morgan.

'He was married. He had a child,' Claire exclaimed.

'I know, I know. It's a shock. But hey, it'll be all right,' said Morgan. 'It's not the end of the world. I mean, everybody's got a past. And Eden's just a kid. You can't blame her...' For one moment Morgan was glad that she was single and un-encumbered by messy relationships. 'This is just one of those bumps in the road.'

Claire gazed at her in disbelief. 'Bumps in the road? He betrayed me. I can never trust him again.'

'Now, don't go ballistic...I mean, I'm sure Guy regrets not telling you. He should have told you, obviously. But think about it. If you'd known all this, I'm sure that wouldn't have changed your feelings about him. This just seems worse than it is because you're so down, emotionally and physically. It's not that bad,' Morgan insisted.

There was a murmur of voices, and the occasional

sound of laughter from the living room. 'They all knew about it,' said Claire. 'And nobody told me.'

Morgan sighed, knowing that she was right. 'Well, I guess…they thought it wasn't their place to say anything.'

'They were laughing behind my back,' said Claire bitterly.

'Now, honey, that's just not so,' said Morgan. 'Nobody's laughing at you. If anything, they seemed almost as surprised as you were that Guy hadn't told you. Now don't start thinking this was some kind of conspiracy. Everybody came here today to celebrate. Really.'

Drew pushed away from his mother's breast with his little fingers and began to fuss. Claire looked at him helplessly. She bent down to kiss his little round head, but he was fighting against her, flailing his tiny fists.

'What?' Claire cried to her baby. 'Oh, Drew, what is it?' Morgan lifted the baby from Claire's arms. 'Maybe he needs changing. I'll do it.' Morgan carried him to the changing table in the corner of the room. She marveled at how light, almost birdlike, he felt in her arms.

Claire murmured something, which Morgan didn't hear. 'What?' Morgan asked, turning to look at her.

'I said, I can't do it,' said Claire. 'I can't go on.' Morgan felt as if a cold hand had clutched her heart. She held the baby close, her hand around his little round head, as if to shield his ears from his mother's words. 'Claire, don't talk like that,' she insisted. 'Don't even say such a thing.'

Claire turned her head, and gazed out the bedroom window.

The afternoon sky had completely clouded over, and the breeze had stiffened. It blew the crisp, desiccated leaves away from the trees. Separated from their branches, they were lifted for a moment, and then, still tumbling helplessly in the wind, they drifted to the ground. She shook her head. 'Fine,' said Claire softly. 'I won't say it.'

THREE

MORGAN ROLLED HER SUITCASE into the waiting area of her departure gate. She set the bag beside a bank of battleship gray, molded plastic chairs, and sat down on the end seat. There were only a few other people scattered through the lounge. A middle-aged couple dressed in drab colors and sensible shoes sat a few seats down, facing her. Several rows behind them, a man was sleeping, slumped across two seats, his mouth open. The flight to Heathrow was not scheduled to depart for another three hours, but Morgan had arrived with time to spare. She liked to be early. Especially for an international flight.

She pulled the Sunday newspaper she had bought from her voluminous leather shoulder satchel, but though she unfolded it in front of her, she was too excited to read. She finally lowered the paper and just sat there with her eyes closed, imagining the month ahead, the gorgeous villages and countryside she would visit, the colleagues she would meet. Her doctoral thesis on Harriett Martineau's life and work was outlined, and some of it was written, but this trip would provide the needed detail, the visual images she could keep in her head as she revised and polished. Simon had called earlier in the week to describe the manor house turned hotel which he had booked for them in the Lake District. Sometimes, after she talked on the phone to Simon she worried that she had little to say that was truly interesting. But this conversation was different. They had both been equally excited about the adventure which lay ahead. All week she could barely sleep, she was so giddy with excitement.

Giddy and, truth be told, a little guilty. She had left West Briar on Sunday, checking out of the Captain's House early the day after the christening. When the innkeeper asked her how it went as she was checking out, Morgan pretended enthusiasm. In fact, the party had been a disaster. Claire refused to leave her room, and the guests left as soon as they could bolt down a plate of food. Morgan tried to bring a plate of food to her, but Claire refused to touch it. Morgan felt terrible for Claire, but she also knew that she couldn't straighten out the problems in Claire's marriage to Guy. 'By the time I come back,' she told her friend, 'everything is going to seem much better. Eden will be gone, and life will be back to normal. You'll see,' she told the weeping Claire, who did not even beg her to stay as she had in the past. Claire let her go like an exhausted shipwreck survivor releasing her hold on a floating spar—numbly, hopelessly.

Thinking about it now, Morgan felt her spirits sinking, and she warned herself to stop. You're bumming yourself out. Let it go. You can worry about all these problems when you get back. Right now, just enjoy the moment. Morgan's smile returned. She deserved this happiness. She had earned it. She had applied for, and received, a grant to do her research in England. This wasn't her first trip to England, but it would be the most special—this time she would be with Simon.

This grant was only the latest in a long string of scholarships and prizes she had won for her academic work. From the moment she had left the misery of her uncle's house in upstate New York, she had found more than escape in university life. At her college, she found a place where she belonged, and a family in her fellow students.

Once she had her doctorate, she would have the security she craved, and a chance at a faculty position. She wondered if Simon would ever consider seeking a position at a US university. He was well known for his poetry in academic circles. He could probably secure himself a place if he tried. Whoa, girl, she thought. You're getting ahead of yourself. You haven't even been to bed together yet. See how this trip goes. But she couldn't help daydreaming about the life they might have together, if all went well.

Morgan's contented musings were suddenly interrupted by a song by Alanis Morissette, which was the ringtone on her cellphone. She reached into the pocket at the front of her sack and pulled it out. She frowned at the unfamiliar number in the window, opened the phone and answered it. 'Hello?'

There was no answer—just a cacophony of noise and muffled voices.

'Hello?' Morgan said again.

'Morgan?' said a familiar voice, softly.

Morgan frowned and sat up in her chair. 'Claire? Is that you?'

'Yes,' said Claire. Her voice was flat.

'How are you doing?' Morgan said.

Claire did not answer. 'Where are you?' Claire asked.

'You caught me at the airport,' said Morgan, admittedly feeling worldly and sophisticated as she said it. 'I'm waiting for my flight.'

'Where are you going?' Claire asked.

Morgan felt a moment of annoyance. She knew that Claire was overwhelmed by her new baby, by all that had happened, but Morgan had told her repeatedly how much she was looking forward to this trip. 'I'm going to do my research. In England. I'm going to meet Simon. Remember I told you?'

There was a silence at the other end. 'Right,' said Claire at last. 'That's right. Never mind. I'm sorry.'

'It's all right. I'm glad you called,' said Morgan. 'I'm not leaving for hours. I have time to talk.'

There was silence at Claire's end.

'Claire? What's going on?' Morgan asked.

'No. I shouldn't have called you. I always call you.' There was a note of real regret in Claire's otherwise affectless tone.

'That's all right,' said Morgan without conviction. If she was honest with herself, she had to admit that she felt slightly...nettled by the call. She didn't want to think about Claire's problems. She didn't want anything to spoil this day. She had done her best for her friend, and now she just wanted to think about her own trip, and the glorious weeks ahead. But immediately she realized she was being petty, and was ashamed of her own impatience. 'Don't be silly,' she said warmly. 'Of course you should call me. What's up?'

'Something has happened,' said Claire.

It was an innocuous statement. But Morgan instantly felt alarm coursing through her veins, although she couldn't say why. 'What's happened?' she asked warily.

'Guy,' said Claire. 'And...' Claire's voice cracked. 'Drew.'

'What about Guy and Drew?' Morgan asked. Her heart was beating fast.

'They're...dead,' said Claire.

'THEY'RE DEAD!' Morgan cried. Chills ran through her, criss-crossing her arms and legs. 'Oh, my God. Claire...Oh, my God.'

The middle-aged couple across the way facing Morgan looked up at her, their eyes filled with concern.

Morgan hunched over in her seat, turning a shoulder to

them, and gripping the phone with both hands. 'What do you mean? What happened? Were they in an accident? Oh Claire, I can't believe this.' Guy and Drew both dead? For one brief, selfish moment, Morgan thought again about herself. Her trip would have to be postponed. She thought of Simon describing the romantic old hotel, and then she was instantly ashamed of herself for even thinking about such a thing when Drew... Morgan pictured her godchild, the tiny, innocent baby, resting in her arms only days ago. Tears filled her eyes and she felt an actual stabbing pain in her heart. 'Oh, my God. Nooo...'

'It wasn't an accident,' Claire said in a dull voice. Through her confusion, through her own shock, Morgan suddenly realized that Claire was not crying. Not screaming. And then, simultaneously, she registered what Claire had said. 'It wasn't an accident? What do you mean? What was it then? What happened?'

'Morgan, I need you here,' said Claire.

Morgan sighed and released the handle on her carry-on luggage. 'Of course, Claire. I'll come right away. But how... What happened?'

'They were...killed,' said Claire. 'Murdered.'

Morgan put a hand to her chest. She could feel a pulse beating beneath her clavicle. 'Oh, my God. It can't be. Who? Where did this happen...?'

'At our house,' said Claire.

'Jesus, Claire. I don't understand. Were you there when it happened? Oh, I can't believe this. Are you all right?'

Once again there was silence at Claire's end. Morgan realized that she needed to get a hold of herself. Claire was obviously in desperate need of someone to lean on. She was not helping Claire by being hysterical. She needed to take charge. She forced herself to think, to speak calmly. 'Claire, are you hurt? Where are you right now?'

'I'm at the police station,' said Claire.

'OK, good,' said Morgan. 'At least you're safe.'

'They've been asking me questions,' said Claire.

'Questions? My God. What's wrong with those people?' Morgan cried. 'You should be at the hospital. You're probably in shock. Look, you tell the cops that you will answer their questions later. Or let me talk to them. I'll tell them. Is anyone with you? Astrid? Or Lucy? Anyone who could take you to the hospital?'

'No,' said Claire.

'All right, look. Call someone to come and take you to the hospital or at least a doctor's office.'

'I can't call them,' said Claire softly.

'Why not?' Morgan demanded.

'The police told me I only get one call,' said Claire.

'One call? That's ridiculous...' Morgan began to protest. And then, in the next moment, the enormity of what Claire was saying registered in Morgan's mind. 'Wait a minute, wait a minute...' Morgan pleaded.

'I called you,' said Claire simply.

Morgan felt dizzy, as if the airport lounge was tilting. 'What...are you talking about? Are you saying that they're questioning you because...they think that you...?'

'They've arrested me,' said Claire.

For a moment it was Morgan who was silent. Like everyone else, she'd heard of innocent people being arrested, convicted. But that was an aberration. Normally if you were arrested, it was because the police had reason to believe you were guilty. Or she had always believed that until this moment. But Claire...? No. Claire kill her husband and her baby? It was...impossible. Almost... laughable. For a moment, Morgan felt as if she was in some bizarre dream, that this call wasn't even real. But it was real. 'Claire,' she said. 'I don't know how this has happened, but I do know that it's some awful mistake. Oh, my God...' Morgan glanced at the clock on the wall facing her. How long will it take me to get there, she thought? She had taken the airport shuttle to get to Kennedy. She would have to go back to Brooklyn, and get her car. She was calculating hours. It would take too long. Claire needed help right away. 'Look,' said Morgan. 'You need to have someone with you. Do you and Guy have an attorney that you use...?'

'No,' said Claire. 'Not really.'

'Well, listen. I don't know what's going on, but I know you shouldn't say another word to the police until you have an attorney with you. It doesn't matter if you're innocent. We've all seen enough TV shows about this sort of thing to know. This is how innocent people get into trouble. You just tell the police you can't say anything more to them until an attorney gets there, OK? Then when the attorney arrives, you explain everything to him. He will tell you what to do.'

'It doesn't matter,' said Claire.

Morgan could picture her friend, her eyes vacant, shaking her head. Morgan wished she could reach through the phone and shake her by the shoulders. 'It definitely does matter,' said Morgan. 'Claire, you have to listen to me now. That's why you called me, right? You called me so I could help you. So, listen. You tell them to get you an attorney. If you ask them to do that, they have to do it.'

'It's too late,' said Claire.

'It's not too late,' said Morgan. 'You just tell them that. Say you want an attorney and then don't answer any more questions or say another word. I will be there as soon as I can.'

'I already told them,' said Claire.

Morgan's heart skipped a sickening beat. 'Told them what?'

'That I did it,' said Claire. 'I killed them.'

FOUR

'WHAT?' MORGAN ASKED WEAKLY.

There was the sound of shuffling and voices getting louder in the background. She could hear the muffled sound of Claire's voice, dull and leaden. A conversation was going on between Claire and a brusque male voice, and then Claire returned to the phone. 'I have to go, Morgan,' she said sounding almost like a child. 'I did what you said. I told them that I want an attorney.'

'Let's go,' the male voice rumbled in the background.

'I have to go now. They're putting me in a holding cell,' said Claire. 'Please, hurry, Morgan. Please. I need you.'

Morgan's mouth was so dry that she wondered if she could utter a sound. 'I'll come,' she tried to say. The phone was dead before Claire could reply.

Morgan snapped her phone shut and put it back into her satchel. For a moment she sat there, staring down at the industrial-looking carpet on the lounge floor. The middle-aged woman across the aisle leaned over, and spoke to her, searching Morgan's face. 'I couldn't help overhearing. Are you all right?' she asked.

Morgan met her sympathetic gaze with a confused look in her eyes. 'No,' she said, after a moment. 'No.' Morgan stood up on shaky legs, and gripped the handle of her rolling carry-on bag. 'No. I have to go.'

Morgan hesitated for a moment and then went to the ticket counter, which was still deserted. 'Excuse me,' she said to the lone agent who was working there.

The ticket agent, a black girl with perfect make-up and a slicked-back ponytail, and a name tag which read 'Tanisha', looked up at Morgan. 'Yes?'

'I...am supposed to be going on this flight,' she said. 'To London.'

'Yes.'

'I can't go. I have to leave,' said Morgan. 'Leave the airport.'

'Are you ill?' she asked.

Morgan shook her head. 'I just got a call. A death...in the family,' she said.

'I'm sorry,' the girl named Tanisha asked in a gentler tone. 'Do you want me to reschedule your flight?'

'Oh, no,' said Morgan, her mind racing, as if trying to flee from the admission she had just heard from Claire. The real world felt unreal to her, as if everything she recognized was just a false facade. Everything she ever knew had been a lie. She fumbled in her jacket pocket and handed her boarding pass to Tanisha. 'I don't know what I'm doing. No. Just cross it out. Cross me off the list.'

Morgan started to leave the lounge and then hesitated, and sat back down in one of the far chairs. She had to tell someone, had to talk about it. She looked at the time on her cellphone, made a mental calculation, and then punched in Simon's number.

He answered on the third ring. His voice sounded tinny and far away. In the background she could hear the sounds of music, and people talking and laughing. 'Simon,' she said, her voice shaking. 'It's Morgan.'

'Morgan,' he said, sounded pleased. 'I can hardly hear you. I'm at a drinks party in Belgravia. You'd adore these people. Here, let me step into another room...'

His inference that she would soon meet his friends was consoling. She heard the noise diminishing at the other end and then Simon came back on the line. The sound of his soothing English voice made her want to weep. 'There we go. Let me just...OK. Well, I'm glad to hear from you but, shouldn't you be off to the airport by now?'

'I'm at the airport,' she said. 'But I have to leave. I have to...I can't come. Not tonight.'

She heard a sharp intake of breath. 'Can't come? Morgan, what's the matter? Why ever not?'

Morgan took a deep breath. 'My best friend, Claire, just called me. Remember, I told you. She just had a baby.'

There was a silence at his end.

'I was the godmother.'

'Oh, yes,' he said. 'Right.'

'She's been arrested. They're both dead. The baby and her husband. The police think that she...' Morgan began to cry.

'What?' he said.

Morgan sniffed. 'They think that she was the one who...killed them.'

'Good God. That's horrible,' said Simon. 'There, there. Now, take it easy.'

'It is horrible,' Morgan sobbed.

'No wonder you're upset.'

'Claire is my best friend. She's like a sister to me.'

'But, I'm not quite clear on why you're canceling the trip. I mean, you're not a solicitor. There's not all that much you can do for her.'

'I can stand by her,' said Morgan angrily. 'She has no one else.'

'Well, of course,' he said soothingly. 'That's true, of course. But you realize that these...situations can take a long time to be resolved.'

Morgan was silent.

'Well, I mean, they do. It's just that simple.'

'I shouldn't have bothered you,' said Morgan. 'I have to go.'

'Now, hold it there. Steady on. That was boorish of me. One can't think of one's self at a time like this. I'm just a bit…disappointed, that's all. I was so looking forward to our…journey.'

Morgan nodded, but didn't speak. Part of her wanted to say 'me too', and part of her wanted to rail at him for being so unfeeling.

'You've had a shock. Why don't you call me back when you know more,' he said gently. 'We'll sort it out. Maybe we can rebook.'

Morgan felt as if her heart was frozen. 'As you said, it could take a long time.'

Simon was quiet, considering her reply. Finally, he said, 'Circumstances often change. Let's just wait and see what happens. Shall we?'

IT WAS TWILIGHT BY THE TIME Morgan arrived in the town of West Briar. On previous visits she had walked on the beach, and visited the shops downtown, but she had never had occasion to notice where the police department was. She pulled up beside an elderly man who was walking his dog and asked him for directions. It turned out that the police department was headquartered in a historic building across the street from the firehouse. She probably would have found the place without directions, because of the uproar on the sidewalk outside of the building, where reporters and news vans were clustered. Morgan had to park her car several blocks away and wend her way through the milling representatives of the media to reach the entrance.

The weathered, cedar-shake façade of the police department building resembled those of its near neighbors—

a whaling museum and a pastry shop. But as Morgan pulled open the door, it was immediately obvious that only the outer shell of the building was of a historic vintage. Inside, the building had been renovated to include all the latest equipment, surveillance cameras, humming computers and ergonomic office furniture. The white-haired desk sergeant asked Morgan her business.

Morgan frowned. 'I'm here to see…Claire Bolton.'

She did not have to explain who Claire Bolton was. The desk sergeant's ruddy face turned a shade redder, and his eyes narrowed. 'Are you another reporter? I already told you people. There will be no interviews with the prisoner.'

The prisoner. Morgan turned the word over in her mind. How could it be? How could he be talking about Claire? 'No,' she said. 'I'm not a reporter. I'm her…' She started to say 'friend', and then immediately stopped herself. Mere friendship would probably not gain her access to their most notorious prisoner. She was pretty sure of that. 'I'm her sister,' she said.

'What's your name?' the desk sergeant demanded. 'Morgan Adair.'

'And you're her sister?' the sergeant said skeptically. Morgan nodded. 'She called me and asked me to come. I just arrived in town.'

'Just a minute,' he said. He picked up the phone on his desk and spoke into it. 'Yeah, she says she's the sister. Morgan.'

The desk sergeant waited, and then nodded. 'Awright,' he said. He put the phone down and turned to Morgan. 'The van for the county jail is on its way to pick her up. You can visit with her until it arrives. But that's it.'

'Thank you,' said Morgan humbly.

'Hardiman, front and center,' the sergeant bawled.

A heavyset female officer came up to the desk. 'Yessir.'
'Take this lady to see her sister. The Bolton woman.'

'Yessir.'

'Stay down there with her. She can go in the cell,
but pat her down before she goes in and again when she
comes out. We don't want any fuck-ups here till we get
her moved to county.'

'Yessir,' said the officer, a square-shaped, acne-scarred
woman in her forties. She turned to Morgan solemnly.
'Come with me.'

Morgan followed the straight-backed officer through a
set of locked doors, which she opened by putting her palm
against a scanner. They entered a freshly painted room in
which there was a bathroom without doors on either side
as you entered, and then four barred cells, two on each
side. There did not appear to be anyone in the first two
cells. Morgan wanted to call out, but she didn't want to
break any rules. She took off her shoes and submitted to
a wanding, and then a patdown by the officer. She obeyed
as the officer told her to stay put. Officer Hardiman went
to the cell on the far left.

'Your sister's here,' she said abruptly.

There was no reply. The officer gestured for Morgan to
come to where she was standing. Her heart beating fast,
Morgan approached the cell door. Officer Hardiman unlocked the barred door with a card key and motioned for
Morgan to go in. After Morgan entered, she slammed it
shut behind her.

'I'm right here,' said Officer Hardiman. 'I'm not going
anywhere. And I'll tell you when you have to leave.'

'Thank you,' said Morgan meekly.

The cell was much darker than the corridor, but only
because of the absence of windows in the room. The
walls looked freshly painted, although they were de-

faced by obscene graffiti. It was clearly a facility only meant for short-term imprisonment. The cell had a small metal table, a chair and a bed, but no toilet or sink. Claire, dressed in her own stained sweatshirt and jeans, was sitting on the edge of the cot. Her short, wedge-cut hair looked flat and without shine. There were dark circles around her eyes. Her flawless complexion was waxy in the dim light. Her huge, dark eyes were fixed on Morgan as she entered the little cell.

Now that they were face to face, Morgan found herself almost afraid to meet that familiar gaze. She was afraid that she would not see the person she knew when she looked into Claire's eyes. The person she recognized. The whole way home from the airport and en route to West Briar, Morgan had tried not to think about the words she had heard Claire say. 'I did it. I killed them.' The story was already on the radio, and Morgan had been forced to change the station, and finally switch on her iPod to try and avoid hearing multiple recountings of the day's terrible events.

Now she was locked in a jail cell with Claire, and there was no avoiding it any longer. She looked at her dearest friend. Claire got up from the cot, crossed the cell to Morgan, and put her arms around her.

'Thank God you're here,' Claire whispered. Then she let out a sob.

Morgan could smell baby powder on Claire's sweatshirt, mixed with the odor of dried milk and spit-up. In her mind, she saw Drew's tiny face, his rosebud lips and bright little eyes, and she felt herself stiffen as Claire's arms enfolded her. She placed her hands lightly on Claire's trembling back. Normally, Claire's grief would have been enough to make Morgan want to cry too. But not today. Morgan's questions buzzed in her mind, like bees in a hive. Was Claire crying over the loss of Drew and Guy? Or was she crying because she was a prisoner here in this cell? It seemed…perverse for her to cry over her loved ones if she was responsible for their deaths.

Seeming to sense Morgan's hesitation, Claire dropped her arms and stepped back, folding her arms over her narrow chest and rubbing her own forearms, as if she were freezing. 'Sit down,' she said, indicating the chair.

Morgan nodded. She pulled the chair out from the table and sat. She licked her dry lips and glanced up at Claire who was watching her. 'Sorry. I'm just trying to…' Morgan's voice faded away.

Claire resumed her seat on the edge of the bed. She folded her hands in her lap, kneading them together.

'Are you OK?' Morgan asked. 'Physically, I mean.' Claire nodded without speaking.

'Did the lawyer come?' Morgan asked.

'Yes,' said Claire.

'What did he say?' Morgan asked.

Claire rubbed her eyes with the heels of her hands. Then she took a deep breath. 'She. It was a woman. Noreen was her name. Noreen…something. She left a card. There, on the table.'

Morgan looked down and immediately saw the cream-colored business card. 'Noreen Quick, attorney-at-law,' it read over the address.

'Noreen, then,' said Morgan. 'What did she say?'

'She's pregnant,' Claire said, and her eyes filled with tears. 'Any minute she's going to have her baby.'

'Claire!' Morgan spoke sharply. 'What did she say? About your case.'

Claire shook her head and sighed. 'She said it was a difficult case because I confessed to the police. Honestly, Morgan, I can't remember much of what she said. I'm so exhausted. I just kept wishing I had a tranquilizer or something to knock me out so I could sleep. They won't give me anything in here.'

Morgan felt an unreasoning flash of anger. Tranquilizers? That was all she could think of after all that had happened? How could you admit to killing your husband and your child and then forget how your lawyer had advised you? How could you admit to killing at all, and just want to sleep. 'Never mind,' said Morgan coolly. She slipped the card into her own jacket pocket. 'I'll talk to her.'

Claire looked up at her gratefully. 'Would you, Morgan?'

'Yes, of course,' said Morgan stiffly. 'I came here to help.'

'Thank God for you,' said Claire. 'I feel like I have no one else in the whole world. Guy's family won't help me.'

'You can't blame them,' said Morgan sharply.

Claire blushed beneath her sallow skin and looked down at her lap. 'No,' she whispered. 'Of course not.'

Looking at that familiar bent head, Morgan felt a sudden, unexpected rush of tenderness. This couldn't be true. There had to be some mistake. This wasn't some crazed killer. This was Claire, with whom she had shared dorm rooms and apartments and hotel rooms on the road. Claire, with whom she had streaked her hair, taken long walks discussing the meaning of life, laughed till she cried remembering how they had stalked the science teacher they both had a crush on in junior high. Claire, who was closer to her than a sister.

'Oh Claire,' Morgan pleaded. 'Tell me this is some big misunderstanding. I mean, you couldn't kill anyone. Let alone your baby...'

Claire remained silent. A tear trickled down her cheek.

'How did it happen? Just tell me what happened...' Claire gripped the sides of her head as if it were pounding.

'Don't make me say it all again.'

'Why?' Morgan cried. 'Why would you ever do such a thing?'

Claire looked up at her with torment in her eyes. 'I don't know why. I keep going over it in my mind. I mean, the baby had been so...fussy. And Guy...I threw him out. I was so angry at him for lying to me about his daughter.'

'Wait,' said Morgan. 'If you threw him out, how come he was at the house?'

Claire shrugged. 'I let him come back home that night. To the guest room. I was trying to get over it but every time I looked at him...'

'So that's why you killed them?' Morgan said incredulously. Even as she said it, it seemed preposterous. Impossible. 'Because of Eden?'

Claire shook her head. 'Maybe. I'm not sure.'

'I don't understand,' Morgan wailed. 'How...' How could you, Morgan wanted to say.

Claire misunderstood. 'It was very early this morning. It was still dark. I was in the bathroom. With Drew. He was in the tub.'

'What were you doing with the baby in the bathroom at that hour?'

'I...don't know. I guess...I was giving him a bath.'

'In that big, clawfoot tub? He was so little. He was barely big enough for the sink.'

Claire seemed to be staring past Morgan at the scene in her mind. 'There was water in the tub. Drew was in the water. Guy came into the bathroom and I...we had an argument. And, I don't know. I guess, maybe, we struggled. And Guy slipped. He hit his head on the edge of the cast iron tub. There was a lot of blood. Everywhere.'

'So, you're saying it was an accident,' said Morgan skeptically.

Claire looked at her hopefully. 'It must have been.'

'And Drew?'

'Oh, Morgan…' Claire's voice broke. 'He drowned in the tub. My baby…'

Morgan felt physically sick. She gasped for air, trying to force herself not to vomit. 'Claire. You let him drown in the tub? Jesus Christ.'

'Don't sound like that, Morgan,' Claire pleaded. 'I didn't mean to. I know I didn't mean to. Don't you be mad at me too.'

'You didn't mean to? You sound like a child,' Morgan upbraided her. 'This isn't like swiping some bubblegum from the 7-Eleven.'

'I know that,' said Claire, suddenly angry.

Morgan jumped up from the chair and began to pace the small cell like a tiger in a cage. She raked her hand through her hair, trying to process this information. Trying to imagine Claire…

Officer Hardiman's walkie-talkie emitted static, and the officer responded, speaking in a low voice.

Morgan forced herself to calm down. She had to calm down for Claire's sake. Claire had no one else to support her. No matter what she had done, their years of friendship required some kind of allegiance. Yes it was appalling, but accidents did happen. Perhaps it had been a series of horrible accidents. Accident or not, Claire needed Morgan to be on her side. Everyone deserved someone to be on their side. Morgan turned and looked at Claire, who sat slump-shouldered on the bed, her gaze far away.

'I'll do what I can to help you, Claire,' Morgan said. Claire looked up at her, anguish and gratitude in her eyes.

'County van is here,' announced Officer Hardiman.

'Two officers are on their way down here to escort the prisoner.' She inserted the key in the door and slid it open far enough for Morgan to emerge. 'Ma'am, I'm going to have to ask you to leave.'

Claire reached out and grasped Morgan's hand.

Morgan had to pull her hand free from her friend's grip. She could hear the heavy tread of boots approaching. 'I have to go.'

Claire nodded and wiped her eyes. 'I know. But Morgan, one more thing. Will you be sure to feed Dusty?'

It took Morgan a moment to realize what Claire was asking.

'Your cat?' said Morgan in disbelief. 'You're worried about your cat?'

'Please,' said Claire.

'All right. All right,' said Morgan. 'I will.'

'OUT. NOW,' roared Officer Hardiman. Morgan jumped, and hurried to obey.

FIVE

PHOTOGRAPHERS' FLASHES POPPED like fireworks in the dark as Claire was escorted, handcuffed, a burly state trooper on either side, out of the West Briar police station toward the waiting van. Across the street, Morgan watched as her best friend, so tall and comely that people sometimes mistook her for a fashion model, now stumbled down the walk in a filthy sweatshirt and jeans. Her sallow face, ashen eyes and sunken cheeks made her look like a malnourished street urchin. Reporters shouted her name, but Claire did not respond. She let herself be boosted up into the van, as one cop scrambled up into the seat beside her and another slammed the back doors behind them. Then he turned and faced the crowd. 'OK folks,' he cried. 'Show's over.'

The newspeople began to disperse, ready to move on to the next story, as the van which transported prisoners to the county jail pulled away from the curb. Morgan knew that she needed to return to her car. She needed to decide what to do next. Where she was going to stay. All of that. But, instead, she remained where she stood, as if rooted, still trying to absorb, like a series of blows, all that she had seen and heard.

A silver, ostentatiously large, late-model SUV with black-tinted windows pulled up to the curb in front of her and idled there, blocking her view across the street. The passenger-side window descended, and the driver leaned across the seat. Morgan frowned. Some rubbernecker wanting details on what had happened, no doubt. She was prepared to snap back at any such request.

'Morgan?'

Morgan frowned, surprised to hear her own name, and peered into the car. It took her only a moment to recognize him. Sandy Raymond was successful and wealthy, but no one would call him a handsome man. He was a stout man, not fat, but not muscular either. His brown hair was longish, and always looked a little greasy. His face was scarred from teenage acne, his nose crooked from having been broken, and his blue eyes were small and keen.

Although Claire and Sandy had dated for a year before they got engaged, Morgan had never spent much time with the couple. Although they did go out, and attended the odd charity event, Claire often told her that Sandy had a reclusive nature. Sandy divided his time among several impressive homes, but he liked to live informally, and didn't care much for entertaining. Morgan was frankly surprised that Sandy even knew her name. 'Hello,' she said. 'What are you doing here?'

'Same thing you are,' said Sandy abruptly. 'I'm…concerned about Claire.'

'Really?' said Morgan. The skepticism in her voice spoke louder than words. Why would he want to support the woman who had left him the day after their engagement party? The New York tabloids had had a field day with the public humiliation of a most eligible, wealthy man dumped for a chef with a catering business. It would have been understandable if Sandy took a little satisfaction from the terrible turn of events in Claire's life.

'Yes, really,' said Sandy irritably.

'I'm just surprised,' said Morgan.

'Why? I almost married the woman. Naturally I'm concerned about her.'

Sandy didn't know that Morgan had also seen him in the choir loft of the church during Drew's baptism, where he was clearly not welcome. Morgan pressed her lips together and looked away from him. Sandy Raymond's actions were very hard to understand. But she was not about to admit it. 'Right,' she said.

'Are you going to stick around town?' he asked.

'Yeah,' she said, thinking of Claire's concern that her cat be fed. It still struck her as bizarre, in light of Claire's murderous rampage against her family. 'I guess I'll stay at Claire's house.'

Sandy frowned and shook his head. 'That's not going to happen,' he said.

Morgan bristled. 'Excuse me?'

Sandy did not seem to notice her chilly tone. 'Well, it's just that the house is a crime scene. The police probably have it closed down until they're finished in there. They won't let anyone stay there tonight.'

'Oh,' said Morgan, immediately realizing the truth of what he said. 'I suppose that's true.'

'Look,' he said, 'I have that great big house. You've seen it. I've got six bedrooms and it's just me and my girlfriend there. Why don't you stay at my place?'

Morgan noted the mention of his girlfriend. Clearly he had moved on. Morgan thought about Sandy's huge house, a house she had only visited once—on the night of the ill-fated engagement party. It was a sprawling old mansion, tastelessly renovated with anachronisms like a sports bar, and a screening room. Still, the offer was tempting, if only for the luxury of it all. But it just didn't seem right. 'Well, that's very nice of you, but I can get a room somewhere,' said Morgan. She thought fleetingly of the comfortable, cozy Captain's House, now closed. 'I can find something…'

'Look Morgan,' he interrupted her abruptly. 'You've got to be as blown away as I am. It might help us both to air it out. Talk about it. You'd be doing me a favor if you stayed at my house,' he said. 'Really.'

Morgan hesitated, but there seemed to be honest chagrin in his tone. She recognized it, because she felt it herself. 'I don't know…' she said. 'I don't want to bother you.'

'No bother. Do you know the way?' he asked, as if she had already agreed to his proposal. 'Do you want to follow me in your car?'

'No,' said Morgan. She had vivid memories of that stately old house, built on the oceanfront, its gardens leading down to the dunes. 'I can find my way. Thanks.' Morgan was weary from the day, from the upheaval in her plans and, most of all, from the shock of Claire's arrest. Her confession. She felt overwhelmed in the face of it all. But she had come here to help. And Claire was worried about her cat. If Claire wanted her to feed the cat, then Morgan would do that. 'There's something I have to do first,' she said.

'OK. Well, we'll be home all evening,' he said. 'You do what you need to do and I'll see you when you get there.'

Morgan nodded, and straightened up. 'Thanks. See you later,' she said.

Before the words were out, the passenger window of the SUV rose, blocking the driver from sight.

MORGAN HAD NO IDEA if there was cat food in the house, or if she would even be allowed to enter the house, so she stopped at a mini-mart and bought a few cans of cat food. Then she continued on to Claire and Guy's cottage. As

Sandy had predicted, the house was dark and had been sealed off by the police. The balloons from Drew's christening were still tied by limp ribbons to the mailbox, but they had lost most of their air, and no longer danced. Instead, criss-crossed crime scene tape flapped in the night breeze. The house looked forlorn. It was only last Saturday, as she arrived on the day of the baptism, that Morgan had seen Dusty on the front step, and the whole picture was one of an ideal home, an ideal life. Morgan sighed, and parked the car.

She got her flashlight out of the glove compartment, picked up the sack of cat food cans, and walked down the driveway. 'Dusty,' she called softly. She scanned the yard with her flashlight, but there was no sign of the cat. Dusty was a Tom, a feral cat whom Claire had found, investigating a dumpster behind the local Shop-Rite. Though he had been easily house-trained, he was wary of people, and Claire was the only one he would allow to pet him. He came and went from the house at will, using a cat door which Guy had installed for him. He avoided human social gatherings, and kept strictly to his own schedule. Morgan wondered where his wanderings had taken Dusty tonight. He could be somewhere out in the neighborhood. Surely all the commotion with the police today would have scared him away. But, Morgan thought, as she cautiously circled around to the back of the house, calling to him, he might have gone back inside.

Morgan went up to the back door which led to the kitchen. The yellow crime scene tape was loose in the back, whipping back and forth in the breeze. Morgan climbed up the back steps and peered in the kitchen window, looking for the glow of a cat's eyes. All she saw was darkness. It made Morgan shudder to look into the house, to think about the horror that had occurred there.

Guy, dead on the bathroom floor, and baby Drew, face down... She forced the thought from her mind. She would be glad to be away from this place and she was grateful now for Sandy Raymond's offer of hospitality. I'll just put out the cat food and leave, she thought. She could leave the food outside for Dusty. Surely he would find it there.

But then she realized that she had nothing to put the food into. She needed a plate, a bowl—something on which to dump the contents of the can.

Morgan hesitated, wishing she had stopped somewhere and bought a dish. She looked around the backyard for some sort of plate. There were a couple of flowerpots on a table in the backyard. The flowerpot saucer might do, she thought. As she pondered this, she absently turned the doorknob on the back door. The door swung open.

'Oh, God,' Morgan exclaimed, startled by the yielding of the door.

She had to let her heart calm down a little bit as she held the door ajar. It wasn't locked. No big deal, she told herself. Don't get carried away. She shone her flashlight around the kitchen. The cat dish was on the floor, near the sink. That was simple. She would just empty the can into it and leave. Even if Dusty was outside, the cat was sure to come in through the cat door searching for food.

OK, time to go in. Just do it. She pushed the door in a little way, and edged through it. For a moment she stood there in the darkness, listening. The house was silent as a tomb. It felt as if every vestige of happiness that had ever existed in this house had leaked away, like air through a pinprick in a balloon. She imagined that the house was waiting for something, the silence within these walls was of voices stilled. Morgan's stomach started to churn. She reminded herself that she hadn't eaten in hours. It isn't the house, she told herself. You're just tired and hungry.

Part of her wanted to go further into the house, to go to the bathroom where it had happened. She had a morbid desire to see it with her own eyes. But when she got right down to doing it, the idea was simply too frightening.

Feed the cat and get out, she thought. Don't linger. Setting her flashlight on the counter, she bent down and picked up the two bowls. One had a picture of a dripping spigot on it. The other, comical, brightly painted cats. She emptied out the cat's drinking water and changed it. Then she cleaned out the other bowl and refilled it with cat food.

'Dusty,' she said in a loud whisper. There was no sign of the cat. Carefully, she crouched down with the two full bowls and placed them back on the floor. Suddenly, she felt as if she were being watched. The hair on the back of her neck stood up. For a moment, she was frozen, afraid to look. Then, defiance kicked in and, with a rapidly beating heart, she whirled and looked into the darkness beyond the kitchen, out in the dining room.

Something was moving in the dark. Morgan stifled a scream and scrambled to her feet, groping on the counter for the flashlight. 'Who's there?' she demanded. She switched on the beam with trembling hands and jerked it toward the movement she had seen. Suddenly there was a horrible screeching cry, and she felt something hit her from behind in the legs, buckling her knees.

Morgan let out a cry as she felt her legs being clawed through her pants. She jumped and pointed the torch down. Dusty was standing on his hind legs, gripping her calf with his claws and growling like a demon.

Morgan yelped and shook him off. Dusty jumped back, raising his back and hissing, his eyes flashing yellow in the dark.

'Dusty, goddamit,' Morgan swore. Although at the

sight of the cat she felt almost relieved. She was not afraid of an angry house cat. She glanced back at the dining room, but whatever movement she had seen was no longer visible. She told herself that it must have been Dusty skulking through the house. She began to edge toward the kitchen door, shining the flashlight in the cat's eyes. 'Go on and eat. And leave me alone.'

Morgan fumbled for the doorknob behind her, and started to turn it.

Suddenly, the door was jerked open from outside and Morgan cried out and fell back into the kitchen, as a dark figure filled the doorway.

SIX

'HEY,' AN ANGRY VOICE DEMANDED.

Morgan found herself averting her eyes from another flashlight beam. When her eyes adjusted, she saw the outline of a uniformed police officer at the foot of the back steps. 'Oh, God, you scared me,' said Morgan.

The policeman frowned. He was young and had a wide girth and a double chin. 'Who are you? And what are you doing in this house, miss?'

Morgan decided that the truth was best, and as little of it as possible. 'I'm a friend. I'm feeding the cat,' she said.

'This is a crime scene. Didn't you see the tape?'

'What tape?' Morgan asked innocently.

The cop frowned, and looked around, finding the broken end of the tape caught on a cedar shake. 'This tape,' he said. 'Don't tell me you don't know what that means.'

Morgan lowered her head and hurried down the steps. 'Sorry. I was just worried about the cat,' she said. 'The door was open.'

'Is that your car parked out front?' he asked.

'Yes,' said Morgan. 'I wasn't sneaking in. I just didn't realize I wasn't supposed to come inside.'

The cop looked at her with narrowed eyes. 'You're a friend of the people who live here?' he asked.

Morgan evaded the question. 'Yes. I'm just taking care of their cat,' she said.

'Don't you know what happened here today?' he asked. It sounded almost like an accusation.

Morgan hesitated. Then she nodded. 'Something terrible,' she said.

The cop snorted. 'You can say that again.'

'Am I in trouble?' Morgan asked.

The young cop thought it over, and then shook his head. 'No,' he said. 'Just go.' He turned his flashlight on to the driveway and Morgan hurried into the path of the beam, not waiting for him to change his mind.

It WAS MORE DIFFICULT TO FIND Sandy Raymond's house than Morgan had anticipated. Part of it was that her nerves were jangled from the trip to Claire's cottage. But it was also because the driveways along that winding stretch bordering the sea were tucked between large trees, and there were no signs or lettered mailboxes to identify the occupants of these huge homes. After turning into several driveways, only to find an unfamiliar house when she emerged from the tree canopy into the clearing, she finally took the correct one. She recognized the house the moment she saw it. It was an imposing, gray stone house which would have fit perfectly into the English countryside.

Morgan pulled up into the graveled parking area beside which four expensive luxury vehicles, from a Mercedes convertible to the silver SUV, were already parked. She looked up at the symmetrical façade of the house with its tall multi-paned windows and surrounding patios. The carriage lights bracketing the front door were not illuminated, and Morgan immediately felt ill at ease. Sandy hadn't even bothered to leave the lights on. This oversight seemed to say, louder than words, you are not really welcome here. Morgan hesitated. She remembered that Claire often said that Sandy didn't like company. Or maybe, she thought, Sandy was playing some kind of mind game with her, to pay her back for Claire's betrayal. Whatever the reason, it wasn't too late to get a motel room somewhere. She didn't need something nice like the Captain's House. Anything would do. Morgan replaced the key in the ignition and turned it.

Suddenly, the front door of the mansion opened, and Sandy, dressed in a hoody and baggy sweatpants, came out and peered down at the circular drive. Then he ducked back into the house and the carriage lights were suddenly blazing.

Morgan frowned, and sat in the idling car. Sandy reappeared on the front patio.

'Morgan,' he called out. 'Come on in.'

Morgan hesitated. Then, she removed the key from the ignition, and got out of the car. She went around and opened the trunk of her car. She still had the same rolling bag she had been planning to carry on the plane. When she arrived back in Brooklyn after leaving the airport, she did not want to waste time repacking. She had tossed the bag into the trunk of her car and took off. Now, she swung the bag out of the trunk, pulled up the handle and rolled it to the foot of the stone steps where he stood. 'The lights were off,' she said, 'so I wasn't sure…'

Sandy shook his head. 'Sorry about that.' He did not descend the steps to help her with her bag. Morgan jerked the densely packed, wheeled carry-on bag up the stone staircase. As she started to walk inside, Sandy turned and reached for the handle of her rolling bag.

'I've got it,' said Morgan firmly.

'Suit yourself,' said Sandy. He led the way into the house. The front hallway, with its curving staircase, was flanked by two huge living rooms, each boasting large ultrasuede sofas and chairs in shades of beige, taupe and chocolate. The window treatments were silken and formal, but they were also of neutral shades and blended into the walls. The rugs were sisal, and the whole appearance of the rooms was pristine, bland and safe. Morgan could still remember how disappointing it had looked to her the first time she was here. The decor, which was probably tailored by an expensive interior designer to Sandy's casual bachelor life, was a distinct let-down after the elegant façade of the house.

A computer with a mountain-range screen saver was set up on a blond-wood, ergonomic-looking station which stood beside the unlit fireplace. Sandy sat down in front of the screen, his back to her, and began to tap at the keyboard. He indicated with a vague gesture the armless, overstuffed chairs. Morgan sat down and looked around.

'You want a beer?' he asked, lifting a green bottle from the top of the computer desk, his eyes fixed on the screen.

'Do you have any wine?' Morgan asked.

'Like, a whole cellar,' he smirked. 'Farah,' he bellowed. 'Bring a glass of wine.'

'What kind?' a faraway voice called back.

He turned to Morgan. 'Red or white?'

'Doesn't matter,' said Morgan.

'Montepulciano,' he called out.

Farah, Morgan thought? Was that his girlfriend, or the household help? Judging from his tone, Morgan figured it must be a housekeeper he was summoning.

Sandy turned his swivel chair around to face Morgan. 'She'll be here in a minute. It's a big house,' he said apologetically, but with unmistakable pride.

Morgan nodded. 'It's a beautiful house. It's just so... impressive.'

'Any trouble finding it?'

Morgan shook her head. 'I remembered from the...'

'Engagement party,' Sandy said. He frowned and turned back to his computer. Then he brightened as a beautiful girl with glossy brown hair halfway to her elbows appeared. She wore a soft, form-fitting pink terrycloth hoody, half-zipped so that the tops of her breasts were visible, and gray leggings. She was barefoot, and carrying a glass of garnet-hued wine in either hand.

This is not a housekeeper, Morgan thought. This had to be the new girlfriend. Sandy had, indeed, moved on. And he wanted her to know it.

'There you are,' said Sandy, speaking to Farah. 'This is Morgan. She's an old friend.'

The girl brought one of the glasses to Morgan and handed it to her with a sweet smile. 'Hi. I'm Farah,' she said.

Morgan could not help comparing this girl to Claire. Where Claire was graceful and elegant, with her short, stylish haircut and sinewy model's body, Farah had the body and hair of a centerfold. Where Claire was cool, this girl was hot. When Morgan looked in Claire's eyes she saw humor and intelligence. When she looked into Farah's eyes, she saw openness, sweetness. Each was a beauty in her own way, but they were nothing alike. 'Thanks, Farah,' said Morgan.

Farah glided over to the sofa and curled up on the cushion like a cat. 'Sandy,' she chided him gently, 'can't you tear yourself away from that screen? We have a guest.' Sandy sighed and swiveled around, looking at Farah. She beckoned to him with one finger. He obediently rose from the desk chair, picked up his beer from the top of the computer desk and joined her on the sofa.

'Move,' he said, and Farah acquiesced, scooting over

so he could have the corner seat. He draped his forearm around her narrow shoulders.

Morgan took a sip of her wine. It had a bold, rich taste. She hoped it would not make her dizzy. She hadn't eaten in hours.

'So, Morgan,' said Sandy, without preamble. 'What was the story with Claire and her husband? Was he beating her up or something?'

From under the shelter of his arm, Farah looked up at Sandy innocently. 'Who are you talking about?'

'My old girlfriend,' said Sandy casually. 'Claire. Morgan's an old friend of hers. Claire was arrested today for killing her husband and baby. Don't you ever watch the news?'

Farah shrugged and smiled apologetically at Morgan. 'Not really.'

'So what was it?' Sandy asked. 'Was he cheating on her?'

Morgan frowned. 'No. No, nothing like that. They were happy.'

'They couldn't have been that happy,' Sandy observed bluntly.

'I guess every marriage has its problems,'Morgan conceded. She thought about Eden, but she didn't want to mention the secrets Guy had kept from Claire. It seemed pointless, now that he was dead. 'Claire has had a tough time since the baby came along.'

'Don't get me wrong,' Sandy interrupted. 'I'm not shedding any tears for Guy Bolton. I paid him a small fortune to come to my house and make an engagement party, and he ran off with my bride-to-be.'

Farah sat up straight and looked at him in amazement. 'No way.'

'Oh, yeah. I figured you knew. It was all over the Net.

They thought it was a riot that the dot-com mogul got dumped the day after his engagement party,' said Sandy. Then he caressed the young woman's shiny mane. 'That's right. You don't read.'

'I read,' Farah protested, punching him playfully before snuggling down next to him again.

Sandy took a pull on his beer bottle. 'So, why did she do it?' Sandy asked.

Morgan sighed. 'I don't know. It seems...unbelievable.'

'But she confessed,' said Sandy sharply.

'She did.'

'Jesus.'

'I know.'

'Who's her attorney?' he asked.

'I don't know. Some woman named Noreen Quick.'

'I never heard of her.'

'Claire seemed to like her.'

'What does Claire know?' Sandy demanded impatiently. 'She can't be trusted right now. She doesn't know what the hell she's doing. Obviously.'

Morgan felt a little put off by his abruptness, but there was truth in what he said. 'Maybe not,' said Morgan. 'But it's still her choice.'

Sandy shook his head and took another pull on his beer, wiping his upper lip on his sweatshirt sleeve. 'Claire needs the best criminal attorney money can buy. Is money a problem? Cause I can pay for it,' Sandy offered, waving his beer bottle expansively.

'That's so nice of you,' said Farah. She looked at Morgan, wide-eyed. 'Isn't that nice of him?' She lifted her head like a baby bird and kissed his cheek. He did not seem to notice.

'Yes, it is nice of him. And I agree with you that she needs a really good attorney, but it's not up to us,' said

Morgan. 'Thank you, though. That's so generous of you. Especially after…all that's happened.'

Sandy held his hands wide apart, as if to say that he had nothing to hide. 'The woman's in big trouble,' he said. 'I'm just trying to help.'

'I appreciate it,' Morgan said. 'I'm sure that Claire will too.'

Sandy shrugged. 'It's no problem for me.'

Morgan studied his coarse features, his small blue eyes. He tried to appear casual, expansive. But the tension in his shoulders and in his jaw told a different story. She thought about the fact that she had seen him at Drew's christening, hiding in the shadows. She decided not to mention it. Morgan put her wine glass down on the cocktail table in front of the sofa. 'You know,' she said, 'I am beat and I have a feeling tomorrow is going to be a long day.'

Sandy nodded. 'Farah, take her up to the middle guest room.' Farah immediately began to uncoil herself from the couch. 'And get her something to eat if she's hungry,' Sandy ordered. Then Sandy looked at Morgan. 'Are you hungry?'

Morgan stood up. She disliked the way he ordered his companion around. Had he treated Claire like this? She had spent almost no time with them as a couple, but Morgan couldn't imagine Claire allowing any man to treat her that way. No wonder she left him, Morgan thought. What she could not understand was how Claire had gotten involved with him in the first place. Despite the generosity, the hospitality he offered, there was a deliberate lack of finesse about him. As if he wanted to emphasize the point that he had earned a fortune without bothering to be polite. Morgan did not want to defy his wishes, especially in his house, but no matter what he said, Morgan also did not want Farah to have to wait on her like a servant. 'Just point me toward the kitchen. I'll grab something myself.'

'No,' he said. 'Let Farah get it. That's her job around here.' Then he reached up and slapped Farah on her small, firm derrière. 'She's got to earn her keep somehow.'

Farah's mouth dropped open in feigned outrage. Then she grinned, bent over, murmured something in his ear, and kissed him as if to reward him for being amusing.

Sandy shoved her gently away. 'Yeah, yeah, OK. Go on, now,' he said.

Farah straightened up and looked at Morgan brightly. 'Follow me,' she said.

SEVEN

THE VOICE OF ALANIS MORISSETTE invaded Morgan's deep sleep, and it took her a moment to realize that it was her cellphone. She opened her eyes in the darkness, and found herself sunk into the comfort of a king feather bed, in one of Sandy Raymond's many guest rooms. She fumbled to switch on the lamp and slid off the silky sheets and out from under the weightless, warm duvet to rummage through her bag for the phone.

'Hello,' she murmured, frowning.

'I'm trying to reach Morgan Adair,' said the woman's voice at the other end.

'Yes,' said Morgan, 'that's me.'

'This is Noreen Quick's office calling. Ms Quick is calling on behalf of her client, Claire Bolton. Would it be possible for you to come and see Ms Quick this morning? She has a few important matters to discuss with you.'

'Yes,' said Morgan. 'Yes. Absolutely. I can come. I'll be there right away.'

Groggy though she was, Morgan got the directions and entered them into her phone when the secretary hung up. Then, she stumbled off to the pristine, marble-surfaced bathroom for a quick wash-up. She dressed quickly and grabbed her satchel. She thought about taking her suitcase with her, but that seemed rude in light of Sandy's hospitality. She would come back for it, and thank him properly. She found her way downstairs in the huge, silent house. She left the house without seeing Sandy or his girlfriend, stopped at a convenience store for coffee and a roll, and arrived, on time, at the lawyer's office.

According to the neatly scripted sign which hung from a lamppost, the offices of Abrams and Quick were located in a clapboard-sided cottage in a narrow street off of the main thoroughfare in downtown Briarwood. Morgan parked in front of the building, opened the gate in the picket fence and walked in the front door. She nearly tripped over a furry, dun-colored Airedale who was stretched out across the hallway, his head resting on his front paws. He raised his eyebrows and looked up at Morgan, but didn't bark, or stir. Bemused, Morgan stepped over him and entered the room marked reception.

The woman at the desk, whose sign read 'Berenice Hoffman', was middle-aged, with black horned-rimmed glasses. Her gray hair was pulled back in a short ponytail and she was wearing a black turtleneck beneath an Adelphi sweatshirt. Berenice looked up from her computer and smiled at Morgan. Across from the desk was a small playpen, currently occupied by a toddler in red overalls with a halo of golden curls who was playing quietly with some foam blocks. The child looked up at Morgan and made a gurgling sound.

Morgan smiled at the toddler. 'Hi yourself,' she said. Then she turned back to the receptionist. 'My name is Morgan Adair. You called me earlier...'

'Yes, right.' Berenice pointed to the toddler with her pen. 'Ms Quick is with Kyle's mother right now. But if you'll take a seat, she's almost done, and then she'll be glad to talk with you.'

'OK,' said Morgan. She sat down next to the playpen and waggled a finger at the baby, who rewarded her with a radiant, toothless grin.

Morgan turned back to the receptionist. 'Whose dog is that in the hall?' she asked.

'Mine,' said Berenice. 'That's Rufus. He barks all day from loneliness if I leave him at home and then the neighbors hate me.'

Morgan nodded. She was a little surprised by the informality of this office, but she liked it, all the same. 'He seems pretty…calm around people.'

'He likes company,' said Berenice, rolling her eyes. 'Ms Abrams and Ms Quick do mainly divorce and custody work. So we get lots of kids in here. He loves that. He lets them crawl all over him.'

Morgan nodded, smiling. She thought about what Sandy had said last night. Claire needed the best possible criminal attorney. Obviously, criminal law was not the specialty of this firm. Morgan worried that this was not the right firm for Claire's case. She decided to reserve judgement until she met Noreen Quick.

Berenice returned to her computer, and Morgan looked around the reception area which had a decidedly female atmosphere. There was a glass jar of candy on the end table and mounds of tattered parenting magazines, as well as *Ladies Home Journal* and *US News and World Report*. Along with some framed university plaques, a rainbow quilt hung on the wall. Morgan felt more as if she were in a pediatrician's office than a law firm.

She heard a door opening out in the corridor, and a woman's voice thanking someone profusely. In a moment, a young woman came into reception, and her gaze turned immediately to the playpen. 'Hey Kyle,' she crooned. 'How's my sweetie?' The young woman wore a midriff-baring shirt and torn jeans and had messy, strawberry-blond hair. There were deep circles around her eyes, and she was carrying an enormous diaper bag, festooned with ducks and rabbits. 'Were you a good boy for Berenice?'

'Ma…' cried the baby, clambering up and bouncing as he held on to the edge of the playpen.

The woman reached in the diaper bag and pulled out a checkbook.

Berenice murmured an amount and the woman quickly wrote a check while the baby continued to yelp for his mom.

'Thank you so much for watching him,' the young woman said, as she bent over the playpen to lift the child out. 'Come on, sweetie. Let's go say hi to Rufus. Thanks again, Berenice.'

'No problem,' said the older woman. The phone rang on her desk. Berenice picked it up and nodded. She hung the phone up and looked at Morgan. 'She can see you now. Go out in the hall and take the second door on your left.'

'Thanks,' said Morgan. She went out into the hall. The toddler was on the floor, pulling at Rufus's ears while his mother made a call on her cellphone. Rufus, true to his reputation, remained tranquil.

A door opened in the hallway and a woman appeared there. She was short, with curly orange hair, freckles and no makeup. She was dressed casually in stirrup pants, and a large, sky blue sweater which covered a distended, obviously pregnant belly. She probably had a reasonably trim little figure when she wasn't pregnant, but the belly, combined with short stature, gave her body a certain troll-like appearance. Noreen extended a hand to Morgan. 'Hi, I'm Noreen Quick.'

Morgan shook her hand. 'Morgan Adair.'

'Come on in, Morgan. Can I call you Morgan? Thanks for coming.'

Morgan followed her into an office which was painted yellow and had family pictures on every flat surface. Noreen appeared to have children, but not a husband, if the pictures were any indication. Morgan glanced at her left hand and saw that Noreen did not wear a wedding ring.

On the wall of the office there were also framed newspaper articles extolling Noreen Quick's professional and charitable efforts on behalf of Planned Parenthood and an organization called Mothers At Work. Noreen sat down behind her desk and Morgan took the visitor's chair. Noreen leaned forward and folded her hands.

'How are you and Claire related, Morgan?' asked the attorney.

'We're old friends. More like sisters,' said Morgan.

Noreen peered at her. 'She has no close blood relations?'

'Not really. Some cousins in Oregon. Her mother died several years ago. She and I are very much in the same boat. We've come to rely on one another.'

Noreen held up a document. 'Well, obviously she has a lot of faith in you. I saw Claire first thing this morning and she indicated that she wanted you to have general power of attorney while she's incarcerated.'

'Power of attorney? What does that mean?' asked Morgan.

'You will be in charge of managing her assets, her financial affairs, that sort of thing. Obviously, she trusts you to safeguard her interests.'

'Wow,' said Morgan.

'Are you willing to act as her agent?' asked Noreen.

The idea of it was daunting, but Morgan wasn't about to refuse. She had promised to help, any way she could.

'Yes. Of course,' said Morgan. 'Whatever she needs me to do.'

'All right. I'll have this recorded with the state.'

'But I don't know exactly...what her interests are...' said Morgan.

'Some things she can tell you herself. And when you are able to get into the house you'll be able to access her computer, her paperwork, etc.'

'Do you know when that will be?' Morgan asked. 'The police have the house blocked off right now.'

'I'll call and find out when you can get in,' said Noreen.

'Oh, thank you. That would be a big help.'

'No problem,' said Noreen. She made a note on the pad in front of her.

'How's she doing today?' Morgan asked.

'Excuse me?' said Noreen.

'Claire. How's she doing?'

Noreen spread her freckled hands. 'As well as can be expected, I suppose.'

'Can we get her out of there on bail?' Morgan asked.

Noreen sighed. 'Bail's a problem. If it was just the baby, that would be one thing. In our justice system, that is actually considered the lesser crime. The fact that the husband was also killed...Bail's not gonna happen. And, they have her on a suicide watch right now. Which is, in my opinion, a good idea.'

Morgan blanched. 'You think she's suicidal?'

Noreen looked surprised. 'Obviously, she is at a high risk right now.'

'So that's all the more reason to get her out of there,' Morgan insisted.

Noreen frowned. 'Even if we could, she needs constant supervision. This is a responsibility that you do not want to take on. Trust me. I'm having her examined by a psychiatrist today,' said Noreen.

Morgan had a sudden image in her mind of Claire, last night, being led to the van for the county jail—the vacant, exhausted look in her eyes. 'That's probably a good idea,' Morgan admitted.

Noreen frowned. 'Her state of mind is a cornerstone of my defense. I'm going to plead temporary insanity. She is suffering from an extreme form of post-partum depression. Actually it's called post-partum psychosis.'

'Psychosis? I was with her last week,' said Morgan. 'She didn't seem that disturbed.'

Noreen looked at her with raised eyebrows. 'She killed her husband and her baby. It doesn't get much more disturbed than that.'

Morgan reddened. 'I know. I know you're right. But the way she told it to me, it sounded almost…accidental.'

Noreen gave a mirthless chuckle. 'I'm afraid it would be impossible to sell "accidental". Maybe one or the other death might have been an accident. But both of them? No. That's out of the question.'

This attorney was undeniably forceful. Morgan felt her objections being slammed down like badminton birdies. But Morgan felt both weighted down, and emboldened by the fact that Claire had legally entrusted her with all her affairs. It gave Morgan the right, the duty in fact, to speak her mind on Claire's behalf. 'You're probably right, but, please don't take offense, but shouldn't Claire have a criminal defense lawyer?' said Morgan.

Noreen spoke in an equable tone. 'No offense taken. I offered to argue this case pro bono because I am an expert on women's issues, and I think I can present the most convincing case. But if you want to try and find another attorney, by all means, feel free.'

'It's just that I've known Claire for so long,' Morgan pleaded. 'I can't imagine her ever deliberately doing such a thing.'

'Look,' said Noreen, 'Women who suffer from post-partum psychosis have hallucinations, they hear voices telling them to kill their children, they have suicidal fantasies.' Noreen seemed to be gaining energy, intensity as she spoke.

'When a woman is in this state of mind, she is not really responsible for her actions. All she wants to do is stop the voices, stop the pain. A woman with post-partum psychosis thinks that she is doing something good for her baby by killing that child. That she is carrying out God's…commands, if you will.'

'I'm sorry,' Morgan interrupted. 'I've read about women like that, but it just doesn't seem like Claire was that…'

'Crazy?' Noreen looked at Morgan with a shade of impatience. 'You don't have to take my word for it. As I told you, Claire is going to be examined by a psychiatrist. Once the psychiatrist confirms post-partum psychosis, we'll have an expert opinion. Then we can proceed.'

'Proceed how?' Morgan asked.

'Well, I'll argue not guilty by reason of temporary insanity. Obviously, no mother in her right mind would kill her baby. So, she has to have been in a deranged state of mind. When her husband tried to intervene, they struggled and she "accidentally" pushed him. According to the coroner's report, he cracked his skull on the edge of the cast iron tub.'

'I see,' said Morgan, shuddering.

'You know, in other civilized countries, they wouldn't punish a woman for infanticide. They would see to it that she got the help she needed. I want that for Claire.'

Morgan nodded, as if to agree, but her stomach was in a tight knot. There was no question that Noreen Quick had a point about post-partum depression. But Morgan kept picturing Claire, weeping, and saying how much she loved Drew, and how she didn't want to fail him. She never mentioned hallucinations, or the impulse to kill him, Morgan thought. Wouldn't she have mentioned that to me? And if she was suffering from those kinds of thoughts, how could I not have noticed?

'If we win…' Noreen continued.

'She'll be free?' Morgan interrupted.

Noreen frowned. 'No. There's virtually no chance of that. Claire will be remanded to a mental health facility. She'll stay there, probably for a period of years, until the judge finds that she is fit to be released.' Noreen, her presentation accomplished, sat back in her chair.

'A mental hospital,' said Morgan. 'For years.'

Noreen nodded. 'With any luck.'

'That's the best she can hope for?' Morgan asked.

Noreen narrowed her eyes and studied Morgan as if she were being deliberately obtuse. 'Your friend confessed to killing two people, Miss Adair. What did you think she was going to get for that? A parade?'

EIGHT

LEAVING THE LAW OFFICE, Morgan felt stunned, as if she had taken a blow to the head. Somehow she had not yet faced the fact that Claire was going to be put away for a long time. For years. But the bluntness of the attorney's assessment had brought the reality home to her. Morgan sat in her car without moving, staring out over the wheel, trying to imagine herself visiting Claire, year after year, in some hospital for the criminally insane. It didn't seem possible, but, clearly, it was imminent. When Morgan finally raised her key to fit into the ignition, she suddenly remembered that, while she knew where she was going, she did not know how to get there. She needed directions. Not for the first time, Morgan wished she had a GPS. But in the city, they were a magnet for thieves. She Googled maps on her internet phone, but she knew she couldn't read those little directions and drive at the same time. She was forced to get out of the car and return to the office. There, the helpful Berenice printed her out directions. Morgan thanked her, and studied the map with a heavy heart. Then, she returned to her car and drove directly from the office to the county jail.

The jail was located forty minutes from West Briar in a neighborhood distinctly less upscale and scenic than the Briars. Although the surrounding area was dense with old trees, the large, cinder block institutional building had been built on a sparsely vegetated patch of clay-like soil, surrounded by a chain link fence topped with barbed wire. The procedures for visitors were much stricter than they were for the holding cells at the rear of the Briarwood police station.

Morgan was directed to the female side of the jail, waited for buzzers and passed through numerous locked doors. The building was relatively new, even clean-looking, but the smell in the hallways was a rank combination of sweat and bathroom cleaner. Morgan held her breath. She was frisked by a female corrections officer, and then told to wait in several lines. She was careful not to complain or raise any objections. Finally, after standing among a group of weary men, women and children, who all seemed familiar with the procedures, Morgan was yanked from the line and led down a hallway and into an office to stand in front of the desk of a chubby, brown-skinned woman in a tweedy brown pantsuit. The sign on her desk read Elva deLeon, Assistant Warden.

'You're here to see Claire Bolton?' the woman asked, tapping on her desk with a gel pen.

'Yes, ma'am,' said Morgan.

'She's being examined by a psychiatrist right now. If there's any time left when the shrink leaves you can see her. But I doubt you will have much time for a visit. Why don't you come back another day?'

'That's all right,' said Morgan stubbornly. 'I'll take my chances.'

'Whatever you want to do,' the woman said, dismissing Morgan with a shrug. A guard escorted Morgan back to the waiting area. The other visitors had disappeared, presumably to see their loved ones. Morgan waited, until finally, after nearly forty minutes and several inquiries, she was told that she could go to the visiting area. This was a bare room, with armed guards at the doors, a few vending machines and some wooden tables and chairs, occupied by prisoners in drab blue jumpsuits and their visitors.

'Do I sit?' Morgan asked one of the guards.

The woman nodded, unsmiling. Morgan found an empty table, sat down and looked around. In a minute, she saw Claire appear at the doorway, escorted by a guard.

Morgan jumped up. 'Claire,' she called. Claire turned her head at the sound of her name and her eyes registered recognition when she caught sight of Morgan. Recognition, but nothing more.

'Sit back down,' said the guard.

Morgan resumed her seat. Claire was escorted to the table. Morgan wanted to stand up and hug her, but she was reluctant to defy the guard's order. When Claire sat down and folded her white hands on the table in front of her, Morgan reached over and covered them with her own. Claire's hands were icy cold.

'Are you all right?' Morgan asked.

Claire was almost unresponsive. 'Sure,' she managed to say.

'Did you see the psychiatrist? How did that go?'

Claire lifted one shoulder. 'All right. I guess.'

Morgan wondered if the shrink would tell her anything about their conversation if she asked him. It was worth a try. 'What was the shrink's name, Claire?'

Claire shook her head. 'Beekman...Bergman...I don't know.'

'Don't worry, I'll find out.' Morgan leaned forward and forced Claire to meet her gaze. 'I've just been to see your lawyer, Noreen Quick. She told me that you assigned the power of attorney to me. I was surprised, but I appreciate that you trust me so much. And I'll do my very best for you. You know that.'

Claire seemed to be gazing at her from a great distance. 'I do know that. That's why I wanted you to do it.'

'Claire,' she said carefully. 'Noreen Quick. She seems very bright, very capable. But I'm just worried that she wants to make a point with your case. She plans to use post-partum depression as your defense.'

'I have no defense,' said Claire dully.

'Don't talk like that. You told me it was an accident,' Morgan insisted. She was amazed at herself, that she could even entertain such an explanation. That in twenty-four hours her disgust, her revulsion at the crime, was being replaced by her determination to save her friend, no matter what. Situational ethics. There's nothing you can do for Guy or Drew, she reminded herself. All you can do now is try to help Claire. 'You need to be sure. Even if you're acquitted with the post-partum defense, you'll have to live in a hospital. Maybe for a long time. If it was truly an accident, you might…not be found guilty.'

'Oh Morgan, how is that possible? How could I have killed them both by accident?' asked Claire hopelessly.

Something about that question made Morgan's palms break out in sweat. She had the sudden impression that Claire had no idea what the truth was. Morgan stared at her friend. 'What do you mean? Don't you know what happened?'

'Yes, of course,' said Claire, looking away.

'Well then how could you ask that question? Did it actually happen the way you said? Claire, this is critical. You confessed. That means nobody is going to try to help you. But if you don't really remember what happened…'

'Stop it, Morgan. Stop. I don't want to talk about it.' Claire squeezed her hands into trembling fists. 'I did it. That's all you need to know. Let it go.'

Morgan wanted to press her but then she thought better

of it. Claire looked like she was ready to collapse. She was hunched over, her head bent, her shoulders rounded, like someone trying to wait out a hail of blows. She was steeled against these questions. Steeled against Morgan.

Morgan knew that she had to take another tack. She searched her mind for a different subject to ease the tension. 'I went to feed Dusty last night. He attacked me.'

Claire looked up at Morgan. 'He did? I'm sorry. He's very…possessive…of the house.'

'I noticed,' said Morgan.

'Is he OK?' Claire asked.

'Yeah,' said Morgan. 'He's fine.'

'Wrap it up,' the guard called out.

Morgan realized that she had to return to the most pertinent matter. 'Yes, all right. Of course. But let's get back to the attorney. I was talking to Sandy Raymond…'

'Sandy?'

'I stayed at his house last night. He's very concerned about you, Claire. He thinks you need a criminal attorney. Maybe we should consider that, Claire.'

Claire reached out and touched Morgan's forearm. Her touch was clammy. Her gaze was unfocused. 'Listen, there's something else I need you to do. I want to attend the funeral services for…for my husband and my baby. Can you arrange that for me?'

Morgan's stomach began to churn. The idea of Claire attending Guy and Drew's funeral was almost ghoulish. 'I don't know if that's allowed,' she said.

'I asked the assistant warden. She said it might be possible if the family would agree. Will you ask them for me, Morgan? You can convince them…'

Morgan did not believe for a moment that Guy's family would ever agree to it. 'I'll do my best,' she said.

'And don't worry about the lawyer,' said Claire. 'It doesn't matter…'

'Doesn't matter!' Morgan cried. 'We're talking about the rest of your life here. Everything matters.'

Claire was silent for a moment. Then she said, 'Will you take him if I…'

Morgan had no idea what she was saying. 'Take who?'

'Dusty. Will you take him for me?'

'Let's not get ahead of ourselves,' said Morgan. 'Maybe you're going to get out of this.'

'No,' said Claire. 'No. It's over.'

Immediately, Morgan remembered what Noreen Quick had said. Claire was under a suicide watch. Morgan grabbed her chilly hands again. 'Listen to me, Claire. Nothing is settled yet. Don't you dare give up. You need to hang in there.'

'I don't know, Morgan. What for?'

'Well, for…me. For one thing. I need you. We're…each other's family, remember? Look, I won't give up on you. I'll fight for you.'

Claire did not smile or nod. 'I don't deserve it,' Claire said.

'Time,' the guard intoned.

Claire stood up and Morgan followed suit. 'Don't you dare do anything…wrong,' Morgan concluded feebly. She did not even want to breathe the word suicide.

Claire allowed herself to be led away. She looked back over her shoulder. 'Thank you for everything,' she said.

'You hang in there,' Morgan insisted. She could feel herself trembling all over. 'Claire!' But Claire did not turn around or look back at her.

NINE

MORGAN STOPPED AT THE FOOT of the church steps and glanced over at the newer section of the historic cemetery, where two men with a small backhoe were digging two graves, side by side, one half as large as the other. In a sickening instant, Morgan realized that the graves were probably being prepared for Guy and baby Drew. Even though she knew that they were dead, in a way she had not allowed herself to contemplate it. She had acted as if she were here on a visit and simply hadn't seen them yet. But watching the preparation of the graves gave her a sickening dose of reality. She turned away, her heart aching.

Around the churchyard it seemed to be a day for maintenance. An overall-clad painter was standing beneath the tall, mullioned church windows, daubing white paint on the sill from a quart can which he held in his hand. Morgan ascended the church steps, pulled open the door and looked inside. The church was silent, the warm autumn light spilling across the empty pews.

'Damn,' she whispered.

'Can I help you?' the painter asked.

Morgan started. She turned to him to explain that she was looking for Father Lawrence and realized that the bespectacled painter in the white papery cap was, in fact, the minister himself.

'Oh,' said Morgan startled. 'I didn't expect to see you there, Father,' she said.

The minister smiled sheepishly, and carefully wiped off his brush on the rim of the paint can he was holding. 'I like painting,' he said. 'I find it relaxing. My wife and I used to own an old house at my last parish, but when we moved here a new rectory had just been built. There's nothing for me to do on this place. So, I touch up the church building. Is there something I can do for you?'

'Actually, I was looking for you,' said Morgan. 'I was hoping you might be able to help me.'

Father Lawrence set his brush down on a plastic drop cloth and pressed the top back on to the paint can. He pulled a rag from his pocket and wiped off his fingers. 'If you want to go inside to talk,' he said, 'just give me a moment to get cleaned up.'

'No, that's not necessary,' she said. 'It's fine out here. It's a nice day.'

'We've met before, haven't we?' the minister asked, looking at her with narrowed eyes.

'Yes,' said Morgan. 'Yes we have. I was here last week.' Morgan took a deep breath. 'For the christening. Drew Bolton's christening. I was his godmother.'

The expression in the minister's eyes grew pained. 'I'm so sorry,' he said. 'Such a tragedy.'

Morgan glanced back over at workmen digging in the cemetery. Then she looked back at the minister. 'Yes,' she said. 'It is.'

The minister came around and sat down on the church steps. He gestured for Morgan to sit down beside him. A chilly breeze rustled through the leaves, but the steps were in sunlight. Morgan took a seat at the edge of a tread.

'So, you were the godmother. Were you related to them? The victims,' he asked.

'No,' said Morgan. 'The...' Morgan hesitated. She refused to say 'killer', even if it was true. 'Claire, Drew's mother, is my dearest friend.'

Father Lawrence drew in a breath. 'I see.'

'I've come to see you because of Claire,' she said.

The minister remained silent.

Morgan glanced at him. He had taken off the painter's hat, and was wiping his brow with the back of his hand. 'Look,' said Morgan, 'I know that she did a horrible thing. I mean, I've known her most of my life and it was just a complete shock. I haven't really been able to accept that she would even be capable…'

'I'm sure it is a shock,' he murmured. 'I've spoken to the family, of course. They are suffering greatly.'

'I know,' said Morgan miserably. 'I know they must be.' His observation reminded her of where she had to go from here. She had to ask the family for permission for Claire to attend the services. That was a duty she was truly dreading.

'And Claire,' Father Lawrence said, shaking his head. 'She seemed to be such a lovely, nice woman. She must have been tormented to do such a thing. Out of her right mind in some way…'

'Yes,' said Morgan, grateful for even this hint of understanding. 'And she is suffering too, believe me. She's in a terrible state. In fact, I'm afraid for her life.'

The minister frowned. 'Really?'

'Yes,' said Morgan. 'Absolutely. She's under a suicide watch at the county jail, but you know, if a person is determined enough they can find a way…'

Father Lawrence nodded. 'Yes, of course,' he said.

'Look,' said Morgan, 'I'm sure it sounds crazy for me to say this but Claire always had a lot of faith. I was thinking that maybe it would help if you could try to talk to her. I don't know what the official church policy is when someone does something as bad as this, but…I'm really worried. She's over her head.'

Father Lawrence smiled slightly. 'The official policy, as you say, is that we're all sinners, and that no sin, no matter how terrible, is unforgivable.'

Morgan faced him hopefully. 'Could you go to the county jail and tell her that? I mean, I am really afraid for her. For what she might do.'

'I guess I just assumed she'd have a spiritual advisor at the prison. Someone…familiar with the place.'

Morgan could see that he was balking at the idea of visiting the prison. He'd probably never had to visit an accused murderer from his parish before. She wasn't about to let him off the hook. 'No. She liked you,' Morgan insisted. 'She trusted you.'

Father Lawrence turned the painter's hat in his hand, frowning. Finally he said, 'I suppose I can do that.'

Morgan pounced. 'Soon?' she asked.

Father Lawrence nodded. 'I think the rest of the painting can wait,' he said.

Morgan sighed with relief. 'I was hoping you'd say that.'

'I won't guarantee that I can improve her state of mind.'

'But you'll try,' said Morgan.

Father Lawrence nodded. 'I'll try,' he said.

THE BOLTONS' WAS THE only house, built on a promontory, at the end of a cul-de-sac. It was a sprawling, modern house of one story, with a multitude of windows overlooking the sea. It was surrounded by windswept gardens and today there were cars wedged along the shoulder of the isolated road, with several police cars among the vehicles parked there. Dick Bolton was well off now, but he had friends from all walks of life in the Briars, dating back to his lifeguarding days. Morgan suspected that many of those people were turning up to offer condolences.

Morgan took the parking space of a couple who were driving away from the house. The woman in the front seat was wiping her eyes with tissue. Morgan sat in her car for a moment, looking up at the house, marshaling her forces. Finally, she got out of her car and slammed the door. She walked up the flagstone walkway, past Mexican laborers, dressed in jeans and sweatshirts, who were tending the gardens. Dick hired a multitude of Mexican workers every summer, obtaining temporary work visas for them so that they could do his gardening, clean fish in his warehouse and wash dishes in the Lobster Shack. Morgan could feel the curious eyes of the men in the crew on her, as she passed by, and she wondered if they knew about the tragedy which had befallen the family inside. Morgan rang the bell, and the door was opened by Astrid Bolton.

At first, Morgan felt relieved that it was Astrid, her shiny crown of pale blond braids a stark contrast to her black sweater and pants, who had come to the door. She was a stepmother, and Morgan knew, from conversations in the past with Claire, that Guy had a testy, difficult relationship with both his father and his stepmother. Surely, Morgan thought, Astrid would feel slightly less animosity toward Claire and Morgan than would Guy's blood relations. But up close, Morgan could see that Astrid's oval face was deeply lined, and her lavender eyes were red-rimmed and glittered with tears. She made no effort to be welcoming. 'What is it?' Astrid asked hoarsely.

'Astrid, I'm terribly sorry…' Morgan began.

Astrid lifted a manicured hand. 'Don't,' said Astrid.

'If you're going to start making excuses for her, don't do it. Save your breath.'

'Believe me,' said Morgan, 'I have no excuses. I am as baffled by this as everyone else.'

Astrid was trembling. She was a quiet woman who, despite the ethereal fairness of her looks, seemed to have a solemn nature. The few times that Morgan had met her, Astrid had struck her as someone who maintained an even keel. But her customary composure seemed to have deserted her. 'Please, if you don't mind, we are just…destroyed by this loss.'

'I understand,' said Morgan. 'And I'm so sorry. But I have to talk to you. You and Dick both, if possible. Lucy too, if she's here.'

Astrid frowned. 'What about?'

Morgan took a deep breath. 'It's important. May I come in?'

'Dick is in no shape to see anyone. Much less a friend of Claire's.'

'Believe me, I wouldn't be intruding if I didn't have to be here,' said Morgan.

Astrid hesitated and then, reluctantly, stepped aside and allowed Morgan to enter. As Morgan walked into the house, she glanced back at the gardening crew, who continued to look curiously at her. Astrid closed the door behind Morgan and indicated that she should come into the main room. There were clusters of people talking quietly in the low-ceilinged, folk-art decorated living room, and the dining room table was covered with platters of food.

'Follow me,' said Astrid grimly.

Morgan's stomach was churning and she wished she could turn and run. But she had promised Claire. As she followed Astrid through the house, she came face to face with Fitz, his hair a mass of curls, a tweed sports coat stretched across his broad shoulders, coming out of the powder room. 'Oh, hi,' she said, realizing she would welcome even his leering smile at this point.

Fitz's eyes were red-rimmed and his face was puffy. It seemed to take him a minute to register that he was looking at Morgan. He looked startled to see her at first, and then his expression hardened.

'How are you?' she asked.

'Just great,' said Fitz balefully.

'I know,' she said. 'I'm sorry.'

Fitz frowned at Morgan. 'Do you really think you should be here? After what Claire did...?' He stopped and pressed his lips together. Without waiting for her reply, he turned away and walked past her.

Shaken by Fitz's reaction, Morgan tried to steel herself as she caught up to Astrid who was pushing open the door to a darkened room at the end of the hall.

'Astrid?' A voice called to Astrid from inside the room. Morgan could see that this room had all kinds of beach photos, surfing trophies, and electronic equipment on its custom-made shelves. The plasma-screen TV picture was on, but there was no sound. The far wall was windowed, and overlooked the sea.

Huddled in a club chair in the corner, covered by a Burberry plaid throw, was Dick Bolton, dressed in a gray sweatshirt that seemed to mirror his complexion. A sportsman, an outdoorsman, Dick was normally a robust figure. He had seemingly dwindled in his grief. He looked up at Morgan with empty eyes.

'This is Claire's friend, Morgan,' said Astrid, and her voice had an edge. 'She wanted to talk to you.'

'And Lucy, if possible,' said Morgan. 'This affects all of you.'

Astrid avoided Morgan's gaze. 'Lucy's not here. She's...'

'She's too busy,' Dick said bitterly. 'Too busy to be with her family when her brother has just been killed.'

'Now darling,' Astrid chided him. 'She's terribly upset. This is very difficult for her. She has to deal with this in her own way.'

'She's spoiled. And she's selfish and you're the one who spoiled her,' said Dick accusingly. 'You have babied Lucy ever since you set foot in this house. Fussing over her diet, and her vision problems and her schooling. Thanks to you, she thinks this condition of hers makes her so special she doesn't have to do the normal, decent things that people do,' he cried hoarsely.

Astrid's face was white. 'I've only tried to take care of her,' Astrid said.

Dick put his hand over his eyes and let out a sob. The room was silent except for his muffled gasps. Then, he reached out with his other hand, groping the air, and Astrid took hold of it. 'Sorry, darling,' he whispered. 'That was unfair. I'm out of my mind. I'm sorry.'

'It's all right,' said Astrid soothingly.

'You've been an angel with Lucy. With both of my children.'

Morgan, taken aback by Dick's outburst, wished she could disappear. Instead, she was rooted to the spot.

Astrid swiped one of her knuckles over her own tears and struggled to maintain her composure. 'Morgan has something to say to us,' she said, lifting her small, pointed chin. She nodded at Morgan. 'Go on.'

'Mr Bolton,' said Morgan. 'Astrid. I can't begin to tell you how sorry I am for your loss.'

'Thank you,' Dick said dully. Then he peered at

Morgan. 'I remember you,' he said. 'You were at the baptism.'

'Yes,' Morgan admitted. 'I was Drew's godmother.'

Dick Bolton covered his keen blue eyes with a shaking hand and his voice was a wail. 'Why? Why did she do this to us?'

Morgan shook her head without replying.

Dick Bolton dropped his forearms heavily to the arms of the chair. He looked dazed. Astrid looked at her husband with sorrowful eyes. She folded her arms over her chest. 'Well,' she said to Morgan. 'What is it you wanted to talk about?'

Morgan looked from one to the other. 'First I wanted to say how sorry I am. All I can tell you is that the Claire I have always known...'

'What is she talking about?' Dick asked miserably.

'Please,' Astrid said in a warning tone. 'Just be brief. We're very upset.'

Morgan drew in a deep breath and plunged. 'All right. Here's the thing. I've been to see Claire today. She asked me to come here and...and ask for your permission... She wants to attend the funeral.'

Astrid's eyes widened. 'Oh no, you can't mean that.'

'It's up to you,' said Morgan. 'Whatever you say, that's what we'll do. She wouldn't be standing or seated...with you. She'd have to stay off to the side. With guards.'

'Are you insane? That woman killed my son. And my grandson,' Dick exploded.

Astrid shook her head, and blew her nose into a tissue. Morgan did not try to offer any explanation. There was no way for her to make this request less onerous. She assumed that they understood that. It was simply up to them to render a verdict. The last word.

The room was silent. Finally, Astrid broke the silence.

'I don't know how she could ever think to show her face there.'

Morgan stifled a sigh. She did not have the heart to protest or plead Claire's case any further. What could she say? These people had a right to their anger.

Suddenly, there was a tapping on the door of the den. Then the door opened, and Fitz stuck his head in. 'Excuse me,' he said.

Astrid looked at him impatiently. 'Fitz, not now…'

Fitz raised a hand. 'Um…Eden's grandparents just showed up here from West Virginia. They are looking for their granddaughter. What do I tell them?'

Morgan frowned. It was really the first time she had even thought about Guy's daughter, who had appeared so inopportunely at the christening. 'Guy's daughter?' she asked. 'Is she still in town?'

Dick Bolton seemed to summon some of his old spirit. 'They have the nerve to come here? Those insane rednecks?' Dick muttered in disgust. 'Don't let them in.'

'Dick, don't,' Astrid murmured. She turned to Fitz. 'Did they try the Spauldings? That's where she was staying.'

Fitz shrugged. 'I think they did.'

'Well, then I don't know,' said Astrid wearily. 'I haven't seen her since the night before…since the night of the dinner.'

Eden, Morgan thought. She had almost forgotten that Eden had been the spark that ignited this tragedy.

'Are you expecting Eden to show up here?' Fitz asked.

'I don't know,' said Astrid. 'She certainly hasn't called to offer her condolences for our grandson…' Astrid's voice cracked. 'Or my stepson.'

'Tell them to go home,' Dick thundered. 'We don't

know anything about that kid. Tell them to leave. They're not welcome here.'

Astrid took a deep breath. 'No. No, darling. Wait. That would be rude. They've come a long way and they're worried about their granddaughter.'

'After what they put us through,' Dick cried. 'I don't owe those people a thing.'

Astrid ignored his protest. 'Offer them some food or something to drink and tell them to wait, if you would, Fitz. I'll be with them in a minute,' said Astrid calmly.

Fitz nodded in agreement and withdrew, closing the door. Astrid turned to Morgan. Despite being middle-aged, she had a still-refined face and erect carriage, which seemed to only be sharpened by her grief. 'Look, you'd better go,' she said. 'This is a family matter. This is not really the place for you.'

'Yes, all right,' said Morgan.

'Just tell Claire we said no,' said Astrid. 'No, she can't come. Our lives are ruined because of her.'

'Wait a minute.' From his club chair, Dick Bolton's voice interrupted with surprising strength.

Morgan turned and looked at him in mild surprise. She was ready for him to hurl a parting insult at her.

'On second thought, maybe she should be there. Yes. Tell her she can come,' he said. 'To the funeral.'

Astrid turned on him. 'Dick,' she exclaimed.

'I want her there,' said Dick. 'I want to see her face.' He looked from Morgan to Astrid. 'That's final. She can come.'

Morgan felt a chill. She did not dare look at Astrid, who was gasping with dismay. Of course Morgan realized that there was menace embedded in Dick's permission. How could Claire expect any reception at this funeral other than a completely hostile one? Still, it was the answer Claire wanted, and Morgan would bring it back to her. She only hoped that Claire would not regret her choice. As she murmured her goodbyes, Morgan did not ask about arrangements, or press Dick Bolton for his reasons. She would find out the arrangements. Whatever his reasons, Morgan felt certain that they had nothing to do with compassion.

TEN

AT A TINY STOREFRONT health food place called Nature's Pantry, Morgan sat at one of the five tables and ordered a California sandwich from a college student-aged waitress. While she was waiting for her food, Morgan called the county jail and asked to speak to Claire. She was told that prisoners couldn't receive calls until five o'clock. Morgan said she would call back. Then she called Noreen Quick's office and asked to speak to the attorney.

'I'm sorry,' said Berenice, who recognized her name right away. 'That's not gonna be possible. She's at the doctor's. She started having contractions.'

'Oh,' said Morgan. 'Really? Was that…expected?'

'She's not due for another month,' Berenice confided.

'Do you happen to know if she found out about Claire's house from the police?'

'What about it?' asked Berenice.

'Well, I don't know when the police will allow me to go inside,' said Morgan.

'Oh, I don't know anything about that,' said Berenice. 'Why don't you go over to the station house and ask them yourself? Do you know where the police station is?'

Morgan thought grimly of her visit to Claire in the holding cell. 'OK, I can do that. I guess you don't know if Ms Quick will be back at work tomorrow. I suppose it all depends on the baby.'

'Well, even if it's a false alarm, I can tell you that she

was on complete bed rest with her last baby for at least a month before it was born.'

Morgan was somewhat surprised to be apprised of such personal information about the attorney's life, but it certainly seemed in keeping with the estrogen-saturated atmosphere of that law office. Morgan found the openness rather disarming. 'I'm just worried about the case,' she said. 'You know, my friend Claire's defense…?'

'Oh, Ms Quick'll still be working. She'll just have to work from home. From her bedroom. Until the baby's born. Believe me, it won't slow her down much. She's a dynamo.'

'Yes, she seems to be,' said Morgan.

'Just drop by the police station and ask them about the house. Somebody there will help you.'

Morgan told Berenice that she would handle it, and tucked her phone away as her waitress appeared carrying a sandwich on brown bread stuffed with alfalfa sprouts. Morgan ate her food, bland to begin with, without tasting it, paid the cashier, and hurried out the door.

Although she did not know the village of West Briar very well, she was not about to forget her way to the police station. She went in, and asked the sergeant on duty if she could speak to someone about Claire Bolton's case.

The sergeant spoke on the phone and then looked at Morgan. 'Detective Heinz can see you for a few minutes. He's in the squad room, second door on the left.'

Morgan thanked him and followed his directions to the squad room. She entered timidly and looked around. Uniformed officers and men in ties and shirtsleeves were mingling at the desks in the large, white room which took up half of the first floor of the building. A good-looking young man in uniform asked if he could help her. 'I'm looking for Detective Heinz?' she said.

The young man pointed to a large, bald-headed man with half glasses and a goatee scowling at a computer monitor in the corner. He was wearing a blue-striped shirt, a gold knit tie and a large, elaborate-looking watch that could probably track the time in three time zones. He did not look up as Morgan approached his desk. 'Detective Heinz?' she said.

'Just a minute,' he said without looking up. He finished tapping something into his computer, and then rolled his chair back about a foot. He frowned at Morgan. 'What?' he said.

'My name is Morgan Adair. I'm a friend of Claire Bolton's,' she began.

'I see,' he said. His face showed no emotion.

Morgan pulled her power of attorney papers from her tote bag and turned them toward the detective so that he could see them. 'Claire has asked me to…help get her life in order. She gave me power of attorney while she's in jail.'

Heinz raised an eyebrow and folded his arms over his chest. 'And what does this have to do with me?'

'Well, I need to get into her house to sort through her papers and…you know…take care of her business. And her cat. I have to feed her cat. And I hope to stay at the house while I'm in town. Yesterday I wasn't allowed to enter the house because of your investigation.'

Heinz raised a hand and waved it, as if to wave away her concerns. 'You can go in. We're through with the place. We don't need anything in there.'

'You're sure? Nothing?' Morgan asked.

Heinz shrugged. 'The investigation is closed. Your friend confessed.'

'So, you aren't looking into any other possibilities?' Morgan asked. 'I mean, don't you keep digging?'

Heinz folded his hands on the top of his desk, in a fashion which suggested that he was restraining an urge to reach out and shake her. 'You've got real life confused with television shows. Do you see these files, Miss?' Heinz asked, inclining his bald head toward a tower of Manilla folders on the corner of his desk. 'These are investigations I'm still working on. Lot of it is small stuff. Break-ins. Fraud. Domestic disturbances. Every one of them's got to be addressed. So, no, I don't really have time to keep digging, as you say, in a case where I have a videotaped confession. That's the gold standard in any courtroom in the land. She did it. It's a slam dunk. End of story.'

'Well, actually, she's going to plead not guilty, as I understand it.'

'Good luck to her,' said Heinz sarcastically.

'Claire just seems a little…confused to me,' Morgan persisted in the face of his uninterest. 'She mentioned something about an accident.'

A gap-toothed smile spread across the detective's face and he shook his head. 'Did she now? She's calling it an accident. Hey Jim,' he called out to a rangy, brown-haired man at a neighboring desk.

The other detective looked up from his computer. He had a smoker's complexion, and folds in his eyelids.

'Meet Jim Curry,' said Heinz. 'We questioned your friend together. He and I were both there when she confessed to murdering her husband and her baby. Jim, this gal's a friend of Claire Bolton. Seems like our Claire is now thinking that it might have been an accident.'

Jim Curry smiled wryly and shook his head. 'Yeah. Right,' he said.

Morgan felt that he was twisting what she was trying to say. 'I didn't mean that,' Morgan protested. 'I just said…'

'You're wasting my time, miss. Now, I'm a patient man…' said Heinz.

Morgan gazed at the detective. She doubted that very much. He seemed explosive, and anything but patient. For a moment she tried to imagine Claire—confused, depressed Claire—being questioned by this domineering man. 'Maybe she was frightened,' Morgan said.

Heinz took a deep breath, as if he was going to lash out at her. Then, suddenly, his manner changed and he spoke to her slowly, and not unkindly, as if she were a child in preschool. 'Listen to me, Miss. I know you're upset about your friend. None of us wants to think that the people we care for could do something like this. But this was a heinous crime. Innocent people do not confess to a heinous crime. They just don't. Guilty people confess. Your friend is guilty.'

Morgan met his gaze without flinching, but in her heart she knew that what he said was clearly true. She had heard of cases where people confessed to a crime they didn't commit. But in those cases it always seemed to be someone with a low I.Q. Or a young kid. And even then, there were always lingering doubts. When it came right down to it, it was impossible to imagine confessing to such a crime if you were innocent. And Claire was not claiming to be innocent. Claire was guilty, and Morgan was going to have to find a way to live with it. Morgan nodded. 'I understand that what you're saying about a confession is true. I mean, who would admit to such a thing if they didn't do it? It doesn't make any sense.'

'No, it doesn't,' he said.

'It's just so hard to believe that Claire could have done this thing.'

'I'm sure,' he said.

'So,' said Morgan with a sigh. 'I'm...I appreciate, you know, that you're letting me get into the house.'

'No problem,' said Heinz, inclining his head toward her.

'I'm sorry I bothered you about this.'

'That's all right,' said Heinz calmly, swiveling in his chair so that he was once again facing his computer. 'I'm here to help.'

DRESSED IN THE CHICEST of workout clothes and listening to her iPod, Farah skipped down the steps of Sandy Raymond's house. Morgan approached and called out to her. Farah lifted her earbud from her ear, and beamed in welcome.

'I came for my things,' said Morgan. 'And I wanted to thank Sandy.'

'He's inside. Guess where?' said Farah inclining her head toward the house. Her shining, wavy brown ponytail bobbed like an actual horse's tail, falling halfway down her back.

'On the computer?' Morgan guessed.

'Inside. Playing Wii. It's a beautiful day!' she cried in exasperation.

'Yes, it is,' said Morgan.

'Second floor,' said Farah. She glanced at her watch and waved as she broke into a trot.

Morgan thanked her and started up the steps to the house. She entered the foyer and called out to Sandy. A voice responded from upstairs. Morgan climbed the staircase, and searched the rooms on the second floor until she came to a room which looked like the control room on the Starship Enterprise. Sandy was standing with a wand in his hand, facing his virtual opponent on a giant screen. He was jumping back and forth, whacking at the air with the wand.

'Sandy,' she said.

'Yeah,' he replied without looking at her.

'I came for my things. The police said it was all right so I'm going to stay at Claire's house for the time being.'

'Oh. OK.'

'I just wanted to thank you for your hospitality.'

'No problem,' he said, lunging at the screen.

'I'll just go get my stuff,' said Morgan, backing out of the room. She tried to recall what Claire had said about her life with Sandy when they were engaged. She seemed to remember that they used to go out in the evening, rode bikes now and then, and went for walks. They even went horseback riding once on vacation. She did not remember Claire ever saying that Sandy was a computer addict, but that was the impression that Morgan now had of him.

She went down the hallway until she found the room where she had slept. The curtains were still closed and the bed was unmade as she had left it when she ran out in the morning. Her suitcase lay open on a long tan suede ottoman at the foot of the bed. Morgan pulled back the drapes and quickly threw her things into the suitcase, and zippered it up. She set the wheeled bag down on the floor. Then, she hesitated, wondering whether to remove the sheets from the enormous bed. Normally, when she stayed in someone's house, she would take the sheets off so her hostess wouldn't have to do it. But she had never stayed in a house the size of a hotel before. Obviously Sandy needed a household staff to maintain the place. Well, household staff or not, she decided to err on the side of being a considerate guest. She leaned over the bed and began to remove the pillowcase from one of the pillows.

'Just leave it.'

Morgan turned and saw Sandy standing in the doorway, his arms folded over his sweaty T-shirt. 'Are you sure?' said Morgan.

'The housekeeper will change them tomorrow.'

'Ah,' said Morgan, replacing the pillow in its case, and pulling up the sheet and the duvet. She smoothed the duvet out as best she could.

'How's Claire doing?' Sandy asked.

Morgan turned, and reached for her suitcase, lifting the handle. Then she shook her head. 'Not too well. Very depressed.'

'Not too surprising,' said Sandy.

'No. Under the circumstances,' Morgan admitted.

'She shouldn't have left me,' Sandy said.

Morgan frowned. 'What do you mean?'

'Well, you have to admit,' said Sandy. 'Her life would have turned out differently.'

'It's not as if her life is over,' Morgan said.

Sandy shrugged. 'It might as well be.'

Morgan stifled an angry retort. If that's what he wanted to think, let him, she thought. It wouldn't do any good to argue with him. She would not be giving up on Claire so easily.

Morgan rolled her suitcase past him out into the hall and headed for the stairs. 'Thank you for having me last night,' she said stiffly.

'Don't mention it,' said Sandy. 'Tell Claire I said hi.'

ELEVEN

MORGAN GLANCED AT THE DEFLATED balloons still tied to the mailbox, and made a mental note to get scissors and cut them down. Their continued, bedraggled presence was like a reproach to Drew and Guy's memory. She continued up the path to the house while Dusty sat tensely on his haunches in front of the door and stared at the creature coming toward him.

'Hey, Dusty,' said Morgan. 'Remember me? I'm the one with the cat food.' Dusty's gaze was impassive. Morgan was on her guard. She really did not want to be clawed again. She had already had enough of this day. After she left Sandy's house, she had visited the funeral home and checked on the arrangements, and then stopped for a few groceries and bought herself dinner at a little Italian place in the same strip mall as the grocery store. While she waited for her order of pasta, she had called Claire again at the prison. This time she was able to get through.

Although her voice had sounded weak and fatigued, Claire had been grateful to hear that she would be allowed to attend the services. 'I have to warn you. I'm afraid that Guy's father may be setting you up,' Morgan had told her. Claire insisted that it didn't matter, she didn't care. She fretted, however, that she had no black clothes to wear. Morgan told her that she was on her way to the cottage, and would find the clothes she needed and bring them to the prison.

Now, edging past the cat, Morgan mounted the step and ran her hand along the trim above the door looking for the spare key in the spot where Claire told her it would be. She knew she could try the back door, but she suspected that the cop had locked it after he found her in the kitchen the night before. Morgan pulled the key down and inserted it in the front door lock. She opened the front door, and stepped inside.

Flipping on a lamp by the door, she looked around. Claire's normally tidy cottage was in disarray. Every drawer and cabinet seemed to have part of its contents sticking out.

At first, Morgan was alarmed by the sight and then, all at once, she realized that this must be the result of the police search. With a sigh, Morgan began a cursory effort to straighten up. She stacked books, files and papers back into their drawers and on to their shelves. After a while, the place looked better. Morgan glanced down the hallway which led to the master bedroom. The worst chore awaited her. She knew she had to go in there, to get the clothes which Claire wanted. They might need washing or pressing. But the clothes were all in the closet adjacent to the bathroom where the crime had occurred. Morgan's stomach felt like a clenched fist. It was not going to get any better, she thought. Just do it.

She walked down the hall, and hesitantly entered the master bedroom. The room was a mess with clothes strewn on the floor and the bed unmade. Once again, Morgan knew she should pick the room up, but she just wanted to get the clothes and get out. Avoiding looking at the bassinet or the changing table, she went straight to the dresser and rifled through the drawers. She found the underwear, panty hose and black sweater which Claire had asked for. Then she went over to the closet. Beside the closet, the door to the master bathroom stood ajar. Morgan tried not to look. She pulled out a slim black skirt and draped it over her arm. She knew she should turn and walk out, not look, but her gaze seemed to be drawn to the bathroom. The scene of the crime.

Just last week, Morgan had guided Claire into the large, white tiled bath, to help her get ready for the christening. Morgan had run a bath in the cast iron claw-foot tub, and filled it with bubbles, set out a fluffy white towel and even shampooed Claire's short, fashionably cut hair. Claire had finally pulled it together and at that moment, to Morgan, it had seemed to be a day full of hope. And now, all that hope was over. Hesitantly, Morgan reached past the bathroom door to the switch on the wall and turned on the light.

Her gaze swept the room and she gasped. The walls and floors of the white room were spattered red with blood. A formerly white towel sat in a wet pool on the bathroom floor, stained an uneven pink and rusty red. There was still water pooled in the bottom of the bathtub and flies buzzed over it. The smell in the room was off, metallic, turning fetid.

Somehow Morgan had expected that the only sign of the tragedy which occurred there would be some intangible feeling in the air. Instead, the police had left it as it was, a roomful of violence and its aftermath. Morgan's stomach lurched, and she thought she might be sick. She turned her face away from the appalling sight, and made her way blindly from the bedroom out into the hallway, and down the hallway to the living room.

Morgan flopped down on one of Claire's overstuffed, chintz-covered loveseats, leaned her head back against the high cushions and took a few deep breaths. She tried not to think about the bloodstained bathroom but it was difficult to banish the image from her mind's eye. She had never intended to sleep in the master bedroom, but just knowing it was there, in that condition, made her feel as if there was something festering in the center of the house.

Suddenly, Morgan felt overwhelmed. What am I doing here, she thought? Everything around me is in chaos. I'm a stranger in this town, going around making excuses for a confessed murderer. This isn't my battle. I'm not even related to Claire. But even as she thought it, she knew it was only exhaustion that was making her think that way. Yes, Claire had confessed, but that didn't mean it was time to walk away. Of course it was Morgan's battle. She was closer to Claire than anyone else, and she intended to see her through this nightmare. It was just that these last few days had been nothing like she expected them to be. She thought longingly of her aborted trip to England. Today, she would still have been in London, poring over some of Harriet Martineau's manuscripts in the British Museum, and having dinner with Simon. Tomorrow, they would have been setting out for the Lake District. She had been there several times, but only briefly. This would be a luxurious visit. Stately English homes, set like jewels in the boulder-strewn hillsides which sloped down to the crystalline lakes. Their hotel was a former manor house, with a forest surrounding it. The hotel's brochure, which Simon had sent her, promised tea by the fire, in the most fragile of cups…

A pounding on the front door made Morgan jump, and she stared at the door as if it were alive and shouting at her. The knocking continued. Morgan lay Claire's funeral clothes carefully over the arm of the sofa, smoothed down her own rumpled clothes, and got up to answer.

The couple at the door looked to be in their sixties. The man had sparse white hair sticking out from under a ball cap, a pouchy red face and rheumy eyes. He had on a worn plaid shirt and jeans. The woman's hair was dyed a Creamsicle orange. She was a soft-bodied woman with a shy smile.

'I'm Wayne Summers. This here is my wife, Helene,' said the man in a rough voice with a Southern drawl. 'I'm looking for Guy Bolton's house.'

Morgan cringed inside. She hated to have to explain about Guy. She wondered how much she had to say to this stranger. 'This is his house,' she said. 'I'm sorry to have to tell you this, but I'm afraid that Guy is dead.'

'I know he's dead,' said the old man bluntly. 'His wife killed him and the baby. Couldn't have happened to a nicer fella. No, we jest come up here from West Virginia and we've got to be getting back home. We're looking for our granddaughter. Eden? Thought she might still be here.'

'Eden is your granddaughter!' Morgan exclaimed.

'Do you know Eden?' Helene said hopefully.

'Well, not really. I mean, I did meet her…when she first arrived.'

'Where'd she go?' Wayne demanded.

'I'm afraid I don't know…' said Morgan.

'You see a friend of ours from church saw on the CNN news what happened to Guy Bolton and that baby,' explained Helene. 'We tried to call Eden on her cellphone but we couldn't reach her and we got worried about her. I mean, we knew she came up here to try and meet her father. We figured she might be all upset by this, and we better come see if she needed us to bring her home.'

Wayne Summers sighed and shook his head with exasperation. 'I told you this was a waste of time, Helene. That girl hasn't got the sense God gave an acorn…'

'That's not so, Wayne. She's a very smart young

girl,' Helene corrected him staunchly. Helene turned to Morgan. 'Our Eden is highly intelligent. Her psychologist told me so. But she has some emotional problems...'

'Emotional problems,' Wayne scoffed. 'That psychologist is just stealin' our money. Eden's not right, Helene. It's a fact of life. Her mind is...off...'

Morgan could see that Eden's grandfather had little patience for her. Morgan knew what it was like to live in a house where you felt unwanted under your own roof. Even though the death of her parents in the hotel bombing had left Morgan with a trust fund for her expenses, Morgan could remember how her uncle would curse his late brother, with whom he had never been close, for visiting this extra child on his household. It sometimes seemed that he wanted her to hear it, wanted her to feel guilty for existing. She wondered, briefly, if that was what Eden's life had been like. She was a grandchild, whom these people had never intended to raise. 'Eden's been through a lot this last week,' said Morgan. 'She finally met her father...'

'How did that go?' Helene asked anxiously.

'I guess, not too well,' said Morgan.

Helene sighed. 'I was afraid of that.'

'Who are you anyway?' Wayne Summers asked suspiciously. 'I'm... My name is Morgan Adair. I'm a friend of Guy's wife, Claire.'

'The one who killed him?' Wayne asked.

Morgan looked at him coldly, trying to formulate a reply. 'Hey, don't glare at me, little lady. I've nothin' against her. In fact, I'd like to shake that Claire's hand.'

'Wayne Summers, you hush,' Helene insisted.

'I won't,' he said stubbornly. 'Guy Bolton finally got what was due him.'

'Why do you say that?' Morgan asked.

'Why? He killed our Kimberlee, that's why.'

Helene gave her husband a look full of warning. She turned to Morgan and rolled her eyes. 'Don't pay any attention to him. He's a mad dog on this subject.'

'Like hell. It's the God's truth,' Wayne exclaimed. 'I don't care what the police said. He killed her as sure as I'm standing here.'

Helene ignored him. 'Maybe Eden's back at the Spauldings by now. That's the woman who sent her the article from the paper about the baby. Our Kimba worked for them one summer. They've got a hotel called the Captain's House and our daughter was a chambermaid there.'

'The Captain's House,' Morgan exclaimed. 'Sure, I know that place. I stayed there.'

'Well, then you know what a nice lady that Mrs Spaulding is. She never forgot about Kimba. Or Eden. She sent Eden a Christmas card with five dollars in it every single year,' Helene explained amiably.

'Don't call her by that niggerish name,' Wayne protested. 'Her name was Kimberlee.'

Morgan could hardly believe her ears. 'Niggerish?' she said.

Helene apologized for her husband. 'Don't mind him. She decided she wanted to be called Kimba back when she was going to art school in New York City. More modern, I guess.'

'More colored,' Wayne scoffed. 'Sounds like a name straight out of Swahililand.'

'That girl of ours could sew anything,' said Helene wistfully. 'She won a contest and she got a scholarship. She wanted to be in fashion.'

'When I catch up to Eden...' said Wayne in a threatening tone, interrupting his wife's reverie about their long-lost daughter. 'Helene, come along.'

'I'm coming, dear. I just wondered,' said Helene, turning to Morgan. 'Would you mind very much if I used your little girls' room?'

Immediately, Morgan remembered the bloodstained bathroom off the master bedroom, and shuddered. 'Uh, yes, of course,' she said. 'Just use the one up the stairs. On your right.'

Helene started up the stairs.

'I'll wait in the truck,' said Wayne. 'If Eden turns up back here, you tell her I'm too old for her games. She best get on that bike of hers and head for home. And tell my wife I'm outside.' Before Morgan could reply, Wayne left the house.

In a few moments, Helene returned to the living room. 'Your husband's waiting for you outside,' said Morgan.

'Oh thank you. And don't mind him. He's just old-fashioned,' said Helene as she started for the door.

As if racism was some sort of charmingly nostalgic trait, Morgan thought. But as offended as she was by the old man's remarks, she was most curious about something he had said. 'Wait,' said Morgan. She put her hand on the woman's sleeve. Helene's arm was as soft as a marshmallow. 'I can't help wondering. What did your husband mean about Guy killing your daughter? I thought your daughter died in an accident.'

'Well, it *was* an accident. They were on their honeymoon and they were scuba diving. Kimba had no business doing that. But she wanted to please him, no matter what. Kimba wasn't as experienced divin' as Guy, and she was still physically real weak from having the baby. They think she panicked and went toward the surface too fast. There's something called the "bends"...'

'Yes, I've heard of that,' said Morgan.

Helene shrugged. 'They had a...you know, a hearing

and all. It seems that the two of them were with a group, exploring some sunken ship, so there was witnesses. Guy wasn't even with her when it happened. He was in plain sight of some other diver. Kimba was in another part of the wreck. They couldn't find nothing wrong with her equipment. She just panicked. They told us that panic is the number one cause of accidents for scuba divers...'

'So why does your husband still blame Guy?'

'Well, Guy Bolton, may he rest in peace, was no gentleman. He got our daughter pregnant and he really didn't want to marry her. But after the baby was born, they did get married. Who knows? It might have worked out for them.'

Morgan was taken aback at this unexpected news. 'Does Eden know about this?'

Helene sighed. 'Now, she does. When she was so determined to come up here and meet Guy, Wayne told her all about his belief that it was no accident. Wayne hoped it would stop her from comin'. It didn't stop her, as you can see.'

'But you told her that it wasn't true?'

Helene nodded. 'Of course I did. Right away. There's no reason on earth for her to go thinking a thing like that about her father.'

There was a loud blast of a car horn. Helene looked out the front door at the pickup truck parked in front of the house. 'I've got to go. Thank you for your help. If you see my granddaughter just tell her Mom-mom loves her, and wants her home. Will you do that for me?'

'Yes,' said Morgan.

'Bless you,' said Helene. She hurried out the door and across the yard to the truck.

Morgan went to the door and watched until their truck was out of sight, but all the while her mind was turning

over all she had heard. She tried to imagine how Eden
had felt when she heard this story about her father. Maybe
she didn't want to believe it at first. And then, she arrived
here, in West Briar, to a chilly reception from Guy, how
did she feel then? There were a million questions buzzing
in Morgan's head. But there was no one in the family she
could ask. It would have to be someone who remembered
those days, and what had happened. All at once, she had
an idea.

Morgan went into the kitchen where Guy had his computer on a built-in desk in the kitchen, as well as piles of
recipes, and notes taped to the monitor. She searched his
files and in no time, she found what she was looking for.
She wrote down the information, stuffed it in her pocket,
and picked up her car keys. Then, just as she was turning
off the kitchen light, her gaze fell on a pair of scissors on
the counter. She picked up the scissors and took them with
her. She would clip those balloons off the mailbox right
now, on her way out. She didn't want to have to look at
them again.

TWELVE

ON A ROAD THROUGH THE WETLANDS which led to the Briarwood Marina was a row of old fishing shacks built on pilings, where, at high tide, the water rose almost to the decking. Many of these modest dwellings had been cunningly rehabbed, in recent years, to be small but comfortable getaway homes. Others remained resolutely authentic, with ripped screens and patched roofs. Fitz lived in one of the latter.

Morgan checked the number she had lifted from Guy's computer, parked on the street, marched up to the front door and banged on it. She could see the lights on inside the house, glowing warmly against the windows. All the way over, she had been pondering what she had heard from Eden's grandparents. It turned out that Eden had yet another reason to hate the father who had rejected her, and her own grandfather was convinced that she might not be of sound mind.

Morgan probed the thought the way she might probe an aching tooth with her tongue. What if Eden had decided to seek revenge? Morgan knew how tender-hearted Claire was. What if Claire, out of some misguided feeling of pity and responsibility, had decided to save the girl and take the blame? It made more sense to Morgan than the idea that, even in the depths of depression, Claire could have killed her husband and her child. Morgan knew it was much longer than a long shot, but it was all she had.

In a moment the door opened. Fitz, wearing a T-shirt

and jeans, ran his hand self-consciously through his curly hair as he recognized his visitor. Caught by surprise, he smiled at the sight of her. 'Hi,' he said.

'Hi,' she said.

'What's up?' he asked.

Looking at Fitz, she flashed back to their reckless moment at Claire's wedding. If he was thinking the same thing, it did not show in his face. 'I had a few questions. I thought you might know the answers. Do you have a minute?'

'Sure. I guess so,' he said. 'Come on in.'

Morgan hesitated. If she went into his house, would he think this was a ploy to rekindle their liaison? That was the last thing she wanted to do.

Fitz frowned at her. 'Come on. It's chilly out here.' Morgan shivered, and nodded. She followed him into the small house. Inside it was sparsely furnished, but it was warm, and surprisingly neat. As she glanced around she saw bookshelves, a table with two chairs, a TV and two well-worn leather chairs facing it with an ottoman between them. The floor was warmed by an oriental rug. The small room was bathed in the amber glow of a table lamp and a standing lamp. It looked way too rustic for a bachelor pad.

Fitz indicated that she should sit in one of the chairs. 'Something to drink?' he asked.

Morgan shook her head, and sat on the edge of the cushion. Fitz settled himself in the neighboring chair and put his feet on the ottoman, looking relaxed. 'I'm sorry to bother you,' she said.

Fitz nodded. 'No problem.' He offered her no further encouragement. He obviously wasn't going to make it easy.

Morgan took a deep breath and launched into her explanation. 'I'm here because I was just talking to Eden's grandparents. They came by Claire's house, looking for Eden. Her grandfather told me a very bizarre story about the death of Eden's mother. You've known Guy forever. You were his best friend. I thought you might know something about it.'

Fitz gripped the armrests on his chair. 'Oh. Right,' he said in a bored voice. 'You mean that Guy was to blame for Kimba's accident? Didn't matter what the inquest said. The old man blamed Guy and he didn't want to hear anything different.'

'Yes,' said Morgan. 'Well, I was just thinking that Eden came to town with that weighing on her mind. Maybe she wasn't quite sure whether or not to believe it. And then, Guy blew her off at the baptism.'

'Well, yeah, but then they got together and they got along.'

'They did? When?' asked Morgan, startled by this news.

Fitz shrugged. 'After the baptism. When she came here to see him.'

Morgan shook her head. 'Came here?'

'You didn't know about that? I thought Claire must have told you.'

'No, I'm sorry. Told me what?'

Fitz sighed. 'Well, after the baptism, Claire and Guy had a big argument about Eden and his marriage to Kimba, and Claire threw Guy out.'

'Oh, yes, she did tell me that,' Morgan remembered. 'Well, he came over here and stayed with me for a couple of days. But he kept calling Claire, begging for her to forgive him, going over there to talk to her. Finally, she let him come home. He was exiled to the guest room upstairs, but she did let him back in the house. Unfortunately.'

Morgan ignored the implication. 'And you're saying that he saw Eden during that time?'

'Yeah, he saw her,' said Fitz. 'A couple of times. Well, look. I told him that he owed it to the kid to talk to her. She came all this way to finally meet him. He knew I was right. That was the right thing to do. You never really knew Guy, but he was a good man. He didn't want to hurt that kid any more than she'd already been hurt. I mean, it never was his fault that he couldn't see her. The grandfather wouldn't allow it.'

'So, he invited Eden to visit him here,' Morgan prompted him to continue.

'Right,' said Fitz. 'I told him to ask her over. She came a couple of times, before he moved back in with Claire. In fact, she may have even visited at their cottage, after Guy moved back home. Anyway, they got along all right. And I know for a fact that they all went to a family dinner at Dick and Astrid's that last night.'

'Claire too?'

'Yeah. Claire was going, as far as I knew.'

'I thought Dick didn't want anything to do with Eden.'

'He didn't. But Astrid felt sorry for the kid. She wanted to help. And in the end, Dick went along with it. He's not a bad guy. He loves his kids, but he has a hard time showing it. Like lots of guys. But let me tell you, when Eden's grandfather tried to blame Guy for Kimba's death, there was nobody who defended Guy more than Dick. When the death was ruled accidental, the old man threatened a civil suit. Dick was a tiger about it. He told the old guy he'd be living in his truck if he kept it up. He was fierce, defending his son. I always thought Guy didn't give him enough credit. Dick was in his corner all the way.'

'And yet, Guy thought it was OK to treat his own daughter like an intruder.'

Fitz sighed. 'I'll grant you, that wasn't Guy's finest moment. But she ambushed him that day. He was freaked out.'

'He was the adult. He should have tried a little harder,' Morgan insisted.

To Morgan's surprise, Fitz nodded. 'You're right. He should have. And I know that he did when they got together. They talked for a while. I mean, obviously it was strained because Claire had kicked him out, but Guy was trying to make a connection with Eden. He took her out for a hamburger. They did all right together. She showed him some pictures she had brought of herself as a little girl. You know, that kind of stuff.'

Morgan shook her head. 'So, I guess she didn't believe her grandfather's story about Guy. I mean, not if she and Guy were hitting it off.'

'I don't know anything about that,' said Fitz. 'I mean, after Guy moved back home we didn't get much of a chance to talk about it. But from what I saw, they were fine with one another.'

'You're sure about that,' Morgan said skeptically.

Fitz shrugged. 'It looked that way to me,' he said. Morgan glanced at him, and looked away. She could feel his gaze on her.

Fitz cocked his head and looked at Morgan curiously. 'Why all the questions about Eden anyway?'

Morgan hesitated. The lamplight encircled them in a warm glow, and Morgan felt the impulse to tell him what she had been thinking. He certainly seemed interested. She decided to risk it. 'It's just that I was thinking that no one could blame Eden for wanting revenge.'

Fitz shook his head, as if she were speaking a foreign language. 'Revenge? Revenge for what?'

Morgan was instantly hesitant, but it was too late to take it back. 'I don't know. I'm just speculating. What if Eden decided to pay her father back for what he had done to her and her mother?'

'He didn't do anything to her mother,' Fitz reminded her. 'They got married and she died in an accident. Period.'

'But, what if Eden still believed that he was to blame?'

'What if she did?' he said.

'Well, someone killed Guy. And his new baby.'

Fitz looked at her in disbelief. 'Someone? Your friend, Claire, confessed. Remember?'

'Maybe Claire knew it was Eden, but she felt guilty or sorry for the girl, and decided to take the blame.'

Fitz reared back in his chair. 'Whoa. Wait a minute. Are you crazy? Are you insane? You're really trying to blame these murders on Eden now? On that poor kid?'

'Kids can be very...erratic. They can act without thinking,' Morgan said defensively. Now she regretted revealing her thoughts to him.

Fitz gaped at her as if she had grown another head. 'That's pathetic. That is truly pathetic. I mean, I can see that you're looking for excuses. Any excuse. For Claire. But to try to pin it on an innocent kid... And then act like Claire was some kind of hero.'

'It's not an excuse. I'm just trying to look at the possibilities rationally,' Morgan said archly.

Fitz snorted and pushed himself up from his chair. He turned on Morgan. 'Rational? You call that rational? It's...obscene. You'll grab at any excuse. For Claire, and for yourself.'

'Myself?' Now Morgan stood up as well, not allowing him to look down on her. 'What do I need an excuse for?'

Fitz pressed his lips together as if he was trying to prevent his thoughts from escaping.

'Go ahead,' said Morgan. 'Say it. Say what you're thinking.'

Fitz's eyes narrowed. 'You're avoiding the obvious. Your friend confessed to this crime. Don't you feel a little bit responsible?'

'How am I responsible?' Morgan cried.

'Oh, I don't know. Maybe, if you'd been paying attention, you would have figured out that your friend was off the deep end… And if you had, maybe *my* best friend and his child would still be alive.'

Morgan blinked fast, blindsided by his accusation.

'You must have noticed that Claire was going nuts, but maybe you felt it served her right. Maybe you were a little bit jealous of all the good things that had happened to old Claire,' he accused her.

Morgan's mouth fell open in disbelief. 'How dare you say that? You don't even know me,' she said.

Fitz pounced. 'You told me that yourself. At their wedding. After about your tenth glass of champagne, you said how much you envied Claire. How men fell in love with her at first sight and made fools out of themselves for her. And how that never seemed to happen to you.'

'I never said that,' Morgan protested, although she knew it might indeed have been something she said. It was certainly something she had felt, but she wasn't about to admit it. She felt the need to strike back. 'I'll admit that I drank a lot of champagne,' she said coolly. 'Sorry. I don't really remember much of anything about that wedding, to be honest with you. It's mostly just a blur.'

Fitz held up his thumb and forefinger, almost touching, and squinted through the tiny opening. 'Oh come on. Tell the truth. Didn't you feel just a wee little bit of satisfaction that Claire was depressed in spite of all her good fortune?'

Morgan struggled to keep her expression impassive.

'You don't know what the hell you're talking about,' she said flatly.

'Are you sure?' he said. 'I do know you a little.'

Morgan ignored this reference to their brief encounter. 'Don't flatter yourself,' Morgan retorted coldly. She turned away from him and left the shack, slamming the door behind her. She held her head high as she walked back to the car. By the time she got into the driver's seat, he had closed the door to the house. She stared out at the dark, peaceful wetlands, moonlight shimmering on the still waterways, her heart pounding with anger. But beneath the anger, for some reason she could not explain, she felt humiliated. Her cheeks flamed at the thought of his scornful appraisal of her. It was completely unfair. Unjust. She had acted out of friendship, done all that she could for Claire. She was here for no other reason. But to her surprise, tears began to run down her face.

Morgan folded her arms on the wheel, and rested her head against them. She felt weary to the point of exhaustion, and her heart was aching. Fitz was an arrogant fool, but a small part of her could not dismiss what he said. As much as she would deny it, in her heart of hearts she knew that she had felt a little jealous of Claire and even somewhat abandoned by her. If Morgan was acting purely out of friendship, wouldn't she have noticed that Claire was descending into mental illness? Wouldn't she have insisted on taking her to a psychiatrist? Claire would have resisted, but ultimately, she could have been convinced if Morgan had only tried harder. Perhaps Morgan could have prevented the tragedy that ensued.

Guilty feelings rushed, like a virus, through Morgan's system. But after a few seconds Morgan lifted her head and shook it. True or not, it was too late for regrets. There was no time for that now. She reminded herself that she could not afford to fall apart, to give way. She had to stay strong now. God knows, she thought, someone has to. Insufficient as she might be, Morgan was the only one Claire had left.

THIRTEEN

THE FEMALE GUARD behind a Plexiglas shield at the county jail visitors' desk looked up at Morgan impassively, 'You're too late,' she said.

Morgan glanced at the clock and struggled to maintain a civil tone. 'I've still got ten minutes,' she said.

'Your friend already has a visitor. Asked not to be interrupted.'

Who, Morgan wondered? She knew better than to ask. 'Maybe they'll leave early. I'll wait,' she said.

'Suit yourself. Sit over there.' The guard pointed with a pencil.

Morgan sat in one of the molded plastic chairs, leaving a chair empty between her and a mother, a toddler squirming in her arms, who was also waiting. She put her head back against the wall and closed her eyes. She had spent an almost completely sleepless night in the upstairs guest room of Claire's cottage. She had been startled by every sound, and, despite her exhaustion, had felt as jittery as if she had drunk a quart of coffee. Every time she started to doze, images of the blood-spattered bathroom downstairs rose in her mind, waking her. She finally fell into a coma-like stupor at dawn, and did not even hear the alarm, which she had set on her cellphone, go off.

When she awoke and saw the time, Morgan threw on some clothes and ran out of the house without breakfast. Morgan drove above the speed limit and squealed into the parking lot. She rushed through the security procedures, handing over the paper shopping bag she was carrying which held the black clothes Claire wanted to attend tomorrow's funeral. The security guard had taken it, refusing to assure Morgan one way or another that the clothes would be delivered to Claire. Morgan felt as if her frantic effort to arrive under the wire may have been in vain.

Now Morgan's stomach was churning with nothing in it but acid. Although she kept her eyes closed, there was no chance of her dozing off in this prison waiting area. The smell alone was enough to prevent sleep, not to mention the cries and curses which erupted in the bowels of the building and echoed down the hallways.

'All right,' said the guard from behind the desk. 'Visiting hours are over. Everybody out.'

Morgan opened her eyes and sighed. She would not be seeing Claire until the funeral tomorrow, and she doubted whether she would have a chance for a conversation with her then. At least she had delivered the black clothes for Claire to wear. The rest was up to the discretion of the prison authorities.

Morgan got up and followed the straggling queue of visitors down the hallway and through the several sets of doors which led out to the parking lot. Several people were trudging up to the bus stop out by the highway, some holding the hands of children. They looked so weary. As she got into the car, she wondered if she should offer them a ride. The ringing of her cellphone distracted her from the guilty impulse.

'Ms Adair? This is Berenice Hoffman at Noreen Quick's office.'

'Oh yes, sure,' said Morgan. 'How are you?'

'Fine. Ms Quick wants to talk to you. She's at home, on bed rest. This is her address. I'll email you the directions.'

'What's this about?' Morgan asked.

'I don't know. She said it was important.'

'When does she want to see me?' Morgan asked.

'ASAP,' said Berenice.

Morgan glanced at the time on her dashboard. 'I can be there within the hour,' she said. As she drove through the prison gates she glanced over at the line of prison visitors now slumped on the bench at the bus stop outside the gates. The children circled the bus stop restlessly, but the adults sat with blank faces, resigned to the wait.

NOREEN QUICK LIVED FAR from the shoreline, in a quiet cul-de-sac of 1950's era split-level homes built on a former potato field, now surrounded by mature trees and gardens.

Noreen's yard was casually tended with a plastic jungle gym and a life-size plastic dollhouse flattening the grass and turning it brown beneath them. Morgan walked up to the door and knocked.

A tall, angular woman with a wide, gap-toothed smile and a cap of blond-tipped, wildly curly hair answered, wiping her hands on an apron. Morgan introduced herself. 'I'm here to see Ms Quick,' she said.

The woman stepped aside to invite her in. 'Follow me,' she said. She started down the hallway of the light-filled, pleasantly cluttered house and glanced into the living room at two young children with red hair who were watching Barney the purple dinosaur on the television. 'Turn that down,' she ordered. 'We'll all be deaf.' The older child, a boy of about four, dutifully pointed the remote and lowered the sound.

'After Barney's over, come in the kitchen and get your lunch,' she said.

The younger child, an adorable cherub with freckles, looked up eagerly. 'Nanabutter?' she exclaimed hopefully.

'You got it, babe,' said the woman with a genial smile. She turned back to Morgan. 'Down here,' said the woman, continuing down a hall filled with plants, an overflowing bookcase and framed family photos. She opened a bedroom door at the end and stuck her head into the room. 'Nonny, your client's here. Keep it short.' The tall woman turned to Morgan. 'She doesn't do resting very well.'

'I'll bet,' said Morgan.

The tall woman rolled her eyes. 'You have no idea. Go on in. If it lasts too long I'm coming in there.'

Morgan nodded and slipped into the room. Noreen Quick, her red hair standing up like a cockscomb, was lying in a four-poster bed, surrounded by files and papers on the counter-pane, a computer glowing at her bedside and a Bluetooth phone in her ear. She was wearing a thermal Henley shirt which was stretched out over her large stomach. She gestured to Morgan to come and sit down in the rocking chair beside the bed.

Morgan took a seat. 'How are you feeling?' she asked.

Noreen waved a hand dismissively. 'Fine. This is a pain in the ass, but the same thing happened last time. Bed rest. I hate it, but I deal with it.'

Morgan nodded.

'I'll get right to the point,' said Noreen. ''Cause if I don't, and you're in here any length of time, Gert will come in and kick you out.'

'That's what she indicated,' Morgan murmured.

'She'll do it, too,' said Noreen.

Morgan detected a note of pride in the attorney's voice, as if it made her feel precious, to be guarded so fiercely. Morgan could understand that. 'That's fine with me,' she said. 'What's this all about?'

Noreen sighed, and pressed her lips together. 'It's not good news.'

Morgan's heart sank. 'What does that mean?'

'I just got a call from the psychiatrist we hired. His conclusions based on his interview with Claire.'

Morgan frowned. 'And…?'

'Well, it's a little disappointing. He claims that Claire does not have PPP. Not now. Or at the time of the…incident as far as he's concerned.'

Morgan's heartbeat seemed to flutter with anxiety. 'I don't understand…'

'Post-partum psychosis?' Noreen said. 'Don't you remember I explained this?'

'Yes, of course, I remember. But this doctor is saying that Claire wasn't depressed? That's just not true,' Morgan insisted.

'Depressed, yes,' said Noreen. 'But lots of people are depressed. Hell, everybody gets depressed now and then. That's not a defense. Psychosis is a defense. Delusions, compulsions, hearing orders from God. That's what we need to establish. That she was suffering from a psychosis.'

Morgan frowned. 'In a way, this confirms what I've been thinking. She was down, definitely, but she just didn't seem that crazy to me.'

Noreen looked at her coldly. 'Well, don't be too pleased with yourself for agreeing with his diagnosis. Unless we can prove psychosis, the prosecution is going to say that this case is not about mental illness. They're going to say that Claire was very angry at her husband, because of the daughter he never told her about who showed up out of nowhere. They're going to say that Claire did this deliberately.'

Morgan shook her head helplessly. 'That's just not possible. I mean, she was angry about Eden, yes, but... Well, what can we do?'

Noreen studied the report she was holding for a moment. 'Obviously, we need to hire another expert, perhaps one who is more...accustomed to being a defense witness. Someone who will recognize the PPP symptoms in a way that this gentleman did not. However, the services of such a witness can be expensive. As the person with power of attorney over Claire's finances, I wanted to clear it with you before I proceeded.'

Morgan looked at her with narrowed eyes. 'You mean you're going to bribe him to say what we want?'

'Not at all. This will be a credible witness. A licensed psychologist.'

Morgan thought this over. 'Will the prosecution have a psychologist interview her too?'

Noreen nodded. 'Yes, they certainly will.'

'What if their expert comes to the same conclusion as this first doctor?'

Noreen rolled her eyes in exasperation. 'We have to see to it that our expert proves more convincing.'

Morgan grimaced. 'It seems...risky.'

'Risky? Try to understand this, Morgan. We don't have all that many options,' said Noreen impatiently.

Despite the attorney's impatience, Morgan felt compelled to continue. 'But what if... Look, I learned something yesterday. Eden—that's the long-lost daughter—had good reason to hate Guy Bolton. Her own grandfather blamed Guy for the death of Eden's mother...'

Noreen raised her eyebrows. 'Was Guy responsible for her death?'

Morgan shook her head. 'No. Apparently not.'

'Where was the old man when Guy was killed?'

Morgan took a deep breath. 'In West Virginia. But

Eden was here and she knew about it. She may have believed it and decided to...'

'Stop,' Noreen raised her hands. 'Try and understand something, Morgan. Claire confessed. Whether you like it or not, she confessed to this crime. Now, as I was saying, because our defense rests on Claire's state of mind, we need an expert who will testify she was unbalanced as a result of post-partum psychosis. It's that simple. And I will find us such an expert. Unless you'd prefer that your friend spend the balance of her life in prison...'

'No, of course not,' said Morgan.

The door to the bedroom opened, and Noreen's partner entered carrying a steaming teacup. 'Nonny,' she said in a warning voice. 'I want you to drink this.'

Noreen looked directly at Morgan. 'That means "leave",' she said.

Morgan got up stiffly from the rocker.

'Just let me do my job,' said Noreen, accepting the proffered teacup. The tall woman reached behind Noreen's back, plumping her pillow. 'Gert, I'm fine,' Noreen grumbled, but she was suppressing a smile. She turned back to Morgan. 'Don't worry,' she said more gently. 'Trust me. I've got this under control.'

FOURTEEN

ONLY TWO CARS WERE PARKED in the sandy lot, surrounded by beach plum bushes and brittle-looking shrubs. One was a white minivan with a swarthy-looking man asleep in the front seat, a cap pulled down over his eyes. The other was a dented compact car with a sparkling blue bumper sticker which read, 'Don't drive faster than your Angels can fly.' Morgan parked at the far end of the lot and got out of the car. She had been here once last summer and the parking lot had been impossible to negotiate, filled to capacity with late model BMWs and Lexuses. Autumn definitely brought a slowdown. The path to the beach wound through grass-covered dunes, and Morgan could hear the sea pounding in the distance.

She started down the empty path, walking toward the beach. Despite the turmoil in her heart, she was distracted from her worries by the magnificence of the azure sky with thin clouds adrift on the horizon. She stepped out on to the sand, and took off her shoes and socks. The sand was cool and felt slightly damp between her toes. She walked toward the water, toward the divide between the gray wet sand and the eggshell white dry, and stayed on the dry side as the waves rushed up and tried to reach her, before they collapsed with a noisy crash into a spray of foam just inches from her feet.

The last time she had walked here was with Claire, when she was already far along in her pregnancy. Claire, with her canvas pants rolled up so she could walk in the water, holding her stomach, already protective of the child inside. She had talked excitedly about her plans for this child. The addition she and Guy would build on to the cottage, or maybe they would move back to France. She hoped to regain her figure and go back to work as a graphic artist when the baby was a few years old. Cheerful, exciting plans. This, the same woman who had confessed to killing her baby, her husband.

Morgan sighed, but her sigh was drowned out by the restless tide. She thought about the psychiatrist's report—how could anyone suggest that Claire's were the actions of a sane woman? Maybe Claire wasn't as severely depressed as some, but she was surely out of her right mind to have to done such a thing. Wasn't there more than one way for a person to exhibit mental illness? Wasn't the murder of a child, and a beloved husband, all the evidence you should ever need?

A lifeguard's boat with a ragged hole in its wooden hull was overturned on the beach, slowly being buried by the sand. Morgan stopped and sat down on it, sticking her legs straight out in front of her. The very thought of all this made it seem impossible for her to keep walking, as if her very strength was sapped out of her. She sat and stared down the lonely beach. A few hundred yards away, a young woman had set up an easel in the sand, and was seated on a camp chair, daubing paint thoughtfully on a canvas. Another person in a blue anorak was walking in Morgan's direction, bending over repeatedly, picking up rocks or shells and placing them into a bucket while two dogs gamboled around her, kicking up sand, and chasing one another, yapping. It took Morgan a few minutes of staring absently at the shell collector to realize that she was looking at Guy's sister, Lucy.

Morgan's first impulse was to turn away. She didn't

want to encounter Lucy, or have to speak to her. She stood up from the boat, but before she could flee, Lucy straightened up, and peered at her, frowning. Then, recognition, though not pleasure, dawning in her face, she lifted a small hand in an anemic greeting.

Morgan sighed, and waved back. She hesitated a moment and then walked to meet her.

Up close, Lucy looked ghostly. Her cottony blond hair was being whipped around her face by the wind. Her glasses were dusty with sand. Lucy said hello, and gazed down at Morgan's bare feet. 'Aren't you freezing?' she asked.

'Honestly, yes. It's a little too cold for this.'

Lucy frowned at Morgan. 'Astrid called me. She said Claire is coming to the funeral.'

'That's right,' said Morgan. 'I brought some black clothes to the prison this morning.'

'Why did my father say it was OK?'

Morgan shrugged. 'I don't know. But he did.'

'That's a mistake,' Lucy said bluntly. 'Her coming.'

'I agree with you,' said Morgan.

An awkward silence fell between them. Morgan glanced down into the bucket at Lucy's shells. Lucy moved the bucket to her other hand, as if to shield the shells from Morgan's prying gaze.

'What made you start working with shells?' Morgan asked, trying to be friendly.

'It was Astrid's idea actually. I was always good at jigsaw puzzles. Prader-Willi children are known for that,' said Lucy matter-of-factly. 'Astrid thought I might like putting shells together like puzzle pieces. Turned out I did.'

Morgan was about to make a comment about that fortuitous insight, when Lucy said abruptly, 'I thought you'd be gone by now.'

Morgan tried not to take offense. 'I'm going to the funeral too.'

Lucy's gaze was far away. 'Right. You were Drew's godmother. Not me.'

'I'm sorry if that hurt your feelings,' said Morgan sincerely. Lucy waved her small, flaccid hand. 'Doesn't matter. Guy would never pick me,' she said.

Morgan felt pained by the casual cruelty that Lucy's remark suggested. She wanted to change the subject. 'Have you heard anything from Eden?' Morgan ventured. 'Her grandparents showed up looking for her. I didn't know what to tell them.'

Lucy stared impassively out to sea. 'She's been at my house.'

'She has?' Morgan exclaimed. 'She's been staying with you?'

'She is my niece,' said Lucy.

'Oh, I know. I didn't mean… It was nice of you to invite her,' said Morgan.

'Everybody acts like I don't know how to have someone over,' said Lucy indignantly.

'I'm sure that's not true,' said Morgan.

'After it happened,' said Lucy, 'nobody cared about Eden's feelings. I told her to come stay with me.' Lucy shook her head. 'The others all forgot about her.'

'Well, I'm sure everybody was in shock,' said Morgan sadly.

'Everybody in the whole town was in shock,' Lucy exclaimed. 'Every time I think of what Claire did to that helpless baby…'

Morgan noticed that she didn't mention Guy. 'Claire was seriously depressed,' said Morgan.

Lucy looked disgusted. 'So depressing to have a beautiful new baby.'

Morgan immediately remembered Claire's story about Lucy in the genetic counselor's office. She decided to ignore the barb. 'Fitz said that Guy and Eden were becoming close before he died,' said Morgan.

Lucy's gaze was as cold as the sea. 'Eden wanted him to like her,' Lucy said. 'She was trying so hard to make him love her. Even after he was mean to her and hurt her feelings.'

Morgan studied Lucy's pale, slack face. She sensed some personal animus in that assessment. She couldn't help wondering about the torment that Lucy had endured in her life for being a little bit different, a lot less pretty and coordinated than the other girls. Some siblings rose to the defense of a feebler sibling. Others just joined in the jeering, wanting to distance themselves from the weak, and be on the side of their normal friends. Was Guy one of those people, she wondered? 'You didn't have a very high opinion of your brother,' said Morgan.

Lucy looked at her coldly for a long minute, and seemed to be struggling to reply. Finally she said, 'That's my business. He was still my brother. Claire shouldn't have killed him. Or that...' Lucy's voice cracked, and she cleared her throat impatiently. '. . . baby.' Abruptly, Lucy turned away from Morgan, called the dogs and began trudging toward the overgrown entrance to the beach. The dogs swirled around her legs, barking and playing.

Morgan walked behind her until she reached the overturned boat. Then she stopped and sat down on the hull to brush the sand off her feet and put her socks and shoes back on.

Lucy turned and looked back at her. 'Are you leaving after the funeral?' she asked.

'As soon as I can,' Morgan said.

'Good,' Lucy nodded. 'You should go.'

ON THE DRIVE BACK to the cottage, Morgan thought about how much she dreaded the funeral tomorrow, coming face to face with all the people who had cared for Guy and rejoiced in the birth of his son. As she pulled up in front of the cottage, she saw that there was a car parked in the driveway, a dark gray, late model Jeep. As she got out of her car, it took her a minute to recognize Dick Bolton's vehicle. She walked past it, and peered inside. The normally energetic Dick Bolton was slumped in the passenger seat, staring through the windshield. Morgan hesitated, and then tapped on the side window. Dick jumped slightly, turned his large, handsome head and looked over at her. Before she could say anything to him, he looked away, as if he did not see her.

Her face reddening, Morgan straightened up and went up the path to the house. Dusty was sprawled out in the fading, leaf-strewn flower bed of dahlias and zinnias, watching Morgan through slitted yellow eyes. Morgan let herself into the cottage. Immediately she noticed a garment bag draped over one of the dining room chairs, and she could hear sounds coming from the kitchen. 'Hello,' she called out.

'In the kitchen.' Morgan recognized Astrid's lilting accent. She walked into the kitchen and saw Astrid taking items from the counter and placing them in a cardboard box.

'Hi Astrid,' said Morgan. 'I saw Dick in the driveway.'

Astrid wore a black cape over her clothes and her crown of braids looked uncharacteristically off-kilter, wisps loose around her face. Her ivory complexion was deeply etched with lines, and her eyes were more gray than lavender. She looked up at Morgan. 'I see that you've been staying here,' Astrid said.

'I probably should have asked you and Dick first,' said Morgan. 'If you'd like, I'll get a motel room.'

'Oh, I don't care,' said Astrid wearily. 'What does it matter now?'

'I just saw Lucy at the beach,' said Morgan.

Astrid's face softened and she looked at Morgan hopefully. 'How is my little girl? Is she all right? I've been so distracted.'

'She seems…kind of angry.'

Astrid sighed. 'Well, it's easier for Lucy to be angry than to admit that she is sad.'

Morgan could remember that from her own childhood. Anger was a kind of shield for her own intense sadness. And, obviously, Astrid knew Lucy better than anyone, but to Morgan it seemed that Lucy was not the least bit sad. Not about Guy, anyway.

'She does seem sad about the baby,' said Morgan carefully. 'I got the impression that she and Guy weren't that close.'

Astrid sighed. 'Well, you know it was never easy for Lucy. She had a lot of developmental difficulties, because of this condition she has. Guy, of course, was attractive and smart. Everyone wanted to be his friend.'

'It seemed as if Guy might not have been exactly her… champion, shall we say.'

Astrid was vague. 'I don't know about that. There was an age difference. They never spent much time in the same company, you know. They weren't in the same schools at the same time. That sort of thing.'

'Still, kids can be so mean.'

Astrid's temper flared. 'Are you saying that Guy was mean?'

'I don't know,' said Morgan.

'Of course he teased her a little. As brothers do. But he was never cruel. I can tell you that. His father and I wouldn't have allowed it.'

'You're right. I'm sorry. I just...got an impression from what Lucy said.'

'Well, it's the wrong impression. I ought to know. They were my children,' said Astrid with a catch in her voice.

'I know. This is difficult. It must be so hard for you to even walk in this house,' said Morgan. 'A lot of memories.'

Astrid stared blankly out into the other room. Then, she shook her head, as if waking herself from a dream. 'Look, Morgan, you may as well know, I've got some professional cleaners coming in to take care of the bedroom and the bath,' said Astrid with a shudder. 'The police recommended them. I suppose I should do it myself but I can't face it. Dick said he'd send over a couple of the Mexican workers from the Lobster Shack, but I...I don't want them to see this.'

'Professionals are probably a good idea. I can't even bear to look in there myself,' said Morgan.

Astrid nodded, unsmiling. Then she closed the lid on the box. 'I guess I've got what I need.'

'What have you got there...?' said Morgan, nodding at the box.

Astrid sighed. 'I had to pick up some clothes for Guy and the baby to wear...' Her voice choked for a moment. Then she recovered herself. 'For the funeral tomorrow. And these are a few other things. To put in the coffin.'

Morgan shook her head sadly. 'This is such a nightmare,' she said.

'Yes. Well...' Astrid lifted the box from the counter, and then walked past Morgan into the dining room where she picked up the garment bag and slung it over her arm. 'We must face it…' she said.

'Do you need help with that?' Morgan asked.

Astrid shook her head. 'No. It's under control.'

Morgan went with her to the front door and opened it for her. Astrid walked out on to the front step and looked over at the car where her husband waited. Dick sat there looking dazed, and made no move to get out of the car.

'I can open the trunk for you,' Morgan offered.

Astrid lifted her chin. 'I can manage,' she said. 'I have to.'

FIFTEEN

THE TINY WHITE CHURCH, so recently the site of Drew's christening, was overflowing with mourners, who were lined up out the door and down the sidewalk. Morgan, waiting in line, was grateful that the weather was cooperating, not dumping rain on the assemblage. The first person Morgan saw when she finally entered the church was Fitz, standing among the other dark-suited pallbearers at the back, looking uncharacteristically grim. Morgan tried to remain inconspicuous in the line which snaked down the side aisle of the church, hoping he would not notice her.

The people waiting to file past the open coffins at the front of the church inched along. As she edged forward Morgan had plenty of time to observe the church and the crowd. The altar and the two coffins were banked with a profusion of elaborate, stiff-looking flower arrangements. The members of the Bolton family formed a receiving line beside the coffins. All except Eden. Though Morgan scanned the church as she moved slowly toward the front, she saw no sign of Guy's daughter. Dick, his normally tanned complexion now pasty white, stood stoically beside Astrid, who leaned against him, weeping into a crumpled hanky. Lucy, who flanked her father on the other side, was dry-eyed and wearing an ill-fitting black pantsuit and a turtleneck with Dalmatians on it. Father Lawrence waited, almost out of sight, near the altar, talking quietly with various mourners who approached him.

As those who had come to pay their respects passed by the coffins, the sight of Guy's body seemed to cause weeping and head-shaking, but the sight of the tiny baby, Drew, in his christening dress, resting on satin in the miniature coffin, provoked wails and despair. Despite the coolness of the day, it was warm in the tiny church, and Morgan felt almost overcome by the raw emotion surging through the crowd, the cloying perfume of the flowers, and her dread of approaching the open caskets. Why did they have to leave them open, she thought? Wasn't this whole thing awful enough without having to view the embalmed bodies?

The sound of raised voices at the back of the church caused Morgan to turn around. Eden had arrived, dressed in her black leather jacket and jeans, and looking as if she had rolled in the dust. She and Fitz seemed to be having an angry discussion. Eden was agitated and wild-eyed, while Fitz spoke quietly to her. Morgan could not make out the words for the cries of the mourners and the lugubrious music of the organ. Eden started to march defiantly down the center aisle of the church, but Fitz caught her by the arm and held her back.

Eden protested and shook off his grip, scowling at Fitz like an angry child, while Fitz continued to murmur in her ear, pointing to the Bolton family and explaining something to her as she shook her head and clenched her jaw.

Suddenly the woman behind her poked Morgan in the ribs. 'Go on,' the woman hissed. It was Morgan's turn. Startled, Morgan lurched forward on wobbly legs, and hesitantly approached her godson's bier. Looking at his small, round face, she found herself remembering a long-forgotten religious teaching that newborns were free from sin and welcomed into heaven. Despite her lack of faith, Morgan found the thought strangely comforting.

Tears began to run down her face, and she did not bother to wipe them away. She remembered plans she had secretly made for this baby—that she would take him to the monkey house at the zoo, and ice skating at Rockefeller Center for Christmas, and ball games at Shea Stadium when he got older. She would be Aunt Morgan, and he would look forward to her visits, maybe even think she was a cool godmother. Morgan kissed her own fingertips and placed them briefly on the baby's cold, plump cheek. 'Goodbye my angel,' she whispered. She couldn't bear to gaze for long at the baby. She noted that there was a white prayer book with a gold cross in the corner of the coffin, and a stuffed brown bear which Claire had kept in Drew's bassinet. Even if she had wanted to, it was impossible to linger, given the press of the crowd behind her, and Morgan moved on.

Weeping freely, she approached Guy's coffin. He had been dressed in a dark suit and tie, his face still handsome, even in death. Morgan had learned things about him in these last few days which had made her wonder what kind of man he really was. Not a saint, or a superhero. Only human, she reminded herself. Gazing at him now, all she wanted to remember was Guy, Claire's husband, who was exuberant and made her laugh. Who loved her best friend to distraction. His chef's toque, his red sash, and the block of carving knives he had received as a parting gift from his master chef in Lyon were placed beside him in his coffin. Morgan thought about Astrid, collecting a box of belongings from the house yesterday, creating her tribute to Guy and his baby son. She had given thought to the dead, and gathered up material things that had mattered in life to place beside them. Propped up against the open lid of the coffin was a heart of white roses crossed by a ribbon, which read, 'Beloved Son'.

Morgan reached out and touched Guy's cold hand gently. As she passed the family, Morgan murmured her regrets with a lowered gaze. Then she turned and stumbled up the aisle toward the first seat she could find.

'Morgan,' she heard someone hiss. She looked around, through her tears, and saw Sandy Raymond gesturing to her to come and sit beside him and Farah. Gratefully, Morgan dropped down into the corner of the pew which Sandy had vacated for her. Farah, chic in a black designer minidress with jet beads, and a black spotted veil, smiled brightly at Morgan. Sandy, who was wearing a denim work shirt under his blazer and running shoes on his feet, reached out and patted her forearm.

'This is a freak show. Can't believe they have open caskets,' Sandy whispered in his gravelly voice.

Morgan wiped her eyes and murmured some non-committal reply. The sight of those two bodies in repose had shaken her more than she thought possible. They were both so young. They were in the early days and years of their lives. Now over. Finished. Morgan could not force her mind to contemplate it for long. She wished she could just close her eyes and drift away from here, and forget about the grief that was weighing on her heart.

Just then, a loud, anxious murmur raced through the church, and everyone seemed to turn at once, galvanized by the sight of the group which had appeared at the back.

Plain-clothes officers in dark glasses and uniformed guards surrounded their prisoner. Claire, her cheeks and eyes sunken, her skin gray, and her hair barely combed, walked with manacled hands, wearing the black skirt and sweater which Morgan had brought to the county jail. Her eyes dry, Claire stared up the center aisle at Guy and Drew's coffins. One of the officers held her arm as another, looking in every direction for trouble, led the police procession toward the open biers. A gasp arose from the assembled mourners.

'Claire,' Morgan whispered and she rose to her feet just as Claire passed by the pew. She reached out a hand toward her friend.

'Sit down,' growled the uniformed officer who was clearing the aisle. He glowered at her, and Morgan quickly resumed her seat. Claire did not look at Morgan, but kept walking, her eyes wide and focused on the caskets.

Morgan looked up at where the family stood at the front of the church. Lucy and Astrid seemed shocked by the sight of Claire. But Dick Bolton, who had been visibly sagging, suddenly straightened, and his tranquilized gaze popped, as if he had been given a jolt of caffeine. He stuck out his jaw like a bulldog and began to shake his head, as if he was not going to be able to restrain himself. Morgan thought she could actually hear him growling. He took a step toward Claire. One of the plain-clothes officers walked quickly to him and spoke to him in low, sympathetic tones. Claire paid no attention.

The line of mourners was held back by another officer as Claire was allowed to approach the caskets. Claire held up her manacled hands to the guards, a questioning look on her face, but the guards roughly shook their heads. Removing her handcuffs was clearly not possible. Claire's shoulders slumped in obedience.

Morgan felt her heart breaking as she watched her friend's profile. Claire bent her head over the casket of her baby son and stared, dry-eyed, at the tiny, waxen face. Her eyes widened, but otherwise she betrayed no expression.

Cry, Morgan thought. Let it out, Claire.

All through the church, Morgan could hear the loud murmurs of disapproval, disbelief. Claire raised her manacled hands and pointed to her baby's fingers. The guard hesitated, and then nodded briefly. Moving her linked hands as one, Claire reached out and put her index finger on Drew's tiny hand. Her eyes closed, and her body was shaking from head to toe.

'OK,' said the guard gruffly, signaling that she had to move on.

Without looking at him, Claire obeyed. She edged over to Guy's coffin and tilted her head to look at her husband's face. Her gaze remained impassive, still as death itself. Once again she lifted her manacled hands in supplication. Once again the guard nodded assent.

Slowly, Claire lifted her hands up over the edge of the coffin. She put her fingers up to Guy's cold face. She studied his still features as if she was searching them for some answer. Some explanation that he would now take to his grave. She whispered something, her lips moving feverishly.

Dick Bolton's voice cut through the shocked hush in the church. 'Keep your filthy hands off them,' he thundered. This, Morgan thought, with a sickening certainty, was the moment he had been waiting for, the reason he had agreed to allow Claire to come. His chance to rage at Claire, excoriate her, was now at hand. He did not miss it. 'How can you even look at them? Those two good, innocent souls. They never hurt you. They thought you loved them. You will burn in hell for what you've done. After you've spent the rest of your miserable life in prison, that is.'

'What a bastard,' Sandy murmured. 'Can't he see the state she's in?'

'I was afraid of this,' said Morgan.

'All right, all right,' said the guard. 'Take it easy now. Everyone take it easy.'

Claire blinked several times, but she did not look at Dick. The guard spoke in a low voice to Claire. 'Come on, now. That's enough.'

Claire nodded, although her gaze was glued to her dead husband's frozen features.

Then, before anyone could realize what she was about to do, much less stop her, Claire leaned forward. With her shackled hands she reached for the block of knives which had been tucked into the coffin, deliberately grasping the largest handle and jerking it from its resting place.

Sandy jumped to his feet. 'Claire, don't,' he cried.

'What's she doing?' Morgan demanded.

'Hey stop that,' the guard insisted. But he was too late.

It all happened in a moment. As the guard lunged for her, and the seated mourners in the church rose to their feet, crying out, Claire closed her eyes, lifted the knife and plunged it into her own chest. Morgan, paralysed with horror, watched helplessly as Claire slumped forward, a gush of her blood soaking into the satin lining of the coffin, as she fell across her husband's lifeless body.

SIXTEEN

THE GUARDS FROM THE COUNTY JAIL did not wait for an ambulance. They lifted Claire's limp body themselves, and, yelling at the hysterical crowds to part, rushed her down the aisle, and out to the waiting van which was idling at the curb, waiting for the prisoner's return.

Pandemonium broke out among the mourners, and Father Lawrence got up into the pulpit and pleaded for calm.

Sandy set his jaw. He grabbed Farah by the hand. 'Come on. We have to get out of here.'

'They haven't even started the service,' Farah protested.

'The hell with the service. Come.' He turned to Morgan. 'You coming?'

Morgan nodded and followed him out into the center aisle which was swamped with people talking loudly, weeping, and crying out. Sandy bulled his way through the crowds and Morgan managed to follow in his wake. Once they reached the sidewalk, Farah dug in her stiletto heels, shaking her head. 'What is that woman's problem?' Farah said. 'She'll do anything to draw attention to herself.'

'We have to get to the hospital,' Sandy said evenly.

'I don't want to go. I hate hospitals.'

Sandy looked taken aback at her resistance. 'You won't go with me?'

Farah shrugged. 'Look, she did a terrible thing to her

husband and that little baby. I don't even see why you would want to go.'

Morgan wasn't about to wait out their quarrel. 'Well, I'm going. I've got my own car,' she said.

Sandy's gaze was locked with Farah's. Neither one looked as if they wanted to give way in the argument. Morgan turned her back on them both and headed for her car.

BRIARWOOD HOSPITAL HAD NOT been able to give Morgan any patient information. Morgan asked to be connected to the Emergency Room as she drove with one hand and tried to talk on the phone. She wondered if perhaps Claire had been taken right back to prison, to the infirmary there. She didn't know whether to continue on to the hospital or head directly to the county jail. As she was pondering these unappealing options, a woman's voice answered. 'Briarwood ER.'

Morgan heaved a sigh of relief and asked about Claire. The woman on the other end did not hesitate. 'She's in surgery.'

'How is she? What kind of surgery…?'

'I can't tell you anything,' said the receptionist.

'But she's my best friend,' Morgan pleaded.

'The privacy laws are very strict,' said the receptionist. Then she hung up. Morgan slipped her phone in her bag, and made the next left turn. She still remembered, from the days surrounding Drew's birth, the way to the hospital.

It took her a while to find the waiting room for the surgical theater, but she finally found the correct hallway. She instantly knew she was in the right place when she spotted the guards in uniform who were milling around outside the closed double doors. Morgan took a seat and waited. The guards glanced at her and then looked away. After a while, a woman garbed and masked in blue, blood-spattered scrubs, emerged from the operating room. Morgan jumped up and tried to inquire, but the woman held up a hand to silence her and kept walking, hurrying away on quiet, crêpe-soled shoes. The guards looked curiously at Morgan but made no effort to speak to her. Morgan was the only person waiting for news of Claire. Obviously, Farah had won the argument with Sandy, Morgan thought. The fact that no one else seemed to care whether Claire lived or died made the whole situation seem even more tragic. Morgan put her head back against the wall and closed her eyes. Please God, she thought, don't let her die in there.

After what seemed like an hour, a man in scrubs emerged from the operating room, pulled off his mask and gloves and nodded to the guards, speaking to them in a low voice. He seemed to be answering their questions but Morgan could not hear what they were saying.

When the man, whom Morgan presumed to be a surgeon, left the guards, she summoned all her courage and approached him. 'Excuse me, doctor,' she said.

The man slowed down and looked at her impassively. 'I'm...Claire is my best friend. Is she alive? Is she...?' Morgan felt tears welling in her eyes.

The doctor hesitated, and then he nodded. 'She's alive. But she's critical. She tore herself up pretty well. The next forty-eight hours will determine the outcome.'

'Are they going to take her back to the prison?'

'No,' he scoffed. 'They can't care for her there. She's on a ventilator. She'll stay here.'

'Thank you,' said Morgan. 'Thank you for saving her.' The doctor nodded and walked away. Morgan sank back down on the chair, and took a deep breath and whispered a prayer of thanks to the God she often doubted. Claire was still alive. People always said that where there was life, there was hope. So, she would keep hoping. After a minute's relief, Morgan realized how hungry and exhausted she was. Forty-eight hours. There was nothing to do now but wait. She decided to get herself some coffee and a bite of something to eat. As much as anything else, she wanted a change of scene. She got up from the chair where she had sat for so long, and made her way to the elevator and the cafeteria on the ground floor.

Numbly, she went through the cafeteria line, took a cup of coffee and a roll and found a table in the corner with her back to the door. As she was stirring some milk into her cup, Father Lawrence, in his black suit and collar, walked up to her table and pulled out the chair across from her. 'May I?' he asked.

Morgan nodded. 'Sure,' she said. 'Is the funeral over?' Father Lawrence nodded. 'Somehow, we got through it.' He took a seat and looked at her sadly through his steel-rimmed glasses. 'How is Claire doing?' he asked.

Morgan sighed. 'She came through the surgery. But she's in critical condition.'

'I'm glad to hear that she survived the surgery,' said the minister.

'That's nice of you to say,' said Morgan.

'I mean it. Are you all alone here?' he asked.

Morgan tried to smile. 'Just me and the prison guards.' Father Lawrence shook his head. 'I don't understand why she did this…'

'Well, it was horrible for *me* to see Guy and the baby like that. Imagine what it was like for her,' said Morgan.

Father Lawrence shook his head. 'I spent some time with her at the prison yesterday.'

'They told me that she had a visitor. Was that you?' Father Lawrence nodded.

'What did she say?'

Father Lawrence folded his hands on the Formica tabletop. 'I urged her to confess. To seek absolution. I told her that God would forgive her anything, if she was truly repentant.'

'So did she do that? Confess?' said Morgan, taking a sip of her coffee.

Father Lawrence frowned.

Morgan waved a hand. 'Never mind. I know you can't talk about that. Even I know that a confession to the clergy is sacrosanct.'

'No, that's just it,' said Father Lawrence. 'There was no confession.'

Morgan looked up at him. 'What do you mean?'

'She said that she was beginning to think that she did not kill them.'

Morgan's heart thudded. 'What?' she said.

'She told me that all she could remember now was waking up and finding the baby in the bathtub.'

Morgan peered at him, as if he were speaking a language she could barely understand. 'But she told me that she did it. She described the whole thing to me. Why in the world would she say that if it wasn't true?'

Father Lawrence shook his head. 'I don't know.'

'She confessed to the police. You don't just admit to a murder you didn't do…'

'Well,' said Father Lawrence with a sigh, 'I'm afraid that she may be starting to deny the truth to herself. It's all too overwhelming. And then today…'

Morgan's gaze was on the priest, but her mind was beginning to race. 'Or…'

'Or what?' he asked.

'Or maybe she's finally realized the truth. That she didn't do it.'

Father Lawrence looked at her balefully. 'Now, Morgan. There's nothing to be gained by clinging to a false hope.'

'You don't know her, Father,' Morgan pleaded. 'Not like I do. It's never seemed possible to me.'

Father Lawrence's eyebrows were knit together in consternation over the steel rims of his glasses. 'Morgan, the police knew that Claire was guilty before they even started to question her.'

Morgan stared at him. 'How could they know that?'

'Apparently,' said the cleric with a sigh, 'Guy was found alive. He implicated her before he died.'

'NO,' Morgan cried out. The other diners in the hospital cafeteria looked around at her in alarm. Morgan lowered her voice. 'That's impossible. Claire told me that he was dead.'

'She also told you that she killed him. Which is true?'

'No,' said Morgan. 'She couldn't have mistaken that…'

'Claire is not a doctor,' the clergyman reminded her. 'She might have assumed he was dead, when, in fact, he wasn't.'

'Who said that he was still alive?' Morgan demanded. 'Who told her that? Who said he implicated her?'

'The detectives who were interrogating Claire told her that Guy explicitly accused her before he died.'

'I never heard anything about that,' Morgan protested. Father Lawrence dismissed her protest with a wave of the hand. 'Well, he did. And, Claire is doing herself no favors by denying this now. When a man names his killer with his last breath, there isn't anyone who would doubt it…'

'No, I know that,' Morgan admitted. Her mind was racing. 'This is something we just have to accept…'

Morgan was silent for a moment. 'What if he didn't?' she said. 'What if he *was* dead, and he *didn't* implicate her. What if they only said he did?'

Father Lawrence frowned. 'Oh come now, Morgan. You can't believe that. The police have no reason to lie about it.'

Morgan was not listening to the clergyman's words. 'I guess it would be easy enough to find out,' she mused aloud.

Father Lawrence grasped Morgan's forearm and leaned toward her. 'Morgan, stop this. Claire has a chance to make peace with her God, and with her fellow man. She was in a very disturbed state of mind, and people will understand that. God will understand that. But she has to heed her conscience. Denying that it ever took place is not the answer. As her friend, Morgan, you have to encourage her to take responsibility for her actions.'

Morgan nodded automatically, as if she were agreeing, but her mind was elsewhere, nurturing a glimmer of hope, and impervious to every word he said.

SEVENTEEN

THE NURSE AT THE ER DESK looked up at Morgan with a hint of impatience in her eyes. 'Yes?'

Given her recent, jarring reminder about the medical privacy laws, Morgan knew better than to simply ask for the information she wanted. Although she was not in the habit of being deceptive, she did know how to do research. She had stretched the truth on occasion to gain access to rare documents. She was ready to do it now, for Claire's sake. Luckily, she was still wearing her good black suit from the funeral. She pulled her university picture ID from her handbag and flashed it at the nurse. 'My name is Morgan Adair. I'm an investigator from the prosecutor's office. I have a question pertaining to one of your recent admissions.'

Immediately the nurse looked less hostile, as if she liked the idea of participating in a legal matter. 'Yes?'

'Sunday morning, a gentleman by the name of Guy Bolton was transported here by ambulance.'

The nurse nodded.

'There seems to be some question,' Morgan continued. 'Was Mr Bolton still alive when he arrived at the ER? Could you look it up for me?'

The nurse looked at her warily. 'This isn't about some lawsuit against the hospital, is it?'

'Oh, heavens, no,' said Morgan. 'I work for the county.' The nurse nodded. 'OK. When was that, again?'

Morgan gave her the date and time.

The nurse punched a few keys on the computer. Then she shook her head. 'Nope. He wasn't brought here. Are you sure you have the right hospital?'

Morgan frowned. 'I…don't know. I thought so.'

'Did the incident occur here in Briarwood?'

'West Briar,' said Morgan.

The nurse cocked her head. 'Well, they should have brought him here.' She frowned at her computer screen. 'But they didn't. I don't know. But you can find out from the EMTs on the Rescue Squad.'

'Are they here in the hospital?' Morgan asked.

The nurse shook her head. 'They work out of the Briarwood Fire Department. You'll have to ask there.'

'I will,' said Morgan. Her search was narrowing. 'Thanks.'

The Briarwood Fire Station was housed in a small brick building which adjoined the several bays where the hook and ladders and ambulance were parked and serviced. Morgan parked in a lot behind the bays, and entered the brick building. It looked more like a men's social club than a city service building. There was a pool table, a bunch of small tables and chairs, and a serving bar through which you could see the long galley kitchen. A couple of men wearing dark blue work clothes were playing cards at one of the tables. Another man was busily cooking something in the kitchen redolent of tomato sauce. The door leading to the bays was open, and Morgan could see that there were several men working on the equipment out there.

The card players looked up as she entered. 'Can we help you?' a fit-looking, white-haired man asked pleasantly.

'My name is Morgan Adair. I'm looking for an EMT from the Rescue Squad.'

The white-haired man instantly threw down his cards and stood up. 'What's the problem?'

'I'm sorry, no, not like that,' said Morgan gesturing for him to sit back down. 'I just had a question for someone who was on duty on Sunday.'

The man gave a little sigh of relief and resumed his seat. 'That was us. My partner and I were working Sunday. We work twenty-four hours on, and then forty-eight hours off. So, we just got back today. How can we help you?'

'I was wondering. Could I ask you about a call you made on Sunday morning?'

Instantly the man looked wary. 'What call was that?'

'Um. It was in West Briar. A man named Guy Bolton and his infant son.'

The younger man, who had a shaved head, set down his cards. 'Are you a reporter?' he asked.

'No,' said Morgan innocently. 'I'm a friend of the family.' When he spoke again, the white-haired man's tone was chillier. Clearly, he still suspected Morgan of being a reporter. 'We can't give out information about the calls we make.'

Morgan pressed on. 'Oh, I understand. The media is looking for every scrap of information. The family is being pestered night and day by reporters. But, I thought if I came here, the news vultures wouldn't make the connection.'

The two men exchanged a skeptical glance. 'What are you after?' the younger man demanded.

'OK, look, the family's in shock from all that has happened, as you can imagine. It was such a...terrible thing...'

'That's for sure,' murmured the younger man.

'Nothing I can say is of any real comfort. But it occurred to me that Guy might have had some last words for the family, you know? Some few words that they could take comfort from. I was figuring he might have spoken to a nurse or a doctor or even an orderly. Someone. So I went and asked at the ER in the hospital in Briarwood. I was just assuming that's where you would have taken him. I mean, it's the closest hospital to the Bolton's home. But they looked it up and said he was never admitted there. The nurse told me to come over here and ask you which hospital you brought him to.'

The white-haired man frowned and chose his words carefully. 'We didn't bring him to any hospital.'

'I'm confused. You didn't answer that call?' said Morgan.

'We answered it,' said the younger man.

'So…how come you didn't take Guy to the hospital?' Morgan asked.

'There was no reason to transport him,' said the white-haired man.

'Why not? Are you saying that he was dead when you arrived?'

'That's correct.'

Morgan shook her head. 'But, don't you have to treat him anyway, just in case…I mean, in case he's still alive? No disrespect, but you're not doctors, right? I mean, don't you have to try and treat him just to be on the safe side?'

The older man nodded. 'Yes, of course. Unless it's completely obvious—a decomposing body or something like that—even if the person appears to be dead, we begin treatment. And we call a paramedic to the scene. He administers an EKG.'

'And what does that do?' she asked, frowning.

'Well, it determines if the person is alive or dead. If it's a flatline the person is pronounced dead and turned over to the police for the Medical Examiner to determine cause of death.'

'Just like that?'

The older man looked at Morgan as if she were some kind of crackpot. 'At that point, there's really no debating it.'

Morgan's heart was pounding. 'And that's how you found him? That's what happened with Guy?'

The older man nodded. 'Yes.'

Morgan wanted to let out a completely inappropriate cry of joy. This was proof that the police had lied to Claire, played some kind of mind game on her. She didn't know what it was worth, or if it was worth anything, but it lifted her hopes all the same.

'Sorry we couldn't help you,' said the older man.

Morgan remembered to look sorrowful. 'That's all right. I was just hoping...'

The men seemed relieved that her question had been a simple one that they could answer without compromising their professional responsibilities. The white-haired man leaned back in his chair. 'No, I'm afraid Mr Bolton was already well past the point of last words when we arrived.'

Morgan gave them a brave smile. She tried to remind herself that this was no proof of anything, other than that the police had stretched the truth when they questioned Claire. Claire had still confessed. There was no denying that. But, Morgan could not help feeling, in spite of everything, that something was finally, finally turning Claire's way. 'Well, thank you. Really. You have helped me. Believe me. It's always better to know for sure.'

EIGHTEEN

NOREEN QUICK WAS HAVING A BATH. Morgan said she would return later, but Gert indicated that Morgan was welcome to go into the bathroom to speak with the attorney in the tub. Reluctantly, Morgan opened the door, and a cloud of steam escaped. The room was lit by candles and smelled of verbena. Noreen was immersed to her shoulders in the jacuzzi-style tub. Morgan had expected the attorney to at least be covered with sudsy bubbles, but that was not the case. Noreen's red hair was wet and plastered to her head. Her breasts and huge stomach were visible, seeming to wobble beneath the gently swirling water of the tub. Morgan didn't know where to look.

'Excuse me,' Morgan said. 'Gert said it was OK for me to come in. I thought you must be in a bubble bath.'

'No, that bubbly chemical shit is not good for the baby. Oh, sit down there on the john and make yourself comfortable. It's just us girls.'

Reluctantly, Morgan did as she was bid.

'I'm glad you're here,' said Noreen. 'I was just going to call you to let you know that I have hired another shrink. It's a woman this time. I talked to her at length and she has a very profound understanding of post-partum mental illness. I think we can be almost guaranteed of a favorable result. Especially after what Claire did at the funeral. What a scene. How is she doing anyway?'

'She's...critical,' said Morgan.

Noreen shook her head and some of the droplets landed

on Morgan. 'Horrible. Tragic. But I have to say, this is becoming a no-brainer. Obviously, Claire needs psychiatric treatment. I hate to sound ghoulish but this latest stunt is nothing if not helpful to our case,' said Noreen. 'With all this, our expert will have the jury in tears.'

'Maybe,' said Morgan.

'No maybe about it,' Noreen asserted. 'This is going to work to our advantage.'

Morgan hesitated, and then decided to be frank. 'Things have changed. Look, yesterday Claire told her minister that she didn't remember killing Guy and the baby. She now has doubts that she was the one responsible.'

Noreen smiled wryly and paddled the bathwater with her hands. 'She has doubts.'

'Yes,' said Morgan eagerly. 'And it turns out that the police lied to her.'

'About what?'

'They told her that Guy had implicated her as the killer before he died. But I asked the EMTs who were in the ambulance. They told me that Guy was dead by the time they arrived at the scene.'

'Morgan, you've got to stop this.'

'But what the police told her just wasn't true,' Morgan protested.

'I saw the tape of her confession,' said Noreen.

Morgan was taken aback. 'You did?'

'I have a copy of it. It's in my office files. The prosecution sent it over as part of the discovery process. So, yes, I've seen it. There's no mention by the detectives of Guy implicating her. This is just another thing Claire is imagining.'

Morgan's heart sank. 'But why would she say that?

Why would she tell Father Lawrence that she doesn't remember killing them now?' she persisted.

Noreen's eyes widened. 'Why does she say anything? Claire is mentally ill. Look, I'm not a shrink. But you don't have to be a shrink to see it. Morgan, you have to accept this. Claire is not the same gal you used to go shoe shopping with. This woman killed her own family. Then she stabbed and critically wounded herself today. She is suffering from severe post-partum depression. She told you herself that she did it. What does it take to convince you?'

Morgan sighed. 'I don't know.'

'Claire needs help. She's not a criminal. She's sick. She almost succeeded in killing herself. She needs serious, professional help. As her friend, I should think that's what you would want for her. That's certainly what I intend to convince the court.'

'How can you even go to court?' Morgan asked, frowning at Noreen's large, freckled belly.

'Don't worry. By the time this gets to trial,' Noreen said, patting her stomach, 'this guy will be cutting his first tooth.' Noreen planted her hands on the rim of the jacuzzi and began to lift herself up. 'I got to get out of here. I'm getting pruny.' The water began to cascade down as she rose. 'Grab me that towel there. Can you help me?'

Morgan jumped up. 'Wait. Be careful,' she cried. 'Let me call your partner.'

'Just give me a hand,' said Noreen.

'No, I'm afraid,' said Morgan. 'What if you slipped? Let me call her.'

Noreen scowled, and sank back down, parting the waters in a mighty splash. Morgan escaped from the steamy, candlelit bathroom, yelling to Gert for assistance.

HUNGRY AND WEARY, Morgan returned to the cottage, and let herself in. Dusty purred around her legs as Morgan went into the kitchen. First she pulled out her phone, and checked it again to see if she might have missed a call from Simon. There were no missed calls registered. With a sigh, Morgan called the hospital. The nurse would only say that there was no change in Claire's condition. Morgan put her phone back in her pocket and rummaged in the refrigerator until she found the fixings for a sandwich and something to drink. She slapped together her sandwich, placed some food in the cat bowl and then carried her plate and glass out to the empty dining room table. She sat down to eat, although the food tasted like cardboard in the mouth. She had swallowed two bites when she heard a knock at the door. Cursing beneath her breath, Morgan got up, walked to the front door and opened it.

Fitz stood at the door, his face drawn, his eyes wary. Startled at the sight of him, Morgan considered slamming the door, but didn't.

'Morgan, I need to talk to you,' he said. 'Can I come in?'

'I'm busy,' she said.

'Look, I'm sorry about the other night… About what I said…'

Morgan turned away from the door and returned to the table and her sandwich. Fitz hesitated, and then stepped inside and closed the door behind him. He walked carefully to the table where she was sitting as if he were traversing a field of landmines.

'Mind if I help myself to a beer?' Fitz asked.

'I don't care what you do,' said Morgan, chewing, avoiding his gaze.

Fitz went into the kitchen, and then returned to the

dining room with an open bottle of Heineken. He sat down opposite Morgan.

'How's Claire doing?' he asked.

Morgan gave him a cool, level gaze. 'Like you care,' she said.

'Hey, it's been a tough day for all of us,' he said, staring at the beer bottle he rolled between his hands.

Morgan was about to make a sarcastic remark when she remembered that Fitz had watched his best friend be buried today. She let it go, and continued to eat her sandwich. The thought of offering Fitz a sandwich crossed her mind, but only fleetingly. She was not feeling hospitable. 'What are you doing here?' she asked. 'I have nothing to say to you.'

'I shouldn't have been so rough on you. I'm sorry,' he said. Morgan did not look at him or reply.

Fitz took a deep breath. 'I don't know if you noticed, but Eden was at the funeral today.'

'Ah yes,' said Morgan. 'Eden. The innocent kid.' She remembered seeing them at the church, Fitz clearly trying to reason with the wild-eyed girl.

'Are you interested in hearing this?' he asked.

Morgan was curious, in spite of herself, and realized that she had to modify her tone if she wanted to hear what he had to say. 'Hearing what?'

'Well, she said she had come there to spit on her father's corpse.'

Morgan grimaced in surprise. 'Eden said that?'

'She said he deserved to die. She said he was an evil bastard.'

Morgan stared at Fitz.

'I told her that wasn't true. I tried to remind her of how Guy had been trying to get to know her. She told me that it was all a lie, that he was a terrible person and that I didn't really know him. Well, I couldn't help thinking of your suspicions,' he said.

Morgan looked at him, wide-eyed.

'I know it sounds crazy 'cause Claire confessed…' he said.

Morgan felt as if she had been zapped with an electric current. 'Did you ask her what she meant?'

'Of course I asked her. But it was impossible to talk to her. She was very agitated…almost as if she was on drugs or something. She was very nervous. She said she had to leave. That she didn't know what to do.'

Morgan began to tremble all over. She tried to put things together in her mind.

'Why didn't you go after her?'

Fitz rolled his eyes. 'The funeral was about to begin, and I was a pall-bearer. I couldn't exactly leave at that moment. I told her that I wanted to talk to her afterwards.'

'So? Did you?'

Fitz shook his head. 'I looked for her as we were leaving the cemetery. She was gone. Since then I've been trying to call her cellphone, but no luck.'

'Did you try Lucy's?' Morgan demanded. 'She was staying there.'

Fitz shook his head. 'She wasn't with Lucy. Lucy told me to try the Captain's House. I went over there. She's not there. Mrs Spaulding hadn't seen her.'

Morgan stared at him. 'I wonder what she meant.'

He sighed. 'So do I. But in the meantime, I thought you should know about this. Maybe your suspicions weren't that far off.'

Morgan hesitated. She wanted to tell him what she had learned on her own. But the last time she trusted him he had turned on her. In spite of her misgivings, she blurted out one thing that she had learned. 'The police told Claire, before she confessed, that Guy implicated her as his killer, but it wasn't true. It wasn't true. I asked the EMTs. He was dead when they arrived on the scene.'

'Really?' said Fitz.

Morgan nodded. 'I know what you're thinking. It doesn't really explain her confession. None of this does.'

He sat there staring at his beer, and for one minute, she thought he was going to stand up and ask her where the recycling can was, and wish her good luck with it. Instead, he began to absently peel the label off the bottle, frowning at it intently.

'What?' Morgan said.

'Do you know anything about false confessions?' Morgan immediately thought about her theory that Claire might have confessed to protect Eden. 'You mean, like, if you plead guilty to protect someone else?'

Fitz shook his head. 'No. That's…no. You mentioned that last night. But no. Nobody does that.'

Irritated at being dismissed, Morgan said, 'Well, what then?'

Fitz took a deep breath. 'When I got my master's in counseling I took a whole course on how to interview abuse victims. Kids.'

'I thought you were a wrestling coach,' said Morgan.

'Part-time. My main job at the school is in guidance. I like working with kids. I'm hoping to have my own practice someday.'

'Really,' said Morgan.

'Disappointed?' he said. 'Thought I was just a jock?'

'No,' said Morgan, flustered.

'Anyway, in custody cases, kids are often coached to lie, or, sometimes, if the abuser is an authority figure, they lie because they're afraid. And sometimes, they are so suggestible that they accuse adults when nothing really occurred. This course I took was about the techniques you use to get at the truth.'

Morgan shook her head. 'What's that got to do with Claire? Are you saying you think that Claire was an… abuse victim?'

'No,' he said. 'No. I didn't mean that. It's just that… it's difficult to get at the truth sometimes. There are all kinds of interviewing techniques professionals use, even well-meaning people—doctors and social workers—even when they're trying to help—that cause children to admit to things that sometimes never happened.'

'Claire's not a child,' Morgan said cautiously. 'She knows the difference between reality and fantasy.'

Fitz frowned. 'I know. Look, I have to admit I'm not an expert on this. And it was last year when I took the class.'

Morgan's feelings of hope faded. 'Right.'

'But,' he said, pointing the neck of the beer bottle at her, 'my professor was an ace, and he's written a couple of books about this. He would know. He's the one to ask. Are you interested in talking to him?'

'It might be worthwhile. How would I reach him?' she asked cautiously.

Fitz reached in his pocket for his phone, flipped it open, and scrolled down the names in his address book.

'What are you doing?' Morgan asked.

'Calling him,' said Fitz.

'Now?' Morgan asked.

Fitz frowned at her, holding the phone open in his hand. 'This seems pretty urgent to me. Don't you think?'

Morgan nodded.

'I probably still have his number. I do.' He punched a number on the phone and waited.

Morgan watched him, her eyes wide. He held her gaze as he spoke.

'Professor Douglas?' Fitz asked. 'Yeah. This is Earl Fitzhugh. I'm sorry to bother you. I was in your class on interviewing techniques last year. Yeah. Graduate student. That's right. Look, do you think, would you have a few minutes to talk about something really important? I need the uh…benefit of your expertise. Well, if you had time now… Yeah, the sooner the better. Where can we meet? OK, and I'm bringing someone else. Great. Thanks.'

Fitz flipped his phone shut and grinned at Morgan. 'Finish that sandwich,' he said. 'We gotta go.'

NINETEEN

OLIVER DOUGLAS'S WIFE, a slim woman with a cap of short gray hair, greeted Fitz and Morgan at the door and directed them to a studio out behind the house.

They picked their way carefully across the dark backyard, and knocked at the screen door on the small, brightly lit, peaked-roof building at the rear of the property.

'Dr Douglas,' Fitz called out.

The inner door to the studio opened, and a white-haired man in stained overalls and a flannel shirt peered at them over the top of his half glasses. He pushed out the screen door. 'Come in, come in,' he said, stepping aside.

Fitz went in first. 'Dr Douglas, thanks for seeing us.'

'Happy to. How are you doing, Earl?'

'Good. This is my friend, Morgan…'

'Adair,' said Morgan.

The old man wiped his hands on his overalls. 'I'd shake your hand but I'm covered with glue,' he said. He pointed to a beat-up sofa against the wall. 'Have a seat.'

Fitz and Morgan sat down on the sofa. Morgan could feel the sofa springs through the well-worn cushions. She looked around the walls of the studio. They were covered with collages, odd and whimsical, fashioned from calendar pictures, leaves and pebbles, pipe cleaners and newspaper lettering. Somehow she had expected piles of books and a computer.

'What do you think of my work?' the old professor

asked. Morgan gazed at the collages. 'They're so…joyful.' Professor Douglas looked around fondly at his bright, fantastical creations. 'My field of expertise is rather grim. It deals with the dark side of the moon, if you will. People who spend their lives preying on the most vulnerable among us. Well, Earl knows. He's involved in this same sort of thing. But one needs a break from it. This is how I get away from it all.'

Morgan studied his creations. 'I see that.'

'How's your work at the high school going, Earl?' Professor Douglas asked.

'It's tough, but I feel like I'm doing some good. I'm thinking about going back to get my PhD though, so I can open my own practice. Work with adolescents.'

Oliver Douglas, who was amassing an assortment of colorful photos into a file folder, nodded. 'Wonderful idea. There's a great need.'

'That's the truth,' said Fitz.

'So,' said Douglas, picking glue off the tips of his fingers. 'What was so important you had to see me tonight?'

Fitz looked at Morgan. 'Well, I explained to Morgan that one of your books was about authorities getting people to confess to crimes they didn't commit…'

'Interrogation Techniques in False Confessions,' said the professor, his avuncular manner disappearing as he recited his title.

'Exactly,' said Fitz. 'Well, Morgan's best friend from childhood is in jail. She confessed to killing her husband and her infant son.'

Professor Douglas turned one of the worktable stools to face the sofa, and sat down on it, folding his arms across his chest. 'The Bolton woman?'

'That's right,' said Fitz. 'You know about it?'

'Of course,' he said. 'I've been reading about it. The

woman with post-partum depression.' He turned to Morgan. 'What about her?'

For a moment Morgan felt tongue-tied, as if she had to make the most important presentation of her life, and she didn't want to blow it. She took a deep breath. 'I've known Claire Bolton since we were twelve,' said Morgan, 'and even though she told me herself that she did it, I couldn't believe that she would be capable of such a crime...'

'I'm sure that every prisoner in San Quentin has a friend who would say the same,' said Professor Douglas calmly.

Morgan hesitated, feeling chided, and then continued. 'When she first confessed, I believed her, even though it seemed impossible. But now, I have doubts.'

'What's changed?'

'Well, for one thing, Claire is beginning to say that she can't remember doing it.'

'Did she confess to you in some detail?' he asked.

'Her description of the crime was...vague,' said Morgan.

The professor's expression was inscrutable.

'And I now know for a fact,' Morgan continued, 'that the police lied to her.'

Professor Douglas leaned forward, his gaze intent on her face. 'Really? Tell me about that.'

'Well, the police told Claire that her husband, Guy, implicated her before he died. But that isn't true. I talked to the EMTs who responded. Her husband was dead when they arrived on the scene.'

'You did your research.'

Morgan blushed. 'Force of habit.'

'So they told her that her dying husband accused her. You're certain of that.'

'Positive. She said so.'

'And is her confession on tape?'

'Yes,' said Morgan. 'The lawyer saw it. But she said there's no mention of Guy's accusation on the tape.'

Professor Douglas frowned. 'Well, the interrogation of a suspect begins on the scene, continues in the squad car and so on. Sometimes only a small part of an interrogation is actually on the tape. Tell me about the depression,' he said. 'How severe was it?'

Morgan shrugged. 'Her attorney wants the shrink to say that it was post-partum psychosis, which is much more severe than...'

Professor Douglas was nodding in a way which indicated that he did not need an explanation. Morgan did not belabor the point.

'One shrink has already said that she wasn't psychotic. And I don't think she was either. She never seemed out of touch with reality to me. Just...depressed.'

Professor Douglas frowned and looked away.

'Does that sound like someone who would make a false confession?' Fitz asked.

'I can't say that, based on what I've heard,' said Professor Douglas.

Morgan's heart sank.

'Normally we associate false confessions with young people, or people of low intelligence who can be easily manipulated—in almost every case, male. I assume that would not describe your friend,' Douglas said.

Morgan shook her head glumly. 'Obviously not.' Professor Douglas tapped his upper lip with his index finger. 'Although it's interesting,' he said, peering out into the distance.

Fitz looked at Morgan, and then back at his former professor. 'What?'

'What was her home life like?' he asked abruptly.

'Well, they'd only been married a short time...' Morgan began.

'No, I mean childhood. Strong father?'

'No father,' said Morgan. 'He left when she was tiny. She never knew him.'

The professor nodded, as if this is what he had expected to hear.

'Well,' said Fitz. 'What do you think?'

'Well, false confession is also associated with states of extreme stress. The idea of post-partum depression as extreme stress does fit a certain pattern. I mean, here we have a woman who already *feels* guilty because she is not the picture of happy motherhood, the way she is supposed to be, the way society expects her to be. And most people are not sympathetic to this kind of depression. It's as if you were questioning your good luck in having a healthy child. So, your friend is exhausted, probably sleep-deprived, and wrestling with the fact that she is not responding as expected to this great blessing in her life.' Douglas drifted off into another thought.

'And?' Morgan prompted him.

'She's a law-abiding person, correct? Never in trouble with the law.'

Morgan shook her head. 'Never.'

'And the police, whom she trusts, tell her that her own husband accused her before she died and she has no reason to doubt them. There she sits, tired, guilty, in despair.' He paused to collect his thoughts. 'Obedient to authority, still leaking milk from her lost baby. For the police she is simply the obvious suspect. They have her in custody and may just want to clean up the case quickly. So, they bend the truth to see if they break her.'

'And she confesses,' cried Fitz.

'It's a possibility,' Professor Douglas cautioned.

Morgan knew that the professor's assessment should be comforting. But her heart still felt like a stone. 'I mean, OK, everything you say makes sense except for the part where she admits to killing these people if she didn't. No matter how hard I try, I can't understand that.'

Professor Douglas sighed. 'Everyone thinks that they would never do that. Let me tell you something. You'd be surprised at what you might do under duress,' he said. 'Very often, we aren't as brave or as honest or as strong as we'd like to imagine ourselves to be.'

Fitz nodded. 'There could be another suspect. Guy's teenage daughter.'

Professor Douglas shook his head. 'The police aren't going to be interested in other suspects. Unless her confession is discredited, your friend, Claire, hasn't got much going for her. And a confession is one of the most difficult pieces of evidence there is to discredit. For exactly the reason you just stated, Morgan. Jurors say to themselves, I would never confess to a crime I didn't commit. It's against human nature.'

'But it does happen,' said Morgan.

'In a perfect storm of circumstances, most certainly,' said the professor.

Fitz leaned forward. 'So, do you think that's what happened in this case?'

The professor shrugged. 'I couldn't say.'

Morgan and Fitz exchanged a glance. 'But I thought… you could help,' Morgan said.

'Well, I've tried to. Granted, that's an abbreviated summary,' said the professor.

Morgan stood up. 'What about Claire?' she asked.

'What about her?' asked the professor.

'Well, if you think she's innocent…'

'I don't know Claire. I was simply speculating,' said the professor, 'with the information you gave me.'

'So this is just kind of like a parlor game for you?' Morgan demanded.

'It's not his problem, Morgan,' said Fitz under his breath.

'It's all right, Earl,' said the professor.

'Would you talk to her lawyer?' Morgan asked.

'If her lawyer wanted to talk to me, of course,' he said equably. 'But I don't think she will. She dismissed your question about the taped confession, didn't she? I'm acquainted with Noreen Quick. Ms Quick's expertise is in family law. And she's a crusader for women's causes. She is not a criminal attorney. As I understand it from the newspapers, she wants to win on the PPD defense.'

'But if Claire didn't do it... If it's not true...' said Morgan.

'That confession will still remain the chief piece of evidence against her,' said Professor Douglas. 'Believe me, all investigating ceases when a suspect confesses. It's generally agreed that the police don't need anything more.'

'Isn't there anything we can do?' Morgan cried.

The professor scattered another folder of magazine clippings on to his worktable like an envelope of giant confetti. He was silent for a while, moving the colorful pieces around on the board in front of him.

'Let's go,' said Fitz. 'Thanks for your time, Professor.'

'NO,' said Morgan stubbornly. 'There's got to be something.'

Professor Douglas frowned at the design he was making. Finally, he spoke without looking up at them. 'I could tell you more if I could see the confession,' he said.

TWENTY

Morgan stared out the window on the passenger side of Fitz's car. In the moonlight it was possible to see the bay, its water dark and shining, but Morgan wasn't focusing on the view.

'What are you thinking?' Fitz asked.

Morgan shook her head.

'I thought he was saying that Claire probably did make a false confession,' said Fitz encouragingly.

'He was a little hard to pin down,' said Morgan.

'Still, it's a hopeful sign, right?'

'It's better than nothing,' she said.

They rode along in silence for a few moments. Then Fitz said, 'How long are you going to stay around here? I mean, don't you have classes for your PhD or something?'

Morgan was faintly surprised to realize that he knew that much about her. 'I'm supposed to be in England right now, doing research for my thesis. In fact, I was in the airport, ready to board a flight to Heathrow when Claire called.'

'That's a bummer.'

'Well, my…boyfriend wasn't too happy that he had to cancel all the hotels and everything. He was going to try and get the money back.'

'Your boyfriend was going with you?' Fitz asked. Inwardly Morgan cringed, knowing that Simon would never describe himself as her boyfriend. It sounded like they were teenagers instead of… What exactly were they, she thought? She felt discouraged when she thought about Simon. He had not called her back to ask about Claire. Although he probably didn't want to bother her. He was probably waiting for her to call him. 'Simon lives there actually,' said Morgan. 'He's a poet and he lives in London.'

Fitz was silent.

Morgan glanced over at him. 'What?' she said.

Fitz shrugged. 'Just thinking that it was a lot to give up. Most people wouldn't do that for a friend.'

In the darkness of the car, Morgan blushed at the compliment. 'Claire would do it for me,' Morgan said firmly. 'Besides, I'm not giving it up. I'm just postponing it.'

Fitz drove with one hand on the wheel, looking casual. 'Are you in a hurry to get back? I live just up there. Next right.'

'I know where you live, Morgan said, and the hostile outcome of their encounter at his house seemed to hover in the air between them.

But if Fitz had any remorse about how that visit had turned out, Morgan could see no evidence of it on his face. 'Right,' he said. 'Well, you want to come over for a drink or something?'

Morgan frowned. She felt grateful to him for taking her to meet Professor Douglas, but she didn't want him to think that she was interested in a relationship. That possibility was off the table, and going to his place for a drink would surely give him the wrong impression. 'Thanks,' said Morgan, 'but not tonight. It has been a long day. I'm really exhausted...'

'OK, all right,' said Fitz. 'I'll just run you back to Guy's place.'

'Thanks,' said Morgan.

Fitz nodded. 'No problem.' There was an awkward silence between them. 'So,' he said at last, 'what do you do next? Do you think you can get your hands on that tape of Claire's confession?'

'I don't know,' she admitted. 'There's no use in asking the police.'

'None,' he agreed.

'And I don't think that Claire's attorney has any interest in pursuing this idea of a false confession.'

'Not from what Professor Douglas said,' said Fitz.

'I think I'm going to have to insist that Claire get a criminal attorney. I mean, Noreen Quick did generously offer her services to Claire pro bono, and I was grateful for that. I think Noreen wanted the case because it is so high profile. But that may not be in Claire's best interest. I probably should have just hired a criminal attorney in the first place. Her former fiancé even offered to pay for it,' said Morgan.

Fitz frowned. 'Who? That dot-commer that she dumped for Guy?'

Morgan nodded. 'Sandy Raymond.'

'Why would he pay for it?' Fitz asked.

'I don't know,' said Morgan. 'He was worried about her.'

'That seems a little bizarre,' said Fitz.

Morgan glanced over at him. 'You seem to find it odd when anybody tries to help a friend.'

'No,' he said indignantly. 'Not at all.'

As soon as she had said it, Morgan regretted it. He had been a true, longtime friend to Guy, and she knew that losing him had wounded Fitz terribly, despite his jaunty appearance to the contrary. 'I didn't mean that. I know you were a great friend to Guy.'

'It's hard to picture my life without Guy in it,' Fitz admitted.

'How long were you two friends?' Morgan asked.

Fitz frowned, and Morgan saw that his eyes were glistening. He cleared his throat. 'I don't know. A long time. We met when we were kids. His mother—his real mother—and my mother were friends from some group they belonged to. There was a rodeo in Jersey somewhere and they decided to take us. Cowtown, it was called. It was a long drive. We spent the night there at some dinky motel but we thought it was great. Oh man, did we love that. Bronco busters and bull riders. Fantastic. That was the first time I met Guy. And Lucy. God, poor Lucy.' He chuckled.

'Why do you say that?' Morgan asked.

'Oh, I remember she wanted these red cowboy chaps. Nothing else would do and finally her mother bought them for her. They looked so comical on her...' Fitz shook his head. 'Guy and I teased her without mercy.'

'Making fun of a child with a handicap? Fond memories indeed,' said Morgan stiffly.

'Lucy's not handicapped,' Fitz protested.

'She suffers from some kind of genetic syndrome,' said Morgan.

'I know, but come on. She's a little different, but she's always seemed normal to me. Besides, we weren't making fun of Lucy. We were making fun of the chaps. Because they were stupid. The truth was that with those little glasses and her hair flying every which way and those crazy little chaps, she looked kind of cute. But that's what older brothers do. They tease you.'

'I happen to know that Lucy has never forgiven Guy for his cruelty.'

'Cruelty?'

'What do you call it?' Morgan asked.

'Treating her like a little sister is what I call it,' he said.

'Paying attention to her. Making her laugh. Hell, I can still make her laugh if I mention those chaps.'

'That's what people do when they're being bullied. They laugh. They try to pretend they don't care,' Morgan said.

Fitz jerked the car to a halt. His jaw was set. Morgan looked around and they had pulled up in front of the cottage.

'Fine,' Fitz said. 'You would obviously know better than me. Guy and I were a couple of bullies.'

Now that they were back, Morgan dreaded going inside the cottage. And she felt faintly guilty for criticizing Fitz when he had tried to help her tonight. 'Look, I wasn't there. Maybe she didn't mind being teased about the chaps. I just know that Lucy still thinks very badly of Guy. She told me that her brother was mean and didn't care about other people's feelings.'

'If you say so,' he said.

'I'm not judging you, Fitz. I'm just telling you what she said about Guy. I'm sorry if it sounded like I was accusing you. I'm so stressed out by everything.'

'Right,' he said.

It suddenly seemed important to Morgan to make amends. 'Do you…would you want to come in for a while?'

'I better get home and get some rest. I'm taking ten seniors to a wrestling clinic for a couple of days,' he said curtly.

Morgan was surprised at the disappointment she suddenly felt. 'Really? Where's that going to be?'

'Westchester,' said Fitz.

'Sounds like fun,' she said.

'Kids always enjoy it,' said Fitz.

Morgan opened the car door and started to get out. She

looked back at him. 'Thanks for telling me about Professor Douglas. And for taking me to see him. I really do appreciate it. And I didn't mean to insult you. I'm sorry if it sounded that way.'

Fitz nodded. 'No problem,' he said without looking at her. The moment Morgan slammed the door, he pulled away from the curb, and didn't look back.

SHE TOOK A QUICK BATH, and went to bed in the guest room. She was asleep before she knew it. A tinny, singing voice awakened her and she groped for the light, and for her phone on the night table. She felt utterly disoriented, and when she looked at the time, she understood why. It was four thirty in the morning. Her first thought was of Claire, and fear coursed through her. She had called the hospital before she went to bed, and her condition was unchanged. But anything could have happened in the interim.

'Yes, hello,' Morgan managed to gasp out, trying to sound as if she wasn't fast asleep when the phone rang.

'Morgan,' said a cheerful voice.

It took her a moment. 'Simon?' she said.

'Yes. I felt I had to call you,' he said.

Irritation warred with the pleasure she felt at the fact of his call. 'Simon, it's four thirty in the morning here,' she said.

'Oh, God, of course it is,' said Simon. 'I'm sorry. I wasn't thinking.'

Morgan closed her eyes. He just forgot, she thought. 'What is it?' she asked, trying to sound somewhat less surly. After all, she had been hoping he would call.

'Well, we just arrived and I have to tell you, this place is fantastic. You are really going to love it when you finally get here. It is exquisite.'

'What place?' she mumbled. 'Where are you?'

'I'm at the hotel. The Manor. You know, where we were planning to stay?'

'What are you doing there?' Morgan asked, confused.

'Well, they refused to return the deposit. Absolutely refused. I admit I was a little bit steamed at first, but then I decided it would be foolish to just waste the money,' he said.

Morgan was silent for a moment. 'You're at our hotel?' she said. 'You went without me?' She heard her own voice sounding possessive, pathetic. She wished she could take the words back.

'We just arrived and they are going to set us up in the breakfast room. It looks out over the most gorgeous formal gardens…'

'We…?' said Morgan.

'Oh, my friend, Tim, and I,' said Simon offhandedly. 'He's a chap I know from the literary magazines. I asked him to come along.'

Morgan's first impulse was to be glad that Simon was with a man. Not another woman. And then Claire's words came back to her. Why hadn't he ever made a move on her? Why would he take a man to this most romantic of hotels? Was she kidding herself after all? Was this Tim a friend, or was it something else? Her heart felt small, dark and dense, like a peach pit. Ask him, she thought. Settle this, for once and for all. But she knew that she wouldn't. It was too demeaning to have to ask.

'You called to tell me that you went without me,' she said flatly. 'Gee, thanks.'

Simon was silent at his end. Finally he sighed and said, 'Perhaps that wasn't the thing to do.'

Morgan looked at the time again and made up her mind. Normally, she might have stayed on the line, hoping he would say something that she could cling to, as proof that he did indeed have fond feelings for her. Somehow, tonight, that seemed too little to hope for. 'Perhaps not,' she said, and pressed a button to end the call.

TWENTY-ONE

WHEN SHE ARRIVED at the hospital in the morning, Morgan learned that Claire had been moved again. Morgan sought out the room, and tiptoed in. The blinds were half closed, rendering the room dim. The bed by the door was empty. Although the face of the patient on the window side of the room was obscured by the privacy curtain, Morgan knew that she had the correct room because Sandy Raymond was slumped in a chair at the foot of the bed, staring at the bed's occupant.

'Sandy,' Morgan whispered.

Sandy looked up at her in bleary-eyed surprise, as if he had been awakened from a dream. 'Oh, hi,' he said.

Morgan tiptoed to the foot of the bed and looked at her friend. Claire had tubes snaking out from her nose, her arms, and out from under the covers. Bags full of blood and fluids, which fed the tubes hung, suspended on hooks over her bed, like ghoulish balloons. Claire's skin was yellow and waxy and her eyes were closed, sunk into dark hollows in her face. Her hands lay open in a position of supplication atop the white thermal blanket. Her mouth was open and she was breathing in and out with juddering gasps. 'Oh, God, she looks so…bad,' Morgan whispered.

'No need to whisper,' said Sandy. 'She's out of it. Completely.'

Morgan looked over at him. 'I'm surprised to see you here,' she said.

Sandy kept his gaze trained on Claire's face. 'I've been here for a while. I couldn't sleep.'

'Where's Farah?' Morgan asked.

'I don't know,' he said. 'Probably having a manicure.'

Morgan realized that he was not going to discuss Farah. 'Sandy,' she said, 'I'm glad you're here. I've been thinking about what you said.'

Sandy frowned. 'About what?'

Morgan looked back at Claire. 'About the criminal attorney. I think Claire needs to get rid of the attorney she has, and get a good criminal attorney.'

'If she needs an attorney at all,' said Sandy, a desolate note in his voice.

Morgan walked around to the side of the bed and took Claire's freezing white hand in her own. 'She's going to get better.' Morgan leaned down and spoke softly into Claire's ear. 'You are going to get better. Do you hear me? You have to.'

Claire's eyelids fluttered, and she licked her lips. Then, every sign of life subsided again.

Morgan straightened up and looked at Sandy. 'I don't believe that this post-partum depression defense is the right one,' she said. 'I don't think she killed them. I think she was coerced by the police into confessing.'

Sandy frowned, but he sat up, and leaned forward in the chair, his eyes narrowed. 'You have some reason to think that? This isn't just part of some misguided "best friends forever" mantra, is it?'

'No,' said Morgan. She started to elaborate, and then decided against it. 'When I stayed at your house, you mentioned that you could find Claire the best criminal attorney around. Is that offer still good?'

'Sure,' he said. 'I can put you together with a guy

named Mark Silverman. He's the man. When do you want to meet with him?'

'Well, first things first. I feel I have to explain things to Noreen Quick.'

Sandy waved his hand impatiently. 'No, no,' he said. 'That's not a good idea. You should talk to Mark first, and then present it to Noreen as a done deal. That's the way these things are done.'

'But we need the tape of Claire's confession. And she has it,' Morgan protested.

Sandy shrugged. 'We need everything she has. But we're not going to get it from her. Any research she did is work product. She'll dig in her heels and refuse to give it up.'

Morgan peered at him. 'You know an awful lot about the law,' she said.

'Hazard of my job,' he shrugged. 'I get sued a lot.'

'So what can we do?' asked Morgan.

'Whoever the new attorney is will demand copies of everything from the prosecutor's office, and he'll get it. Eventually. Till then, we wait.'

'How long?' Morgan asked.

Sandy shrugged. 'Could take months.'

'No, that's no good,' said Morgan. 'We can't wait for that.' She reached down and brushed some damp hair off of Claire's forehead. 'She needs some hope. Now. When she wakes up, I want to have good news for her. If she has to go back to jail with no hope…I'm afraid of what she'll do.'

'I know,' said Sandy, gazing at Claire's masklike face. 'Look, do you want me to set up a meeting with Mark Silverman?'

'Yes, I'd appreciate that. Do you have my number?' Sandy nodded.

'In the meantime, maybe I could get a copy of the tape,' said Morgan thoughtfully.

Sandy frowned. 'How?'

'I'm…not sure. I have to think about it,' said Morgan.

'Look, I don't know what you're up to, but don't go outside the usual channels. Mark can't use evidence if it's tainted…'

Morgan gazed down at her friend, struggling to breathe, unable to awaken. 'I have to know for sure,' she said. 'We can do anything, once we know for sure.'

Morgan bent down and kissed Claire on the forehead. Claire's forehead was almost as cold as her hands. Morgan looked over at Sandy. 'I'm gonna go,' she said.

Sandy kept his gaze on Claire. 'I'll just stick around for a while,' he said.

MORGAN PARKED ACROSS THE STREET from the offices of Abrams and Quick, and stared at the building, trying to think of what she could say to get what she wanted. She knew that she needed to circumvent Noreen, but without Noreen's permission, she doubted she would succeed. As pleasant as that receptionist, Berenice, was, she would surely refuse to allow Morgan access to Claire's file without first calling Noreen. Morgan began to try out lies on herself, shifting in the seat and trying to gauge how close she was coming to a convincing story. Some sounded plausible. None perfect. None would give her enough time or opportunity to do what she needed to do.

Should I just wait, Morgan wondered? Let the process of lawyers and courts take its time? Obviously she could not wait here in West Briar. She had a life and classes to get back to. By the same token, she could not imagine leaving Claire alone here. For the moment, Sandy seemed to be concerned for her, but how long would that last, once Claire awoke and was able to tell him that she still didn't love him? And after this suicide attempt, serious and nearly successful, Claire had proved that she felt she had nothing to live for, no reason to go on. Morgan knew that keeping her best friend alive, when and if the doctors had saved her, would take more than reassurances and good wishes. This was a person who had lost the will to go on.

Morgan glanced into the car's side view mirror, and saw her own face, looking drawn and tired. How do I make you want to live, my friend, she wondered? How can I convince you that you are not to blame, when I have no idea what really happened? Her spirit felt mired in sludge. She sighed, and turned on the engine. It was no use. She could not convince anyone of her intentions in this condition.

All of sudden, the front door of the law office opened, and a dog, restrained by a leash, came bounding out, dragging his owner out and down the path. Berenice, her silvery hair in its customary ponytail, was wearing a plum-colored fleece vest over a plaid shirt and jeans. In one hand she held Rufus's leash as the dog barked and dragged her forward. In the other hand, she held a scoop and plastic bag, which indicated that they were headed out on a doggy relief mission.

As she was dragged away from the office, Berenice pulled the door to, but Morgan could see, even from across the street, that the door was standing open a few inches. Morgan inhaled sharply at the thought which rose to her mind. Berenice hurried to the corner behind Rufus, and turned down the next block. Before she had time to talk herself out of the idea, Morgan made up her mind. She reached into the shelf beneath the CD player in the car and swiped one of the CDs still in its plastic box.

She stuffed it into her bag, and got out of the car, looking both ways before she loped across the road. Morgan went up the path, and before she had reached the front step she could see, to her great relief, that the door was indeed open. She looked all around her, slipped inside, and waited for a moment, holding her breath.

Then she walked past the reception area and glanced casually inside. There was no one in the waiting area. Business was obviously slower with Noreen incapacitated.

Determining that she was alone in the building, Morgan realized that she could proceed. Swiftly, she went down the hall to Noreen's office.

For one moment she thought that the office door might be locked, since Noreen was home on bed rest. But apparently, Berenice had occasion to go in and out of Noreen's office during the workday, and left the door to it wide open. Morgan wondered, briefly, who Abrams was, and why she never seemed to be at the office. She forgot the thought as she slipped inside. She thought about shutting the door, and then decided against it. It was better if she could hear what was happening in the foyer and the corridor.

The office was neat, not having been used since Noreen went on bed rest. The people in the family photos were now real people to Morgan, but she did not linger to study them. She glanced at Noreen's desk. It had a computer, of course, and if it were to hold the information that Morgan wanted, she knew that it would be a much more daunting task. She was not a hacker. She'd have no chance of getting into Noreen's files. But Morgan was looking for a physical object—a DVD which contained the confession. Physical objects that were evidence had to be stored in the real, not the virtual world. She went quickly to the file cabinet behind Noreen's desk and opened it.

The volume of files was daunting. But the alphabet was on Morgan's side. She found Claire Bolton in the top drawer. She reached in, carefully pulled the file out, and before she could even open it, a DVD disc in a plastic case slid out the side of the file. Morgan caught it in her hand, and looked at the label. It was an official label from the prosecutor's office with Claire's name, the date and time on it.

The date and time told Morgan all that she needed to know. This was the tape of Claire's confession. 'Yes,' she whispered. She put the DVD into a zippered compartment in her sac and hoisted it on her shoulder. Then, quickly, she replaced the file in the drawer. Just as she was sliding the drawer shut into the cabinet, she heard the sound of the front door opening and then, immediately, the frantic barking of a dog.

Morgan's heart, already racing, began to thud.

'What is it, Rufus? What? Who's there? Is somebody there?' Morgan scanned the room, but there was no other exit. She was going to have to go out into the hallway. She did her best to assume a calm, cheerful demeanor. She squared her shoulders, as the barking escalated, and stepped out into the hallway.

At the sight of her, Rufus began leaping up, straining at his leash and barking. Berenice looked frightened at first and then, when she realized that it was not some masked intruder, her expression turned to irritation.

'Rufus, hush. I mean it, hush,' she insisted.

The dog simmered down and sat down beside her. 'Now,' Berenice demanded, turning to Morgan. 'What are you doing here? You're not supposed to be wandering around these offices.'

'I'm so sorry,' Morgan said innocently. 'The front door was open so I came in.'

'Was it? I thought I closed it,' Berenice said fretfully.

Morgan raised her shoulders. 'No, it was open.' Berenice frowned, and Morgan could tell that she was mentally retracing her steps. Then, she peered at Morgan.

'But what are you doing in Ms Quick's office? You know very well that she's out on bed rest. You've been to her house.'

Morgan could feel herself reddening as she prepared to attempt her audacious lie. 'Well, when I was at Noreen's house, I liked the music that was playing. Gert lent me this CD and told me to bring it back when I was finished listening to it,' said Morgan, reaching into her bag and pulling out the Corinne Bailey Rae CD which she had taken from her own car. 'I was passing by, so I thought I'd leave it here, on Noreen's desk.'

'I'll do that,' Berenice said. She told Rufus to lie down. Then, she lifted the CD in its plastic case from Morgan's fingers, walked around the desk, opened the drawer and slipped it inside.

'Is that OK?' said Morgan. 'I guess I should have brought it back to the house.'

Berenice sighed, apparently relieved at the innocence of the intrusion. 'It'll be fine here. I send stuff over there all the time.' Now that the crisis was past, Berenice was clearly anxious about her own part in it. 'I don't usually leave that outer door open. I'm very conscientious about that as a rule.'

'I'm sure you are,' said Morgan in a reassuring tone.

'Noreen would not be happy if she thought I went out and left the door standing open,' said Berenice.

'It's not worth mentioning,' said Morgan in a reassuring tone.

Berenice nodded as she stepped over Rufus who was lying in the hallway. 'No reason to make her worry,' she said.

Morgan stepped over Rufus as well, and bent down to scratch his furry head. She was almost home free. In a few moments she would be out the door, with the disc in her bag. 'No,' Morgan agreed, smiling. 'She has enough to worry about.'

TWENTY-TWO

THE IMAGE ON THE SCREEN was flat gray and white, a woman sitting alone in a chair at a desk. A male voice could be heard questioning her, but no one else was visible on the screen. In the corner, white numbers indicated the date and time. The woman was slumped in the chair, her eyes vacant, her face slack. One of her hands rested, trembling, on the desktop.

'All right,' said the male voice. 'This is Detective Roland Heinz and I am here with Detective Jim Curry. We are interviewing Mrs Claire Bolton. Now, Mrs Bolton we're going to go over the events of the evening which ended in the death of your baby son, Drew, and your husband, Guy. Before we begin, have you been apprised of your rights?'

'Yes.' Claire nodded.

'And you are making this statement of your own free will?' Claire nodded.

'Can you say the word "yes", Mrs Bolton? We need it to be audible.'

'Yes,' said Claire.

'Now, you told us earlier that on Saturday night you went to a family dinner at the home of your in-laws. And what was the purpose of this dinner? Just a get-together?'

'My husband's...daughter was there. Eden.'

'So, the dinner was in her honor. Eden's honor.'

Claire grimaced. 'Sort of,' she said.

'You agreed to go even though you were angry about this long-lost daughter.'

'Yes. I didn't want to go. We weren't really speaking.'

'Who wasn't speaking?'

'Me and my husband,' Claire admitted. 'But it wasn't Eden's fault.'

'It was *his* fault, for not telling you about her. Is that correct?'

'I suppose,' Claire whispered.

'And how did the evening go?'

'Terrible,' said Claire.

'Now according to witnesses, your baby had been crying, and carrying on intolerably, is that correct?'

'Yes,' Claire whispered.

'Did he do that during the dinner?'

'Yes,' said Claire with a sigh.

'You weren't able to soothe him.'

'No,' said Claire. 'Nothing I did…worked.'

'Were you…embarrassed by this?'

'Embarrassed?' Claire asked.

'Well, you appeared an incompetent mother in front of your husband's family.'

Claire frowned as if she were trying to remember. 'I guess so,' she said.

'After dinner you and your husband went home. And how were you feeling that night when you went to bed?'

'Very, very upset. And tired,' said Claire. 'Very tired.' Claire sniffed, and wiped her nose on her sleeve.

'You and your husband were not sleeping in the same room.'

'No. He was sleeping in the guest room.' There was no emotion visible in Claire's face. In her eyes.

'Because of this ongoing argument.'

Claire nodded, and then realized that she had to say the word. 'Yes.'

'The baby woke you up again at what…four a.m.' Claire hesitated, as if balking at the question. 'I think so.'

'Is that a yes or no?'

'I'm not sure.'

'You heard the baby and got up,' the man's voice instructed her.

Claire sighed, and slumped over. 'Yes, I must have.'

'You took Drew, who was very small—only seven weeks old—into the bathroom adjoining your bedroom, and ran water in the tub.'

Claire frowned, and a few tears ran down her face. She wiped them away. 'I don't…'

'This is what you told us, isn't it?'

'Yes,' said Claire. 'I think…yes.'

'With the intention of drowning the baby to silence him.' Claire shook her head in misery, and lowered it on to her arms.

'Mrs Bolton? Isn't that true?'

'I was so tired…' she said.

'You put the baby face down into the tub.'

Claire raised her head and looked pleadingly at the man who was speaking to her. 'I don't remember doing that. I must have just wanted to wash him up.'

'We've been over this, Mrs Bolton,' the man's voice said impatiently.

'Yes,' said Claire hopelessly. 'For some reason, I guess I did…'

'For some reason?' the man asked in a mocking tone. 'You didn't know that a newborn infant would drown if he was placed face down in the tub?'

'Yes, of course,' she said. Her voice was choked with tears. 'Of course.'

'Now, Mr Bolton, hearing the baby's cries, came downstairs and found you drowning your own baby.'

Claire stared straight ahead, not speaking.

'Mrs Bolton?'

Claire did not turn her head to look at her questioner. 'He was shouting at me. He wanted to get the baby... He...pushed me away.' Claire's eyes seemed to be peering at some dimly remembered scene.

'That infuriated you, didn't it? After all, he had caused the whole situation. You were so mad at him that you wanted to kill him.'

Claire started to shake her head in protest, and then she stopped.

'Weren't you, Mrs Bolton? We've talked about this, remember?'

Claire began to cry. 'I didn't mean to hurt him. But then he fell and hit his head on the edge of the tub. There was blood everywhere...'

Claire began to sob, lowering her head on to her arms again. 'You called nine-one-one,' he said.

'Yes.'

'Do you remember what you said?'

Claire shook her head. 'No.'

'You told the nine-one-one operator that they were both dead. You implied that you found them that way, didn't you?'

'Did I?' Claire asked.

'Even though that wasn't true,' said the voice, ambiguously. Claire began to weep silently, wiping away the tears. 'That wasn't true, was it? Remember what we talked about?'

'It wasn't true,' Claire whispered.

'But they did both die. And it was your fault.'

Claire closed her eyes. There was a long silence.

'Mrs Bolton?'

'Yes,' she whispered. 'Yes. It was my fault.'

'Thank you, Mrs Bolton. This ends our interview…'
The screen went blank.

Morgan, who was sitting at a student desk in Oliver
Douglas's empty classroom, rubbed the heels of her
hands against her eyes. She had tracked Professor Douglas down, waited through his eleven o'clock class, and
convinced him to skip his lunch hour in order to watch
the tape. He had not been difficult to convince. His curiosity was piqued by what he had already learned from
her and Fitz, and he had agreed to the plan. As soon as
the classroom had emptied out, he had popped the DVD
into the player.

It had been agony to watch the tape, even though
Morgan knew what she was going to see. She took a deep
breath, and looked over at the professor, who had been
watching the DVD with her, and making an occasional
note. He was staring at the empty screen, frowning.

'What do you think?' said Morgan.

Oliver Douglas shook his head. 'This is not a confession,' he said.

Morgan's heart leaped in her chest as if she had just
learned that she won the lottery. 'Really? Why do you say
that?' she asked.

Douglas continued to shake his head. 'Unbelievable.'
Morgan leaned forward, hungry for affirmation. 'How
so?'

'It's classic. They only film her—not themselves. It's
a proven fact that this technique of isolating the suspect
in front of the camera suggests guilt to a jury. Plus, there
was no narrative on the part of the accused. She didn't
actually say anything, except yes, or maybe. Her interro-

gator described the incident. He even described how she felt. She merely agreed with him.'

'She could have said no,' Morgan offered gingerly, trying to play the devil's advocate.

'Didn't you hear him telling her that they had gone over this before? That's virtually code for coercion. They were reminding her of her dying husband's accusations. Accusations, it turned out, that he never actually made. There are witnesses who can testify to that. Correct?'

Morgan nodded. 'Absolutely.'

Professor Douglas got up and took the DVD out of the machine. He popped it back into the case and handed it to Morgan. 'I can't believe her attorney hasn't raised hell about this.'

'Is it that bad?' Morgan said hopefully.

Douglas, dressed today in sports jacket and tie, and corduroys, looked far different than he had in his workroom, among his colorful collages. He looked distinctly professorial as he hoisted himself up on the edge of the desk, keeping one Hush-Puppied foot on the floor. 'It's worse than bad, Morgan. This poor woman has been browbeaten to breaking point. Not a difficult task, given her condition.'

'So, you don't think she did it,' Morgan exulted. Professor Douglas raised a hand in warning. 'I can't speak about that. But she did not confess to the crime. That much is certain. Any respectable judge should throw this out.'

Morgan frowned. 'You don't sound sure that they will.'

'Well, the prosecution may get it introduced, if Mrs Bolton's attorney is incompetent, or has another agenda...' he said, raising an eyebrow in Morgan's direction.

Morgan understood what he was saying. 'I'm getting

her a different attorney,' said Morgan. 'It's already in the works. Some fellow named Mark Silverman.'

'Oh, good. Good. I know Mark Silverman. He is a capable criminal attorney. Mark Silverman will have this confession suppressed. And even if the judge should decide to admit it, I'll help Mark tear it apart on the stand.'

Morgan felt tears spring to her own eyes. 'Oh, thank you,' she said.

'Now,' said Oliver Douglas, 'that doesn't mean that Claire couldn't still be convicted. The circumstantial evidence is strong. And of course, there's forensic evidence…'

'But that could also exonerate her,' said Morgan.

'Although…' Douglas said, gazing at the DVD player.

'What?' Morgan asked.

'Some of it was true. I feel quite certain of that.'

Morgan's stomach started to lurch. 'What do you mean?'

'It's an impression. But my work revolves around analyzing these interviews.'

Part of Morgan wanted to take the DVD and flee, before he could say another word. But she found that she couldn't resist asking, that she was rooted to the spot until she heard his answer. 'Tell me what you mean,' she said.

Oliver Douglas frowned. 'Well, the business about the evening with the in-laws was obviously true.'

'Well, yes,' said Morgan. 'They did have dinner together at Dick and Astrid's.'

'The baby was fussy and Claire was ashamed of her own seeming incompetence and very, very tired.'

'Easily verified,' said Morgan. 'But that's hardly a damning admission. The fact that she went out to a family dinner.'

Professor Douglas continued as if she hadn't spoken. 'I think that she was also telling the truth about her husband coming downstairs and finding her with the baby, drowned in the tub. I think it went just that way. He was yelling at her. They struggled. He fell on a wet, slippery bathroom floor and hit his head on the edge of the tub. She didn't really equivocate about that.'

Morgan slumped down against a desk. 'This is no help,' said Morgan. 'You're saying that she killed him.'

Professor Douglas shook his head. 'It was obviously an accident. Given his size, her weakened physical condition, and the lack of any weapon, he could easily have overpowered her in a struggle.'

'So, that's good,' said Morgan carefully. 'That's not a crime.'

'No,' he said.

Morgan stood up, clutching the plastic box to her chest. 'OK. Then, she's OK…'

'She was lying about the baby,' he said.

Morgan wanted to squeeze her eyes shut and put her hands over her ears. 'You don't know that,' she pleaded.

Professor Douglas was thinking aloud, and did not seem to hear her. 'They led her by the hand through the part about the baby. That came through clearly on the tape. She wasn't recalling any of that.'

'How could she not remember it?' Morgan demanded angrily.

Oliver Douglas shrugged. 'Trauma. And guilt. You can't discount guilt.'

Morgan felt completely frustrated. 'Guilt? I don't understand. First you say she didn't do it. Then you say she did it. Which is it?'

Professor Douglas arched his eyebrows. 'Oh, I'm not saying she felt guilt about *killing* her baby. No. She felt guilt about being depressed after the baby's birth. Guilt because, from time to time, she was so frustrated that she had given birth to this child, and couldn't seem to care for him. Tremendous guilt about that.'

'So you think that she feels…guilty about what happened to the baby.'

'Of course. She's his mother. And, I think she's trying to somehow make her perceptions consistent with the facts. But they don't actually…agree.'

'I'm lost,' said Morgan, throwing up her hands. Professor Douglas frowned. 'Claire agreed that the baby was in the bathtub, and that her husband must have heard the baby's cries and come running. But that doesn't make any sense. People come running when they hear something unusual. Guy was used to hearing the baby's cries. Probably wouldn't even wake him up. I mean, wasn't that part of what precipitated Claire's depression? The baby's constant crying? Guy had been hearing that night and day for two months solid. Why would he come running for that?'

'I don't know,' said Morgan miserably.

Professor Douglas shook his head and tapped his lip with his index finger. 'No. He wouldn't.'

'We know he came running. It doesn't really matter why,' Morgan said wearily.

Professor Douglas smiled. 'Oh, but it does. Guy came running because he heard something unusual. It wasn't the baby he heard screaming. He heard his wife screaming.'

Morgan frowned at him. She shook her head. 'Why would Claire be screaming?'

'Claire was screaming,' he said slowly, as if visualizing the scene in his mind, 'because of what she saw in the bathroom. When Guy rushed in and found her there, and the baby lying face down in the tub, he jumped to the ob-

vious conclusion. Claire had snapped, and tried to drown
the baby. Of course the two of them struggled. He was in
a panic. Angry and horrified. Trying to get to his son. To
save him. And Claire was probably desperate, trying to
make him understand.'

'I don't get it,' Morgan pleaded. 'Understand what?'

Oliver looked at her calmly. 'The truth, of course. That
she found her baby like that. Drew was already drowned
when Claire went into the bathroom. The baby was already dead.'

TWENTY-THREE

IN THAT MOMENT, MORGAN COULD see it, in her mind's eye. Her baby godson's death was suddenly more brutally vivid to her than it had yet been. Bile rose in her throat, and she thought she might have to vomit. She took a deep breath and mulled over what she had just heard. And then, in the next instant, Morgan felt almost jubilant. Such an evil deed was perverse, frightening. But if it was not Claire who had committed it… 'Professor Douglas, if that's true…'

Professor Douglas looked back at her and nodded. 'If it's true, then someone else drowned the baby.'

'Oh, my God.' Morgan thought about this for a moment and then peered at him. 'But who?' she asked.

Professor Douglas shook his head. 'Sorry. I don't know anything about these people. I can't help you with that.'

Morgan tried to organize the possibilities in her head. Her thoughts again turned to Eden—the rejected child who arrived on the christening day of a cherished baby. Eden. Who probably wanted to make her father suffer as she had suffered. Could she have chosen such a heartless way to retaliate?

'There's probably forensic evidence that can help determine who else was in that bathroom,' Oliver Douglas said.

'Yes, but…the police would know that by now, wouldn't they?' Morgan asked.

Professor Douglas demurred. 'You forget. They're not looking for anyone else. They have a confession.'

'But if you were to tell them what you found out...'

'Morgan, you're an academic. You know the difference between a hypothesis and facts based on tangible proof. This is a hypothesis. The confession, by their lights, is proof.'

'We can't just leave it like this...' Morgan protested. 'They need to be looking for that other person who... came in and killed the baby.'

Professor Douglas smiled. 'I'm glad you like my theory so well. As I told you, when Claire gets to trial, the confession may be discredited. There's every hope of that. It may be suppressed even before she gets to trial.'

'No. That's not good enough. The police need to be looking for another suspect. Can't we force them to collect more evidence? And test it?'

Professor Douglas stood up and buttoned his jacket. 'I don't know. I'm not an attorney. It may be that Claire's attorney can request that new tests be made. Look, Morgan, I've got another class, so I'm going to have to run. Ask Mark Silverman about the evidence when you meet with him.'

Morgan nodded, her mind racing. She shook hands with the professor. 'Yes, you're right. I will do just that. And I can't thank you enough, Professor Douglas. Thank you. Really. You've given me hope.'

ON THE RIDE BACK TO TOWN from the campus, Morgan felt both excited and sickeningly anxious about this glimmer of possibility for Claire's vindication. Professor Douglas's reconstruction of the events made sense in a way that nothing else did. If she really thought about the improbability of proving him correct, the anxiety took over.

She tried to force herself to focus on hope. As she turned down Claire's street, she saw a yellow van parked in front of the cottage. The name Servicemaster was painted in red on the side of the van. For a moment, she thought it might be some sort of delivery service. Then, as she drew closer, she saw a trio of workers in uniforms unloading vacuum cleaners, buckets and mops clustered at the front door of the cottage. The foreman of the crew, a muscular man who looked to be about forty, was inserting a key in the lock.

Morgan pulled up behind the van, threw the car into park and jumped out. 'No,' she cried out. 'No. Stop. Don't go in there.'

The foreman looked up at her in confusion. 'Excuse me?' he said.

Morgan's heart was pounding as she ran across the lawn to where the crew stood waiting, armed with their cleaning implements. 'NO. You can't clean that house.'

The foreman reached into his pocket and pulled out a copy of a receipt. 'We have a work order, here,' he said.

Morgan waved it away. 'I know. I know you do. Mrs Bolton told me that you were coming.'

The crew foreman looked at Morgan suspiciously. 'So, what's the problem?'

'The situation has…changed,' said Morgan. 'There's… evidence that needs to be protected in that room. This place needs to be sealed up again.'

The man frowned at her. 'Are you from the police?'

'NO,' said Morgan. 'But…I know I'm right.'

The foreman shook his head. 'Sorry, ma'am. We were hired to come and clean this place today. Unless Mrs Bolton tells us not to…'

'OK,' said Morgan. 'Wait. Just wait one minute. I'm going to call her. OK? If she says that you should wait…'

The foreman glanced at his watch and then looked at Morgan skeptically. 'I'll call her,' he said in a tone that indicated he did not trust Morgan. He pulled his phone from his pocket, flipped it open, and tapped in a number from the receipt. He avoided Morgan's gaze as he waited. Finally he said, 'Yeah, Mrs Bolton. This is Steve. From Servicemaster. Yeah. We're at your son's house, and there's a lady here who doesn't want us to clean it. Yeah. I don't know. Just a minute.'

The foreman turned to Morgan. 'What's your name?' he asked.

'Morgan Adair.'

The foreman repeated her name into the phone and then listened to the voice at the other end. After a moment, he held the phone out to Morgan. 'She wants to talk to you.'

Morgan grabbed the phone gratefully. 'Astrid?' she said.

'Morgan, what is going on?' Astrid demanded.

'Look, it's a long story but… The bottom line is this. I've been talking to an…expert who analyzed Claire's confession. He thinks that someone else may have killed the baby.'

'What?' Astrid cried. 'What are you talking about?'

'Look. I know. I know. It sounds…bizarre. But if it's true…If there's any truth to it, the police need to go over the crime scene again and look for evidence of someone else being there. Once these people clean it up, every trace of evidence is going to be gone.'

Astrid was silent for a moment. 'Did you speak to the police about this?' she asked. 'This idea of finding new evidence?'

'No. Not yet,' Morgan admitted.

'So this is just some…crazy scheme of your own,' Astrid said caustically.

'I know it sounds crazy,' said Morgan. 'But, I need a little bit of time to take care of all this. I mean, surely you can understand. If Claire is…if she didn't do what they said, I have to try and help her.'

'She admitted she did it,' Astrid said flatly. 'She confessed.' Morgan was silent for a moment. She wasn't about to say the word's 'false confession' to the family of the victims.

'Astrid, she's my best friend. All I'm asking for is a little time.'

'I don't see how you can ask another favor of me on Claire's behalf,' Astrid said. 'As it was, she turned the funeral into a horror show. Really, Morgan…'

'Look, I understand and I don't blame you. I'm not asking you to leave the house like that for good. I'm only asking for a day or two. What difference will a day or two make in the overall scheme of things?'

'It smells foul in that house,' Astrid protested. 'Flies are starting to buzz around in there…'

'I know it,' said Morgan. 'It's disgusting. I'm going to leave here myself and get a room. But I need these people to back off for a day or two. Please, Astrid, I'm begging you. Just a day or two. It can't matter to you.'

There was a silence on the other end of the phone. Then Astrid sighed. 'All right, let me speak to Steve.'

Morgan handed the foreman the phone. 'She wants to talk to you.'

Steve put the phone to his ear. 'Yeah,' he said. He listened for a moment. 'OK. OK, I'll call you when I'm back in the office and we'll reschedule.'

Morgan closed her eyes and breathed a prayer of thanks. 'Let's go.' He turned to Morgan. 'We're going to clear out of here, for now,' said Steve. He closed his phone and put it back into his pocket. He led the other workers off the front step and down the path back to their van.

Morgan sank down on the front step, relieved and exhausted. Now that they were gone, she wasn't sure what to do next. Dusty came slinking silently out from one of the flower beds, and sat down on the step beside her. Morgan reached out a hand and Dusty allowed her to pet him, as if it were a sacrifice, meant to offer her moral support. Morgan rubbed a hand absent-mindedly over the soft fur, warm from the midday sun.

If she had arrived back a few moments later, she thought, the scouring would already have begun. Any trace of the baby's killer would be removed. Morgan did not question her acceptance of Oliver Douglas's theory. It now seemed to her that it was the only plausible explanation. She tried to imagine that night. Claire arguing with Guy, who went upstairs to sleep in the guest room. Someone sneaking into the house, past Claire who was exhausted and probably in a deep sleep. It took nerve to think that one could get away with such a heinous act—drowning an infant—without waking that baby's mother. Morgan tried to imagine the killer, tiptoeing through the room, picking up baby Drew and… That was the point at which she could no longer bear to imagine it. The idea of taking that tiny, innocent baby and holding his face down in the water. Morgan shook her head as if she could shake the thought away. How much hate would that despicable act require? Was Eden capable of that kind of depravity simply to punish Guy?

Suddenly, Morgan realized she was assuming that Drew's killer was trying to hurt and punish Guy. But there was another possibility, of course. The possibility was that the killer's hateful act was directed at Claire.

After all, Claire was Drew's mother. No matter how depressed she might have been after his birth, Claire loved that baby with all her aching heart. If someone wanted to hurt Claire, what better way…?

A silver SUV pulled up in front of the house, and stopped. The driver got out and started to walk across the brown grass toward the step where Morgan sat. Sandy Raymond's T-shirt was untucked beneath his hoody, his hair was uncombed, his hands in his pockets. When he saw her staring at him, Sandy gave her a brief wave.

'Hey,' he said.

Morgan nodded, and looked down at the cat, her heart pounding. She felt as if she had summoned Sandy Raymond with her thoughts. She had seen Sandy hiding in the shadows at the christening, and sitting in the congregation at the funeral. She had found Sandy sitting by Claire's hospital bedside, willing Claire to survive, and that had seemed rather touching. But now, as he came towards her, Morgan wondered. Was that what he was really doing at Claire's bedside? Was he worrying? Or was it possible that he was enjoying the results of his own vengeful acts?

'I've been looking for you,' he said. 'You never came back to the hospital.'

'No. I've been busy,' said Morgan evasively.

'Look, I called Mark…Silverman. The attorney,' he said. Morgan found herself doubting his simplest statement. She reminded herself that this was good news.

'You did? What did he say?'

'His secretary told me he's tied up in a big trial right now. I told her that I needed him to get back to me. ASAP.'

Morgan nodded, thinking about the murder house, the crime scene, which loomed behind her. Unsealed. The crucial evidence which might save Claire was in there, available to anyone who might wish to destroy it. And Sandy, promising an attorney whom, now, it seemed, he couldn't deliver. 'Well, OK,' she said.

'OK what?' said Sandy.

'Well, if he's not available, I might need to get someone else,' she said calmly.

'Hey, keep your pants on,' said Sandy angrily. 'I told you. This guy is the best. He'll call me. I promise you.'

Morgan nodded. She avoided his gaze.

'What's the matter with you?' Sandy asked. 'You're acting weird.'

'Nothing,' said Morgan defensively. 'It's just been a strange day.'

'Hmmph. That's for sure,' said Sandy. He leaned over and reached out a hand to Dusty. The gray cat hissed, and raked his claws down the back of Sandy's hand.

'Jesus,' Sandy cried, jumping back and rubbing the blood off of his hand.

Dusty bolted off the steps at the sound of Sandy's cry. 'That little bastard,' said Sandy. Then he frowned at Morgan. 'I never liked that cat. Can I come in and wash this off?' he asked.

Morgan stood up, her heart pounding. She felt ridiculous saying no. But she had to. She didn't want him inside. Especially now that it occurred to her he might have had a motive. 'I'm sorry,' Morgan said. 'They changed the locks.'

'Who changed the locks?' Sandy demanded.

Morgan shrugged. 'Guy's parents. They don't want anyone in there. I was just about to leave.' She indicated the path out to the cars.

Sandy looked ruefully at his bleeding hand. 'That mangy cat has been crawling around in the dirt. Isn't that how you get tetanus? From dirt?' He began to accompany Morgan down the path to their cars.

'I have no idea,' said Morgan. She also had no idea where she was going when she got into the car, but she knew that she wanted to get Sandy away from the house.

'Sorry about the delay. I'll call you when I hear from Mark,' said Sandy as he got into the front seat of the SUV. 'Shit, I'm going to get blood on my leather seats.'

Morgan pretended to fumble with the radio console on her dashboard, until Sandy revved up the engine and pulled away from the curb. Morgan followed suit, not wanting him to look in his rear-view mirror and see her still sitting there, or worse, getting out of the car. She wasn't sure where she was going. The house and its contents were safe for the moment. But where one worry receded, others immediately arose to fill that space. She had to find an attorney and somehow get that further testing ordered. Or at least have new tests done on the evidence that the police had collected. She could manage without Sandy's help. But the question seemed to pursue her, and inhibit her effort to make a sensible plan. Could it have been Sandy who killed the baby?

Stop this, she told herself as she drove aimlessly along. Now you suspect Sandy. And Sandy has been kind, considering everything. You have no reason to think that Sandy had anything to do with this. Or Eden, who was just a mixed-up teenager. But somebody killed that baby. Somebody, who had wanted to destroy Claire or Guy, or both of them.

Morgan sat idling at a stop light with her blinker on, getting ready to turn. Across the street, a pretty colonial-style house was decorated for Halloween with pumpkins and hay bales and goblins hanging from hooks on the front porch. Tied to the mailbox was a trio of Mylar balloons printed with ghosts and witches. Morgan gazed at them for a moment without really thinking about them. And then, just as the light changed, she was galvanized by another thought.

She suddenly remembered those bright balloons which were tied to Claire's mailbox, heralding Drew's christening. The balloons she had cut down with the kitchen scissors, which were still in her coat pocket. Perhaps someone had seen those balloons and ribbons on the mailbox and been filled with envy or loathing at the good fortune of the people inside. She remembered reading a news story like that, not long ago. A woman had entered a stranger's house, alerted, by balloons and signs in the yard, to the fact that there was a newborn inside. Of course, in that case, the woman had stolen the baby, intending to keep it for herself. But the story reminded Morgan that the intruder could have been a stranger.

Morgan felt overwhelmed by the possibilities. Claire had confessed and the police weren't looking. It seemed that she was the only one dissatisfied with the police version of the crime. The only one determined to expose it as a lie. And she didn't know where to begin. In that moment of flagging confidence, Morgan reminded herself that one important fact remained. If Professor Douglas's theory was true, then stranger or intimate, the baby's killer was at large, and Claire, despite her guilt and all her fears, was not the one to blame.

TWENTY-FOUR

THERE WAS A CAR, packed with suitcases, parked in front of the closed garage doors at the Captain's House. The sign out in front said 'Closed for the Season', but the car indicated to Morgan that the owners were still there. She walked up to the front door and began to ring the bell. She could hear it chiming through the empty guest house, but no one came to answer it.

Morgan peered into the window lights alongside the door, but could see nothing but darkness inside. She pressed the bell again, knowing that somewhere inside, the proprietor, Mrs Spaulding, was wishing that whoever it was would just go away. Morgan was not going away.

After what seemed like ten minutes of waiting, and pressing on the bell, she heard footsteps shuffling up to the front door, and then the door was pulled open. Paula Spaulding looked out, her normally pleasant expression twisted into a frown.

'We're closed,' she said. And then managed to force a smile at the sight of a former customer. 'Oh, hi,' she said. 'Miss…'

'Adair. Morgan Adair.'

'Right. Of course. I'm sorry, Morgan. I thought I told you. Last weekend was our last available weekend. We're leaving for Sarasota today.'

'You did tell me,' said Morgan. 'I'm not here for a room. Well, I need a room, but that's another matter. You did tell me that you were closing. I'm not here about that. Actually, I'm looking for Eden.'

Paula Spaulding looked surprised. 'You know Eden?' Morgan quickly explained her connection to Claire.

'Oh, my gosh,' said Paula. 'So, that baptism you were on your way to last week… That was for…'

'It was for Eden's half-brother. Drew. My godson.'

'Oh, dear, come in,' said Paula. 'I'm so sorry. Here. Come in and sit down. I didn't mean to be rude. Really. I'm just in a hurry to finish up here. My husband'll be back any minute and ready to go. But oh, I'm so sorry about your godson.'

'Thank you. So am I,' said Morgan.

Paula indicated one of the wing chairs in the parlor and Morgan sat down. Paula sat down too. 'I'd offer you something to drink…' said Paula, 'but I've cleaned out the refrigerator…'

'That's all right,' said Morgan. 'Really. I'm just wondering. Is Eden still staying here?'

'She was. But she left for home,' said Paula. 'I mean, I thought she was headed back to West Virginia after her father's funeral. But her grandparents called me and it seems she hasn't arrived home yet. I guess she took a detour,' said Paula.

Morgan nodded. Then she said carefully, 'Did Eden tell you who sent her the clipping about Guy and Claire's new baby?'

'Oh, I did,' said Paula.

'You did?'

'Yes. Although I wonder now if it was a mistake.'

'You mean, because of what happened.'

Paula nodded. 'You know, I felt responsible in a way because her mother was working for me when she got pregnant with Eden. And then, after Kimba's death,

Eden's grandfather wouldn't allow her father to come near the child. I was sure that Kimba would want Eden to know her father. After all, a child has a right to know her own parents, don't you think?'

'Yes. I think so,' said Morgan.

Reassured, Paula continued. 'Eden was happy when she first got the clipping. She called me, and I invited her to come up and stay. I'm sure you think I'm a busy-body and I should have stayed out of it, but Kimba was... very dear to me. She came to work here as a chamber-maid the summer after her first year at art school. She and her friend Jaslene. They were so much fun. Oh, those girls made me laugh.' Paula smiled fondly at the memory. 'They were just a couple of young girls wanting to live in a beach town, work hard, and enjoy being young...'

Paula's cheerfulness collapsed into a sigh. 'Of course, once Kimba got pregnant... Well, you know...'

Morgan didn't want to stem the flow of her recollections. 'Sure,' she said.

'Anyway, I was so happy to have Eden here for a visit, motorcycle and all. I never dreamed it would all end the way it did...' Paula said, shaking her head.

'No. No one could have foreseen that,' said Morgan.

Paula grimaced as she continued. 'The papers all said that your friend...killed them because she was mad about Eden. Do you suppose that's true?'

Morgan wanted to deny Claire's guilt, to explain her new theory. But she stopped herself. Instead, she shook her head. 'No. I don't think that was it.'

'To be honest with you, in spite of everything, I felt a little bit sorry for your friend. I mean, I had the baby blues myself after my second child. It's no fun. And I kept asking myself, how could her husband not have told her about Eden? Or his marriage to Kimba?' Paula wondered.

'I don't know,' Morgan admitted. 'You know, Eden seemed very angry at the funeral.'

'Well, naturally. After all, she'd just met her father, and then he was gone. I suppose that would upset anyone.'

'It was more than upset,' Morgan insisted. 'She was definitely angry. At Guy.'

'Sometimes people—especially when you've had a lot of fantasies about them—they can be disappointing.'

'That's true,' Morgan conceded.

'Eden had a lot of information coming at her. She wanted to find out all that she could about her mother, too. She pumped me about everything I knew. I thought Jaslene might be able to tell her more than I could. She and Kimba were such good friends. Jaslene is a big shoe designer in New York City now,' Paula said, as proudly as if she were talking about her own daughter. 'Have you heard of Jaslene Shoes?'

'No, but I'm not that fashionable,' said Morgan.

'Well, success hasn't gone to Jaslene's head the way it does with some people. I encouraged Eden to give her a call. Unfortunately, it turned out that Jaslene was in Milan. So Eden left her a message. Then she went to stay with her aunt for a couple of nights.'

'Yes. Her Aunt Lucy told me that Eden spent some time with her.'

'That's right,' said Paula. 'And then yesterday, after the funeral, Eden must have come in the house, gathered up her stuff and left. She left a note, thanking me, saying she'd be in touch. And, as I said, I haven't heard from her since. Those motorcycles can be dangerous,' Paula fretted.

'She seemed to be able to handle it pretty well,' said Morgan in an effort to be comforting.

Paula sighed and stood up. Her expression was worried, but she nodded in agreement. 'I suppose. Well, I'd love to sit and talk but I've still got a few things to do before we're ready to leave.'

Morgan stood up as well. 'Thank you for your time. I've got to be going too. I've got to go find myself some place to stay. I wish you were open until Christmas. This is such a beautiful house.'

'Oh heavens,' said Paula. 'I'd be completely burned out if I was open until Christmas.'

Morgan smiled. 'I can understand that. Well, thanks again.' She shook hands with Paula Spaulding and headed for the front door.

'You know,' said Paula.

Morgan turned and looked at her.

'I've got a house-sitter coming next week. But I wouldn't mind having someone staying here until then. Of course, you'd have to check the heat, take in the mail, water the plants and all.'

'You mean, stay here in the house?' said Morgan.

'I wouldn't pay you. But I wouldn't charge you either. And you'd have to wash your sheets, and make sure the kitchen was spic and span.'

'Oh. I'd gladly do that. That would be great,' said Morgan.

Paula smiled. 'Well, that might work out for both of us. Come on with me. I'll give you a quick tour.'

WHEN THE TOUR WAS OVER, Morgan, thanking Paula profusely, left the guest house and went back to Claire's cottage to pick up her things and feed the cat. She did not linger in the cottage, for she was all too aware of the sickening smell which Astrid had remarked on earlier. She was careful to lock all the doors when she left, wondering how long she had before Astrid overruled her objections and blanketed the place in house cleaners. Morgan knew that she had to find another attorney, but short of the Yellow Pages, she had no idea where to look.

She thought about calling Oliver Douglas but she knew that he would advise her to wait for Mark Silverman. Besides, she had asked enough of Oliver Douglas. She needed another plan, but she was at a loss. It seemed as if she was completely alone in this quest to help her friend. Alone and inadequate. She knew nothing about attorneys or the law, yet she had to do something. Her head ached at the thought of it. She reminded herself that at least, for now, she had a place to stay.

Morgan stopped in at the hospital briefly to see Claire. Claire's face seemed to be somewhat less yellow and waxy than before, but otherwise, there was no change in her condition. Morgan pulled a chair up beside the bed, took Claire's hand and whispered into her ear, 'Someone else killed Drew. Not you, Claire. Someone else did it, and we're going to find out who. I'm going to be staying at the Captain's House for a while. The lady who owns the Captain's House is letting me house-sit. So don't worry. I'm fine there. And I won't leave you alone.' If Claire heard Morgan's whispered promise, she gave no sign.

By the time Morgan returned to the Captain's House, Paula and her husband were already gone. A cheery note on the door told Morgan to make herself at home and enjoy her stay.

Morgan let herself in to the lovely old house and turned on a few lights to dispel the shadows of dusk. The house, so inviting when Paula was at the desk, now seemed isolated and gloomy. Morgan set her bag down in the maid's room behind the kitchen which Paula had indicated would be hers. A far cry from the spacious guest rooms upstairs, the maid's room held only a twin bed, a ladder-back chair and a small dresser. But the wallpaper was a beautiful yellow and blue toile pattern, and the room had a circular mullioned window which gave the tiny room a distinct charm. Morgan set her bag down on the chair, and rummaged in it for a sweater to put on against the chill. After she had pulled the sweater over her head, she pulled her abundant chestnut hair up into a ponytail. Paula wanted the heat kept low, now that there were no guests, because the house was so expensive to heat. Morgan intended to be the perfect caretaker.

Morgan unzipped her boots and left them beside the bed. Then she padded into the kitchen in her stocking feet, and opened the refrigerator. As Paula had announced earlier, the refrigerator was all but empty. She closed the door, and went into the long, narrow pantry, searching among the foodstuffs until she found a can of chili to heat up. She took it back to the counter, found a bowl into which she poured the contents, and then slipped the bowl into the microwave. While she waited for the chili to heat, she looked out the window at the darkening sky. The lonely sliver of moon hung high, a platinum crescent against the vast, deep blue, while a metallic ribbon of ocean rippled at the horizon, beautiful and cold.

Morgan shivered, as the timer dinged. She had no sooner sat down with her bowl when her cellphone rang in her pocket. She fished it out and answered.

'Morgan. It's Fitz.'

'Hey,' she said, surprised, and, actually, happy to hear his voice. 'How are you?'

'OK,' he said. 'Sorry I got a little testy with you about Guy.'

'That's all right. I shouldn't have said those things about your friend,' Morgan assured him, eager to have their rift mended. 'And I'm really glad you called. How's the wrestling camp?'

'Bunch of knuckleheads,' he said fondly. 'Two injuries so far and counting.'

'Hmmm,' she said. 'That's too bad.'

'Ah, it's normal,' he said. 'What's happening there? How's Claire?'

'She's the same. But I am very grateful to you.'

'Really,' he asked, sounding pleased. 'Why?'

'For taking me to meet Oliver Douglas,' she said. 'Because you did that, I finally have some hope.' Briefly, she told him about Oliver's analysis of Claire's confession, and her own need to find a criminal attorney. Fitz listened quietly. Morgan began to think that she had said too much. She waited for him to dismiss her concerns and hang up. Finally, he spoke.

'Forget the other lawyer,' said Fitz. 'You haven't got time to waste. Go and tell the lawyer you've got. Tell her what you just told me.'

'Noreen? She's not going to listen to me,' said Morgan.

'You make a very persuasive case,' said Fitz.

'She's just going to get mad at me for interfering in something I don't know anything about,' said Morgan.

'Or…she's going to be persuaded because she admires what you're trying to do for your friend,' he said.

'Do you really think she would listen?' Morgan asked.

'Well, I don't know,' he said. 'But you haven't got another attorney. And you can't let the time get away from you. I say it's worth a try. Not that my advice is worth anything,' he said.

'As a matter of fact,' she said, 'I think your advice is just what I needed.'

TWENTY-FIVE

'WE'RE JUST ABOUT TO WATCH Finding Nemo,' said Gert.

'I realize this is probably not a good time,' said Morgan. 'But it's very important.'

'I know. It's always important,' said Gert, taking a detour into the kitchen. She waggled a finger indicating that Morgan should follow her. Morgan hesitated and then entered the kitchen.

Gert punched a button on a CD player on the counter, popped out the disc and set it back in its plastic case, which she closed with a clack. Gert handed the CD to Morgan. 'She's good. I loved that "Let Your Hair Down" cut. I figured I might as well listen to it before I gave it back to you,' said Gert wryly. 'Because it's certainly isn't mine.'

Morgan avoided her accusatory gaze by looking down at the Corinne Bailey Rae disc in her hand. 'No,' said Morgan.

'At least you're not trying to con me now,' said Gert, folding her arms over her chest. 'What are you up to anyway?'

Morgan grimaced. 'Did you tell Noreen?'

'Not yet,' said Gert.

Morgan looked at her pleadingly. 'It's a long story and I had a good reason. Please. I really need to see Noreen. I'll explain it to her.'

'Mommy. Come on,' childish voices called down the hall. 'Let's watch the movie.'

Shaking her head, Gert led the way down the hall, opening the door to the bedroom. The two children Morgan had seen at her last visit were snuggled on either side of the flannel-pajamaed Noreen, a plastic bowl of popcorn perched precariously in front of them on the bed-covers.

'Get down for a minute,' said Gert. 'Nonny's got to talk to this lady.'

Noreen frowned at the sight of Morgan, and shushed the yelps of protest from her children.

'Just for a few minutes,' said Gert, deftly lifting the popcorn bowl off the covers, as she shepherded the complaining children down from the bed, warning them to be careful not to kick Noreen. Gert threw Noreen a warning look. 'We haven't got that much time before bed.'

'I'll be brief,' said Morgan, but looking at Noreen's impatient expression, she felt that she could not be brief enough, and her reception was likely to be chilly.

'I hope so,' said Gert, as she herded the children out and closed the door.

Morgan looked anxiously at Noreen. Her red hair stood out around her face like a stiff mane, and was matted flat in the back from the bed pillows.

'Couldn't this wait?' Noreen said.

Morgan shook her head. 'I wouldn't be here if it could.'

'All right, fine. What is it?' Noreen asked.

'I need your help,' said Morgan.

Noreen rolled her hands as if trying to propel Morgan to hurry.

Morgan took a deep breath. 'Claire did not kill her baby. Someone else did. I'm sure of it. And the evidence may still be in that house. Can you prevent them legally from having the house scrubbed down? Or can you make the police retest the evidence from the bathroom? Or let us hire someone to retest it?'

Noreen stared at her without speaking.

Morgan went on. 'I know you think I'm crazy too, but…I took the DVD of her confession from your office…'

'What?' Noreen cried.

Morgan did not stop. 'I had an expert look at it, and when he pointed this out to me it was so obvious that he was right. She made a false confession. She didn't kill that baby, and I don't care how much you want this to be about post-partum depression…'

'Whoa, whoa, whoa,' said Noreen. 'Back up. You took the DVD from my office?'

Morgan stuck out her chin defiantly. 'Yes.'

'Whatever made you think that you had a right to do that?'

'I was desperate,' said Morgan. 'I took a chance.'

Noreen glowered at her. 'Really? And whom did you show it to?' she asked.

'A professor named Oliver Douglas. He wrote a book about false confessions.'

Noreen looked away from Morgan, her hands balled into fists on the top of the bedcovers, her mouth pursed.

'I know a lot of people think that there is no such thing as a false confession, that it's just a trick or a tactic but Professor Douglas has studied this extensively.'

'I know all about Professor Douglas,' Noreen said flatly.

'I know I shouldn't have taken it,' said Morgan, 'but I had to do something. Claire's life is hanging by a thread. And she didn't commit this crime.'

'Everybody's innocent,' said Noreen sarcastically.

'If you looked at the tape with Professor Douglas you'd

see. She's making up the part about killing Drew. She doesn't remember it at all. It's obvious.'

'And her husband's death?' said Noreen.

Morgan sighed. 'Professor Douglas thought that probably did happen the way she said. Guy came into the bathroom and found Drew in the tub and Claire... He was shocked. He probably accused her, or tried to save the baby. Or maybe he tried to take the baby's body from her. They struggled, there was an accident of some kind. I don't know. Obviously she did not overpower him.'

'Obviously not.'

'Guy was sleeping in the guest room upstairs when this happened. I know that for a fact. Professor Douglas's theory is that Claire found the baby and started screaming. That's when Guy jumped up from his bed and came downstairs. It makes sense. Look at the tape and you'll see.'

'How can I do that?' Noreen asked in a cutting tone. 'You have the tape.'

'I'm sorry,' said Morgan. 'I know I shouldn't have taken it.'

Noreen looked at her narrowly. 'If you didn't like the way I was handling this case, why didn't you just get another attorney?' she asked.

Morgan remained defiant. 'I tried to. But now there's no time.'

'Thanks for the vote of confidence,' said Noreen. Morgan felt like they were trading punches with their words.

'Look, I can't worry about your confidence. I can only worry about Claire.'

There was a light tapping on the closed door that made Morgan jump.

'Nonny, we want to watch the movie,' a child's voice pleaded.

'In a minute,' said Noreen calmly. Noreen put out her hand. 'All right. Let's have it. I presume you have the DVD of the confession. You won't be needing that anymore.'

'Oh, yes,' said Morgan fumbling in her bag and pulling out the plastic sleeve. She handed it to Noreen. She pointed to a Post-it note which she had placed on the case. 'That's Professor Douglas's number. He'll be glad to talk to you. He said he would testify.'

Noreen frowned at the writing on the Post-it note. 'You have been quite the busy bee, haven't you?' Noreen asked.

Morgan was unrepentant. 'My friend's life is at stake.'

Noreen chewed the inside of her mouth for a moment. Then she looked up at Morgan. 'So, I imagine you still want an answer to your question. The answer is yes.'

Morgan frowned. 'Yes what?'

'Yes. The defense can petition the court for access to all materials in that house for testing.'

Morgan felt a sudden, cautious elation. 'Really? Will you do that?'

'I will, after I look at this confession again, with what you've said in mind.'

Morgan kneaded her hands together. 'The thing is, I'm not sure that the police did a very thorough job in that house. They weren't looking for evidence of another killer. I think they need to go over that bedroom and bathroom again.'

'Leave this to me,' said Noreen. 'I know how to get this done. It's my job.'

'You believe me?' said Morgan, amazed at the attorney's acquiescence.

'No. Not necessarily.'

'But you're willing to consider the possibility that it

wasn't post-partum psychosis? That someone else killed the baby?'

Noreen gave Morgan a slight smile. 'My plan for Claire's defense was a strategy. Not a religion. I am capable of considering other possibilities.'

'Thank you so much,' said Morgan, almost faint with relief.

'This is an unorthodox way to go about it, but, I have to admit, I'm impressed by your...determination. I am willing to file the petition and have the tests examined for any evidence that might support this theory.'

'I'm sure it's right,' said Morgan.

'And do you also have a theory about who *did* kill Claire's baby?' Noreen asked.

Morgan saw a trap in the attorney's question. She was not willing to voice her myriad suspicions. She was sure that such speculation would only undermine her argument in the attorney's eyes. 'I have no idea,' she said. 'We just need proof that there was someone else in that bathroom the day the baby died. If we can prove that, and Professor Douglas can convince a jury that her confession was coerced...was false...'

'That's a very risky way to proceed,' said Noreen.

'Not if it's true,' Morgan insisted.

Noreen leaned forward and pointed her index finger at Morgan's face. 'All right. Now hear me, Morgan. I appreciate that you are concerned for your friend, but you've interfered more than enough. It's time to butt out of this. If you're right, and someone else killed that baby, you had better not go around voicing your suspicions. Do you understand? That could be dangerous.'

'Yes,' said Morgan.

'I mean it,' said Noreen.

'I understand.'

'All right. So go home. Now, open the door and let my kids in. We've kept them waiting long enough.'

ALL THE WAY BACK to the Captain's House, Morgan turned over the encounter with the attorney in her mind. Noreen had believed her. She felt triumphant at the thought of it. Noreen was going to take it in hand. Even though she was hobbled by being laid up in bed, Noreen still exuded authority, a sense of capability. She would take care of the evidence. She would see to it that Claire's rights were protected. She would confer with Professor Douglas and Claire might end up going free. Tonight Morgan felt as if it had all been worthwhile—her missed trip, the...misunderstanding with Simon. None of that mattered if Claire would simply recover, and be set free. For the last few miles, Morgan sang every show tune she could remember.

The Captain's House looked dark and forbidding when she pulled into the gravel drive and Morgan wished she had left some lights on. It was the kind of house you'd want to invite all your friends and their parents and their children to, she thought, so that people would be rocking on the porch and yodeling out the windows toward the sea. But it was not, Morgan had to admit, the sort of place you wanted to stay in alone. She fished for her keys in her bag, and climbed the steps to the front door, unlocked it, and hurried inside, locking the door behind her.

She did not bother to turn on the lights in the front rooms of the house. Instead, she went through to the kitchen and the tiny bedroom where she was staying. Morgan lay down on the bed, still fully dressed, and the exhaustion she felt after this day rolled over her like a wave. It was a day of progress, she thought. Although she felt low at the moment, she knew that she had done all she could to help Claire today. As much as she would rather have been on her trip to England, there was comfort in that.

The thought of the trip made Morgan think longingly of Simon. Why had she assumed the worst of him? He was unable to get the money back and so he decided to use the reservation. And he invited a friend to join him. That didn't mean…anything. No one wanted to take a trip like that alone. She groped in her bag for her phone and scrolled down to his cellphone number. Still lying on the bed, she punched it in and held the phone to her ear. The moment it began to ring she remembered, too late, the time difference. She glanced at the alarm clock on the bedside table and froze. It was three o'clock in the morning there. 'Oh shit,' she said. Oh well, she thought. He had called her in the middle of the night. Turnabout was fair play.

Still, she felt a little sheepish when a groggy voice answered. 'Simon?' she said apologetically.

'No,' he said, clearing his throat. 'It's Tim. Who's this?'

'I'm trying to reach Simon,' she said.

'Just a minute,' he said irritably. 'Simon,' she heard him mumble. 'Phone.'

She heard a sleepy voice mutter something unintelligible. 'I don't know. Didn't say,' she heard Tim say, and in the time it took to hand a phone across a pillow, Simon answered.

'This is Simon,' said a voice blurry with sleep, but faintly anxious, all the same, at being awakened so late.

Morgan could hear the other man's voice beside him, asking who the caller was.

'Dunno,' said Simon's muffled voice. 'Turn the light on, will you? I can't see. Hand me my glasses. They're on your side. Next to the clock.'

Her face flaming, Morgan ended the call.

In a moment, the phone rang in her hand. She hesitated, and then answered it.

'Morgan, it's Simon,' he said. 'Why did you ring off? Is something wrong?'

Everything, she wanted to say. Instead, she was mute. Frantically, she tried to create rationalizations. The two men were still at a hotel, perhaps in a room with twin beds. The phone was on a table between them. Tim just happened to pick it up because he was a lighter sleeper than Simon and so when it rang, Tim got up from his bed and…

'Morgan, it's three fucking o'clock in the morning. What is going on?'

'I forgot about the time,' she said.

'Oh,' he said.

'I'm sorry I woke you up,' she said. 'You. And Tim.'

Simon sighed. 'Oh, he'll be asleep again in a minute. The man sleeps like a stone,' he said, and she felt chilled by his easy familiarity with Tim's sleeping habits.

'Simon…' she said. She didn't want to ask him, but she was weary of lying to herself. She had to know. Right now. 'Are you and Tim…together?'

He could have laughed, saying that of course they were together. They were on a trip together. She willed him to say it. To make light of her question. But he did not laugh, or make an excuse. 'Yes,' he said.

'I see.' She waited, once more, for him to make an excuse, but he didn't. 'So…to you I'm just…a friend,' she said.

Simon was silent for a moment. Then he said gently, 'Of course you're a friend.'

All her months of hope and fantasy seemed to blow away, like a dandelion puffed on by a child's breath. Her heart felt ashamed, shriveled. 'It's late. I'll call you back another time,' she whispered.

Simon did not protest. 'That might be best. Good night, Morgan,' he said.

For a long while she could not summon the strength to get up from the bed. After a while, she forced herself to get up and take a shower. She went into the den and turned on the television, but she did not concentrate on anything she saw. She kept picturing Simon and Tim, in bed together.

Morgan forced herself to stop. What a fool you are, she thought. Claire had been right all along about Simon, although she had been too kind to say it directly. Even though Simon had flirted with her, clearly enjoyed her company and had agreed to go on this trip to the Lake District with her, the fact remained that he had shown no interest in her as a lover. He had never made the slightest physical overture. She could never even accuse him of leading her on.

But he did, she thought, her heart aching. He acted… interested. Why would he do that, if he was a gay man, she wondered desperately. She tried to piece it together in her mind, to force it to make sense. Was it cruelty? Did he want to embarrass her? That didn't seem like Simon. Or was it just curiosity, to test his own attractiveness, even though he knew he was not going to take it any further? Morgan realized that she could think about it all night, but no matter whether it made sense or not, it was true. Any hope she had ever had for Simon needed to be jettisoned, along with all of those fantasies which were not going to come true.

When she couldn't stand to think about it anymore, she flipped off the television and the lights in the den, and went into the narrow bed where she was going to be sleeping. She was afraid she would lie awake for hours. But she fell quickly into a deep sleep, and was having a complicated dream involving Claire and Fitz and her long dead parents, when suddenly a sound disturbed her sleep and she was instantly, completely awake.

Confused at awakening in the unfamiliar house, she took a moment to get her bearings. She realized that the sound was an intermittent banging noise and that it was coming from the front of the house. For a few moments she lay there, paralysed with fear, and then, chiding herself for her anxiety, she forced herself to flip the switch on the bedside lamp. She quickly pulled on a robe over the T-shirt she had worn to bed. Then, cautiously, she left the cozy room and went out into the kitchen, throwing on the overhead light as she went. She went down the hallway, glancing into the den, and finally entered the main room of the house, walking past the curved banister on the staircase. Immediately, she saw where the sound was coming from.

The front door of the Captain's House was open. The night wind was blowing it to and fro on its hinges. Each time the door hit the frame, it banged back open.

I locked that door, Morgan thought. Her heart was hammering in her throat. The room was still dark, the shadows from the bright moon making hulking creatures out of the antique furniture. Morgan stood frozen to the spot, shivering, trying to deny what she knew was true. But there really was no uncertainty in her mind. She had closed the front door and locked it before she went to bed. And now it stood open.

TWENTY-SIX

FULL OF DREAD, as if she were approaching a scaffold, Morgan walked to the front door and closed it. As she turned the lock, and the howl of the wind was cut off, Morgan heard another sound. Someone on the staircase behind her gasped.

Morgan wanted to cry out, but her own voice seemed to be caught in her throat.

As she wheeled around, Morgan's heart thudded so hard that it seemed to jump out of her chest. She could see a figure standing on the staircase, gripping the banister and staring at her from the shadows.

'Who's there?' Morgan asked faintly.

'Who are you?' the stranger said.

The person cautiously descended a few steps and peered at Morgan. Morgan instantly recognized the pink hair, the dusty leather clothes, the engineer's boots, and the glint of a stud in the girl's nostril. 'Eden.'

'Hey. What are you doing here?' Eden demanded angrily, finally recognizing Morgan.

Morgan caught her breath before she spoke. 'I'm watching the Captain's House for Mrs Spaulding. She left for Sarasota this afternoon,' Morgan explained. 'I thought you left town.'

'I did. I came back,' she said.

'How did you get in?'

'I have a key,' said Eden, waggling a key on a plastic keychain.

'What are you doing back here?'

'You first,' Eden insisted.

'I'm here because of Claire. She's still in the hospital.' The girl assessed Morgan's answer silently, while Morgan studied her, trying to imagine her stealing into Claire's house, looking for the baby. Taking it into the bathroom. Somehow, despite all her suspicions, Morgan could not imagine this teenager taking that next step—drowning a baby.

Eden seemed to ponder her options for a moment and then she made up her mind. 'I left something here. My ring. It must have come off while I was sleeping.'

'So you came back to look for it?' said Morgan.

'Yeah,' said Eden.

'Did you find it?' Morgan asked.

'No. I looked around my room but I didn't see it.'

'Oh,' said Morgan, holding on to the banister.

'You scared me,' said Eden.

'You scared me,' Morgan admitted. 'I didn't expect someone to let themselves in here in the middle of the night.'

'Sorry. You can go back to bed. I'll leave.'

'Shall I help you look again? Maybe you missed it,' Morgan said.

'Why would you help me?' Eden asked.

'Well,' said Morgan with a sigh, 'I'm awake now. I don't think my heart will be back to a normal rhythm for an hour or two.'

Eden did not apologize. 'All right. Come on, then. I was staying upstairs in the lilac room.'

Morgan remembered the room from the tour that Paula Spaulding had given her. The walls were painted a peri-winkle blue with fresh white trim, and the fabric on the curtains and bedspread were sprigged with lilacs. 'OK,' said Morgan, approaching the foot of the staircase. 'What does the ring look like?'

'It's gold. It's got a black stone. Onyx.'

Now that she described it, Morgan remembered seeing the ring on the girl's forefinger. 'I'll bet we can find it between the two of us.'

Eden watched her as she started up the stairs. Her wary gaze made Morgan think of Dusty, Claire's cat. 'You go ahead,' said Morgan. 'Lead the way.'

Eden hesitated, and then started down the hall. She entered a door on the right, and flipped a switch on the wall. A white wicker lamp was illuminated on the bed-side table.

'We'll need more light than that,' said Morgan. She edged by Eden into the room, and turned on the reading lamp beside a slipper chair, and another lamp which sat on the bureau. 'There now,' she said.

Eden looked around the room dejectedly. 'She cleaned the whole room.'

'She might have missed it. Let's look under the bed.'

'I looked there,' said Eden.

Morgan got down on her knees beside the bed, and ran her hand under the dust ruffle. 'Get down at the end,' said Morgan. Eden went glumly to the end of bed, and did the same thing as Morgan.

'Nothing,' Eden announced.

'We need a flashlight,' said Morgan. 'I think Paula pointed one out to me.' She got up off her knees and went out into the hall, where there was a linen closet. She opened the door, and found the flashlight sitting on a shelf of towels. She turned it on, and then brought it into the lilac room. Eden was still groping around under the bed.

Morgan got down beside her, and shone the light underneath the dust ruffle.

'I don't see anything,' said Eden.

Morgan began to shine the light systematically in each corner underneath the bed. Eden sat back on her heels.

'It's probably gone for good,' said Eden.

'Oh, come on now. We just started looking,' said Morgan, keeping her gaze on the flashlight's path. 'You must have been halfway home, and then you came all the way back to look for it. You can't be ready to quit so quickly.'

'I wasn't on my way home,' Eden said. 'I was in New York City.'

Morgan straightened up and sat back on her heels. 'Really? By yourself? That's pretty brave of you.'

'I went to see a friend of my mother's.'

Morgan remembered Paula mentioning the shoe designer, the friend that Kimba knew from art school. 'How did that go?' said Morgan.

Eden stood up, ignoring her question. 'I give up. It's not here.'

Morgan got to her feet. 'Wait. Let's look behind the head-board. It might have gotten wedged in there.'

Eden rose to her feet also, and went around to the other side. Morgan peered down behind the elaborate oak head-board, and then shone the light in. 'I think I see something,' she said.

'Where?' Eden asked suspiciously. She came around to Morgan's side of the bed and peered down to where Morgan was pointing.

'That might be it,' she agreed.

'Let's pull the bed away from the wall,' said Morgan. 'You go around the other side and we'll lift it up so we don't scratch the floor.'

Eden obediently went around, and held on to the bed. 'Now, lift it. Don't drag it,' said Morgan. 'When I say go.'

'OK.'

'OK, go,' said Morgan.

The two of them lifted, and there was a sound of something clattering to the floor. They lowered the bed and Eden crouched down, feeling around under the bed, until she picked the ring up with a cry of delight.

Morgan came around and sat down on the edge of the bed. Eden slid the ring on her forefinger, and displayed it proudly.

'That's a beautiful ring,' said Morgan. 'I can see why you came back for it.'

Eden sat down on the bed beside her, admiring her own hand. 'It was my mother's,' she said. 'My grandmother gave it to me. It's the only thing I have of hers.'

Morgan spoke carefully. 'You don't remember her at all, I guess.'

Eden polished her ring on the thigh of her dirty jeans. 'No. Just the stories my grandparents told me. She was an artist.'

'I guess Paula Spaulding and your mom's friend in New York helped fill in the blanks a little bit.'

Eden shrugged, but her gaze was closed and distant. 'There's lot I don't know about my parents too. They died when I was twelve,' said Morgan.

Eden looked at her with guarded curiosity.

'That's why I think it was good that you came here. I mean, despite everything that happened, at least you got to finally meet your father,' said Morgan.

Eden shook her head. 'I should have listened to my grandfather and stayed away,' said Eden grimly. 'I found out things about him. About my father. Things I wish I didn't know.'

'If you mean that business about your mother's accident,' Morgan said. 'I know your grandfather believes that Guy was to blame, but by all accounts it really was an accident.'

'Not that,' said Eden in disgust.

Morgan tried to hide her surprise. 'Well, Guy didn't give you a very warm reception, which I thought was kind of mean of him. But Fitz told me that you two seemed to be getting along. He said you were having lunch with him and sharing pictures...'

'You don't know anything,' said Eden impatiently.

Morgan did her best not to take offense. 'I didn't know your father well. That's true. But he married my best friend, and from what I saw of him, he seemed to be an OK guy.'

'He was a rapist,' Eden said flatly.

Morgan felt as if the girl had knocked the wind out of her. 'A rapist?'

'See. You don't believe it. You think I made it up,' said Eden, in a tone that suggested she did not expect to be believed.

'No, Eden,' said Morgan, squeezing the girl's tense forearm. 'No. Of course I believe you. Eden, did your father hurt you? Are you all right?'

For a moment Eden looked confused. Then she understood what Morgan was asking her. 'It wasn't me,' said Eden scornfully.

'Oh, thank God,' Morgan said with genuine relief. She was still trying to absorb this terrible accusation about the man she had known. Or thought she had known. Claire's husband. 'So where did you hear that? Did your mother's friend tell you that when you went to see her? What was her name? Jasmine?'

'Jaslene.'

'What did Jaslene tell you?'

'It's none of your business. He's dead now. He can't

hurt anyone else. I have to go. Thanks for helping me find the ring,' she said. Eden stood up abruptly.

'Eden, listen…' Morgan pleaded. 'This could be very important for Claire's court case. Eden, I need for you to tell me. Who was the victim?'

Eden shook her head. 'I promised not to tell. I hope Claire is OK. It wasn't her fault,' she said. 'He deserved to die.' She shouldered her backpack and strode to the door.

'Eden, wait,' said Morgan scrambling to her feet.

But the girl had vanished as if she were made from smoke. All but for the clatter of her boots on the stairs. As Morgan reached the foot of the stairs, the front door was closing. She ran to it, and looked out. She could see the lights of the motorcycle down near the road, and, as she called out Eden's name, she was drowned out by the roar of the bike as it sped from the driveway.

TWENTY-SEVEN

MORGAN WATCHED AS THE motorcycle's lights disappeared. Finally, she went back into the house and locked the door. It was late, but she doubted she could sleep now. Guy Bolton, a rapist? She tried to superimpose that loathsome image in her mind over the impression she had formed of Guy, as a hard-working husband, a handsome partner to Claire. Before Drew was born, Morgan had enjoyed some festive, carefree evenings with Guy and Claire. He seemed to be a man who liked to talk and laugh, and drink a glass of wine as he cooked. And now... Was it true? And if it was, who had he raped, she wondered? And had his victim decided to take revenge?

Morgan sat down in a rocking chair in the front parlor and wrapped the white knitted afghan, which was folded on the sofa arm, around her. She was shivering, partly from the cold in the house and partly from the shock of this news. Think, she exhorted herself. Who knows the truth about this? Morgan felt sure that the key to this was Kimba's friend, Jaslene, the shoe designer. But how to get a hold of her? Morgan didn't even know her last name. I could call Paula Spaulding, she thought. She was probably in a motel somewhere en route to Sarasota. Morgan had the number for Paula's cellphone. And Paula had instructed her to call in an emergency.

Morgan knew that no one else would consider this an emergency. Everyone else saw her hopes to exonerate Claire as futile. As if to remind Morgan that the hour was too late for such a call, the grandfather clock in the foyer chimed twelve times. All right, forget about it, she thought. Calling Paula was not an option, at least for tonight.

Morgan forced herself to get up from the chair. She went to the computer behind the front desk. She pulled up Paula Spaulding's document files and searched for a file which had a directory of names and addresses. Paula had addresses in abundance. Judging by the far-flung addresses, it seemed that Paula had saved the personal information of every customer who had ever patronized the Captain's House. Many people were listed by their full names, but some were simply listed with their first initial. She spent a frustrating hour trying to match, with no success, the New York City phone numbers to the addresses of people whose first names began with a 'J'.

Finally she returned the computer to the home page and sat on the stool behind the desk, thinking. She knew that Jaslene's company was called Jaslene Shoes. Perhaps, she thought, the company phone rang on Jaslene's personal line as well. It seemed unlikely—it wasn't as if there were frequent emergencies in the world of shoe design— but it was worth a try. She glanced up at the clock face and hesitated. Then she chided herself. It was one thing not to call Paula Spaulding at this late hour. But surely, she thought, it was not too late to call a fashionista in the city that never sleeps. She dialed information, had her call connected to the phone line for Jaslene Shoes, and waited while it rang, hoping the elusive Jaslene would pick up. Instead, after about ten rings, she reached the automated service, and left a message, emphasizing that this call was about Eden, and that she needed desperately for Jaslene to call her back.

The temperature in the house seemed to be dropping

lower by the moment, and Morgan began to long for the warmth of a bed. There was nothing more she could do for now, she thought. After checking the locked doors one last time, she went back into the maid's room, and crawled under the covers. For a while she shivered, but then, she began to feel drowsy, and sleep was threatening. As she lay there, she thought about Eden. She remembered Fitz saying that Eden wanted to spit on her father's body at the funeral, and now, Morgan knew why.

Morgan's eyes drooped and closed, in spite of the feverish way her brain was working. She could feel her thoughts veering off the track as sleep claimed her. All of a sudden, thinking about the chain of events led her to a realization. Morgan was jolted awake for a moment. Eden had already been furious at her father at his funeral. And that was before she had ever met her mother's friend, Jaslene. Eden must have learned that her father was a rapist some time before the funeral occurred. That meant that Jaslene was probably not the one who told her.

Morgan felt as if she was rolling backwards down a hill she was trying to climb. She would have to start from zero again, trying to determine where Eden had learned this fact about her father. Morgan tried to imagine possible scenarios, but in a minute her mind was foggy again, and she couldn't think anymore, no matter how she wanted to. She fell abruptly into a deep sleep.

MORGAN WAS AWAKENED by a pounding on the front door. She opened her eyes to a gray autumn day, and felt a sudden loathing for whoever was awakening her, insisting on her attention. In that minute, she understood why Paula Spaulding and her husband left town so early to escape to Sarasota.

Morgan pulled on her robe and got up reluctantly from

the warm bed, muttering, 'Just a minute. Just a minute.'
She shuffled to the front door, turned all the locks and
opened it. Sandy Raymond was standing on the front
porch, wearing jeans and a bleach-stained sweatshirt from
some branch of the University of California.

Morgan looked at him in confusion. 'Sandy.'

'Good. You're up,' he said.

'Not really,' said Morgan. 'You woke me up.'

Sandy barged past her into the foyer. 'You'd better get
dressed,' he said.

'Wait a minute,' said Morgan, pushing her uncombed
russet hair out of her face, her sleepy eyes. 'How'd you
find me? I didn't tell you I was staying here.'

'That's true,' he said.

'I didn't tell anybody,' said Morgan.

'Yes, you did,' said Sandy, a raffish gleam in his eye.
Morgan stood her ground, pulling her robe more tightly
around her. The front door was still open. She wasn't
quite sure she wanted Sandy making himself at home.
'No, I know I didn't.'

Sandy could not keep from smiling. 'You told Claire,'
he said.

Morgan shook her head and peered at him. 'Claire?'

Sandy could barely contain his excitement. 'She's
awake.'

Morgan let out a cry. 'She is. Oh, thank God. When?'

'When I got there this morning, she was awake. She
asked about you. She said you were at the Captain's
House.'

Morgan's mouth fell open as she looked at him. 'That's
impossible.'

'You must have told her,' said Sandy. 'How else would
she know?'

'I...I guess I did mention the Captain's House to her,'

Morgan admitted. 'But I was just babbling. She was unconscious.'

Sandy tapped on her forehead with his index finger. 'The human mind,' he said. 'It's a mystery.'

'She's really awake?'

'Yeah. Hurry up. I'll take you over there if you want.'

'That's OK,' said Morgan. 'Thanks anyway. I've got to get dressed.' She started for her room, but then she looked back to Sandy who was not moving from the foyer. 'Really. Don't wait for me. I can drive myself.'

'OK,' he said with a shrug. 'Whatever. I'll see you there.' He started to turn to leave.

Morgan peered at him. 'You know, I don't get it, Sandy,' she said.

Sandy looked at her with raised eyebrows. 'Don't get what?'

'You. You're always at the hospital. Doesn't Farah mind?'

Sandy's eyes revealed nothing. 'Farah left me,' he said.

'I'm sorry,' said Morgan.

Sandy shook his head. 'I had to bribe her to leave. I gave her my Mercedes.'

'Really?' said Morgan.

'I know what you're thinking,' said Sandy. 'You think it's strange. Me being there all the time for a woman who dumped me for another man.'

'It's true,' said Morgan. 'It does seem strange.'

Sandy's gaze was steady and impassive. 'Well, he's gone now, isn't he?' said Sandy. 'Now, she needs me.'

MORGAN DRESSED, DROVE in a hurry and practically ran down the hospital corridor to Claire's room. When she got there she found Sandy, already seated beside the prison guard on a chair in the hall, his leg crossed so that one sneakered foot rested on his knee, as he read the paper. He lowered his paper and looked up as Morgan arrived and gave her a thumbs up. Morgan identified herself to the prison guard, a stocky, mustachioed Hispanic man. She jiggled impatiently as he checked his list. The guard nodded.

'Hey bro,' Sandy said to the guard, as he stood up and tossed his paper on to the seat of his chair. 'Watch this for me, willya? I want to take a peek in.'

The guard nodded. 'Make it quick,' he said. Sandy followed Morgan into Claire's room.

Morgan looked across at her friend in the hospital bed. Claire was lying still, just as she had been for days, her eyes closed.

Morgan's heart plummeted, and she turned on Sandy, who was behind her. 'Is this a bad joke?' she demanded.

Sandy walked around the foot of the bed and gazed at Claire. 'Don't panic. She's just resting. Claire,' he said, in a slightly louder voice. 'Wake up, you.'

Claire's eyelids fluttered and she looked up at Sandy. The first smile Morgan had seen on Claire's face for a long time lit up her dark eyes, her jaundiced complexion. 'Hey,' she said.

'Hey yourself,' said Sandy, beaming. 'I brought someone.' Claire turned her head and saw Morgan approaching the side of her bed. She lifted a limp hand. Morgan reached out and grabbed it. Claire met Morgan's anxious gaze with a small smile, and then she closed her eyes again and sighed.

Sandy, in an uncharacteristically chivalrous gesture, pulled the visitor's chair around to where Morgan stood. 'Here. You two have a visit. I'll be outside.'

Morgan sat down in the visitor's chair. When she tried

to release Claire's hand, so she could arrange her coat under her, Claire squeezed her hand and wouldn't let go.

'All right. OK,' said Morgan. 'Don't worry. I'm here.'

'I'm so sorry,' said Claire. 'About the funeral.'

'It's all right. It doesn't matter,' said Morgan. 'As long as you're all right.'

Tears trickled down the sides of Claire's face. 'I just felt like there was no hope. When I saw the two of them lying there. They were my heart...'

'I know,' said Morgan soothingly, rubbing her hand. 'I know.'

For a few moments, the only sound in the room was Claire's shuddering sobs. Then, with a great effort, she took a deep breath. 'The doctor says I'll be OK,' she said.

'That's great,' said Morgan.

'Well enough to go back to jail,' said Claire.

Morgan leaned forward, still gripping Claire's hand. 'Claire, listen to me. I have a lot to talk to you about and not a lot of time.'

Claire nodded. 'OK,' she said dully.

'Claire...Father Lawrence told me that you refused to confess. He told me that you said that you no longer believed you were guilty.'

Claire sighed. 'That's true. But what difference does it make now? I confessed to the police.'

'But you meant it, that you are innocent. Right?'

Claire grimaced. 'It's complicated...'

'No, no. Don't start that. Claire, I've been over the tape of your confession with an expert. He studied it with me,' Morgan said urgently. 'He thinks that you were coerced into making a false confession.'

Claire shook her head on the pillow. 'I was so confused about everything.'

'Did the police tell you that Guy had accused you before he died?' Morgan asked.

A spot of color appeared in each of Claire's cheeks. 'Yes,' she whispered.

'Well, that's not true,' said Morgan.

Claire shook her head, as if she did not understand what Morgan was saying.

'Guy was dead before the police got there. He never said anything.'

'But why would they say that if it wasn't true?'

Morgan glanced back at the door, afraid the guard might be there, might be listening. 'They tricked you,' Morgan said.

'But Morgan, I did…kill Guy,' Claire said. 'I didn't mean to…'

'Tell me what you remember.'

'He came in the bathroom. Drew was in the tub. I was trying to get him out. And Guy…He was yelling at me, trying to push me away from my baby…' Claire let out a great sob.

'You struggled,' said Morgan. 'He fell and hit his head.' Claire began to weep, nodding. Her chest, the bandages visible at the top of her hospital gown, began to heave with her sobs. 'The floor was wet. He slipped. There was blood everywhere. Morgan, I loved him. You know that.'

'I know that. And that was not a crime, sweetie,' said Morgan. 'That was an accident.'

Claire pointed feebly to the Kleenex box on the rolling tray behind Morgan. Morgan grabbed a handful of tissues and gave them to her. Claire dabbed in a clumsy fashion at her eyes.

'As for the baby,' said Morgan. She hesitated. She

didn't want to put words in her friend's mouth. She needed to hear what Claire remembered.

Claire began to sob harder at the mention of Drew. 'I took a pill that night to sleep. Something woke me up. I went to the bassinet but he wasn't there. I was frantic. I ran into the bathroom and found him…like that. I don't know how it happened. What kind of a mother am I, anyway? How could I not have realized… Oh, no one will believe me. But I didn't hurt my baby. I would never hurt my baby,' she hiccuped through her sobs. 'I couldn't…'

Morgan got up and leaned over the bedside bars, clutching her friend in an awkward embrace. 'I know you couldn't,' she whispered.

Claire grasped Morgan as if she would never let go. Morgan gradually extricated herself and sat back down in the chair, letting Claire's sobs subside. After a few minutes Claire looked at her, sniffling. 'What happened to Drew? Who would have wanted to hurt my baby?' Claire asked.

Morgan didn't want to blurt out what she had learned about Guy. She approached it cautiously. 'Did Guy have any…enemies? Anyone you thought might have a… grudge against him?'

Claire shook her head on the pillow and dabbed at her eyes. 'No,' she said hopelessly. 'Everyone liked him. Everyone…well, most everyone…'

Morgan's heart beat faster. 'Who are you thinking of?'

'Morgan no. I don't want anyone else unfairly accused,' Claire pleaded.

'I'm not accusing anyone,' Morgan protested. 'I'm just…asking.'

Claire sighed. Finally she said, 'Well, he and his sister didn't get along. But that's normal, I guess. I think she was a little…jealous of Guy. You know. It's understandable. And Guy always said that Astrid spoiled Lucy. Because of her condition. Babied her.'

Morgan felt stunned, appalled by her own blindness. Of course, she thought. Lucy had gone off collecting shells rather than be with her family after Guy and Drew died. Eden had stayed with Lucy before the funeral when they might have talked about Guy. Lucy, who wanted a baby and was scornful of Claire's depression. Suddenly, Morgan remembered Lucy's face when they met at the beach and Lucy said to her, 'My brother doesn't care who he hurts.'

Morgan had thought it was about being teased, being bullied. 'What are you thinking?' Claire said weakly.

Lucy, Morgan thought.

The prison guard appeared in the doorway to the room. 'OK, miss,' he said. 'Better be going.'

Morgan stood up and gave Claire's hand one last squeeze. 'I have to go. Don't worry,' she said. 'I'll be back.'

TWENTY-EIGHT

LUCY'S HOUSE WAS HIDDEN from view by overgrown trees at the corner of a street in a quiet residential neighborhood. It took Morgan several turns around the block before she was sure that she had the right house. The first time Morgan passed by it, she saw a short, dark-skinned man working by himself in a garden, cutting stems of marigolds and placing them in a gardening basket. He looked like one of Dick Bolton's work crew of Mexicans, possibly sent over to Lucy's house to tend the yard. Morgan thought of asking him for the house number, but assumed that he probably didn't speak English. But as she circled the block, she realized that there was no one else around to ask. She made up her mind to pull up and ask the man if knew where number 237 was. She could still remember enough grammar school Spanish to be able to inquire for a house number.

But the next time she rounded the block, the man was nowhere to be seen. Morgan hesitated. She felt pretty certain that the modest house, hidden in the trees, must be Lucy's. She rolled to a stop in front of it, and almost immediately she heard the frantic barking of dogs. This had to be it, she thought. She parked her car and got out. She could see the roof of a white vehicle in the garage. There was no mailbox, but there was a mail slot in the front door, and Morgan saw, as she approached the house, that there were numbers over the door. They were a dull gold color, and hidden by the shadow of the porch roof.

Number 237. This was it. Morgan walked up on to the front porch and knocked. Inside the house, the dogs increased their barking. As she stood waiting, Morgan could not help noticing that the windows were grimy and the front porch light was broken. The house had an uncared-for look, despite the earlier presence of the gardener.

As she had circled the block, she had noticed that a few of the better-kept houses were decorated for Halloween. The ghosts, spiderwebs and witches had the odd effect of making those houses look friendly and inviting. Lucy's house had no pumpkins or goblins to lure the children in. Most kids, Morgan thought, would scurry quickly by this house, with its barking dogs and unwelcoming façade. Instead, beside the front door was a single battered rocking chair with a filthy sheepskin dog bed beside it, and, at eye level, several hooks which held dogs' leashes and choke chains.

From inside the house, Morgan could hear Lucy's voice, chiding the dogs and urging them away from the door. She stood back from the door and waited, as Lucy opened it, and looked out through the storm door at her uninvited guest. Lucy was wearing a stained red apron appliquéd with autumn leaves over her shapeless fleece pants and matching shirt. The dogs leapt up beside her, adding to the accumulation of smears on the inside of the storm door. 'Morgan,' Lucy exclaimed in surprise.

Morgan started to open the storm door, but Lucy shook her head. 'Don't do that. The dogs'll get out.'

'Can't you hold them? I really need to talk to you,' said Morgan.

Lucy shook her head. 'It's not a good time,' she said.

Conscious that she was bluffing, Morgan took a hard tone. 'Look,' she said, 'I don't care if this is a good time or not. This is important. I saw Eden. She told me about Guy. I want some answers.'

Lucy blinked owlishly at Morgan from behind her glasses. 'Told you what about Guy?' she asked.

'I think you know,' she said. 'Not something one would forget.'

To her surprise and relief, Lucy sighed, and her shoulders slumped. She gazed back into the depths of her house with a look of resignation, and stood there, unmoving, as if she were making up her mind. For one terrible moment, thinking that Lucy may have been the victim of Guy's crime, Morgan was almost sorry to be forcing Lucy into this position. But Morgan felt as if she had no choice.

'Come on, Lucy. Let me in. I need to talk to you.'

'Just a minute,' Lucy grumbled. Bending over, she grabbed each of the dogs by the collar, and turned them around, dragging the protesting beasts away from the front door. Morgan jiggled the handle of the storm door but it was locked. For a minute, she thought that Lucy was just going to walk away and leave her there. But there was a sudden muffling of the barking, and then Lucy appeared in the doorway, unlocking the storm door and pushing it out. She did not look at Morgan.

Morgan opened the storm door and followed Lucy into the house. The house had a stale, stuffy smell that was partly doggy. But there was also a cloying odor. It took Morgan a minute to recognize the smell of incense burning. The combination of smells was suffocating. Morgan had to gulp back the bile that she felt rising to her throat.

Although Lucy was still a young woman in her early thirties, the house looked like it had been furnished by her grandmother. The fabrics which covered the furniture were dowdy, with anemically pale watercolor flowers. The stuffing was coming out of the sofa arms. The pale blue shag rug was frowzy from the dogs'claws and table surfaces were scratched. Everywhere in the room were crafts made from shells. A box on the coffee table, a picture frame which held a family photo atop the television, an empty vase on the mantle. There was something oddly touching about Lucy's display of her creations. Obviously, she was proud of her work. Morgan could hear the sound of rushing water from somewhere in the house. The dogs had been shut behind a closed door, which, given the size of the house, probably led to the dining room, and they were baying with displeasure. Abruptly, the sound of the rushing water stopped. Lucy did not seem to notice. She did not offer Morgan a seat. 'All right,' said Lucy. 'Go ahead and talk.'

Morgan looked at the small, plain woman with blond hair that barely concealed her scalp. Lucy seemed so alone. Was it her brother's cruelty which had caused her retreat from the world? It was one thing to lose your mother at a young age. Morgan knew all about that from first-hand experience. But it was another thing altogether to be the victim of a sexual predator. A family member. Was that what had happened to Lucy, she wondered?

'Well?' Lucy prompted her. 'When did you see Eden?'

'I'm house-sitting right now at the Captain's House,' Morgan explained. 'Last night Eden showed up there.'

'I thought you were going to leave town after the funeral,' Lucy said.

Morgan ignored the remark. 'Claire is still in the hospital. Look, Lucy, some new evidence.' Morgan stopped, and then continued. 'It's now apparent that whoever killed Guy and Claire's baby, it was not Claire…'

Lucy immediately bristled. 'That's stupid. She confessed.'

'It turns out that Claire was tricked into making that confession.'

'Tricked,' Lucy scoffed. 'Into admitting to murder? What next?'

Morgan remained calm. 'Somebody else drowned that baby in the bathtub. I don't know why. But when Eden told me about what Guy had done, it struck me as a possible reason.'

Lucy looked at her balefully and then looked away. 'Look, this subject may be horribly painful for you, and if it is, I'm sorry...'

'I don't know what you're talking about,' Lucy insisted.

'If he did that to you, Lucy, no one would blame you for hating him. For wanting to hurt him. Or his baby.'

'I'm not the one he raped, if that's what you're asking,' said Lucy bluntly.

Morgan felt an undeniable relief, both that the subject was out in the open, and that Lucy had not been Guy's victim. 'I'm glad to hear that. I was afraid it might have been you.'

'You thought I killed the baby?' Lucy exclaimed.

Morgan hesitated. 'No, I thought you might have been Guy's victim.'

'Well, I wasn't. Now will you leave?' Lucy asked.

'But you're quite sure that your brother did rape someone,' said Morgan.

Lucy looked back at Morgan, her gaze flickering, as if she was trying to make a decision. Finally she said, 'Positive.'

'Did you hear this from his victim?'

'I was there.'

Morgan felt shocked by the bald statement. 'My God. Lucy.' Suddenly, there was a thud from the direction of the closed door, and one of the dogs let out an ungodly shriek.

'Oh, no,' said Lucy.

From behind the door an accented male voice called out, 'Lucia, Lucia, the dogs. Quick. They knocking it over. The altar.'

'What's going on?' Morgan asked.

Lucy did not reply. She turned and hurried toward the dining room door, throwing it open. Morgan followed close behind her. One of the dogs bolted out, yelping frantically, and began to tear around the living room in circles. Lucy called his name and tried to catch up with him. Morgan looked past her into the dining room and her eyes widened at what she saw.

A small, dark-skinned man with the features of a Mayan, his coal black hair wet and combed back, as if he had just stepped out of the shower, was trying to right an elaborate construction which had been upended on to the dining room floor. He was barefoot, dressed in a sleeveless T-shirt and ill-fitting black pants, and he looked bashfully at Morgan who was gaping at the scene. Then, he went back to his task. The floor was littered with bunches of marigolds, thick sputtering candles and fruit which had rolled out everywhere across the floor. The man was resetting an arch made out of cornstalks against the tower of empty wooden boxes he had reassembled.

Lucy finally convinced the most frantic dog to settle down, and she was on her knees on the floor beside him, combing through his fur. 'Julio, it's wax,' she called out. 'He got hot candle wax on him when the altar collapsed. Poor baby.'

'He knock it all over,' Julio grumbled. He set a small, framed photo of a dark-haired, matronly woman on the makeshift altar. Then he began to dust off a picture of baby Drew in a shell-decorated picture frame. He set it next to the other photo.

'You're OK, you bad dog,' scolded Lucy peeling the wax off his fur, but her tone was indulgent.

Morgan looked again at the Mexican man who was carefully replacing the food, flowers, candles and incense on the flimsy construction. 'What is this?' Morgan asked him.

'It's ah…Dios de los muertos,' he said. 'This week.'

'It's an altar. For the Day of the Dead,' said Lucy, standing up and letting the dogs loose. 'Julio, you better put them upstairs. In our room,' she said. 'We don't want them to knock it over again. They didn't break the sugar skulls, did they?'

'I no see them,' the man said, looking around.

'They were on the table,' said Lucy.

Julio glanced around and then let out a small, triumphant cry. He lifted a flat, narrow box from the dining room table. Four white skulls nestled in the box against a black velvet background.

'Mira. Everything's OK,' Julio exclaimed.

'Oh, good. I'd hate to have to start them all over again,' said Lucy.

Morgan had not missed the words 'our room'. But she pretended to take no notice. She looked in at the box of skulls on the table. 'These are made of sugar?' she asked.

'Yeah. You make them in a mold.' Lucy gazed at her defiantly. 'Julio wanted them. The holiday's not the same without them. I found the recipe on the internet.'

'I see,' said Morgan.

'I bet you do,' said Lucy.

Morgan looked at her directly. 'Look, I'm not trying to meddle in your business, Lucy. I just want to know about Guy.'

Lucy sighed, and, as Julio led the dogs to the staircase,

she sat down heavily and pointed to the other chair. 'You may as well sit,' she said.

Morgan sat down on the edge of the chair.

Lucy did not meet her gaze. 'Julio washes dishes at the Lobster Shack. If my father finds out about this,' said Lucy, shaking her head.

'He won't hear it from me,' said Morgan.

Lucy sighed. 'He's got to know sooner or later,' she said.

'You're a grown woman,' said Morgan. 'You can see whoever you want.'

Lucy looked at her wearily. 'It's a little more than seeing,' she said. 'We got married a few weeks ago.'

'Married?' said Morgan, trying to conceal how truly surprised she was. 'Your family doesn't know?'

She lifted one shoulder helplessly. 'I told Astrid, of course.'

'Astrid won't tell your father?' Morgan asked.

'My father would try to have the marriage annulled. Get his visa taken away.'

'You never know. Maybe your father will be happy for you,' said Morgan.

'My father? Hah,' Lucy laughed without mirth. 'Astrid thinks Julio and I should head back to Mexico. And live there,' Lucy mused. 'I don't really want to go but I have to do something before my dad finds out. Astrid won't tell him. She knows how to keep a secret.'

'From her own husband?' said Morgan.

Lucy sat quietly for a moment. 'Sometimes you have to. Although I'll never know how Astrid did it all these years. How she kept it from my dad.'

Morgan frowned. 'Kept what from your dad?'

'What Guy did...'

It took Morgan a moment to understand. Then her

eyes widened. 'Wait a minute. Are you saying that it was Astrid that Guy…?'

Lucy nodded, frowning. 'Yes.'

'When did this happen?' Morgan said.

'A really long time ago,' said Lucy. She hesitated, uncertain whether to elaborate, and then she seemed to make up her mind. 'About a year after my dad and Astrid got married. Of course, I was…freaked out when they got married so fast. But Astrid was so good. She took care of me like my own mother. I started liking her, but not Guy. Guy hated them both.'

'One day I skipped my swimming lesson and I was in my room. I heard somebody crying. So, I went to the door of my room and I looked out, and Guy was walking down the hall, tucking his shirt in his pants. He didn't see me. I wanted to ask him who was crying but I knew he'd just make fun of me. I kept quiet and let him go.

'But I could still hear the crying. I went down the hall to their room. My father and Astrid's. Astrid was sitting alone on the floor and she was sobbing. It was like somebody died. Her clothes were all pulled down and messed up. She grabbed my father's bathrobe and put it over her when she saw me in the doorway.'

Morgan recoiled from the image. Guy Bolton did that? She was overcome with the feeling that she had never known him at all. 'She told you that Guy raped her?'

Lucy shook her head. 'Not right away, but finally she admitted it. She was just worried about *me* being upset. I wasn't upset. I was just so mad at Guy. I mean, next to my mother, and Julio, I love Astrid more than anyone.'

'I wanted to call my father and tell him what Guy did. First she said, "Yes. Call him." Then, just when I got him on the phone she shook her head. Told me to hang up. I didn't understand it, but I hung up. She said we couldn't tell. She made me promise. She said my father would kill Guy if he knew.

'I didn't care 'cause I thought Guy should be punished, but she said, no, that my dad went through enough. My mother's death and all. She said we had to protect my dad. So, we did.'

Despite the stuffiness of the house, Morgan was shivering. 'God. What a terrible thing to live with,' she said.

'It was worse for Astrid. She did forgive him though. Somehow. So, about Claire's baby—don't go thinking that Astrid wanted some kind of revenge on Guy. That's not the way she is. Lots of times after that I'd see him treat her bad or snap at her, and I'd get so mad I wanted to strangle him. But not Astrid. She turned the other cheek. Astrid isn't like other people.'

'And you never told.'

Lucy shook her head. 'No. I never forgave him. But I never told. Not till I told Eden. I wouldn't have told you, but you already knew…'

Morgan frowned. 'Why tell Eden? Why now?'

When Lucy looked at Morgan her eyes were bitter. 'She was so sad about missing all those years with Guy. I wanted her to know what he was really like. I wanted her to know that she was better off growing up without him.'

'But weren't you worried that, once you told her, it might get back to your father?'

'No one'll tell my father that,' Lucy scoffed. 'Who's going to tell him that about his dead son? No. It's too late for that.'

TWENTY-NINE

MORGAN TOOK THE MEANDERING coast road back in order to have a chance to clear her head. Her spirit was soothed by an occasional glimpse of the sea. But her heart was in a tumult, remembering the appalling story she had heard from Lucy. As she drove along, she realized that she was approaching the Lobster Shack. She had assumed it would be closed, due to the family's traumatic bereavement, as well as the end of the tourist season, but she could see that there were several cars in the small parking lot, and her heart did a surprising flip when she realized that one of the cars belonged to Fitz. He was back, earlier than he had intended to be. She recognized the car, with its Sea-hawks Wrestling sticker, from the night he had driven her to Oliver Douglas's house. She also remembered it from the night of Guy and Claire's wedding, when they had fallen on one another, their formal wear unbuttoned and undone, in the back seat.

Morgan hesitated, and then impulsively pulled into the lot beside his car and parked. The Lobster Shack was an old craftsman's cottage which had, long ago, been mini-mally renovated to accommodate the larger kitchen and tables necessary for a luncheonette. Now that she was in front of the funky old seaside spot, she suddenly realized how hungry she was. Ravenous, in fact.

Morgan got out of the car and went inside, pretend-ing not to look for Fitz as she entered. She hoped that he would spot her. Call out to her. But no one called out, and she was forced to look up, to find herself a table. There were only a couple of tables in the tiny place, and two other customers. She did not see Fitz. Where is he, she wondered? She was certain that she had been right about his car. A young waitress in jeans and a T-shirt arrived promptly at her table and Morgan glanced at the menu, feeling foolish and let down. She decided to get something to go.

'I'll have a pint of that corn and lobster chowder,' she said to the girl.

'We don't have the chowder,' said the waitress. 'That's the weekend special.'

'Oh,' said Morgan, frowning. 'Well, this sandwich plate. To go,' she said.

'You got it,' said the girl, disappearing back into the kitchen. Morgan turned in her chair and gazed out the windows of the restaurant which gave out on to the ocean. There were a couple of tables beyond the windows, on the open-air patio beneath the now empty metal frame which supported a canvas awning in summer. Morgan saw two men huddled at one of the tables. It only took her a moment to recognize Fitz and Dick Bolton. They were both dressed in casual jackets, hands stuffed in their pockets, their backs to the shack, looking out to sea. Fitz would glance occasionally at the older man, uttering something, and then would go back to looking out across the sand to the waves. The breeze off the ocean had blown Fitz's curls back from his face, and Morgan noticed, with a little flash of desire, the elegant curve of his cheekbone when he turned his face to talk to Dick. If Dick replied to him, she could not tell. The older man's shoulders were hunched, as if against the chill. Maybe they would come in soon, and see her sitting there, she thought.

'Hey, Morgan,' said a gentle voice.

Morgan jumped and looked up as Astrid approached the table from behind the counter. Like the waitress, she was wearing a T-shirt and jeans which looked well on her slim figure, and her white-gold braids were pinned loosely to the top of her head. She might have passed for a young woman, but for the deep lines in her face, and the dark circles under her eyes. Looking at her, Morgan could not help thinking of what she had heard from Lucy. Astrid, concealing her stepson's crime to save the family. Forgiving the unforgivable. Or had she forgiven him, Morgan wondered.

'Astrid,' Morgan said in surprise. 'I'm surprised to see you here.'

Astrid shrugged, and sat down in the chair opposite Morgan at the table. She looked at her husband sitting out on the patio. 'I guess Dick and I felt the need to get back to where we started. This place...' She gazed around at the yellowed walls, the red checkered oilcloth on the tables. 'This is where we worked when we first got married. When the kids were young. Before Lobster Shack Seafood took off. I guess we needed to...' Astrid raised one shoulder and her voice trailed off.

'I understand,' said Morgan. 'Back to basics. Kind of a sentimental journey.'

'Kind of,' Astrid agreed. 'Sorry about the chowder you wanted. I just put the pot on with the stock.'

'It doesn't matter. I'm sure everything here is good,' said Morgan. A little silence fell between them. 'I see Fitz is out there talking to Dick,' Morgan said.

'Yeah. Fitz is a good boy,' said Astrid. 'He was Guy's best...' Her voice broke and she struggled to control her tears.

Morgan studied Astrid, puzzled by her grief. It was

hard to imagine after what Guy had done to her. For one moment, Morgan wondered if Astrid's grief was all for show, just a façade. But then she decided that it wasn't possible. No one could fake that sort of misery. Perhaps this is just what people meant by a mother's boundless love for her children?

Astrid glanced at Morgan. 'You're looking at me in a funny way,' she said.

'Oh, no. I'm sorry. I didn't mean to,' said Morgan. 'I was just thinking that Lucy and Guy were…lucky to have a stepmother who cared so much for them.'

Astrid raised her small chin, and her pale lavender eyes glittered with tears. 'I didn't have any children of my own,' she said. 'I wasn't that lucky. But I have loved the ones who were given to me.'

Morgan nodded, feeling uncomfortable. Had Guy begged her forgiveness somewhere along the line? Had he made amends, she wondered? Keeping an eye on the outside table, Morgan noticed, with relief, that the two men had stood up and were coming inside. Dick pulled the door open and entered the tiny restaurant. 'It's freezing out there,' Dick said, shuddering.

Astrid stood up and wiped her hands on the front of her jeans. 'Come back in the kitchen,' she said. 'That's warm.'

Dick noticed Morgan sitting at the small table and frowned. Before he could say anything, Fitz also noticed her. 'Morgan,' he exclaimed. 'Hey!'

Morgan smiled at his obvious pleasure. 'You're back,' she said.

Astrid nudged Dick in the direction of the kitchen, and Dick, after a moment's reluctance, followed his wife's lead.

Fitz came over to the small table, just as the waitress appeared, carrying a brown bag with Morgan's sandwich.

'What's this?' he said.

'Take out,' said Morgan.

'Good! Take it outside to the patio. It's not that cold. I swear. Dick's just a little bit…susceptible, after all that's happened.'

Morgan nodded, pretending to be torn, but actually she was delighted by his impromptu invitation. 'OK,' she said. 'Why not?'

Fitz asked the waitress to bring him some lunch as well, and then he held the door open for Morgan and followed her out to the patio. It was, indeed, a beautiful day, and the sun was warm on them, even though the air was chilly. From the patio, their view of the dunes and the ocean was unencumbered. The sky looked like a baffled quilt of smoky cotton wool, tossed out toward the horizon. The sunlight was diffused and shone, lacy and golden, through the clouds. Beyond the tall brown beach grass studded with persistent stalks of goldenrod she could see blue-gray water breaking on silver sand. Seabirds wheeled and dove into the waves, and salt spray flew up over the shiny, dark rocks which formed a jetty. Morgan took a seat and Fitz sat close beside her. Morgan could feel his gaze on her, and she tried not to blush.

'So what have you been up to while I was away?' he asked.

Morgan said, 'I've been busy. I took your advice and asked Noreen Quick to intervene on testing the evidence.'

'Really?' he said, clearly pleased by this. 'How did it work out?'

'Good,' said Morgan. 'Great, really. She listened to me, and she agreed to file some kind of petition about testing the evidence.'

'Great. That's great,' said Fitz.

'Thanks to you, and Professor Douglas, I think there's some hope for Claire.'

'I still can't imagine who would want to drown a baby,' Fitz said, shaking his head.

Morgan jammed her hands in her coat pockets to keep them warm and felt the outline of the scissors she had taken from Claire's house. 'That's the million dollar question,' Morgan said. 'I was remembering that those balloons from the christening were still on the mailbox. They as much as announced that there was a baby in the house. It could have been…some weirdo. A stranger.'

Fitz shook his head. 'That doesn't seem very likely.'

'Well, we don't know yet,' said Morgan.

'Do you still think it might have been Eden?' he asked.

Morgan shook her head. 'No. I really don't.'

'I'd still like to know,' he said, 'why she was so mad at Guy.'

The waitress emerged, carrying Fitz's lunch and set it down in front of him. She was shivering without any jacket. Her nipples, erect from the chill, showed through the thin T-shirt. 'Anything else?' she asked.

Fitz gave her his winning smile and pressed a bill into her hand. 'No, we're good. This is for both of us. Keep the change. You better get back inside. You'll catch a cold in that.' Morgan felt a completely inappropriate stab of jealousy. The girl thanked him and gladly headed back in. Morgan opened her take-out bag, and the two ate in silence for a moment. Morgan wanted to tell him what she had learned about Guy. But it was difficult to find a way to say it. Suddenly he said, in a tone that was playfully chiding, 'You should have called me while I was at the camp. You knew I was interested.'

Morgan put down her sandwich and wiped her fingers. 'I…didn't have your number.'

'Where's your phone?' he demanded.

Morgan smiled. 'In my pocket.'

'Give it to me,' he insisted.

'Why?' she said. But she reached into her pocket and handed it over to him.

Fitz took the phone from her and began to fiddle with the keypad. 'Because I am going to take care of that. There. Now I'm number one on your speed-dial.'

'What?' Morgan demanded, not wanting to admit that she was flattered.

Fitz handed the phone back to her. 'I was thinking a lot about you while I was gone.'

Morgan had not expected such an unguarded admission. 'You were?' she said.

Fitz wolfed his sandwich down, and brushed the crumbs off his hands. 'Yup.'

'What were you thinking?' Morgan asked. She suddenly felt unable to eat another bite. She stuffed the remains of the sandwich back into the brown bag.

'You done with that?' Fitz asked.

Morgan nodded.

'Here, give it to me,' he said. He took the bag and tossed it into the trash receptacle on the patio. 'Let's take a little walk,' he said.

'OK,' said Morgan.

Fitz jumped off the edge of the patio into the sand below and he held up a hand to Morgan. She took it, and he helped her down. When she was beside him in the sand, he kept a hold on her hand. She thought of pulling it away, but she didn't. They began to walk down toward the jetty, their hands linked. She was hyperaware of his warm fingers, dry and rough, entwined with her own. She wondered what he had been intending to say, when he mentioned thinking about her. He did not keep her guessing.

'I was thinking that you and I kind of…got things backwards.'

Morgan's cheeks flamed. She knew he was referring to their wedding-day tryst in the car. 'I guess we did,' she said.

'I was thinking I'd like to get to know you now,' he said. He looked at her, waiting for her to meet his gaze.

She met it for a second and looked away. She knew she wasn't as brave as he was. 'That's an idea,' she mumbled.

'Hey, come on. Don't look surprised. You're beautiful and you're smart. And sexy. And I admire you. For the kind of friend you are.'

She knew that she should probably tell him all about her thoughts and theories, but all she wanted, suddenly, was to hear him say more about her, about them.

'Thanks,' she said. She felt tongue-tied, as if she couldn't think of a single thing to say. 'Really. That's… really good to hear.'

Fitz squeezed her hand in his. 'Now that Guy's gone,' he said, 'I don't have a friend I could count on like that.'

'About Guy…' she said.

Fitz frowned at her. 'What about him?'

'Well, I found out why Eden was so angry with him,' she said.

'Really? Why?'

Morgan pressed her lips together. Fitz had stopped walking. 'What was it?' he insisted.

She looked at him warily. 'It turns out that Guy…' She felt a sudden pang of guilt. He was looking at her so innocently. She thought about stopping or changing the subject, but, at the same time, she knew it was too late. She was going to have to tell him. 'Someone told me—

and please don't ask me who—that Guy…raped someone.
When he was younger.'

She expected him to ask who it was and where she
had heard this. She wondered if he already knew. He said
nothing, but he dropped her hand.

'That is completely…insane,' said Fitz.

'I'm afraid it's true,' said Morgan.

Fitz shook his head uncomprehendingly. There was a
mixture of disgust and disbelief in his eyes. 'You have
got to be kidding.'

'I'm not,' she said. 'Believe me, I heard it from a reli-
able source.'

Fitz abruptly turned away from her and began to march
through the sand back to the Lobster Shack patio.

Morgan hurried to catch up with him. 'Wait a minute,'
she called after him. 'Wait.'

Fitz climbed up on to the patio and was reaching for
the door handle when Morgan scrambled back up on to
the patio. 'Fitz,' she said. 'I didn't make this up. I'm just
telling you what I heard.'

Fitz wheeled around, glaring at her. 'You really don't
get it, do you?' said Fitz. 'You're talking about my closest
friend. I knew Guy. He would never do that. Never. What
you're saying is a complete and utter lie. Can I make it
any clearer?' he shouted.

Morgan saw Astrid and the waitress behind the windows, looking out, drawn by the sudden commotion on
the patio. They were both frowning, looking concerned.

'Keep your voice down,' said Morgan.

'I don't have to keep my voice down,' he shouted pointing a finger at her. 'First you were trying to pin this on
Eden. That was before you started claiming that Guy
spent his life tormenting his helpless little sister. And

now, you're spreading filth around here about a man who can't even defend himself.

'You're so busy trying to find a scapegoat. Anybody will do. Why don't you pick on somebody who can fight back? Hell, pick on me, why don't you? Maybe I killed the baby. Yeah, how 'bout that,' he cried sarcastically. 'I did it. I didn't want Guy to have to miss his poker night because the baby was crying. That's right. I was the one. Why not? One fall guy is as good as another. Go ahead. Find a way to blame it on me.'

Morgan stood still, frozen in place by his outburst. She did not meet his furious gaze. She wanted to tell him to go and speak to Lucy, but she didn't dare. She knew he was in no mood for her suggestions.

Fitz grabbed the doorknob to the shack and pulled it so hard that it banged back against the patio railing. He strode inside without a backward glance.

Morgan was not about to follow him. She hesitated, looking around the patio. There were a set of steps on the side nearest the parking area. She pulled her jacket tight around her, and fled to her car.

THIRTY

MORGAN WANTED TO JUST RUN back to the Captain's House and hide, but she forced herself to stop by the hospital instead, to see Claire. However, that proved not only impossible, but utterly dispiriting. Claire had been moved back to the infirmary at the county jail, and wasn't allowed visitors until the following day. Morgan returned to West Briar feeling as if she was being punished at every turn for trying to do what was right. She arrived at the Captain's House as the late afternoon darkness was descending, and let herself in to the drafty house.

Morgan turned one lamp on beside the sofa, and sat down, pulling the white afghan up over her. She was shivering from head to toe, and wanted to turn the heat up, but she had promised Paula Spaulding she would keep it low, and so she remained huddled under the blanket, feeling miserable both in body and in spirit.

Fitz's scorn still blistered her heart, all the more so because she had allowed herself to start musing about him while he was away. Why did you do that, she chided herself? It was probably just a reaction to finding out about Simon's sexual orientation. Understandable, she told herself, because she knew that Fitz was straight, and that he had, at one point, desired her. And today, at the Lobster Shack, she had felt that sexual current between them again when he was teasing her about her phone, holding her hand. But that was history now.

A needy part of her wanted to call him, and another

part of her was angry at his reaction. Have a backbone, she told herself. Why would you care what this guy thinks of you? She thought about how cruelly he had mocked her effort to find the truth. His accusation that she was looking for a scapegoat. If that was how he chose to see her, then so be it. She didn't need Fitz in her life anyway. They couldn't seem to get along for more than about five minutes at a time.

Still, disappointment weighed on Morgan's heart. Maybe it was time to go back to Brooklyn, try to figure her life out, and let the legal system take its course. She was tired of digging around in people's secrets, and earning nothing but contempt for it. She thought longingly of her apartment, which overlooked Prospect Park. She could call up a couple of friends, other grad students, and get together for Thai food. Perhaps she could replan her trip. It wasn't too late to get her life back. But even as she longed for all these things, the thought of Claire, lying in the prison infirmary, haunted her, and held her. If she gave up the fight for Claire's innocence, who would be here to help her?

A knock on the door interrupted her thoughts. Reluctantly, she got up off the couch and went over to open it. Astrid stood on the front porch, bundled in a short, wool walking coat and knit gloves, holding a paper bag from which steam and a wonderful smell was rising.

'Astrid,' said Morgan. 'What's this?'

'This,' said Astrid, holding out the bag to her, 'is the pint of the chowder you wanted. I got a head start on tomorrow's batch.'

Morgan took the bag and it was warm in her hands. 'Oh, Astrid. That is so nice of you,' she said.

'Well, you know it helps me to keep busy.'

Morgan hesitated. She didn't really feel like company,

but it seemed rude not to be hospitable after Astrid had gone out of her way. 'Would you like to come in?' she asked.

Astrid shrugged. 'I guess for a few minutes.'

Morgan led the way into the kitchen.

'Cup of tea?' she asked.

Astrid nodded and Morgan turned on the kettle. Then she went to the cabinet and pulled out a mug for the tea. 'I'm going to get myself a bowl for this,' she said, pointing to the bag which contained the soup. 'Can I get you one?'

Astrid smiled and shook her head. 'No. I've been sampling it while I was cooking.'

Morgan got a teabag for Astrid's mug, and, when the kettle whistled, poured her a cup of tea. Then she brought the mug and her bowl over to the counter, and set them down. She pushed the cup across the counter to Astrid, and then took the plastic container from the bag and removed the top. She inhaled the spicy scent of the chowder. 'Oh, that smells divine.' She looked at Astrid. 'Do you mind if I dig in? I didn't really get to eat my lunch.'

'No. Please. That's what I brought it for.'

Morgan sat down on a stool across the counter from Astrid and poured the chowder into the bowl. She held her spoon over the bowl and felt the heat from it rising to warm her face. She dipped her spoon in and blew on it. Then she sipped the soup.

'I guess your lunch with Fitz didn't go too well,' said Astrid. Morgan sighed and shook her head. 'No. He was pretty mad at me.'

'So I gathered,' said Astrid. 'How come?'

Morgan concentrated on her soup. She was not about to tell Astrid what she had learned. 'Just...oil and water, I guess.'

'I had the feeling he was kind of sweet on you,' said Astrid.

Morgan shrugged. 'We have some major differences.'

'How's the chowder?' Astrid asked.

'Good,' said Morgan, eating with enthusiasm, although she found the taste to be a little bit off. Somewhat…metallic. She wondered if the lobster which Astrid had used in the soup might be turning a bit. She hoped not. The last thing she needed was a case of food poisoning.

Astrid blew on her tea and took a sip. 'I spoke to Lucy. She told me that you came by.'

Once again, Morgan kept her eyes lowered and ate her soup. 'Yeah, I stopped by her house.'

'So you know about her marriage. To Julio,' said Astrid. Morgan glanced up at Astrid. 'Yes. She told me.'

'You should be honored that she confided in you,' said Astrid.

'I was a little surprised by that,' Morgan admitted. 'It's a shame she has to keep it a secret.'

'She needs to keep it from her father,' said Astrid calmly. 'Julio has a work visa, like all of Dick's workers, but if Dick finds out about this, he'll have Julio on the next plane back to Mexico.'

'That seems so unfair,' said Morgan.

Astrid shrugged. 'Dick wants to protect Lucy. She's always been…fragile, and every milestone was difficult for her. But he doesn't get it that, if they're in love, there's nothing he can do to stop it. They'll find a way to be together. Dick doesn't think that way. He's a pragmatist when it comes to love.'

'That's a funny thing for you to say,' Morgan observed. 'Didn't you and Dick get married a couple of weeks after you met?'

'Yes, we did.'

'Well, that was a pretty romantic thing to do. Impulsive, you might say.'

Astrid sipped her tea, and avoided Morgan's gaze. 'Yes, it was. But if it hadn't been me, he would have married someone else. Some men need to be married,' she said. 'Besides, he had two children to raise all by himself.'

Astrid spoke offhandedly, but Morgan assumed there must be a lot of disappointment behind her words. 'I guess I pictured your marriage as kind of a fairy tale,' said Morgan. 'I mean, it seemed like the most romantic story when Claire told me about it.'

'In a way, it was,' said Astrid thoughtfully. Then she shook her head, as if to shake off the memories. 'That was a long time ago.'

Morgan understood that Astrid did not mean to discuss her marriage any further. 'But you're optimistic for Lucy and Julio.'

'I hope it's true love,' she said.

She's still a romantic, in spite of everything, Morgan thought. 'Don't you think that Dick wants his daughter to be happy?'

'Dick can be overbearing,' said Astrid, 'like any father, when it comes to his little girl.'

'Maybe it would be better just to tell him,' said Morgan. 'He'll get used to the idea eventually.'

Astrid's smile was sorrowful. 'Oh, you don't know my husband.'

As Morgan was looking at Astrid, she suddenly felt an odd, dizzy sensation. For a moment she felt as if she needed to grip the counter to stay upright. Then the feeling passed.

Astrid frowned at her. 'What's the matter?'

Morgan shrugged. 'Nothing. I'm fine. I'm just over-tired.'

'I'm sure you are,' said Astrid.

Morgan's phone began to ring in her pocket. She pulled it out and answered it.

Fitz's voice greeted her at the other end. 'Morgan. I need to talk to you.'

In spite of herself, Morgan was glad to hear his voice. She reminded herself that he had been very cruel and insulting. It would be foolish to let that pass without a word of apology. 'Oh?' she said calmly.

There was a silence from his end. 'What's the matter?' he said.

'Nothing,' she said.

'Are you OK?'

Morgan's stomach was beginning to roil, and her head to ache. 'Fine,' she said.

'Can I come over and see you?' he asked.

Morgan frowned, squeezing her eyes shut. It was difficult to concentrate on what he was saying. A sudden cramping in her stomach made her want to cry out. But she stifled it. 'No,' she said. 'I don't think it's a good idea. I'm tired. I need to sleep.' That seemed like the straightforward truth to her, the moment she said it.

'Tomorrow?' he said.

'I don't know,' she said. 'Call me tomorrow.'

Before he could protest, she ended the call, setting her phone down on the counter.

'Who was that?' Astrid asked. 'Fitz?'

Morgan nodded.

'He told me about the argument but I had a feeling he'd get over it.'

Morgan took a deep breath, but the stabbing pain in her stomach began again. She folded her arms over her stomach.

'Morgan, what's the matter?' Astrid asked. 'You look

pale.' Morgan hated to admit it, but she was beginning to think that she had been right about the seafood chowder. Her brain felt sluggish, and her stomach was miserable. She didn't want to insult Astrid though.

'I'm just so tired,' she said. 'I hate to be inhospitable but I really need to lie down.'

Astrid slid off the seat, and pointed to the container of chowder. 'Do you want me to put the rest of this in the fridge for you?'

Morgan felt a wave of nausea. She gagged and shook her head.

Astrid looked taken aback. 'Morgan, what is it?'

'I'm sorry,' said Morgan. 'There's something wrong with me.'

Astrid looked at the contents of the plastic container. 'You think it was the chowder?' she asked, her eyes widening.

Morgan shook her head miserably. 'I don't know,' she said. She folded her arms over her stomach and rested her forehead on the cool counter.

'Oh, Lord,' said Astrid. She took the plastic container and poured its contents down the sink, as well as the small amount of remaining soup in Morgan's bowl. She turned on the garbage disposal, and washed out the bowl, spoon and container by hand as well as her own teacup, which she dried and put back in the cabinet. 'Oh, Morgan, I am so sorry. Seafood can be tricky.'

Morgan nodded, but was feeling too ill to speak. 'I'm just going to go…' She gestured vaguely in the direction of her little room off the kitchen.

'Maybe you should go to the doctor,' said Astrid.

'I'll be fine,' said Morgan. 'It just…came over me.' Morgan forced herself to get up from the counter stool. But as soon as she took a step away from the counter, her knees suddenly felt rubbery, and she collapsed in a heap on the waxed wood floor.

'Oh, my God,' Astrid cried, rushing to Morgan's side. 'All right, that does it. You're going to the emergency room.'

'No, Astrid, really,' said Morgan, pulling herself up on the lower rungs of the stool. 'I think if I just…maybe if I throw up.'

'No, no. I read somewhere that's not always a good idea,' said Astrid. 'I forget why. Look. Come on. We're going to the hospital. Don't fight me on this. I feel so guilty. What if it was the soup?'

''S not your fault,' Morgan mumbled. Her breathing was shallow. It was difficult to catch her breath.

'No. I can't just leave you here like this,' said Astrid. 'Come on.' She threaded her thin arm under Morgan's and then around her back. 'Come on. Uppsa daisy.'

Morgan staggered to her feet like a prize fighter who had gone one round too many.

Although Astrid was wiry, she was strong, and she urged Morgan to lean against her.

'My car's just outside. We'll go. Where's your coat?' Morgan pointed to the coat rack by the front door, and Astrid went over and fetched it for her. Morgan slid her phone across the counter and into the pocket of her shirt.

'Need my bag,' said Morgan as Astrid returned.

'No, you don't. They'll just take it from you at the hospital,' said Astrid.

'My insurance…' Morgan protested.

'I'll take care of all that,' she said. 'Now, don't worry. Just let's go.'

Morgan leaned on Astrid, and her limbs felt like she was slogging through jello. Her mouth was dry and the stabbing pains in her stomach were growing more frequent, and more severe. Astrid opened the front door, and the blast of chilly air made Morgan shake all over. Slowly, Astrid guided her down the steps and into her car which was parked at the curb. Morgan collapsed into the passenger seat, and rested her head against the cold windowpane.

'Put on your seat belt,' said Astrid.

It took all of Morgan's strength to pull the belt over her and fasten it at the waist. She could feel drool coming out of her mouth, but she was powerless to stop it.

'All right,' said Astrid. 'You just take it easy. We'll be at the hospital in no time.'

'Astrid,' Morgan muttered, her tongue thick. 'Thank you.'

'Don't thank me,' said Astrid. 'I'm afraid that if it weren't for my chowder, you wouldn't be in this condition.'

Morgan closed her eyes and rested her head against the cold glass. The car began to move, and they were on the road. Morgan felt the torpor enveloping her, while her stomach was being assaulted by pains. She wanted to sleep. Sleep seemed like the only answer. From far away, she heard a familiar song.

'What's that?' Astrid asked, frowning.

Morgan realized that it was her cellphone ringing in her shirt pocket. 'My phone,' she said. She fumbled for it, and pulled it out, opening the phone with wooden fingers and holding it to her ear.

'Hello...' she mumbled.

'Is this Morgan Adair?'

'Yes...'tis.'

'Did I wake you up?' asked a velvety voice, sounding puzzled.

'NO. I'm...sick,' Morgan said.

'Oh. I'm so sorry. This is Jaslene Walker. You left me a message at my company saying you were a friend of Eden's? You said it was important. And I have not had a free moment. I don't know if Eden told you but I am a shoe designer and I have a show coming up, and the problems I have been having this time...'

Morgan felt like she was hearing the breezy chatter from far away. The voice on the phone evoked a mental image of a vibrant black woman with broad features and dreadlocks and the relaxed delivery of a person who spent a lot of time cajoling people on the phone. Morgan felt as if, when she opened her eyes, she would see this woman sitting beside her. 'Yes. Eden told me,' she said, as coherently as she could.

'Should I call you back when you're feeling better?'

'It's OK,' said Morgan. Her head was aching, pounding.

'What did you want to know about?' asked Jaslene. Morgan remembered that she had called Jaslene about the rape story. Wondering if Jaslene had been the one to tell Eden. But now she knew it had been Lucy. 'Ah, it was nothing,' said Morgan. She was eager to hang up. Her head was pounding and her lips were so dry she could barely speak. 'Sorry I bothered you.'

'How's Eden doing? Did she get home all right?' asked Jaslene.

Morgan searched her mind for what to say. She was unable to make a long explanation. She couldn't manage to be that coherent. 'Yes. Fine,' she said.

'Well, I was so glad to meet her at last. She just loved being in Manhattan. I tried to talk her into staying and trying her luck, but she was determined to go back to that awful place.'

Morgan felt confused. She had blanked out for a

moment and forgotten who this voice on the phone belonged to. 'West Briar?' she asked.

Jaslene laughed. 'Is that where you are? West Briar. No. No. Not West Briar. West Virginia. Well, I probably shouldn't judge. I was only there the one time. But that was enough. I went down there for Kimba's funeral. Did you know Kimba? She was Eden's mother.'

'I didn't. No,' said Morgan.

'Well, I'll tell you what. No southern hospitality there. I got to the church, and that grandfather of Eden's let me know that he didn't want any of my kind at the funeral. If you know what I mean by "my kind". It was so insulting.'

Even through her pain and stupor, Morgan recognized this as an appalling piece of information. And very believable from what she remembered of Wayne Summers. 'Terrible man,' she mumbled.

'He WAS,' said Jaslene. 'I had to turn around and go right back to the hotel. I didn't tell Eden that, though. She's a little sweetie. It's not her fault about her grandfather, and I didn't want to lay that on her. I didn't tell about her father either, for that matter.'

Morgan felt as if a small window had cleared in her brain. It was threatening to grow cloudy again, but she had the urgent sense that she needed to keep it clear. 'About Guy? What about him?' she asked.

'Well,' said Jaslene, in a confiding tone. 'He was there, all alone, at Kimba's funeral, looking all sad and hangdog. But he wasn't alone at the hotel. Of course, there is only one hotel in that miserable little town and they stuffed me in some room that used to be a broom closet. Anyway, it turns out he was getting it on with a woman in his hotel room, the very day of his wife's funeral.'

Morgan's hands were gripping the phone. 'Guy did that?' said Morgan. 'At Kimba's funeral?'

'Yes, he did,' said Jaslene. 'It made me wonder if Kimba's father had been right about her death not being an accident. But I was so mad at that old man I just didn't want to give him the satisfaction. So, I packed my bags and left. After all, accident was the official verdict.

'Well, as I say, I didn't mention it to Eden because there's no use in maligning the dead. But I could see him kissing that woman from my one little window in the back. I wasn't peeping mind you. But they had the curtains open. All she was wearing was a bedsheet around her. A skinny little blonde with braids wrapped in a crown all around her head like something straight out of a Nazi wet dream.'

'Who are you talking to, Morgan?' Astrid asked. 'Why don't you call them back? You're in no shape to be talking on the phone. Tell them you can't talk. Here, give me that. I'll tell them.'

Morgan looked over at Astrid. Though Astrid's gaze was on the road, she was holding out her hand for the phone. The street lights filtering in through the car window made her platinum crown of braids look like a halo on top of her head.

THIRTY-ONE

'WHO ARE YOU TALKING TO?' Astrid demanded. Morgan did not reply.

'Have to go. Thanks,' she said into the phone. Then, she slipped the phone into her coat pocket.

'Who was that?' Astrid asked. 'You were talking about Guy.'

'Nothing. It was just…someone…'

'What did they say about Kimba's funeral?'

Morgan couldn't think of a convincing lie, because her brain was in a fog. Try as she might, Morgan could not block the mental image of Guy with his stepmother, in a dark West Virginia hotel room. Astrid, wrapped in only a sheet. 'Wasn't important. I feel better now,' she lied. 'I want to go back to the house.'

'Tell me what they said,' said Astrid. 'I have a right to know.'

Morgan looked out the car window. The street lights were becoming scarcer. Morgan frowned. 'Where are we?' she asked.

'On the way to the hospital,' Astrid said. 'I told you. Now what was that conversation all about? What did the person on the phone say? About Kimba's funeral. Who was it?'

Morgan groaned. 'Friend of Kimba's. 'S all. Please, Astrid. Take me home.'

Astrid ignored Morgan's obvious misery. 'What did they say about Guy?'

'Nothing. Guy was there,' Morgan felt as if she needed to conserve her breath.

'Of course Guy was there. That wasn't all,' Astrid said. 'A woman. In his room.' A wave of nausea rolled over Morgan, and her head felt as if it was being squeezed in a vice.

'Oh, I feel like hell,' Morgan groaned.

'Why are you bringing up Kimba's funeral now?' Astrid said. 'First you tell Fitz that Guy was a rapist. And now this.'

Morgan looked over at Astrid. 'Fitz?'

'After you left the Lobster Shack today, he told me what you said about Guy. He was furious about it. He knew it for what it was—a disgusting lie. You don't care who you hurt. You will say anything.'

'Lucy told me,' said Morgan.

Astrid ignored her. 'Lucy's like a child. She doesn't know any better. You're slandering Guy when he can't defend himself.'

Morgan realized, in a sudden dizzying moment of clarity, that what Astrid said was true. Of course the rape story had been a lie. Guy had not raped Astrid that afternoon at their home. Or any other time. She was willing. It had never been rape. That was a lie Astrid made up to tell Lucy. To cover her affair with her stepson. And ever after, the loyal Lucy kept the secret, hated her brother. Morgan swallowed the bile in her mouth. 'Take me home,' she whispered.

Astrid ignored her and continued to drive.

'Astrid?' Morgan asked.

Astrid did not reply.

Morgan tried to summon her dignity, which was difficult since she was on the verge of passing out, and doubled over in pain. She forced herself to enunciate. 'Please, pull over,' she said. 'I want to get out.'

'You'll get out when I say you get out,' said Astrid. She put her foot on the gas and the car began to fly down the road.

'Astrid, stop,' Morgan said.

'Oh, no. I can see your filthy mind at work.'

'My filthy mind?'

Astrid was shaking her head. 'After all we've been through. I won't let you do this to me. To my family.'

All at once, Morgan realized, through her misery, that Astrid wasn't taking her to the hospital. Wherever they were going, it was not to get help for Morgan. And she was a prisoner in this car, at Astrid's mercy. 'Astrid. Please,' she murmured. 'I'm sorry. I know you've suffered.'

'You don't know anything,' said Astrid.

All pretense seemed to have vanished, and Morgan suddenly knew that she was in danger. Though her brain was cottony, she tried to consider her options. She thought about opening the door and rolling out of the car, but at this speed, that would surely be a deadly move. She thought about the phone in her pocket. She might be able to call the police, but the minute she tried to punch in a number, Astrid would hear the singsong beeps and surely rip the phone from her hand. Morgan knew she was no match for the other woman in this condition. She was too weak. Despite the imminent danger, it was difficult for her to hold on to consciousness.

She thought about her phone and her conversation with Fitz earlier in the day. 'I'm going to make myself number one on your speed-dial,' he had said, as he fiddled with her phone. Had he actually done it? She hadn't checked. She slipped her hand in her pocket and opened the phone. Even in her numbed state of mind, she realized that the minute she pressed a button, Astrid would hear the beep. Morgan needed to mask the sound. Her stomach was churning, both from fear, and from the poison she had ingested. She was sure, now, that the soup had been laced with some drug. Something that was at once making her physically sick and stealing her mental clarity. This suffering was no coincidence.

Don't vomit, Astrid had said in her motherly way. And Morgan had followed her advice. Obviously, Morgan thought, it was time to ignore Astrid's every suggestion. Morgan fingered the flat keypad. She had to hope that she could hit the right number without looking at the phone. She clutched the phone with one sweaty hand, and with the other, she stuck a finger down her throat. As she coughed and gagged, she retched up a viscous mess on Astrid's center console gearshift. At the same time, she pressed the phone's keypad and prayed.

'Stop that,' Astrid cried out in disgust as the car swerved. She pulled it back into the center of the road.

Morgan retched again to cover the faraway sound of a recorded voice in her pocket which said, to her despair, 'It's Fitz. Leave a message.'

'All right,' Astrid snarled. 'That's enough.' She drove over to the side of road. Morgan could hear the sound of waves crashing on the beach. The tide was high, and waves were breaking only a short distance from the dunes. 'Get out.'

'Can't,' Morgan pleaded, shaking her head. 'I'm too sick.'

'Give me your phone,' Astrid demanded.

Morgan hesitated, and shook her head.

'Give it to me. NOW,' Astrid insisted. 'Or I will take it from you.'

Morgan reached in her pocket to pull out the phone.

Groping around, she felt an unfamiliar shape and then she remembered. The scissors she had used to cut down the balloons from the mailbox. They were still in her pocket.

Morgan felt a kind of vague steadying inside herself. She was not helpless. She just needed to pick her moment. She pulled out the phone and handed it to Astrid. Astrid shoved it in her own pocket. Then, she jerked the keys from the ignition and started around to the passenger side. Morgan locked the passenger door quickly. Astrid tried the passenger door, found it locked, and jammed the key in the lock. Morgan tried to hold the door shut, but her limbs felt like they were made out of toothpaste. Astrid jerked the door open.

'NO, please,' Morgan begged her. 'Let's just get to the hospital.'

Astrid grabbed Morgan by the hair, and Morgan let out a howl of pain.

'Come on,' said Astrid. 'You're coming with me.'

'Let go!' Morgan tried to pry Astrid's hands away, but Astrid held the hair tight in her fist. It felt like she was uprooting it from Morgan's scalp.

'Now,' Astrid insisted.

Maybe it would be better to be out of the car, Morgan thought. She tried to do as she was told, but her legs were too weak to obey. Astrid jerked her ponytail and Morgan fell from the car to the ground. She had landed on a mixture of dirt, sand and tall grass.

'I've had enough,' Astrid muttered indignantly, 'of your interference and your legal strategies. You are not going to prevent Claire from being punished for what she did.'

Morgan coughed, relieved, at least, that Astrid had let go of her hair. 'She didn't do it,' Morgan whispered.

'What did you say?' Astrid demanded.

'She didn't kill the baby,' Morgan said.

Even in the moonlight Morgan could see that Astrid's eyes were electric. 'The baby? Who's talking about the baby? I'm talking about Guy.'

'Sorry. I know,' said Morgan. 'He was your son.'

Astrid slapped Morgan as hard as she could across the face. Morgan fell on all fours in the sand, her face stinging, the dampness seeping through the knees of her pants. She wanted to put her head down and rest it there, in the cold sand.

She shook her head to try and clear it, and then rocked back on her heels, holding her stomach to assuage the stabbing pains.

'You don't know anything,' Astrid cried.

To Morgan's amazement, Astrid's eyes filled with tears. She looked out across the ocean, rolling relentlessly in under the impassive moon. 'He wasn't my son. He was my…my fate.'

'Fate?' Morgan whispered.

'From the very first minute we saw each other. When he walked into the lobby of my parents' hotel… He was fifteen years old and I was…older. But we both knew it.'

Morgan blinked at her.

Astrid sighed. 'We knew what the world would think. We had to hide what we felt.' Astrid looked pityingly at Morgan. 'You don't believe me, do you?'

Astrid's tale of love was like some opium dream that Morgan had entered into, as she felt herself sinking, her consciousness fading in and out. 'Yes. I…I do,' Morgan insisted. And, in fact, at that moment, she did.

'I did what I had to do. I married Guy's father and left my home. My family. I did everything so that I could live under the same roof with Guy. And we stole every moment together that we could. For all these years.'

'Oh, my God,' said Morgan. Chills were coursing through Morgan, and she didn't know whether it was from the poison, or the cold, or the fascinated revulsion she felt as she listened to Astrid reminisce about her long affair with her stepson. She had the impression that Astrid had been suddenly released from bondage. That she was experiencing joy in finally telling someone aloud about her love.

Astrid's gaze was far away. 'Nothing could break us apart,' she said.

'He got married…' Morgan remembered aloud. Her mental censor was failing her. She spoke without thinking.

'To Kimba?' Astrid laughed dismissively. 'He was a young man. She meant nothing to him. Kimba trapped him with a pregnancy.' Astrid gave a little half-smile, remembering. 'I freed him.'

Morgan's head was splitting. She felt as if it would soon break open, two halves facing up, under the stars. She knew she should cover her ears. Not listen to one more word from Astrid. But it was a siren song, a tale of love that, perversely, she wanted to hear. Wanted to know. And Astrid meant to tell it.

'I told Dick I was going to a Prader-Willi conference. My husband wasn't suspicious. I often did that. I attended those meetings to learn all I could about Lucy's condition. New therapies. Techniques. I did everything I could to help my Lucy…'

The story was becoming fragmented in Morgan's mind. 'Kimba?' Morgan prodded her.

Astrid sighed. 'Kimba. I knew where they were staying. I'm from the Caribbean. I went there. I knew they would go diving. Guy loves to dive. We both do. They went out on another boat. All the boats stop in the same vicinity because the large turtles feed there. Once we were in the water, I slipped into Guy and Kimba's diving group. It was an easy matter to come up behind Kimba, and turn down the air on her tank. Not all the way, but just enough so that she would notice it. Feel the oxygen diminish. Be afraid. Panic. Break for the surface too fast. I knew she would. She was a novice.'

Morgan was mesmerized, in spite of all her misery. She knew, dimly, that this was a confession of murder. She knew that she should close her ears and not listen to another word. It was so dangerous to know. 'Don't,' she said.

Astrid ignored her. 'I never told Guy. If he guessed, he didn't say…'

Morgan's teeth were chattering but her core was warm. The drugs were suffused through her system now. The pain was almost gone. 'Claire?' she whispered.

Astrid looked at Morgan calmly. 'I gave Claire a sleeping pill that night at our house. She asked me for it. She wanted to sleep. Late that night, I let myself in. She never heard me. I took the baby and put him in the tub. I knew Guy would blame her. Turn away from her when he realized that she had killed their baby.'

Something was pinging in Morgan's brain, a distant, urgent memory, insisting on her attention. 'He loved Claire,' Morgan said dreamily.

Astrid shook her head patiently. 'No. He was just… trying to change things. He said we were addicted and we had to make the break. But you can't break away from a love like that. He'd tried it before. He spent years in Europe. I'd tell Dick I was going to see my grandmother in the Netherlands and I'd rush to Guy. Guy never could resist. He came back to me every time.'

Morgan stared at the double image of Astrid which

shimmered before her eyes. She spoke, in a slurred voice, but gently, almost as she would to a friend. "'S over, Astrid. They'll find out.'

Astrid stood very silent and still for a moment, as if she was listening to a voice that only she could hear. Then she said, with a sad solemnity, 'It doesn't matter. I don't have anything left to live for.'

Astrid reached into the pocket of her coat and pulled up a fistful of something twisted that gleamed in the moonlight. It was difficult for Morgan to focus her eyes. All at once, Astrid swung it, and Morgan saw that it was a circular length of chain. She put up her trembling hands, thinking Astrid was going to hit her with the chain. Instead, Astrid tossed the closed loop of the chain over Morgan's head like a clunky lariat. She gave it a tug and Morgan felt the chain pulled tight against her neck. Adrenalin jolted her, too late, out of her drugged state. Morgan tried to get her fingers between the chain and her neck.

'I borrowed this from Lucy's porch when I went by her house today. It's a choke chain she has for those dogs of hers. I bought it for her. It's to make them obey. She never uses it, of course. Now, if you don't get up and walk,' said Astrid, through clenched teeth, 'I'll strangle you right here.'

Morgan gagged and tried to jam her fingers between her neck and the chain. Tried to pull it away. Astrid jerked the chain.

'Come on. Get up,' said Astrid. She tugged at the chain. 'Come on. Once you get into the water, it will all be over quickly.'

The water, Morgan thought? Oh no. Her drugged-up heart began to hammer. She was in the grasp of a killer. No time left. Now, she thought. She staggered to her feet, and as she did so, she reached into her coat pocket, fumbled around for the scissors and pulled them out. She reached out as best she could, and jammed Astrid's hand, with all the strength she could muster.

Still gripping the end of the chain, Astrid turned on Morgan with rage in her eyes. For one second, Morgan thought that it had worked, that Astrid would let go, that she could pull free. Astrid let the blood run and didn't flinch. She batted the scissors from Morgan's hand as if they were a buzzing fly. She renewed her grip on the chain and began to pull. Morgan had no choice but to try and follow her, crawling and stumbling along, trying to avoid being choked to death. It was no use. Astrid was pulling on the chain with a terrible fury.

Sick, weak, dying, Morgan could not move fast enough across the sand to save herself. She felt freezing cold water rush up, lap over her hands and recede. Astrid gave the chain a mighty tug and Morgan gagged for air, and saw black spots in front of her eyes which were darker even than the darkness. And then, she saw nothing at all.

THIRTY-TWO

FITZ STEPPED OUT OF THE bathroom after his shower, wrapped in a towel. He hunted around the bedroom for his pair of lounging pants with the Las Vegas gambling motif.

His thirteen-year-old niece, Kathy, had given them to him last Christmas and couldn't stop giggling when he opened the box. They were made out of the usual light flannel, but were decorated with playing cards, neon signs and poker chips. Fitz had good-naturedly held them up to his jeans, modeling them, making everyone laugh. But the fact was, he wore them all the time. Fitz found them hanging over the back of a chair, and pulled them on, along with a T-shirt. Then he went out to the living room to see if there was a game on the tube. He picked up his phone, automatically checking, and saw that he had a voicemail. From Morgan.

For one moment, he thought about deleting it without even listening. That was what she deserved. He had done everything he could for her, and still, she kept trashing the people he cared about, and acting like she was the only one who could possibly understand what was going on. She thought she was so smart because she was getting a doctorate. In fact, it had been through his connections that she was able to come up with the idea that Claire might have made a false confession. Why did I try to help her, he thought? All I got was grief.

Tonight when he called her, she said she couldn't talk and had given him that vague 'I don't feel good' excuse.

Wouldn't even commit herself to the idea of talking to him tomorrow. The hell with her, he thought. A lot of girls liked him. He didn't need Morgan Adair.

But that was her number on the phone. Maybe she'd regretted her snottiness. He knew that no matter what he told himself, he liked her more than the other girls he knew. Much more. There was something about her that touched him. He liked her thick, chestnut hair and her great shape and her keen eyes. But it was more than that. He felt...protective of her.

Of course, she'd blow him off if she ever knew that he saw her that way. He had asked Claire about her, after that tumble they'd had at the wedding. Claire had said that Morgan's parents were killed in a bombing in some godforsaken country when she was young, and that Morgan had never gotten over it. She was reluctant to trust anyone. 'Don't go after her,' Claire warned him, 'if you don't mean it.'

He had taken the warning to heart. After all, he wasn't really looking for something serious. What if, in the end, he found that he didn't want a commitment with Morgan? He didn't want to mess up his relationship with Claire and Guy, by hitting on Claire's best friend and then dropping her. So, he didn't call. And, he reminded himself, she didn't call him either.

Fitz stared at the number. Ironically, after all that had happened, now he did know what he wanted. He would happily admit his feelings to her now that she detested him. Today, at the Lobster Shack, before she started spouting lies about Guy, he was feeling sure that there was a spark on her side as well. She had seemed happy to see him there, and let him hold her hand without a word of protest. It had felt like Christmas to be walking along the water's edge with her, holding her hand. And then she started in on Guy. She wouldn't have done that if she were really interested. She would have known better. Maybe there was absolutely nothing there on her part. Hell, he hadn't even kissed her during this whole miserable time.

He looked at the phone again. Still, she had called him back. He wished he could put the phone down and walk away. But he couldn't. He knew he couldn't.

Fitz played the voicemail and listened. He had expected to hear her voice. Instead, he heard someone retching. Sick as a dog. And then a cacophony of sounds. Shouting voices. Something thundering in the background. Fitz broke out in a sweat. What was this?

Maybe it was nothing. This afternoon he had jokingly put his number on speed-dial on her phone. Maybe she had hit it by accident, and he was just listening to normal life going on around her. But it didn't sound normal.

He scrolled back and replayed the message, listening carefully. A woman's voice, harsh and strident, was demanding that she give up the phone. Threatening her. And Morgan, sounding as if she could barely summon the strength to speak, was refusing. He heard the crashing background again. This time he was able to place it. He had lived by the sea all his life. It was the sound of the ocean. Morgan was on the beach with this other…person. His heart was pounding as he listened to it again. This time he heard Morgan say it. Astrid. And then the phone went dead.

Fitz stood there, holding the phone, trying to think. Astrid? Why would Astrid be with Morgan? Threatening her? He knew instinctively not to ask Dick Bolton. Whatever was going on here was going on behind Dick Bolton's back. Which would not, Fitz admitted to himself, be anything new for Astrid. She seemed like the nicest lady in the world. Always helping Dick and fussing over

Lucy. Guy was the only one who hadn't seemed to buy her act. One time he and Guy were talking about Astrid. Fitz remarked that she was great-looking for her age, still attractive. She knows it, Guy said bitterly. She cheats on my father all the time. Fitz had been stunned to hear this. Are you going to tell him, Fitz had asked Guy?

No fucking way, Guy had said. And if I ever hear that you said anything…Fitz had promised to remain silent, and so he had. But it was not hard for him to imagine, now, that whatever Astrid was doing, Dick knew nothing about it.

He thought about calling the police, but what would he say? He could play them the voicemail that he had received, but they would probably laugh at him. Two women fighting over a cellphone. Hardly a police matter.

They were somewhere by the ocean. Well, he thought. That narrows it down. To the coast of Long Island. But even as he thought it, he surmised that they weren't far away. Morgan sounded as if she were really ill. She wouldn't have gotten far.

Fitz hesitated. Part of him wanted to just forget about it. It would serve her right. But at the same time he couldn't take a chance. What if she needed his help? Morgan may have reached out to him. Now was no time to let her down. Well, the first, most direct thing to do, he reasoned, was to call back. He pressed the call-back number and waited.

After a number of rings, a voice answered, sounding breathless.

'Morgan?' he said.

'No,' said the voice. 'She's not feeling well. She's lying down.'

Fitz hesitated. 'Astrid?' he said.

There was a silence at the other end. Then Astrid's voice said warily, 'Yes. Who's this?'

'It's Fitz.'

'Oh hello, Fitz. I think she said she was going to call you tomorrow. She's just feeling so sick tonight. She's got an awful headache. I was just about to leave.'

'Where are you?' said Fitz.

'At the Captain's House. Where Morgan is staying. I was just about to head home. I brought her some soup and she ate and then she fell asleep. I thought she might wake up but she's out of it so I'm going to go. I don't think you should bother her again tonight.'

'Oh, all right,' said Fitz. 'Well tell her I called, will you?'

'I will,' said Astrid. 'I'll leave her a note.'

'OK, thanks,' said Fitz. 'Bye.'

Astrid gave him a pleasant goodbye and hung up.

Fitz stood there, thinking about the conversation. Astrid had answered Morgan's phone. So, Morgan was obviously unable to use it. Maybe that was because she was sick, or maybe it was something else. All the time Astrid was talking, Fitz could hear the roar of the ocean, the waves breaking close to her. Wherever she was, it wasn't the Captain's House. The Captain's House was near the ocean, but that sound he heard was the surf. The water's edge. Which meant Astrid was lying.

Fitz was pulling off the Las Vegas pants as he returned to his bedroom. He pulled on his jeans and a shirt, and grabbed a warm jacket. Then he stuck his phone in his pocket, and found his keys. If they were somewhere on the coast road, he knew he could find them.

ONCE MORGAN HAD BEEN CHOKED unconscious, the rest of it was simple, Astrid thought. They were ankle deep in water when Astrid gave that last furious tug of the chain. Once she had her in the water, the waves did the rest. The tide had just crested, and was going out. Astrid had checked that before she set out tonight. The tide would carry Morgan's body out, away from the beach, out into the dark ocean, and by the time they found what was left of her, there would be no explaining how she got there.

Astrid gave the girl's inert form a gentle shove. Morgan's eyelids fluttered for a moment. Even unconscious she may have been aware of the shock from the cold water. Astrid had a moment's fear that the water might revive her. But her eyes closed again, and Morgan began to float, little by little, away from shore. Astrid watched the first few waves start to take her.

She knew what she would say if, by chance, the body was found, and they found that load of barbiturates in her system. The barbiturates which Astrid had dissolved in the hot chowder. Astrid would sadly suggest suicide. Say that Morgan had expressed desperation, depression, hopelessness, when Astrid visited and brought her the chowder.

Astrid took one last look at the body, peacefully floating. She could still see Morgan's white face, and the rest of her was dark. Her clothes, even her hair was turned dark by the frigid water. Morgan would not be turning over any more stones on Claire's behalf, and uncovering family secrets. And Morgan's death would torment Claire, who would be left without her champion. Astrid shuddered when she recalled this afternoon—Fitz asking her about Guy being a rapist. All these years, Lucy had kept that precious secret for Astrid and now, thanks to Morgan, it was being bandied about. She had to be sure that it was never exposed as the lie that it was.

For one moment, watching Morgan being carried out

into the water by the waves, Astrid was almost tempted to wade in there herself, to let the water take her also. Not for the first time, Astrid was tormented by the memory of how her plan had backfired so horribly. She had meant for Guy to find his baby murdered, and to blame Claire. All the while she planned it, Astrid imagined that Guy would banish his wife to prison and turn his back on her forever. Instead, the finding of their dead child had caused Guy and Claire to get into a physical scuffle and he, improbably, had fallen, hit his head and died. More of Astrid's endless tears seeped from under her eyelids at the thought of it. Guy. Gone forever. She still couldn't imagine her life without him. Couldn't bear to.

Somehow, of course, she had always known that they were doomed. There was a time, early on, when he had begged her to hire someone to kill Dick, so that they could always be together. Astrid was always, nobly, against it. Even the times when he pleaded with her, she resisted, soothed him. Their desire was fueled by the impossibility of their situation. She knew that better than he did. Without frustration, it might end up being ordinary. She couldn't bear that. She knew that she would lose him that way.

And then he met Claire. Like an alcoholic newly committed to AA, Guy had told her that he had found a new kind of life. A life he wanted. He said he was through with their affair for once and for all. She expected him to falter, to come back. But a year had passed, a baby was born, and still he stayed, insisting he was devoted to Claire. And then Claire's depression over the baby had arrived, like a gift in her lap. Astrid had hatched her plan, but she had miscalculated, and now her life was hardly worth living. She reminded herself that she had to stay alive to see Claire sent to prison. Hear sentence pronounced on Claire who had bragged to everyone how much Guy loved her.

Astrid dared not linger here too long. Her own shoes, socks and pants were wet up to the knees and she had to get out to the car and change into the dry clothes she had brought with her. Change, and then quickly drive away. Just before she turned away from the sight of Morgan, floating out in the direction of the dark horizon, she took Morgan's phone from her pocket, and looked at it. Would someone who was suicidal take their phone with them to their death, she wondered? She hesitated, thinking about that, and then decided that they probably would, simply by force of habit. Having decided that, Astrid threw the phone as far and as hard as she could into the water.

Then she turned and began to trudge back toward her car, and the dry clothes which awaited her there. She walked up the beach, her pants getting heavier with every step, weighted down as they were by water and sand. Her hand, which had been washed clean by the ocean, began to bleed again. She approached the car from the back and opened the trunk. She rummaged around and pulled out the dry pants and shoes she had brought along. She closed the lid, and met the implacable gaze of Fitz, staring at her.

'Fitz,' she exclaimed breathlessly, trying in vain to sound normal.

'Where is Morgan?' he said.

'I guess at the Captain's House,' said Astrid. 'Did you try there? I was just out for a walk.'

'By yourself?' he said.

'Well, yes, of course, by myself.'

'What's that for?' Fitz asked pointing to the choke collar which Astrid had removed from Morgan's neck and absent-mindedly rolled around her hand.

'What? Oh, I found this on the beach.'

'Your hand is bleeding,' he said.

'Is it?' she asked.

'Let's go back down on the beach,' he said.

Astrid demurred. 'I think I'm going to go home.'

Fitz took her by the upper arm. 'No. I need you to come with me.'

Astrid felt the shock of his young body close to hers. She had become spoiled by the intoxication of young flesh and for one moment… Then, she shook off the thought. This was not Guy. There was no ecstasy to be had, here. 'I'd rather not,' she said archly. 'Really, Fitz. I'm surprised at you.'

Fitz was not responding politely. 'Let's go down on that beach and look,' he said in a menacing tone. Without waiting for her acquiescence he shoved her forward and down through the dunes and across the sand they went.

'Morgan,' he called out. There was no answer.

He looked over at Astrid, who was watching him pityingly. 'What?' he said.

'Morgan?' Astrid shook her head. 'She's not for you. You deserve better.'

'Where is she?' he demanded.

Almost involuntarily, Astrid's gaze rose to the sea. Fitz felt something cold clamp down on his heart as he turned to where she was looking, and saw the pale face, like a disc of concentrated moonlight, drifting out on the waves.

THIRTY-THREE

MORGAN LAY ON AN ICEBERG in Antarctica, where she lived as a princess among the polar bears. It was a light, white world, where the rays of the sun were so bright that you could hardly stand to open your eyes. She was asleep, although she could see all around her and hear all that was said. The polar bears were talking, saying that in a very short time she would have some special visitors. Though they didn't say who the visitors might be, Morgan somehow knew, and her excitement was fantastic. It was going to be her parents, and she knew she had to awaken to meet them. It was difficult to awaken though. She felt heavy and weighted down. Her royal robes were as dark as seaweed and they seemed to keep her pinned to the iceberg. She had to get up, to get ready to see them. She had to make her home ready for these most wonderful of visitors. But what would she serve them, she wondered? What sort of refreshments would she ever find in this cold, empty place? She was wracking her brain, trying to think what she could offer them when suddenly she heard their voices.

'Morgan, Morgan.' The voice came from far away, and something told her not to heed the voice. Not to listen. In her dream, she opened her eyes, and saw her mother's face, and her father's face, their tender eyes, with light surrounding them. But they were not speaking. They were not calling her name.

Morgan opened her eyes and saw nothing but darkness

and felt the water enveloping her, crushing her with its coldness. She could not feel her feet, her limbs. Her heart stopped from fear. Started again.

'Morgan.'

It was a shout. Someone was there. She turned her eyes toward the shore. Fitz. He was coming through the water toward her. Froth surrounded him and he pushed it away, pushed the water away, pushed everything away and willed her, with his eyes, to hang on.

'Don't,' she wanted to say, but her lips were too numb to move. She felt detached as she watched him surging through the water, as if it were someone else he was trying to reach. She herself was already far away, going home.

As if he could divine her waning will, he shouted, 'Morgan, don't quit. Wait for me.' She wondered what he meant by that, but she couldn't ask him, because her face was frozen, stiff. The waves around him broke against his chest, leapt into the air. A spray of water fell on Morgan's face like steely pellets, striking her. It seemed that he was far away for a long time, and then, suddenly, he was beside her. He grabbed one sodden sleeve of her jacket, and pulled her until he could get his other arm around her. Then he drew her to his chest. She felt the heat of him, the warmth of him. The life.

'Stay with me, babe,' he said. Holding her, he began to push toward shore. Every step was excruciating. She felt as if her hands, her limbs would break off in the water and float away. He was gasping for breath and she could feel the beating of his heart through his jacket. 'Stay awake,' he said. 'I'm bringing you in.'

She tried to speak to him, but her lips wouldn't move. How did you get here, she asked him in her heart? How did you find me? She wasn't sure if her life was leaving her, or returning. There was one thing she had to tell him. She forced her blue lips to move, and it felt like they were cracking, falling from her face. 'Astrid.'

'What babe?' he asked. 'I didn't hear you. Did you say Astrid?' He put his ear close to her mouth.

'Poisoned me,' she whispered.

Fitz threw his head back. 'That bitch,' he cried to the stars. His anger seemed to give him added strength. He pulled her closer and crashed through the waves like a ship's prow. In the distance he heard sirens, and he thanked God he had thought to call the ambulance the minute he saw her in the water. Astrid had not tried to stop him. She fled. His eyes searched the dark beach but Astrid was gone. There was no one and nothing to be seen except for the flashing red lights which had just appeared beyond the dunes.

'Ambulance is here. We're almost to shore. Don't nod off,' he warned her. 'Stay with me.'

LUCY LOOPED THE TWO LEASHES around her hand and allowed herself to be carried down the sidewalk. Sometimes she wondered what it would be like to wear roller skates, and have the dogs pull her. The minute she got up some steam, she told herself, they would turn around or get tangled up in one another, and that would be the end of it.

Lucy knew what her father would say if he could hear her thoughts. Be careful. You're weak. You'll fall.

She glanced up at the house and saw Julio, framed by the front window, and it made her smile. That's what he knew. Her father had no idea how brave she could be. But he soon would. Lucy waved to Julio and he nodded and smiled back at her, but he couldn't wave because he was in the process of putting up curtain rods. He said the house didn't look right without curtains, and that they needed to go shopping and get some. That was the kind of person he was. If there was something wrong, he fixed it. Almost like Astrid, only a man. She knew she should be grateful to her father for this house, but in truth it had always been such a burden to her, with all the chores she was always avoiding or forgetting to do. But not anymore. Not since Julio.

'Lucy…'

Lucy jumped at the sound of a soft voice in the darkness. She looked all around.

'I'm here, in the car.'

Lucy turned to look. She hadn't noticed her stepmother's car parked down the block. But there was Astrid, at the wheel, the car window open. Lucy went over and bent down to talk to her stepmother. The dogs barked their displeasure at the interruption of their walk. 'Astrid,' she said. 'Oh I'm so glad you're here.'

Astrid's face looked strange—wild-eyed and gaunt. 'I need to talk to you,' said Astrid. 'I've had an idea.'

'Me too,' Lucy exclaimed. 'I wanted to tell you. Why don't you come in?'

'No, listen to me,' said Astrid impatiently. 'I've been thinking about this, and there's only one thing to do. You go get Julio, and throw your things in a bag. We'll set out for Mexico right now. Tonight.'

Lucy's face crumpled. 'Oh, no. We can't…Julio's hanging curtain rods.'

'Curtain rods?' yelped Astrid. 'You don't need curtain rods if you're leaving town. Come on. Hurry. I brought money. Lots of money.'

Lucy frowned. 'Astrid, I can't.'

'You have to,' she said. 'Once Dick finds out, do you know what he'll do? Do you understand about these temporary visas? If he fires Julio, and you know he will, he

will drive him directly to the airport and not leave until
he is on a plane to Mexico. Without you. You will never
see Julio again…'

Lucy shook her head. 'Even if I wanted to go, I couldn't
leave my dogs. That's what I was thinking about after you
left earlier today. If hiding the truth from my father means
leaving my dogs… Well, I won't just leave them. I can't.
Not for anything.'

Astrid's silvery eyes were wide and frantic-looking.
'We'll bring the dogs with us. We can manage somehow.
But you have to hurry.'

'I can't do that,' said Lucy slowly. 'Besides, now that
we're married, Julio can stay here, can't he?'

'It doesn't work that way,' Astrid snapped. 'Lucy,
you're being a fool.'

Lucy straightened up, holding the dogs' leashes close
to her chest. 'Don't say that to me,' she protested. 'That's
not right.' She turned away from Astrid's car, and Astrid
jumped out of the driver's side, slammed the door and
followed her up the path.

'I didn't mean it like that, Lucy,' she said. 'Forgive me.
Please.'

Lucy stopped on the front porch steps and looked at
her ruefully. 'I thought you of all people would never talk
to me that way.'

'Darling, I apologize,' Astrid pleaded.

'You always told Guy not to be cruel to me. But just
then, you were being cruel,' Lucy accused her.

Astrid reached out her long, thin hands and pressed
them together, almost like she was praying. 'I'm sorry,'
she said. 'Lucy, I just want to do this for you. Help you
and Julio to get away so you can be together. I can help
you.'

Lucy's gaze softened, and she shook her head. 'I know.

You always did take care of me. But I started thinking, after you left earlier. I don't really want to leave here. Not now that I have Julio. This is my home. If it embarrasses my father that I'm married to a Mexican who washes dishes, too bad. I mean, Guy was Mr Perfect and he married Miss Perfect and look what happened.'

Astrid looked at her helplessly. 'What are you talking about?'

'I'm saying,' said Lucy earnestly, 'that what I have to do is tell Dad the truth. We're always trying to protect him, you and me. But maybe we would be better off just to tell Dad these things.'

'No, Lucy, you can't,' Astrid said wearily.

'Yes, I can. And I'm going to. To tell him everything.' Lucy glanced at the front window, and Julio, on the other side, seemed to sense her gaze. He bent down from the stepstool and waved at her, pointing up at the curtain rods, now in place. Lucy waved back, and gave him a thumbs up sign. Lucy looked proudly at Astrid.

'Actually, I already have,' she said.

Tears sprang to Astrid's eyes. 'No, no,' she said. 'You didn't.'

'I called him and said I had something important to tell him,' said Lucy stubbornly. 'I told him to come over. Give me one good reason why I shouldn't.'

Astrid hesitated, and then she walked up the steps to where Lucy stood. Astrid studied her for moment, with a wistful gaze. Then, she embraced her tenderly. 'You're right, darling. Don't listen to me,' Astrid said. 'I've done everything wrong.'

Lucy looked taken aback. 'You? Oh, heavens. You're the best person I know.'

Astrid wiped her tears away with the back of her hand. 'No. I'm not. When you realize…you'll hate me.'

'That's crazy,' said Lucy. 'I could never…'

'I have to go now.'

'No wait, Astrid. Dad is on his way. He'll be here soon.'

'I'm sorry. I have to go,' said Astrid. 'Right now.'

'Don't you want to be here when I tell him?' Lucy asked. 'For a little moral support? I could use it.'

Astrid put a hand to her mouth and shook her head. 'I can't. Listen, when he gets here just tell him…'

'Tell me what?' said a voice beyond the arc of the front porch light.

'Dad,' Lucy said. 'You got here just in time.'

Astrid turned to face her husband, her face alight, her lips ready with a lie. 'Dick. I'm so glad to see you. I was just on my way home.'

Dick stepped forward, out of the darkness, flanked by a policeman on either side. His normally bronzed face was ashen, and his sandy, surfer's hair shone gray under the porch light. He gazed, flinty and unflinching, into his wife's eyes. 'Really?' he said. 'I would have thought you'd be trying to get away from here. Maybe, flee the country.'

'Why would I do that?' Astrid whispered, her eyes fearful. Lucy looked from her father to her stepmother in surprise. 'How did he know? Astrid, did you tell him?' she demanded, confused.

'Is this your wife, sir?' asked one of the cops.

'Yes, it is.'

The cop walked up to Astrid holding a pair of hand-cuffs and reached for her arms. 'Astrid Bolton, you are under arrest for the murder of Drew Richard Bolton and the attempted murder of Morgan Adair.' He began to recite her legal rights.

Lucy's eyes were wide. 'Drew? Wait! That's not true…'

'You have the right to an attorney,' the cop said.

'Dad! What is going on? This is a mistake. Dad, tell them. Astrid...'

Astrid looked sadly at Lucy, and offered the policeman no resistance. 'I'm sorry, darling,' she said.

Dick stared at his wife, but he spoke to his daughter, shaking his head.

'Don't listen to her, Lucy,' he said. 'Every word she ever said to us was a lie.'

THIRTY-FOUR

'SHE ONCE WROTE, "I am the happiest single woman in England",' said Morgan.

'She never wanted to get married?'

'Her father wanted to force her into an arranged marriage, but Harriet wouldn't have any part of it. She wanted to read and write, and think.'

'That took a lot of courage in those days.'

'And,' Morgan went on, 'we're talking about a woman who had no sense of taste, or smell, and was deaf to boot. And Charles Darwin said of her, "I was astonished to find how ugly she is".'

'Ouch.'

'I know.'

'You talk about her as if you know her,' said Claire. Morgan stopped and looked out across the surface of Lake Windermere to softly wooded banks, and the treeless slopes of the mountains beyond. 'Being here, seeing the house where she lived, and this countryside that she loved so much, I really feel as if I do know her. It's like the last piece of the puzzle. She lived in a lot of places. Traveled quite a bit in her life. But this place was the home that was closest to her heart.'

Claire walked up beside her. 'Well, after two weeks in Cumbria, I feel like she's an old friend of mine, too. And I can certainly see why she loved this place. Who wouldn't? It's so beautiful. I don't know why you agreed to let me come with you. After all, it's my fault it took you an extra six months to get here. But I'm grateful.'

Morgan smiled. 'I just wish you didn't have to leave. It's been like our traveling days of old. And it was worth the wait.'

'Well, all the same, I'm sorry,' said Claire.

The two friends continued on their way, crossing under a canopy of trees to see a small waterfall spilling over a rocky promontory and into a placid pool. As they walked, Morgan's eyes felt soothed and delighted by the sights around her, but her thoughts teemed with harsh images from the last six months. Her own recovery from hypothermia and barbiturate poisoning. Claire's eventual return to health. The day in court when Astrid admitted her crimes, including the murder of Kimba Summers, in front of her stoic husband and, in the row behind him, her weeping stepdaughter and her husband, Julio. Astrid was sentenced to life in prison. Noreen Quick, newly svelte and now the mother of three, was eloquent at the hearing in which all charges against Claire were dropped.

'This is such a lovely part of the world,' said Claire.

Morgan was startled out of her reverie. 'Yes, it is,' she said.

'What were you thinking about?' Claire asked.

Morgan sighed. 'These last six months.' She glanced at her friend.

Claire nodded. 'Never far from my mind.'

'Do you ever…' Morgan hesitated.

'Ever what?' Claire asked.

'Do you ever wonder why you confessed when you weren't guilty? I don't mean to remind you of something so painful, but I have such trouble, even now, imagining you doing that,' Morgan said.

'*You* have such trouble?' Claire said, with a short, bitter laugh. She shook her head. 'No. I've thought about it so often. All I can think is that after I found Drew...' She pressed her lips together until she was able to speak again. 'I think a part of my mind wanted me to be punished... Wanted to die even. I don't think I'm stating that too strongly.'

'Probably not,' said Morgan.

'I can remember feeling so ashamed, so...horrified at how I had failed my baby.'

'That and the lies that the police told you about Guy accusing you...'

'I don't know,' said Claire. 'I'll never know. If I wanted to be punished, I certainly was. I have nothing left. Of that life.'

'I know,' said Morgan. They walked along in silence for a while, their dark thoughts compatible, while the heady scent of spring flowers tickled their noses.

'Look at that little church up there,' said Morgan, pointing across the road to a small stone chapel standing alone. 'That's from the Victorian period.'

'Let's go look,' said Claire.

They left the lake's shore and crossed the narrow street to the church which was set, like a jewel, among clipped box and yew hedges, rhododendrons and shrub roses, all starting to bloom in the April sunshine. They wandered up to the church and looked inside. It was perfectly kept, but empty at the moment. Beside the church was a fenced graveyard.

'Was Harriet Martineau buried here?' Claire asked.

'No, in the end she was buried with her family, in their plot in Birmingham.'

Claire opened the gate in the fence and walked inside, looking from one stone to another. Morgan felt her heart begin to thud a warning as she watched her friend moving slowly among the graves. She stopped at one stone, and crouched down beside it, reaching out to touch it.

'Claire,' Morgan said anxiously.

'These are so worn you can't even read them,' Claire said.

'Hey, I could use some lunch. Are you ready to head back to Ambleside?'

Claire looked up at her, and her eyes seemed to be swimming. She nodded quickly and stood up, brushing her hands off against one another.

This time, they walked along the road, the tall hedge-rows of wildflowers giving the road the air of a secret garden. They walked side by side, but when they heard a car coming, they flattened themselves against the hedge-rows, single file.

The road opened out on to the center of a hilly village with its stone façades unchanged by time, and bright flowers in every doorway and window. At one point, Morgan looked up and saw the back of a tall, curly-headed man ducking into a building in the next block and he reminded her of Fitz. Wishful thinking, she thought. She missed everything about him, as she knew she would, and yet, when he had asked her if he could come over to England with her, she had made excuses. She had told him, truthfully, that Claire was coming with her, even though Claire was only staying for two of the six weeks. She didn't really know why she had done that. For some reason, part of her wanted to keep him at bay.

The two women strolled along the street, looking in windows until finally they came to the local pub, where they entered by mutual consent and sat at a table by the window. The landlord came by and took their order, and then they both looked out at the shoppers with their wicker baskets, and men passing on bicycles.

'Life unchanging through time,' said Morgan with a sigh. 'I know it isn't true, but it looks that way, doesn't it?'

'Deceiving,' said Claire.

Morgan nodded.

'You know, in the churchyard I could tell that you were worrying about me again.'

'Force of habit,' said Morgan.

'I don't want you to worry about me,' said Claire. 'I'm recovering, Morgan. I really am. I get down a lot, but I'm going to be all right. You know that, don't you?'

'Oh sure,' said Morgan too quickly.

'I'm not just saying that,' said Claire, 'I found out that if one person will stand by you, no matter what, it makes you realize that your life is worth living.'

'I agree,' said Morgan.

'You're that one person,' said Claire.

Morgan understood her friend's gratitude. Appreciated it. But didn't really want to dwell on it. She felt that she had done it for herself, because Claire was both friend and family to her. 'And don't forget Sandy,' said Morgan.

Claire smiled, and looked out the window again. 'What's gonna happen with you two?' Morgan asked slyly.

Claire shrugged. 'It's good to have my old job back,' she said evasively.

'That loyalty of his is worth something,' Morgan observed.

'It's worth a lot,' Claire agreed.

'And he threw over a really pretty girl for you,' Morgan reminded her. 'It cost him a Mercedes convertible.'

'I know,' said Claire, with a smile. 'Although I don't really understand him. I was so heartless to him.'

'He and I have talked about it,' said Morgan. She and Sandy Raymond had grown close in the last six months.

At first, she too had been skeptical of his motives, but in time she had come to realize that Sandy, despite his sloppy appearance and his lack of tact, was one of the most quietly confident and tenacious people she had ever met. Once she had told him that she saw him hiding in the choir loft during Drew's christening. He did not deny it. 'I thought maybe if I saw her there, with her baby, that it would force me to admit that I had lost her for good. Didn't work.' He was sure that, in time, Claire would love him again. Sometimes Morgan thought that he might be right. 'He doesn't see it that way,' Morgan said.

'I know,' said Claire. 'It's just too soon to say.'

'Of course it is,' said Morgan.

'What about you?' Claire asked.

Morgan shrugged uneasily. 'You know me,' she said. 'First I think yes, and then…I don't know. I start to wonder.'

'Fitz is head over heels for you, Morgan.'

'I thought a break might do us good. Give us both time to think.'

'Think about what? You love each other.'

Morgan shook her head. 'I don't know,' she said. 'It's been…great. But love isn't any guarantee of anything.'

Claire peered at her. 'Are you thinking about me and Guy?' she asked.

Morgan sighed. 'You have to admit. It makes you wonder.'

Claire shook her head. 'I'm actually not sorry that I married him.'

'You're not?' said Morgan. 'After all you went through…'

'It was terrible,' Claire admitted.

'You almost didn't survive it,' Morgan reminded her.

Claire nodded. 'Yes, I know. But no matter what Harriet Martineau might have thought about marriage, I just hope I'll have the courage to risk it again one day. And the opportunity.'

'Really?' said Morgan.

Claire nodded. 'Someday.'

The landlord came to the table and set down their glasses of ale.

Claire lifted hers to Morgan and Morgan held her glass up and tapped on Claire's. 'To risk, then,' said Morgan. They smiled at one another and drank.

'And ladies, when you're finished with that, the gentleman in the corner over there would like to buy you another round.'

Morgan turned in her chair, expecting to see some dusty workman hunched over a ploughman's lunch. There, in the dark corner of the bar, sat Fitz, his elbows on the bar, and a smile on his face. When she met his gaze, he lifted his glass to her, and his eyes were merry.

'It's Fitz,' Claire exclaimed.

Morgan turned back and looked at her with narrowed eyes. Her heart was hammering. 'You knew about this,' she accused her friend.

Claire smiled. 'I may have known something about it.'

Morgan shook her head. 'How could you?'

'He was so determined. And I owed him one,' said Claire. No, Morgan thought. This isn't right. I didn't invite him here. I have work to do. My thesis research. This isn't a good idea.

'He said something about wanting a proper English wedding,' said Claire.

Morgan looked up at her friend, aghast. 'He must have said "breakfast". A proper English breakfast.'

'I'm pretty sure he said "wedding". I'd consider it, if I were you,' said Claire.

Morgan looked back at Fitz, and found that she could not stop herself from smiling. What are you doing here, she wanted to ask? He met her gaze boldly and the answer in his eyes would have made Harriet Martineau blush. Morgan tried to glare at him, but it was no use. As he got up from his bar stool and started to walk toward her, she thought, for a moment, that if she didn't put her foot down, and send him home on the next plane, there would be no stopping him. He'd be arranging for the vicar, and calling her his wife, and she'd never be in complete control of her life again. They would be setting out together, into the unknown. Her heart was reacting unreasonably, somersaulting with happiness. Morgan knew what it meant. She made up her mind, and stood up to meet him.

* * * * *

REQUEST YOUR FREE BOOKS!

2 FREE NOVELS
PLUS 2 FREE GIFTS!

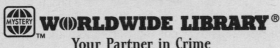

Your Partner in Crime